W9-ASV-690

Pleasant Hurricanes

Pleasant Hurricanes

A Novel by

Sim Shattuck

Dream Catcher Publishing, Inc.
P.O. Box 95783
Atlanta, Georgia 30347-0783

Phone: 404 486.7742   Fax: 881 771.2800
Email: DCP@DreamCatcherPublishing.net
Website: www.DreamCatcherPublishing.net

To the Memory of
Carol Mengis
1913-1920

Library of Congress Control Number 2002106658

Acknowledgments

Thanks go to family and to those friends who helped me materially and emotionally while I was writing: Pat Emerson, Marion Lea, Dennis Minor, Karen Webre, Karen Lewis, Tom Lewis, Ed and Karen Jacobs, and Terri Cahill.

The following people gave me the wherewithal and emotional support I needed: Theda Birdsong, Patrick Garrett, the Lewises, Mona Oliver, Herb Bryant, Dorothy M. Grant, Bob Duplantier, Dennis Minor, Lu McElwee, John and Elaine Bradshaw, and my parents.

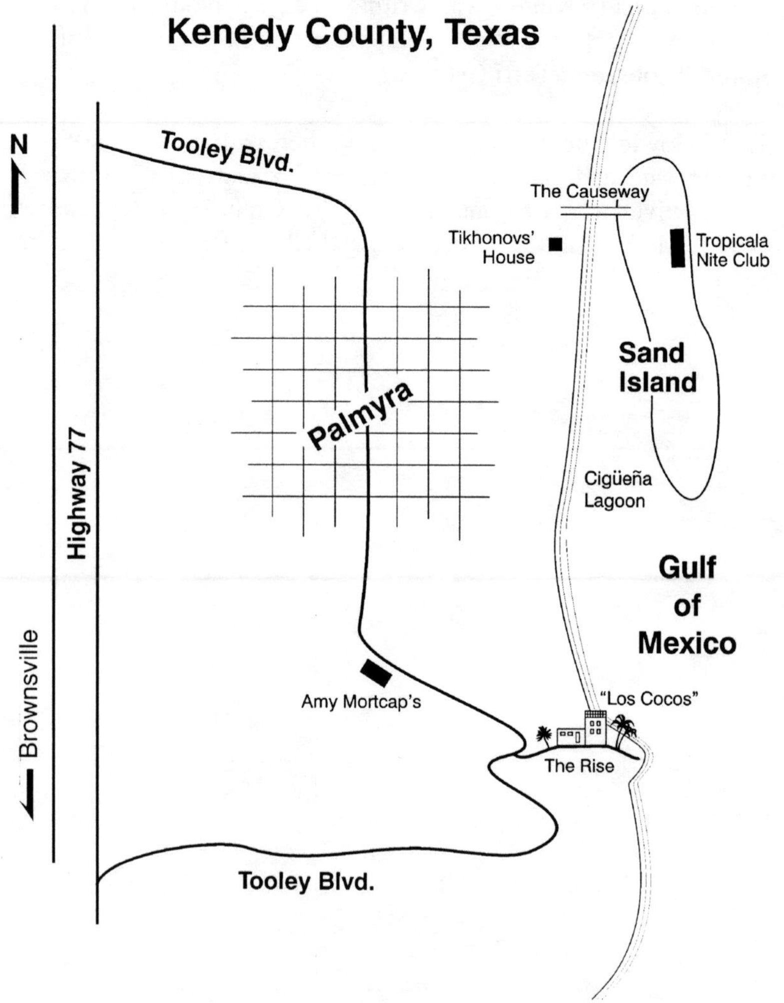
Kenedy County, Texas
N
Tooley Blvd.
The Causeway
Tikhonovs' House
Tropicala Nite Club
Sand Island
Palmyra
Highway 77
Cigüeña Lagoon
Gulf of Mexico
Brownsville
Amy Mortcap's
"Los Cocos"
The Rise
Tooley Blvd.

I First Words

Sundown comes, and since it is the beginning of the summer season, the beaches empty and the town fills up. Café lights blink their fluorescent eyes and pop with that half-audible burp that tells you the electricity is flowing. People in the residential section of town turn on their dining room lights; or because perhaps it is too hot, they sit in their small kitchens next to the hurricane fans that blow ample breezes over wet brows or over hot stoves just finished cooking potatoes.

It is almost never cold here. Last Christmas it was 82 degrees in the shade, and the year before that it was 72 degrees. Occasionally there are cold snaps like the one in 1951 that killed all the citrus trees. But then, that was a long time ago. The breeze is gently warm now.

The town is Palmyra, Texas—permanent population 6000—in the summer and fall months, a seaside resort of 16,000. Palmyra is almost exactly 58 miles north of the Mexican border town of Matamoros, a city known for its interesting restaurants and pleasant winding streets. Palmyra too has a large Mexican population, but it also has an unmistakable Southern small town flavor. The combination of the two cultures makes for an unusual social situation; but here, fortunately, Anglo and Mexican populations are made up of long-time residents who know each other and depend on one another for their livelihoods. Palmyra is pretty much a harmonious place.

Two-lane Hwy 77 is on the west side of town; Cigüeña Lagoon, Sand Island, and the Gulf of Mexico (in that order) are on the east. The town's main drag, Tooley Boulevard, runs north-south, parallel more or less with the highway, though separated by seven blocks of businesses, gas stations, and houses. Local teenagers always joke about "tooling on Tooley" on Friday and Saturday nights. They cruise up and down the neon lit boulevard just hoping for once that something interesting will happen. It almost never does, but then the teenagers are really looking for love, not adventure. Palmyra has its share of bankers, lawyers, drunks, preachers, adulterers, teachers, and every other human type you can think of. Here, as anywhere else, people make decisions concerning their lives and fortunes with the same clumsy informality—and finality—that all people make decisions with. Most residents—about half—have accepted their lot with little disturbance. They have accepted the marriages, mortgages, separations, deaths, and births of this half-population with what equanimity and grace can be found in a very small rural community. These are the people we call normal or "well-adjusted," which means probably that they have found enough meaning in what they do for a living, whom they live with, and the children they raise. If they feel occasional emptiness within, as all people will at one time or another, they attribute the feeling to a nasty, week-long rain or to a headache, or to loneliness—a husband out of town on a sales trip, or a friend who doesn't show up. At other times it is a failed algebra exam or a hangover from a little too much the night before. All in all, however, these people go to their deathbeds contentedly. They fight to survive and prosper, and they generally succeed as the world counts success. Another good thing about them is that they make it through life without cutting a swath of human misery behind them; they raise their children, protect and love their spouses, and are loyal and generous with friends and business associates. By instinct they console grief and toast success. And when they suffer, they whisper about it to their wives or mothers in darkened rooms.

The other half of the population may also do these exact same things and in the same way. But with them, the desperation of everyday struggle may be a little harder to control; the bonds of affection less secure; the strength of their personalities, character, talents, and obsessions less susceptible to guidance. But most are indistinguishable from the other half, as far as you can see from their outer lives. But within, they are all unquiet. It is an Unquiet that is not a tragedy, a failure to have a happy childhood, nor maybe a too-intelligent person trapped in a stagnant place and time. Such reasons are always too easy to speculate on, and our values mislead us because they present only one part of a jittery mosaic.

This is the Palmyra of the two populations. This is the Palmyra of Sorrows, the Palmyra of Joys. This is the Palmyra with a slender black thread of a highway through cane, sorghum, cornfields.

II Working Woman

Having turned on the neons and fluorescents of the Red Arrow Café, Dauphine Candor scratched at her left wrist (she always claimed that metal watchbands irritated her) and went to the coffee station. The busboy who was supposed to keep up with the coffee levels was off somewhere—probably hanging out with that idiot dish washer again, she thought. She added water to the left tank, poured in the pre-measured coffee package, and flipped the black toggle switch. Mr. Rossi, the old bastard who consistently came in five minutes before closing time, would be in early on Thursday night to eat because he had to make his bakery run from Palmyra to Sarita, and his wife usually had Thursday nights off to play cards with her friends.

"So, he comes to me," said Dauphine to herself. "How romantic! Me and Mr. Rossi!"

She laughed to herself and pulled out a cigarette. Frieda would be coming on duty soon, so at least she would have help this evening. She primped for a moment in front of her Max Factor compact and decided her gray and brown hair needed more attention. Stepping over loaded bus trays from the afternoon lunch rush, she cursed the retarded dishwasher and the busboy who could not keep his mind on his work. God knows what depravity those two were planning. She was not afraid of them but she would be glad when the evening cook and Frieda came in. The employees' bathroom mirror was cracked and dirty, but Dauphine gingerly arranged her elaborate bouffant coiffure, oblivious to the squalor around her. She was forty-three and, as she used to say, she "looked every day of it." It was not even that she looked forty-three; it seemed as though someone had temporarily thrown lines around the eyes of a young woman, as if for a staged play. Dauphine always looked as though she was waiting for the makeup crew to walk in and wipe twenty years from her hair and eyes. Ironically, she gave very little thought to her waning youth, her silvering hair. Most of her spare thinking time was caught up in worrying about her daughter Betty Sue, who at fourteen and a half was demanding more freedom every day. Betty Sue was not a bad girl; she was aggressive and friendly, probably a little naive too. That was certainly part of it. But Betty Sue did not play the coy young thing—not Betty Sue! She throws her head back and laughs like a man. If she likes or dislikes you, she'll let you know. She also goes to school dances with boys sixteen and seventeen years old. Dauphine did not like that, especially since Betty Sue had no father to keep her in line. He had left three years before, an increasingly restless, bitter, and maybe dangerous man. But since Palmyra was a small town and Dauphine had not heard anything unflattering about her daughter, she decided to let the girl go out for dance dates. Movie and drag strip dates were still out though; however, Dauphine knew she would have difficulty maintaining her hold on Betty Sue through the summer. On the other hand, the girl usually told her mother what happened during dances, whom she saw, what her current boyfriend said, and so on. And Betty always listened to her mother's advice on clothes and boys even if she did not always agree with everything Dauphine said. Dauphine also got a vicarious pleasure from hearing of her daughter's social vicissitudes. They allowed Dauphine not only the sensation of reliving her own youth, but also the satisfaction of preparing her daughter for the adult life to come. There were problems—growing ones, in fact—but Dauphine knew that raising her daughter was always a matter of crossing her fingers, biting her lip, and hoping the girl would turn out okay.

As she took one last look in the mirror, Dauphine thought to herself, cocking her head: "Did I turn out 'okay'?" Her mother now dead for many years, Dauphine had not thought of herself as a daughter for nearly three decades. She could hardly remember either parent. She did remember the pain of losing each parent, then her life at Aunt Louise's, then the new high school Aunt Louise moved near to. Dauphine herself had been a "bad girl." Really, "wild" would have been a better description. She came in drunk at fourteen, was sexually active by sixteen, and got married at seventeen, two days after high school graduation. Much to everyone's surprise, Dauphine had not been pregnant, nor did she have Betty Sue until ten years later. Also to everyone's surprise, Dauphine and her moody husband had a happy marriage until three and a half years ago. He then began the typical middle-age crazies, partying too much, throwing his money around, picking up young girls. He left one morning after a violent argument with her, and she had not seen him since. She heard someone had seen him in

Houston but she did not try to find out more. She refused child support even though she could have used it.

Dauphine sighed in the mirror. A little cloud formed on the glass and immediately dispersed. No use crying over spilt milk. No use bitching about the past. But sometimes you just can't help looking back. It's all a part of looking at everything. She heard the tinkling of the cheap aluminum bell tied to the front door. It was either Frieda or Mr. Rossi—she did not care which. Another sterling evening at the Red Arrow Café. But it was sort of a home, wasn't it? And where would Betty Sue be going after her dance? She was supposed to go straight home. Dauphine would call to check at eleven. If Betty Sue wanted any privileges this summer, she damn well better be home one hour before midnight. And that was all Dauphine had to say to the cosmos before she combed her hair again and went out to greet whoever was there.

III Pangs of Overeducation and Low Sales

"Janie, can you please come in here for a moment?"

"Yes, Mrs. Banks. I'll be right in."

A few moments later:

"Janie, I didn't get where I am today without (a) setting goals for myself and (b) struggling to reach those goals. I'm beginning to think that some of the girls out front aren't doing enough pushing to get through their sales quotas. It's bad enough with the IRS breathing down my neck every quarter but now I think you girls aren't working very hard. I got where I am today with hard work and goals and that's all there is to it. I want you to pass the word that I'm on the warpath, that I want them to straighten up and fly right or they can shape up or ship out...."

"Hey, that doesn't make any sen....."

"Now Janie, don't try to stop me. Mendoza Realty picked up the sell-vibes on those Sand Island condos and we missed out on the whole deal. My business is falling off and I wonder every night when I go to bed how I'm going to make my car notes or even pay the grocery bill. I have a business to run and if it isn't run right I'm going to find someone to run it right, so help me. I'm at my wit's end with you girls and I've reached the end of my rope. We're burning the candle at both ends and now it's time to face the music and pay the fiddler!"

She slammed down her smiley-face Lucite paperweight. Janie Norworthy walked out of Mary Ann Banks's office and went to her own desk. She thought about the three grueling years she spent getting a Ph.D. in Meso-American Art History. Now she was selling real estate under the heavy aegis of a greedy, frustrated moron who gave a threadbare performance of hiding her viciousness and avarice under a lamination of hackneyed platitudes. Or so Janie thought.

She thought to herself: "what *was* all that education for? I could've stayed in the Anthro. Department if it hadn't been for office politics. Now I'm saddled with a jerk for a husband and two children. Is this hell? I sometimes wonder...."

Little did she know that Mary Ann was not stupid. Mary Ann did not just know real estate; she slept, breathed, ate, and practically lived real estate. She played real estate the way a lovesick gypsy plays the viola. She tangoed all night with real estate to the music of Xavier Cugat. Mary Ann Banks could sniff out a foreclosure miles away with the uncanny, inexorable accuracy of a shark. What Mary Ann Banks lacked in verbal creativity she more than made up for with her elaborate, fantastic land deals. And they all worked out, usually to the buyer's satisfaction as well as her own.

Mary Ann closed up for the evening, pulling loose the scarf around her neck and turning off the window-unit air conditioners. Business was not as bad as she had let on but her sales team was taking their community position as the first-in-sales company for granted. Such attitudes led to decay and...if you don't grow you die in this business, and....

Why couldn't she think? There was something nagging in the back of her mind. Was it something she had to do? The girls' desks were neat except for Janie's. Well, that was not important. Janie was the best in the office. What was bugging her? She realized what it was. She was going home to her empty house now, empty since her husband died seven years before. Bob had been a good man. They used to bowl and go to the movies all the time. Mary Ann knew that she would never find another man she could be so comfortable with. They seemed to have everything in common—hobbies, religion, politics, tastes. She helped him start Banks Real Estate Company when they were two scared kids, he just out of the Army, she just sending their child to school. They had made terrible mistakes at first, but they both went to school nights, they both got their real estate certificates in time. Bob's parents and rich uncle gave him enough capital to get started, and before they knew it they were busy. They had almost gone out of business when they landed the old King Ranch-South account. Mary Ann could never figure out how they had done it. Somehow they had. And from there the reputation of the firm had grown to include most of the larger holdings of the Valley.

Now Mary Ann felt like half a machine running on parts that were invisible. To this day, even seven years later, she had to remind herself that he was dead. She did not hold his memory morbidly close and she did not enshrine him either. He had his bad points while alive, that was certain. Some of his personal habits had grossed her out at the time, but now they only caused a kind of nostalgia. To her he was still alive in some ways and she caught herself asking him questions aloud sometimes. She wondered now and then if she were crazy but she was too busy to consult a psychiatrist.

Other men had occasionally tried to get into her life but Mary Ann politely rebuffed them. She went out to dinner occasionally with important clients. Usually the men who asked her out wanted either her body or her money. It made her feel bitter at times, but the self-assurance and self-acceptance that Bob and she had taught each other never quite wore off. She was, then, neither happy nor unhappy. Mary Ann Banks was getting wealthier, older, more self-assured, and more aware of the world around her. She began to look for patterns behind the world of nature and the behavior of her friends and associates. There seemed to be an intellect emerging from her experience as well. This was a side of her that no one ever saw. And it was a new beast within, one she was not quite sure of yet. From a spring of confusion and loneliness she drew sad waters. Those waters began to encourage questions from her innermost self. She began to read philosophy and physics and history surreptitiously from old college texts bought at garage sales. Those books were among her darkest secrets.

IV An Unusual Home and Its History

When you followed Tooley Boulevard south through the poorer parts of town, you eventually left the city and hit the tin-roofed shacks of the few ex-sharecroppers living in Palmyra. A little farther south of that brought you to an impressive alley of royal palms and a gradual twenty-foot rise that overlooked the Gulf. There was Los Cocos, built in 1935 by Elena Muñoz's father, L. P. Muñoz. Everyone in town had seen Los Cocos and was used to its eccentricities, but outsiders were always mesmerized by its bizarre hideousness. The main building was itself a split-level stuccoed box, the west wing two stories, the east wing three stories and overlooking the Gulf. The third story of this multi-level home was composed entirely of jalousies that could be opened to let in the full sea breeze. The concrete floor of the jalousie level was packed with tropical plants like huge fans and even a few parrots and other birds. Elena sent the birds to Costa Rica by airfreight every winter because she was afraid it would get too cold for them and they could come down with diarrhea.

The two-story portion of this stucco dream was painted a fading midnight blue; the other portion was variously green, pink, or canary yellow in stripes. Superimposed over the blue section were day-glo orange daisies stolen by her brothers on an escapade one night in Corpus Christi. Elena liked the daisies although she did not know where they had come from. Had she known, she would have sent them by air freight back to Corpus Christi as well. Various telescopes and binoculars were mounted on stands looking out to sea and down towards the town. Elena had a recurring nightmare about the townspeople coming with torches and scythes to kill her. She was different from the average Palmyran, but she did not eat babies either. She woke up in a sweat every time she had that dream and would look around the room for Kuon, her vicious German shepherd. Kuon had a spike collar and a suspicious, beady little canine brain. Not even the quietest boattail grackle escaped his notice, nor did anything else elude him for long. Despite his Tauric appearance, though, Kuon was all tailwagging and puppydom for Elena. And he followed her just about everywhere she went. The slightest move that anyone made towards Elena, without her obvious acknowledgment, was met with a whirring mass of two-inch fangs, bristling fur, and a growl that could freeze molten steel. Kuon's only other weakness and distraction was a toy rubber skunk that he chased among the tall, stately palms of the Los Cocos estate.

Everyone in Palmyra knew for certain that Elena Muñoz was crazy, and they all had their favorite stories about her. Most younger residents knew nothing about her past, however, and cared little why Elena was crazy. They knew only that she was harmless and entertaining and that Muñoz Motors hired many workers living in the Palmyra area. Were Elena suddenly to take offense at her treatment in Palmyra and leave, the town would die. But Elena was as shy and diffident as a little girl. It would never occur to her to fire any employees of Muñoz Motors, Inc., which was managed by one of her many brothers. After a nervous breakdown she turned the running of the company over to Raul, but with the stipulation that she retain the power to hire and fire. Raul shrugged and agreed; it seemed a small price to pay to run a successful small engine business. As the years passed, however, Elena had hired no new employees in good times and had let go no workers during bad times. She took great interest in the happiness of her employees and their lives. She always sent the children gifts at Christmas and surreptitiously paid many hospital bills. Parents wanting to know who paid always received the same answer—the BR Foundation of Houston. No one knew that BR was the initials of a boy she had a crush on in high school. He had died of a snake wound on Sand Island while still in the eleventh grade. Elena still mourned for him every May 3rd, his birthday.

Elena's upbringing contributed to her mental problems. She started life at home with her parents in Palmyra. Her father, L. P. "El Lobito" Muñoz, had originally built Los Cocos as part of an ill-planned scheme to make money. Thinking that the Depression would certainly lead to revenue-raising tactics like lotteries and legalized gambling, El Lobito built Los Cocos along the seashore with no other aim in mind than having a swanky casino and nightclub. Using money he had commandeered from running booze and guns at the border, he built the stucco mansion and waited for the Texas legislature to open his front gates and let the money-laden patrons pour into his Hall of Chance. The legislature seriously considered passing the bill—some said for no other reason than to get Muñoz to go legitimate. El Lobito bought his busboy and waiter uniforms and sat back in expectation. Just when things were looking bright, a bunch of fundamentalist ministers from East Texas started squawking about gambling and Communism and Mexican atheists and they said it loud enough over the radio airwaves to stir self-righteous indignation everywhere. The measure was put down by a huge margin. And having invested everything he owned into Los Cocos, El Lobito tactfully blew his brains out in his black Buick on a dry January afternoon. His daughter Elena found him. She was five.

All of Elena's years of desperate searching for love and acceptance stemmed from her unshakeable conviction that she herself had shot her father. She saw the whole thing in her mind. No, it did not happen in the car...it happened in the den, she would say. I picked up his pistol and shot him. Of course it didn't happen that way, and her brothers tried to convince her. It never worked. Elena would carry the self-imposed onus of patricide her whole life—a scarlet "P" attached to her mind.

Elena's mother, a bland, quiet woman originally from Ciudad Mante in Mexico, went silently insane. Night after night she wandered around Los Cocos in her nightgown calling for her husband, Luis Patronio Muñoz. She called him by his full name. Eventually she was caught in a rainstorm and contracted pneumonia. She was then packed off by horrified family members to a sanitarium in Arizona where to everyone's relief she promptly died. Elena was then shuttled back and forth between relatives. Some of them were good to her. One uncle raped her. Another uncle paid for the abortion, put her in college, and then attended her graduation. Elena graduated from the University of Texas at age twenty-one. She started graduate school in English but after one semester dropped out to marry the son of the largest landowner in South Texas. They were married for three years before her husband was killed in a tractor accident. There were no children but Elena had loved her husband very much. They buried him on one of the hottest days Elena ever remembered. It must have been 110 degrees in the shade. They had to bury George van Zelt very quickly because of the weather. Never very stable emotionally, Elena became depressed, skirted suicide, and ended up staying in bed twenty hours a day. Her four conscious hours she spent praying either for sleep or death or both.

After a year she came out of it, and taking her maiden name again, she organized what was left of Muñoz Enterprises and went into business for herself. It helped to have her husband's five million dollars. She got to know other business people in Palmyra, and they all liked her despite her sometimes erratic behavior. She paid a decent wage and listened to smart suggestions, and she ended up quadrupling her wealth just through sales and service of small motors, from toy airplanes to cars. She would not, however, repair tractors. Nor Buicks.

So, to return to this evening, Elena Muñoz, daughter of El Lobito Muñoz, has had her maid Zillah prepare a pitcher of gin and tonics. Kuon serenely chews his rubber skunk at her sandaled feet that are bright-toed with red nail polish. It is Elena's night to look at stars, listen to *The Planets* or other space music, and to wonder about the limitless excitement of a universe she will never get to travel, and maybe decide what to feed a toucan or a cycad.

Meanwhile in the kitchen Otto, her old German butler, neatly shoves stoneware plates into the dishwasher with a faint Pomeranian efficiency. Dinner, like the day, is over at Los Cocos. The old toucan, Popol Vuh (named after the Maya *Book of the Dawn*) looks for a convenient perch for the night. Elena does not care where he chooses, as long as it is not on good furniture.

V Meet the Murphys

Dauphine got off late after cleaning up her station in the Red Arrow Café. It was too late to call home to see if Betty was in bed; she would just see for herself when she got home. She would stop by at Wanda's house if the kitchen light was still on. It wasn't, so Dauphine went to her own house. Dauphine's neighbor and dearest friend was Wanda Murphy, who lived next to her in a small blue and white bungalow.

Wanda and her husband Lanky had been high school sweethearts. Lanky had worked offshore for years, then went to college at Tulane back in 1960. But after a few semesters of what he considered a worthless existence, he came back to Palmyra to work and marry his girl and raise a family. Wanda quit crying all the time now that Lanky was back in town. They went to the movies in Palmyra and occasionally went bowling in Sarita. Once, Lanky took her all the way to Matamoros for a lavish Mexican dinner date. That night in 1963 Lanky Murphy proposed to Wanda Simpson over a delicate silver container of octopus ceviche. The norteña band played some mariachi-type music for them for the rest of the evening—the players knew the two were young lovers in the restaurant that night.

Now Wanda and Lanky often shook their heads as they looked around their poorly-furnished living room.

"Now look at us," they seemed to say. "We have two kids, a pile of debts, a lot of love, a few laughs, and what the hell else?" Their daughter Loren was sixteen, their son Petey twelve. Loren and Petey were very much loved but they fought more than any other two siblings in Palmyra. Despite their age difference, Loren was rather small and Petey was robust. As fighters they were almost evenly matched though Petey was growing stronger every day. Loren knew her hegemony would not endure long. At the breakfast table the next morning:

You rotten little brat!" she said to Petey. "You spied on Betty Sue and I last night!"

"Betty Sue and me" her mother corrected. "Besides, what were you girls doing that you would be ashamed for Petey to find out about, anyway?"

"Why can't he just leave me alone? It's bad enough I have to live in the same house with the little creep. Now he just tags along wherever I go. We can't talk together when he's around. He'll tell everybody what we said."

"What in particular has he said that bothers you?" asked Wanda, lifting her coffee cup to her lips.

"Oh never mind! You don't believe me! I have to explain everything! How come that brat gets all the attention? I hate him! I hate him!"

Actually Loren doted on her little brother; she just did not want him around all the time when she went out with her friends.

"We were talking about boys and Petey came in and started making his stupid frog noises and I was so embarrassed!"

"Hey, pimple-face, hand me the sugar," whispered Petey.

"Mama! He's teasing me! You little twerp!" She pulled his ear.

"Ow! Stop it!"

"Mama, I'm going to kill him!"

Loren chased Petey from the table and into the living room. She tailed him around the coffee table, screaming threats and calling for their mother's help. Loren finally caught him by the back of his collar and yanked him to her. The only sound from the living room then was thudding feet and sharp slapping sounds. Wanda came in and issued an angry ultimatum. But by then the miscreants were laughing at themselves, and they returned willingly to the breakfast table. Another topic of conversation came up. Loren was sixteen and wanted a job this summer. There were several places she could work without previous experience. Aside from business offices, she was restricted from working at Los Cocos (no particular reason--it was just that Mrs. Muñoz was so unusual) and Ed Fernandez's Tropicala Nite Club on Sand Island. Her best bet, everyone maintained, was to get hold of her next door neighbor Mrs. Candor. Working in the Red Arrow may not be the ideal job, but she felt she had the stamina. Besides, boys—some of them cute—occasionally came into the Red Arrow in the afternoon before the movies. In any case, Loren would have to ask Betty Sue's mother to intercede with the owner so she could be hired.

Money was always a problem with Loren. She could not keep up with the wardrobes of her friends. Somehow her clothes never fit quite right, she never had the right colors or accessories. Her friends had beautiful clothes she knew she could never have unless she worked. Maybe working would be character-building. It certainly would not be fun. Work never is. Loren found herself daydreaming in two ways. She dreamt she would find a job or a husband that would provide her with all the money she needed. The other daydream welled up from a deeper source: she wished she did not need the money at all, that she would find a way to spend her life in service to others less fortunate. People scoffed at this ambition. She would show them one day. Either from her Maserati or from the Peace Corps. It did not matter which.

VI Oft-Told Tale

Poor Barry. That's what everyone thought about Barry Madden. He always woke up with a headache because he was a drunk, listening to the radio late into the evening and drinking Four Roses Bourbon. People's sympathy for Barry was mixed with a little bit of stiff-necked Puritan zeal, for although Barry would not ever hurt anyone, no one could understand why he became what he became, when all the world could have been his doormat.

As a teenager Barry was full of promise. He was the Palmyra High Panthers' quarterback, valedictorian, and class president. Barry was also the handsomest boy ever to set foot on Palmyra High's wooden-floored halls. The future was going to be big for Barry—first college, maybe in Austin, or maybe back East—then Standard Oil, or law, or maybe even politics. In any case, Barry knew he would be saying adios to Palmyra when he graduated from high school. And he knew he would never come back except for brief, nostalgic breaks between stages of his lightning-bolt career. All of this glory was to have transpired twenty-one years ago. Instead of drilling for oil in Tibet or serving in a Houston corporate boardroom, Barry was shaking his aching head behind the Tetrapylon Video Game Parlor. His back was stiff and he thought there was hair growing on his tongue. Two small dogs yapped at him from a broken window in the alley where he had passed out the night before.

"Shut up, you stupid mutts," he muttered, pressing his temples and moaning. Barry had given up reflecting on the waste his life had become. It was the smartest move he could make, he figured, since thinking about what might have been would not put food on the table or liquor in the cabinet. It only made his headaches worse and his guilt that much more intense. It obviously was not worth his effort. And he was right.

Barry had gone east to the University of Massachusetts. He lasted a semester, then came home to the University of Texas. He partied constantly, rarely studying, spending all his time and money carousing around Austin. Because of his looks he had plenty of companions. Men liked him because he attracted women and was a fine drinking buddy—always pleasant, generous, and friendly. He could also be counted on to do his part in a barroom fight. But as his grades went down, his friends either flunked out of school and went home or they began to worry and take their studies seriously. One by one, Barry started losing his friends. But his drinking grew worse. When he drank he became insulting and abusive, always ready to pick a fight with the very people who tried to care about him. What was left of his fraternity buddies drifted away in disgust and even fear. Barry was a powerful man and could do crazy, angry things when he drank. More and more he drifted from the college scene to Austin's seedier nightlife dives. He started going home with cocktail waitresses to perform a brief, pleasureless sex act so he could fall asleep at last. He could not count all the strange beds he had awakened in. The spreads usually were tiger-striped or red with a ball fringe. Magnolias on black velvet usually graced the walls. And the "girl" was thirty, divorced, and had two skinny kids hungry for a man's love and attention. They always peeked at him around corners of doors in cinderblock, two-tone shag carpet apartments. Barry avoided the children and almost never came back twice.

Naturally he flunked out of school. He and his father had a terrible fight not long after Barry came home. His father died of a stroke two days later. His mother went to live with a sister in Phoenix. She gave Barry the key to the house and told him to stay in the house long enough to get rid of some of his vices and decide what he wanted to do with the rest of his life. He had been there, deciding for twenty-one years. His mother now dead, Barry had scraped by on insurance settlements, scant oil income from land his father had bought in Oklahoma, and odd jobs. He had spent years blaming his bad luck and the rest of humanity for his failure to accomplish one thing after high school. One time ten years ago he played with the idea of going back to college by correspondence—maybe even returning to a campus. The forms were too much for him to fill out, though, and they sat on the kitchen table for eight months. Then they went into the trash.

Women came and went, usually leaving because of Barry's fits of drunken anger and paranoia. One blue-eyed girl from Houston he had picked up in a diner actually entertained ideas about making Barry shape up into "good husband material." After three weeks of her living in the same house, he hit her and called the sheriff to "escort her out of town." Barry did a stretch in jail for battery. When former friends finally got him out on bail, Barry returned to a ransacked house. The girl had robbed him and left the door open, and vagrants had done the rest. His dog, tied to the fence with a chain, had been stabbed to keep him from barking. Barry was profoundly sad and cried for a week. He decided to pick up the pieces of his life and start fresh.

He got steady work at a paper mill outside of town, but the buddies, the women, and the booze soon got to him again. Whether drunk or sober he was getting difficult to be with. No one ever came over to visit him. He began going on long walks, wild, as if trying desperately to find something he had mislaid. Coming in later, though, he often felt at ease—exercise always did that to him. One walk brought him to the gates of Los Cocos. Of course he had driven by it in high school, and some of his friends and he had spray painted the iron front gate with obscenities. They would have torn the whole property up if they had the chance, but a huge mastiff came lunging at them, throwing himself against the gate with tremendous power, snapping and roaring at the terrified boys. They jumped in their '52 Plymouth and drove back to town. This display of cowardice exposing them to one another, they decided to compensate by laughing and shouting at the old black women hulling peas on gray wood front porches. But the imperturbable old women never even looked up. The young men's shuddering continued under their skins, though, and no boys ever went back to do harm at Los Cocos again.

And yet—here was Barry. The gate had been repainted, probably many times since that night twenty-two years ago. He tried to see through the palms or hear something. Maybe, he thought, he would come here again. The lawn was so green. The house was invisible from here, lost in a sea of straight-trunk royal palms and mimosas in perpetual bloom. A faint sound of distant pipe organ music reached his ears as he began his three-and-a-half mile walk back to town.

"Yes, a lot of water under the bridge since then," Barry thought. A cloud obscured the waning sun. "A lot of paint on the fence, too, I bet." Something irritated his eyes, and he rubbed them.

Thereafter, Barry's walks almost always took him past the entrance of Los Cocos. He saw the German shepherd from a distance and was not close enough to be barked at. Barry wanted suddenly to be invited in to see Los Cocos. He knew Mrs. Muñoz had a reputation for kindness and generosity. There was no way to get to the house with the dog there. He would have to come back every day until he saw someone walking on the grounds. He thought he wanted to ask for a job, but what he really wanted was to belong somewhere. Somehow this house, and its residents, was tied up in his future; he knew it the way he knew the sweat on his own forehead. He wanted to belong to whatever went on at that house.

VII The Four Cruising Teens

The car door slammed. Marti, Betty Sue, Loren, Jeanine. The radio was blasting away on some Corpus Christi FM hard rock station. Loren had miraculously ditched Petey at the house because her folks weren't going to a movie after all. Betty Sue's mother was working late again and probably wouldn't mind Betty going out with her friends for an hour or two. Marti—the athlete—as for her parents! Her parents let the girl drive the family's second car for any reason at all.

"She's so lucky and her parents are so rich," thought Betty Sue.

Marti: "Hey hey hey you guys! Hey what're we going to do tonight?"

Loren: "First let's circle back around the block. I gotta find out if I left the sprinklers on in the front yard."

The rest: "Oh, come on! Good God!"

Loren: "I'm sorry, but I'll get in trouble if I don't turn them off. The yard'll be flooded tomorrow and Petey'll tell on me and I'll be grounded for a whole month."

Marti: "Okay, for you we'll do it. But I want to drive by Madden's house tonight. I think he's really dreamy."

Jeanine: "Aren't you afraid of him? Jesus, I am. Mom thinks he's a creep, some kind of pervert or something."

Marti:" Him? Noooo! Have you seen his picture in the Palmyra High Panther Tracks?"

Loren: "What year?"

Marti: " I think it was '59 or '60 or something like that. He was a doll. Still is, I think."

Betty: "Turn the radio down up there. I'm missing all this!"

Marti: "Oh shut up, Betty! Well, I think he's neat and I want us to drive by his house. Nothing's going to happen. We won't even get out of the car."

Loren: "He must be about 39 now, huh?"

Marti: "No way, Jose! He's thirty-eight."

Loren: "God, when you're that old, one year doesn't make much difference, does it? I mean, he's old enough to be our father!"

Jeanine: "Well, that'll take up all of ten minutes at the most. What do we do after that?"

Loren: "We could talk to your sister again, Jeanine. I thought she was really rad."

Jeanine:" No, Janie has her hands full. I don't think she would want us dropping in without calling first. You know, the kids and all."

Betty: "Did she say anything about babysitting?"

Jeanine: "I mentioned it and she wrote your names and phone numbers down...ooh, turn that up. I love Van Halen. They are so-o cool!...Anyway, she said she'd call you if she needs sitters this summer [snaps her fingers to the music]."

Loren: "How did she ever get a Ph.D.? Especially in weird Indian pottery and stuff? And to end up working at Banks Real Estate office! I mean that's sort of pathetic, isn't it? Marti, turn left here."

Jeanine: "I guess so. I don't think Janie's happy."

Marti:" Hey, who wants a cigarette??"

Loren: "I do—oh LOOK!"

All: "What? What?"

Loren: "It's that creepy Stanley Burgen and Loretta the Hog—on a date!"

All: [variously] "Eewwww! Barf! Yeccch!"

Jeanine: "How did those two find each other?"

Marti: "It musta been in the 'property to rent' ads!" [Laughter]

Betty: "I was sitting in the pew behind Malcolm Dyers, that guy in my algebra class. He was—oh God this is gross--he was messing with a zit on the back of his neck near his collar."

All: "Ewwwww! That's so gross!"

Betty: "That's not all: he popped it!"

All: "EWWWWWW!"

Betty: "Isn't that enough to make you want to absolutely barf? He is kinda cute though—if you can get rid of all his bratty little brothers....Oh, I'm sorry, Loren!"

Loren: "You don't need to apologize. It's okay. Sometimes I agree with you."

Jeanine: "I wish I had a little brother. All I had was a big sister. Things are always so dead at our house. Turn left here on Tooley."

Loren: "Hey I'll make you a deal! I'll sell you Petey for a week!"
All: "Eeeeeewwwwwwwww!"

VIII A Night Club

The Tropicala Night Club, reached by veering off Hwy 77 onto Lagoon Drive north of town, was gearing up for another summer evening. The neon runners all along the eaves—green, pink, orange, yellow—were turned on. Several lights were dead. The tall dark-green neon palm tree saying TROPICALA NITE CLUB! was lit up and blinking itself on. A cooling breeze blew in from the Gulf. Ed Fernandez was happy because it meant that mosquitoes out in the parking lot would not bother his patrons. He might even turn off the air conditioner.

In his own small way, Ed Fernandez was a latter-day El Lobito, trying to make a living serving drinks to summer people, Anglos and Mexicans. Most of the time there was no trouble. When several cantinas opened in Brownsville, Harlingen, and Corpus Christi, the Mexican clientele had gone to them to listen to their own distinctive music and enjoy their own forms of entertainment. The "summers" were easiest to please—usually people from Houston, successful Chicanos and their wives, about ten "regulars" who were drunks but nonetheless inoffensive and amusing, and often college students wanting to escape Texas Southmost and Pan-American University, or maybe the technical school in Kingville. The Tropicala had become something to a hotspot among young people because of its appeal to nostalgia—a piano bar, comfortable overstuffed vinyl chairs, romantic candles on the table—the seaside wall could even be raised to expose the moonlight on the Gulf through a screen wall like a huge front porch.

When you came to the Tropicala, Ed Fernandez greeted you and waited on you, for the first time, himself. Partly this was his way of checking the potential rowdies but it was also his way of making new acquaintances and cementing old friendships. Ed was particularly attentive when regulars—summer or otherwise—brought friends in for the first time. The regulars impressed their guests with the fact that here, if nowhere else, they had pull, they had some clout.

The piano bar featured Edna Parker during the summer months when she and her husband came down from Houston to occupy one of the Sand Island condos so recently stolen from under the professional nose of Mary Ann Banks's real estate company. As she played songs from any era, from Scarlatti to Fats Domino, customers often took their drinks and wandered outside, wading in the surf and listening to the soft piano music mixed with the perfume and murmur of the warm sea. Sometimes they would walk the fifty yards or so to the northern spit of the island, away from the lights of the bar and the condos beyond it, to kiss in the dark beneath a million icy-looking stars. Few lovers got beyond kissing there because the "north spit" was a popular make-out spot. Ed of course did not care what happened on the north spit as long as he got his cocktail glasses back. When Edna was indisposed and could not play, Ed plugged in the jukebox. Some nights you could hear "Telstar" or "String of Pearls" or "Blue Velvet" or any number of nostalgic songs, even from across the lagoon. An old man and woman in the tidy little house on the mainland side heard and smiled; Mary Ann Banks on her front porch sometimes heard and smiled; sometimes the old toucan Popol Vuh cocked his head and listened, his hearing very sharp for something that was nearly two and a half miles away. Stars wheel overhead, it's two o'clock and time to go home. The neon lights go off, the wall comes down, the piano lid shuts. Tomorrow night the lights will go on and the Tropicala will welcome all patrons again.

IX We Want What We Don't Have

The new sun shone through a red and white checked curtain. Wanda poured her best friend Dauphine a cup of coffee. Actually, Dauphine was Wanda's only intimate friend. Wanda had always had problems making and keeping women friends. Before, it was competition; now, it was a lack of common interests that kept her away from the easy society in which women learn to deal with their lives. She clearly felt she was hurt by her isolation, and her friendship with Dauphine was her only bond with the other women of the community. These two women loved each other dearly yet never expressed openly their bizarre envy of each other's life circumstances. Wanda always looked at Dauphine this way:

"I wonder what it's like to be Dauphine, to do anything you want and anytime you want to do it. I love my Lanky and my kids but God! just once I'd like to be free of them, just for a while—just a month. I don't even know what it's like to be alone. Sometimes I dream about walking in a vast desert of beautiful sand dunes and stones. I have on a beautiful white caftan and I'm barefooted. I wander through the night winds of the desert alone staring at the huge moon, wanting the embrace of the stars. I wake up so cold and terrified and grand-feeling. I move away from Lanky in bed and lie stiff as a corpse on my back, my head thinking the craziest things, the strangest childlike feelings. I am too perfect and made of frozen marble, a statue of perfection that no one can have or even touch. After a while the fantasy fades and Lanky reaches over to feel where I am and he puts an arm over me. The desert goes away, the moon goes away, and I think about Loren, Petey, and what I have to do this week. It's really crazy!"

Dauphine thinks:

"I am so tired of the everyday weight of being alone. I have been through hell and back and I don't really need to lean on anyone's shoulder to make my way in this world. The big things of aloneness never bother me. Yes, I know myself very well, and I know from hard experience when to stand alone and when to ask for help. But it's the small things that get to me. I'll look up from a book on a rainy day and suddenly, temporarily, I'll feel lonely. When I carry in the groceries and Betty's not there to help me, I feel so angry that I can't do the job as fast as two, or I'll feel lonely when I get up at dawn to get ready for work. I guess mornings are the hardest time of all; they make me wish someone would touch me—that's all, just touch me and talk to me. How wonderful Wanda's life must be—always having Lanky to talk to, always having someone there to be the father when the father-in-you is worn out. And my God, just once I'd like to stay at home and do little chores and sweet things to please a man—not because he's a god or something, but just to please myself by doing something for someone besides myself."

Sometimes Dauphine did wake in the mornings with a man, but it did not happen very often. She had an example to set for

Betty and it was a difficult job to do. Her time for romance was limited to dates with men who found themselves suddenly free after ten, fifteen, even twenty years of marriage. Some were hurt and felt suspicious of free women. Others wanted to use her. And some came to see Dauphine again and again—sometimes just to talk to her or hold her hand.

Wanda raised her cup to her mouth.

"Sometimes I could just kill Lanky. He pulls such crazy stunts."

"Why? What'd he do?" asked Dauphine casually, looking at the blue rim of her cup.

"He came in from a job in Brownsville and gave me a paper bag. Told me there was something in it for me."

"What was it?"

"I'm just glad I didn't have a heart attack when I pulled out a two-foot rubber snake. Liked to scared me to death. Hey, what are you doing this Friday night after work? Lanky and I are going to get some shrimp and boil 'em. You want to come over and help us eat?"

"I heard this was a good shrimp season—sure, I'd be happy to. Thanks." Dauphine wondered if Wanda was trying to fix her up again. She wondered where Lanky got his friends; they were almost always ugly men with no manners. Funny thing, she thought, they all seemed very tenderhearted. Dauphine always had a good time with Lanky's fix-ups but almost never were follow-up dates arranged. Lanky always shook his head, saying "Maybe Dauphine just doesn't want to get involved." Sometimes Dauphine wondered herself when the same thought occurred to her. Maybe she didn't really want to get involved with someone else. And yet she knew that wasn't true either. She didn't want money, or a powerful husband's proffered place in local society (such as it was), or merely a tenderhearted man—although that was the most important secondary feature. What Dauphine wants more than anything else is—well, what does Dauphine want? Dauphine asked herself that question. Her own blank answer frightened her. She wanted to get alone to think about it, brood over it.

"What do I want?" she asked, moving her silent lips when Wanda wasn't looking right at her.

X The Boss Thinks

Mary Ann came home for a nap that afternoon. Business prospects looked pretty good, but she was tired and decided to take the afternoon off. She knew Janie would run the office with no problems. Mary Ann pondered for a moment, then pulled a book from her nightstand and opened it to the place marked by part of a Kleenex. The book was entitled *Introduction to Philosophy.* She hesitated for a moment before deciding whether to read her philosophy book or open a new trade journal. She decided to read the book. She never could pick up this book without being fascinated by what she learned. It seemed the writers of this book felt everything she felt, thought everything she ever thought about—and more, and explained mysteries to her that she was sure had no answers. Mary Ann learned much from her reading. How much, she wondered, does Janie know about these things? With a Ph.D. she must have some concept of philosophies much higher than her little book. Could it be so? Why had she never talked with Janie about the younger woman's family, education, ideas? Mary Ann knew about Janie's degrees, even considered not hiring her because of them, but she'd hired Janie to help the family and return an old favor from Janie's mother. Surprisingly, it had been a smart move. Janie did her job in an unassuming way, minding her own work and doing as she was told.

XI The Émigrés

Across the lagoon from the Tropicala was a little bungalow with half-moon shutters and a shiny new chain link fence around it. A plastic fountain graced the center of the front yard, ceramic squirrels ran up the chimney, and a small donkey of indeterminate composition pulled a large metallic colored glass globe in a little cart behind him, near the shell driveway. Several pinwheel daisy ornaments fluttered in a late afternoon breeze. A few birds in squatty palms eyed the fountain with mild interest. Could they bathe in this thing?

Mrs. Tikhonov peered cautiously out of her flowered, chintz kitchen curtains. The old sweat, the horrible fever was on her again, and she was sure that they were there again. There was no doubting it, and she was glad Pasha could still raise a gun and fire it. Yes, *they* were there again, no doubt, and the Tikhonov name and property and honor must be preserved at all costs. Mrs. Yelena Tikhonov was sure that gypsies were sneaking through her property. But for them, her life would be an eventless, serene joy; but no, this mockery of American values, American property rights! And it wouldn't matter where the Tikhonovs went: the gypsies had a vendetta against her and Pasha. She crossed herself the backwards-Russian way and went to wake Pasha, asleep in a tattered, green satin easy chair next to a cigar ashtray stand. The TV murmured fitfully in the background. Pasha opened his watery old eyes and looked at Yelena like a stranger.

"Gypsies, Pasha. Gypsies! They're back." Pasha got out of his chair and aimed his old Tsarist rifle out the window. Without even aiming, he loosed a shot that made the air ring and blasted the top half of scrub willows completely into the air. He smiled and looked at small Yelena.

"See, Mama? Now no gypsies." Yelena saw but didn't always believe. Gypsies steal melons! How could they be so cruel to helpless old people in their nineties?

The sorrows and exigencies of old age! Yelena peeked out the front window. The gypsies were gone (probably) and she could return to weeding the tomatoes. But tonight they would return and Pasha would have to get up and search the yard for gypsies. The music from the Tropicala piano bar would never reach this far, but some nights if the crickets weren't too loud the Tikhonovs could hear strains of jukebox music. The Tikhonovs didn't frequent restaurants and bars, so they thought musical ensembles or victrolas played the music.

Yelena made some iced tea at 10:30 that night. She mindlessly lifted from the TV a yellow porcelain planter in the shape of a Pekinese dog and looked it over.

"Do you think," she said, her head cocked at Pasha, "that they'll ever try to get in the house?"

"No, Yelenka," replied Pasha.

"Well, dear, if they do it, please lift your gun up and shoot me in the head because I don't want to live if I'm caught by the gypsies. Just pull the trigger and I'll be dead. Do you understand me, Pasha?"

"Yes, my love, I do," he replied. Yelena sighed comfortably and prepared for bed. Pasha sat in his living room chair and ran his thumb over the sight of his old army rifle. Pasha knew it would be easier to go along with her gypsy-fears than to try to prove the gypsies' nonexistence. Yelena had believed in her gypsies ever since the couple's only son died in 1937. "This is what happens to an old, old woman with regrets who has no grandkids or great-grandkids," he thought. He himself didn't have regrets anymore. Both of them were happy and amazed to wake up every day. Yelena came out in her cotton pajamas, stopped, and stared at Pavel, her husband.

"Oh Pasha...." She touched his shoulder. "How did we get to be so old? What happened?"

He reached up with a tough liver-spotted hand and patted hers.

"I don't know. I don't know. I guess we will be leaving the world soon, won't we? I'm afraid, darling."

"I am too, Pasha. I am too."

XII Dreams of Pyramids, and Stupidity

Janie put down the new book on the Totonac culture of Cempoala and its contribution to Aztec art forms. Well, actually little connection existed between the two, but some poor academic fool had to get his book published to keep his $36,000 a year job. She picked up her tea cup and grunted out one closed-mouthed laugh. What intelligent people have to go through in this country is beyond belief. An angry thought rocketed from her brain to her heart and back again. "I am so bitter. I am so goddamn bitter. God forgive me, I can't help myself."

Lenny would be waking up from his nap before long; then the kids would wake up. (And don't you know, the first thing that dumb bastard will do is turn on the damn TV. Then it will be baseball games or golf or some other mindless moronic sports crap for the rest of the day. For the rest of my life, no doubt. I shouldn't talk this way, but Christ, I can't bear my life any longer.)

XIII Mental Postcards

"What can a man do with someone like her? I offer her a home and food and love. We've got nice kids. I don't understand why she has to slap my head off every time I talk to her."

--Lenny Norworthy

"I am beginning to think about things I've never considered important before. You might say I'm taking the bull by the horns and putting his nose to the grindstone."

---Mary Ann Banks

"Betty Sue is growing up. I thought this day would never come, but now that it's here, it's come too fast. I wish I didn't have to work so hard just to get by."

---Dauphine Candor

"Pavel, I did not hear any gypsies in the yard last night. Do you think they fell off the causeway? I am very happy today. I think I'll watch television some and then take a nap after that. Don't rattle doorknobs, dear."

---Yelena Tikhonov

"I think my barback is dipping in the till. I'm two Chivas Regals short and there's been other talk floating around here. Why the hell can't I find honest people to work in this bar? Why didn't I go into the pre-stressed concrete business with Dad?"

---Ed Fernandez

"Elena Muñoz: I've never really thought much about her. Her life must be wonderful—no money worries, lots of peace and quiet, she really belongs here. She has some place that's all her own and she belongs here. I want to meet her. I never have."

---Barry Madden

"We're getting tired of driving around on Friday nights. Why won't the boys in this town ask us for dates? It's not like we're skags or have leprosy or something. Marti says maybe it's because our breasts are too small. If that's the truth about why we can't get dates, then we are in big trouble. Boys are even stupider than we thought. It just makes us want to gag."

---The four cruising teen girls

"Yes, little birdy, I am afraid there's going to be a reckoning pretty soon because I'm afraid about something Nameless out there—something I can't put by finger on. There's no sense in torturing myself this way. Why do I do it?"

---Elena Muñoz, to Popol Vuh, her Toucan who winters in Costa Rica

Maybe I should leave. Why do I treat my family, my husband this way? I'm no Suor Angelica but I love my kids. Why can't I find peace with my lot in life? It's not so bad, except for the job—and Banks isn't so very bad to work for. She told me something I said yesterday was non sequitur. I wonder where she came up with that. I think that lady knows more than she lets on. Anyway, it all just seems like too much sometimes. I love my children and I worry about them. But I'm dying slowly of brain death, and what's really scary to me is that no one cares! My God, has it come down to that? I could probably resume studies here too if I had the guts to get on and quit whining. I can't wait on anyone but myself. What a bitch I've become.

---Janie Norworthy

XIV Romance and Duty

Mary Ann Banks just finished putting her dishes in the dishwasher. She put her wedding ring back on her right hand and absentmindedly picked up the novel she had started the night before. Putting her ring back on was no longer the difficult ritual it had been just after her husband died; she felt she betrayed him and his memory every time she removed it. But practicalities, as they always do, won out and she no longer gave any thought to the love token's temporary removal. The novel she was reading is entitled *Love's Flaming-Embered Embrace.* Reading this kind of book made her a little uneasy. Mostly it made her think about love, and that was "a can of worms" she would "rather not open just now." And this novel was unbelievably fluffy-minded when compared with her philosophy books. But doing too much of anything gave Mary Ann no pleasure—even thinking, even selling real estate. Which reminded her—she had to call Janie Norworthy about that highway frontage property deal she was trying to swing for Mary Ann.

"That girl sure knows her real estate," thought Mary Ann. "Oh sure, she needs to learn a lot more about the legal side, but she's got the makings, the stuffings, the gumption to be as crafty as a fox and wise as an owl in the real estate business." She walked to the phone, sitting in her brown velvet easy chair.

"Hello?"

"Lenny? This is Mary Ann." (She didn't have to say that but she always did.)

"Hi, Mrs. Banks. Want Janie?"

"Yes, honey. Just for a moment. What's going on over there?"

"Oh, nothing. Same old story. How about your place?"

"Nothing." (What else?)

"Here's Janie...."

"Yes?" a woman's voice answered.

"Hi, Janie. Look, I don't want to disturb you at home but I forgot—"

"I know, Mrs. Banks. The surveyor's report, right?"

"You got it!" said Mary Ann cheerfully.

"Yeah, I thought I'd gotten that squared away before I left Friday, but when I got home I found it in a book in my briefcase. I guess I stuck it in there absentmindedly while I was eating lunch. You want it now?"

"No, Janie. I just wanted to make sure we still had it before closing the deal. I went in yesterday and couldn't find it."

"I was going to look it over this weekend."

"That's fine, Janie. I just needed to know where it is."

"Is that all, then?" asked Janie politely.

"Yes. Okay, see you tomorrow."

"Okay. Bye."

[Click.]

Mary Ann had almost said something, something like "What are you thinking about now, Janie?" Mary Ann wanted to know so much more about the world than she did. She knew nothing about Janie's field of interest; she thought she would go the library and check out books on Meso-American art. Maybe then she could have a talk with Janie about what she learned. Here they were, fifty-eight miles from the Mexican border, yet Janie had never been to Mexico--except for the border towns. Didn't that seem crazy? She should be exploring ruins and going to museums all over Latin America. Yet here she sat in Palmyra, selling real estate for the likes of me, Mary Ann Banks. It's a strange situation.

XV Duty and the Romance of Stars, Also Zillah and Otto

"Wake up, Miz Elena. Wake up! You got to go talk to Mr. Raul!" Zillah gently pulled on Elena Muñoz's white shoulder. The satin sheets gave a hushed hiss as Elena moved her leg across the bed.

"Hm? Mf? Oh, it's you, Zillah. I just had the strangest dream."

Zillah knew Elena had to go into town to talk to Raul this morning. Elena never relished leaving Los Cocos; it seemed to her a violation of the natural order of things. Los Cocos was governed by her concept of the way things should be. The outside world always afforded a series of rude shocks for Elena, and she avoided that other land as much as possible. This is not to say that Elena was ill-equipped to face everyday realities. She would probably survive and even prosper anywhere. But by her very nature she would, like a spider, begin to spin a web of Muñoz charm and romance about her. She would begin with her furniture. Then the strangeness would spread to the outside of her home, then at will elsewhere. To be in Elena Muñoz's home was to be taken into her odd, black-lighted, saturnine world. And yet there were light tunes and even grace notes in this massive fugue, this Los Cocos. What about her orchids, her bromeliads, her aging toucan? The jalousied sea breezes?

Zillah had no time and no desire to consider her employer's contradictory nature. The black maid prided herself on three things: her intelligence (formidable if undeveloped), her ability to run Los Cocos and keep even Otto and Kuon in line, and her extremely practical nature. Zillah despised some of Elena's fruitless worries and concerns. As she helped Elena to the bathroom to wash her face, she remembered what happened the night before: Elena had begun to fidget about 6:30 and decided to think. She went up to the jalousie room overlooking the Gulf. The summer stars pulsated in a huge velvet dome overhead. Indoor banana plants whispered. Elena occasionally came down, wandering through the house, saying, "What am I living for? How come I can't find out?"

She went back to the roof of the jalousie room and lay on her back, Popol Vuh standing on her forehead. The stars glittered from flat horizon to flat horizon, seeming to lift the whole house, to turn it into a star-wandering space ship. She spoke as she lay on the flat concrete roof. "What does this Mystery mean? Why was I even born? I did not ask for this!" Popol Vuh paid no attention but as she moved he would flutter his black wings to compensate. Zillah paid no attention either. She always had to retrieve Elena when she got in one of these moods. Elena put so much into her moods, Zillah thought. Why worry about questions nobody could answer? It would be better to quit asking them because they just made folks nervous. Elena flitted from room to room in her white linen house gown, asking questions no one could answer. Oh, her mother wouldn't agree with that—oh, no! Zillah's mother always listened to Sister Thompson on the border radio station. The purpose of human female existence—said the evangelist Thompson—was to wait on men so they can be ready to wait on God.

This datum means that women are to give their men the kind of homage that God gets (or should get) from man himself. Needless to say, if He exists, God gets the worst end of the deal. At least the men get the satisfaction of being waited on, and the women get the satisfaction of waiting on something that's real and alive. More people believe in waiting on men than believe in the existence of God. Especially men. Elena herself could not accept fully the existence of God (though she hoped it true), nor did she see the desirability of waiting on men who in turn waited on God. God somehow never seemed to want the sandwiches of propitiation man placed on the tray. That sad fact did not, however, worry Zillah's mother. If Sister Thompson said it, it must be so because she gets everything from the Bible. What Zillah's mother, Amy Mortcap, didn't know was that Sister Thompson was illiterate and could not read her own Bible. Plainly, Amy was getting fooled. Zillah knew better, which was sad for Zillah, too, because she knew too much about deception but had few ways of combatting it.

After a crying session on the roof and more stargazing, Elena let herself be led down the steps. Elena said she wanted to go to the moon right now—maybe even Mars. But she would settle for *Star Trek* on television. She had gin on her breath but not a lot. She got out her video tapes of *Star Trek* movies. A glassy wind chime sounded on the roof. Otto the butler had retired to his bungalow after waxing the heavy, ornate wooden dining room furniture. He'd said "Donnerwetter!" and "Himmel!" and "Dieser Verdammte Vogel!" all evening while polishing. Popol Vuh had earlier flown into the dining room. Everyone was scandalized, even Elena. Popol Vuh had been very bad to sneak in and poop on the decorative arabesques and egg-and-dart cornices and claw-feet on the table. Popol Vuh was therefore not allowed downstairs for a month, and he was denied his usual "toucan goodies"—peanut butter cookies, celery, but not the lighted cigarette that Otto would give him every once in a while. To Otto's surprise the toucan liked tobacco, but Popol Vuh's tobacco habit was severely limited by Otto's own stingy nature.

Actually, Otto felt more filial affection for Kuon than for anyone else in Los Cocos except Elena. But Kuon had eyes only for Elena and his rubber skunk—in that order. Otto could recall with deep serenity and pleasure the times he had come in the main house after doing estate inventories and had seen Kuon's massive paws resting contentedly over the tattered little rubber skunk. The dog would give the skunk's head or tail a quick, lively chew with his inch-long fangs. Otto felt a Teutonic kinship with Kuon, but Kuon was really far too sophisticated to assume there was any necessary racial connection between them.

Otto was still large and powerful for a man in his middle sixties. This strength was all to the better since Otto's role as butler often was expanded to include various forms of physical labor such as gardening, house painting, and other outdoor chores. Popol Vuh used to accompany him into the yard but lately the old toucan had moped around the house, fearing no doubt his imminent demise at the claws of Kuon or the snapping beak of some temperate climate hawk.

Otto had passed unconscious throughout the Nazi era in Germany—literally so. He unexpectedly slipped into a coma in

1933 after an ice-skating accident in Baden-Baden and did not recover until June 1945, after the surrender of the Third Reich. Otto had slept for twelve and a half years. He of course had known who Hitler was at the time of his accident, but upon suddenly waking one warm day in 1945 he looked at a shocked nurse and said, "Where am I?" It was the first of many unpleasant questions and even more unpleasant answers. Otto cried and wished he could go back to sleep. Germany had thrown itself into an ashpit, his relatives were dead, and he'd slept through his youth. Now a man in his thirties, he faced the agony of regaining the use of his limbs—all of which had been twisted, tendons tight with disuse. In 1955 Otto came to America, determined to settle where winters would be mercifully short and easy on his always-tired muscles. The way he became a butler was funny: coming through Palmyra and asking directions in German for the location of a restaurant, he made others misunderstand him, and they in turn pointed him to Los Cocos, thinking him some strange drifter looking for work.

Elena heard his story and hired him on the spot, despite his ignorance of butlery. She said that anyone lucky enough to sleep through Hitler would be lucky to have around Los Cocos. He might inspire others in the house to sleep through their worst problems. "After all," said Elena, "what can be worse than a nightmare you wake up into rather than out of?" Otto had nodded his white head in silent agreement.

Zillah, on the other hand, lacked certain subtleties present in other inhabitants of Los Cocos. It was not her fault but the fault of the bad luck that followed her most of her life. Her mother Amy was, and always had been, a raving religious maniac. But aside from her obsession with the will of God, Amy was a kind, attentive if sometimes ignorant mother. When Zillah was born, the Mortcaps moved to Houston where Zillah's father found work. He left when she was five. Amy immediately got two jobs instead of one so her family could eat. Zillah had seven brothers and sisters and could hardly indulge in sorrow over her father's leaving. All he had ever done anyway was get drunk, beat Amy, and make her spit on her religious pictures and blaspheme God. Amy was horrified to do these things, but her husband threatened to kill the children if she didn't. Amy was pretty thick but she knew anger and death might follow each other quickly in her house. Taking all kinds of suffering, Amy finally, passively, shamed her man into departing forever. He had offered no child support and she expected none. She worked for three years to save the busfare to return to Palmyra, got nowhere, and wired home for money. The West Zion B. C. collected the fares for the family of nine. They practically filled the bus.

Consequently, Zillah, the oldest child, had to work from age six onwards. She was given to no enthusiasms, cared not for love, money, religion, or any of the other means by which people persuade themselves that life is worth the effort. Her sole pleasures were sitting in her little room on the second floor of Los Cocos and enjoying a fierce will to survive and to look back on the accomplishment. She shook her head in utter bewilderment at Elena's antics, though knowing Elena's life story she found room in her narrow mind to tolerate and ignore the people and things around her.

Zillah did not believe in God any more than she believed in love, but she felt safe at Los Cocos and rarely ventured to town. Instead she sent one of her siblings into town with the old family truck twice a month to buy groceries. And on weekends she walked the half mile to her mother's tarpaper shack. The house, if one could call it that, had no screens on doors and windows. For some reason that caused shame to Zillah. Flies passed in and out of the kitchen, casually sampling the fare at the Mortcap house. Zillah cried and cursed her mother, her family, and even the God she didn't believe in. Life did not treat Zillah well; she was a shadow at Los Cocos, brightening only when Elena or Otto complimented her cleaning or pastry making. Then her forehead would unknot itself and she would sing "I Know You Got a Chick on the Side" quietly, under her dark breath.

XVI Deceived

Barry, the Sober. Other Matters in Time.

A dim room in an old shack, faded pink lampshade with black horses on it, and a burnout spot where one horse's head should be: this is how you enter the home of Amy Mortcap. Amy breezes herself with a funeral-home fan. On it Jesus opens a gate, lambs look up trustingly, snow falls. Zillah, her daughter, studies the fan. A thought: those lambs trust Him so. Will they be on Jesus' plate tonight? It doesn't pay to trust, never has.
Amy, meanwhile,—

Amy is listening to Sister Thompson's show from station XERK in Mexico. Sister Thompson is saying that adultery is bad. She describes in detail the punishments for illicit lovemaking. Amy listens mesmerized, enthralled. Zillah stalks past her into the kitchen. Kool-Aid is in a plastic pitcher. Zillah looks reflectively into space. She asked herself: "Am I just naturally calm, or am I a bomb ready to go off?" Amy whispers "Amen" in the next room. Zillah hears roaches in the walls, scrabbling up and down like commuters going to work. She speaks quite plainly: (her mother has the radio way up and is mostly deaf anyway) "Mama, Mama, I love you, but you a fool, a sucker." Zillah walks out and fingers a plastic doily on the dining room table. Amy is singing "Since I Found the King" under her breath in a wheezing monotone:

"Since I found the King
You know
You know
You know
I don't need nothin' else.
He's my everything.
I got ta, got ta sing
Since I found the King."

Zillah heard the obvious pleasure in the old woman's sighs. Zillah cannot understand.

Barry Madden woke up with no headache on Saturday morning. He had drunk no liquor the night before, mainly, he figured, due to an oversight. He put on his walking shoes and walked out onto his front porch. Had he heard the laughter of those girls again last night? Who were they? Why did they keep bothering him? Already it was so hot his T-shirt grabbed his sweaty torso and bunched up just under his breastbone, and he knew he would attempt no running today. Barry walked down the streets of Palmyra to make his way to Los Cocos. At times he would stop to have breakfast at the Red Arrow. Today, he would sit next to Mr. Rossi, who didn't like for anyone to sit next to him when he was eating at the counter. Barry picked up the menu, smiled pleasantly at Rossi, and turned to read the menu. Dauphine came to Barry with her order pad (published by Moore Forms, Inc.)

and waited for the man to speak. For a moment Barry considered seducing this older woman, and he eyed her discreetly but appraisingly. Dauphine, was unaccountably angry; she'd certainly been leered at before.

"What are you looking at, friend?"

Barry snapped out of his short reverie and let Dauphine know from the tone of his voice that he considered himself subservient to her, thus making himself like a respectful son. It was all part of his plan, however. He chose to besiege her virtue. Los Cocos and other considerations were temporarily put aside.

"Oh excuse me, ma'am. I didn't mean to be rude. I wasn't looking at you, I'm just thinking about something." He snapped to attention and ordered an omelet and a glass of milk. He noticed that he had a hangover-type headache anyway. How was that possible? The idiot dish washer and busboy that Dauphine despised stuck their greasy heads from behind the coffee station, gleeful grins on their faces. They knew about Barry from their friends, they knew his reputation. But they also knew that Dauphine was no easy pickup. As a woman alone in a small Texas town, Dauphine had long before decided to be discreet in her relationships. She was not too concerned what others thought of her and she was old enough to know right from wrong. It was her daughter Betty she worried about. Dauphine knew what damage small town people could do when they were small-minded as well. Palmyra being a beach town, however, you could see practically anything in the world on Tooley Blvd. or on the beach during the summer. Dauphine remembered the bikers of a few years ago—about 1968. A bunch of Hell's Angels types roared through town tossing beer cans, starting fights in bars and raising hell all up and down the coast. Ed Fernandez had closed the Tropicala for two weeks before the state police moved in and started knocking a few heads. After the bikers came the hippies—most of them drifters on the way to what they considered Xanadu—the lush southern mountains of Mexico. After the hippies came the Hare Krishnas. Dauphine saw them come and go. It usually made her proud to think she was part of something permanent and dependable—a community.

Dauphine knew who Barry was by word of mouth, and he wasn't that much younger than she was. But she was not about to put up with foolishness from him. However, he looked sort of lost, so she softened her stance and, to get the ball rolling, she asked him (in a nicer tone) if he wanted some coffee. He smiled and nodded, she poured it in his cup and went off to tend to the butter pans and some of her other customers. He was handsome, she noticed, in a pathetic sort of way. People like him always get by on their looks, Dauphine reflected. What happens to them when they're old? Dauphine then saw her own face reflected in the pie case she was cleaning. Yeah, what does happen to them?

Barry ate his breakfast and left an unusually large tip. As he left he thought, "I wonder what she's really like." As he left she thought, "I wonder what he really wants."

XVII The Four Teens Go to Brownsville

[The girls sing various songs from a high school choral repertoire. They are all conspicuously good singers for high school girls. Scene: On the highway, headed south. Fields of milo squared off with fences and tall palm trees.]
Marti:" Just tell me one thing, you guys. How did I ever get permission to go to Browntown for a day? Yippee!"

Betty: "'Yippee?' No one says that! It's gross!"

Loren: "What are we going to do while Marti visits her aunt?"

Betty: "Let's go downtown. There might be some boys walking around."

Jeanine: "We could walk over the bridge and see Old Mexico."

Loren: "By ourselves? Do you know what happens to girls who do that?"

Marti: "No, what?"

Betty: "They probably get to see Mexico, that's what! Don't be such a baby, Loren. We can take care of ourselves."

Jeanine: "Well, aside from the fact that our parents would kill us if they ever found out about us going over the border, what harm could come of it?"

The other girls consider [this comment uncharacteristically sarcastic. They look at her with surprise.]

XVIII The Night Before

Ed Fernandez let the wall down at the Tropicala. The sea breeze blew, but the crickets around the lagoon were deafening. Before cutting out the last lights behind the bar, Ed grabbed a stool and propped himself up with his elbows on the shiny wood surface. It was late—probably 3 AM—when he suddenly looked up from his brown study, realized where he was, and got ready to walk slowly out to his car. Business had been good lately. The summer people had more money this year than ever before. Ed reached over the bar and squirted a swallow's worth of beer into a glass. While he took his short drink, he wondered about his business. The Tropicala. It had some nice features—beautiful scenery, romantic setting, comfortable chairs, Edna at the piano. But something was missing. Ed knew if he thought about it long enough he would come up with the answer. Anyway, it was late and he put the disquieting thought behind him and walked out. His mind's eye showed him a holograph of his bed and pillow. He turned the ignition key in his '63 Chevy and drove slowly over the blacktop causeway on his way south into Palmyra. The waters of Cigüeña Lagoon seemed to reach after him as his car pulled off the narrow strip of land. Crickets roared in the mindless black night.

The Tikhonovs, only a few hundred yards from Ed's near approach, were awakened by the sound of Ed's backfiring old car. Pavel looked at the digital clock by his bed. It said 3:15 but Pavel said to himself, "It's much later than we think," and rolled over in bed to put his arm over the arm of his wife. She trembled—gypsies might be in the yard.

XIX Game Show Interlude

Head cradled on his elbows, Lanky Murphy of Palmyra, Texas, looked out his front bay window. A passing jalopy DeSoto, owned by the Armanez brothers Tino and Flaco, sputtered asthmatically around the corner and disappeared behind so many sycamore trees. A few clouds here and there paused over Palmyra as if to yawn; then finding nothing interesting enough to rain on, they floated somewhere else.

His wife Wanda sat in the next room watching Nickelodeon reruns of "Name That Tune" and calling out the names of songs full seconds before the harried contestants, whose minds were preoccupied with the twin prospects of a new Ford and a paid vacation for two in Honolulu.

"DARK EYES"!

Wanda yelled the name of the tune after the first note was played.

"NO, IT'S 'PERFIDIA'!

Her second guess was right. She always had been big on Xavier Cugat....

Lanky wondered why he could not get so engrossed in something—anything. It was just this business of being bored day after day. It wasn't the self-imposed boredom of the man who thought his talents were being ignored or who lived under the delusion that he was somehow meant for better things.

"MOON OVER THE CATSKILLS!" cried Wanda from the other room. No, this was a totally vitiating malaise; it made him want to see just what his reaction would be to anything outrageous. He asked himself things like I wonder what I would feel if I took the tire iron out of the car and bashed Wanda and the kids' heads in. Well, what would he feel?

He fantasized arriving at the Kenedy County police station in Palmyra with his hands cuffed behind him, the police sergeant staring at him in amazed, even fearful disgust, the glaring lights of the jail exposing him guiltily as he submitted to booking and fingerprinting.

"Why'd you do it, Lanky?" the detective would ask, making his face as emotionless as he could.

"I was bored, Officer Teasdell," Lanky would wink and say politely. Then there would be the dark cell and the final realization of what he had done to his poor old wife and two children. The fantasy continued, but Lanky was no longer amused by it.

Having sneaked a pistol into the cell with him, he would say his tragic/pathetic goodbye to the world (or a roomful of snoring drunks), and calmly proceed to decorate a whole wall with the former contents of his head.

Lanky set his coffee mug down and shuddered. The fantasy was too gruesome to maintain. But surely every parent has at least one murderous strain in his personality, a part that never sees the light of day but, like an old tomcat, waits for its children forever in the shade of a dark forest.Usually.

Lanky dismissed the notion from his mind. Life is hard, life is scary, and even fantasies are no escape. Maybe boredom was not so bad after all.

XX Highway Incidents

It happened to Marti first, then to the other girls in the car. It was like passing through a fog patch on the highway, only this one was different. It had no substance—not even a vapor. The girls were headed north out of Brownsville on their way back to Palmyra through the sparsely settled regions of Kenedy County. Two miles from Armstrong they passed through an invisible plasma, some kind of amorphous but definitely real boundary that could be recognized only inside the head.

Marti kept her hands on the wheel but shuddered visibly. She looked to her right quickly to see if Betty Sue sensed what she had sensed. It was comforting in a way to see panic on her friend's face as well.

Marti: "What was that we just went through?"

Loren: "Thank God one of you felt it. I thought I was going crazy. Did you feel it, Betty Sue?"

Betty: "Just barely...something. Weird, huh? What about you, Jeanine? Did you feel it?"

Jeanine: "Oh yes, I'm so glad someone else felt it! Please, Marti, let's hurry up and get home. I'm scared!"

Marti: "No, I have to find out what it is. I could almost, like, feel someone talking to me. Jesus in heaven, what was that?"

Marti pulled onto the shoulder and let a semi pass. She looked to see the expression on the truck driver's face, but she saw nothing but a brief flash of exhaustion. Nothing else. She sighed, and turned around to drive again past the point where she had the strange sensation. The other girls were scared except for Betty Sue. A scrubby little post oak group, then an open field, then—

Again they felt ephemeral, desperate, alien emotions; there was a pause. All four girls gasped. A picture like a negative photographic movie passed through their minds, the emotions undiminished from the beginning of the sensation. Loren felt the emotions of someone trying to make living beings feel a distinct and overwhelming horror.

Marti pulled off the road and turned off the key. Betty Sue formed her mouth to say "Shit!" but the word never left her mouth.

"Bicycle? Mattress?" she said instead.

The mental image changed back to a color positive, and the story unfolded itself in the blink of a fast eye: a pickup truck was going down the same highway. In the back of the pickup was a mattress lay a teenage girl. She could have been any one of them except her clothes were different, her hair in a ponytail, her body slightly overweight. She had a pink ribbon in her hair. Beside her on the floor of the pickup was a girl's bicycle.

It was red with pink plastic streamers coming out of the handlebar ends. The pickup hit a bump, swerved, and the mattress, the girl, and the bike skidded off the truck bed and onto the highway. The girl had no time to roll to safety or even scream; she turned toward the bike, and both were crushed under the automobile behind them. The man who drove the car shrieked and jerked the wheel but it was too late to react.

As abruptly as the vision started, it stopped and there was no more. Marti was staring over the steering wheel, her mouth hanging open. She and Loren were thinking: how can we be seeing this? Is it real? Did the others see the same thing?

Jeanine glanced down at her Calvin Klein jeans. She had wet herself.

But at least the slow, murderous mental film was over. Now some letters appeared from nowhere in their minds, their shapes imperfect but very bright:

"....ALLEMEIST...."

The letters were slanted as if they were moving, and indeed they moved across the scene like ghosts. Marti turned the key, not wanting to hang around for more. Betty Sue and Jeanine were crying. Loren was too stunned to do anything but look out the window. Marti's voice quavered. The car engine was making a strange whirring noise.

Marti: "I don't know what that was, but we have to talk, we have to compare notes! What has just happened?"

Others: "Yes, yes."

Marti: "The word after the picture?"

Loren: "ALLE-something."

Marti: "Yeah, that's it! What does it mean?"

Betty: "I wish I knew. But I'm scared shitless and I want to go home right now!"

She had no argument from Marti. Loren was thinking now, slowly emerging from the cocoon of shock. She had learned two things: she had had her first brush with mortality—it was ugly, stupid, frightening and unfair. She also had reached over the border of that mortality and felt a dead girl's last emotion. She was oddly elated. Under her breath she said, "So. There really is something after death. I've met a dead girl. I always wondered if ghosts were real, and now I have my answer."

On the way home no one spoke. Each girl did not understand what she had experienced. As they reached the south part of Palmyra, Betty Sue spoke first.

Betty: "Maybe Alle-something died on the highway there, but a long time ago. But when?"

Jeanine: "Don't know. But maybe she was trying to reach us, tell us what happened to her. But the question is—why us? And—"

Loren: "But we don't know for sure if she was really alive, but for some reason I feel she was. Jeanine, when we get back we have to ask your sister to help us find info about this girl. You know, court records, newspapers, library stuff like that. I don't know how to use anything but the card catalog."

Jeanine: "Yeah, it wouldn't hurt to ask her what we should do, just in case, I—"

Marti: "Now stop just a minute, you people! Are you crazy? I know we all felt something and saw something. But that's no reason for us to go around telling everyone. Everybody will think we're weird or something."

Betty: "What the hell do you want us to do, Marti? Forget it happened? Pretend we didn't see anything?"

Marti: "No. I'm not saying that. I want to find out as much as you. But I think we shouldn't tell anyone until we've found out the ponytail girl is real. Then we won't look so crazy. That's all I'm saying."

Betty: "I guess that's only fair. Sorry."

Jeanine: "Can a place be haunted?"

Loren: "Huh?"

Jeanine: "You know, what I mean is—could a place like a stretch of highway be haunted?"

Marti: "I don't see why not, if you believe in ghosts. After all, what's a haunted house but a place?"

Loren: "Yeah, like Los Cocos."

[They laugh but the tension relief is not long.]

Betty: "Okay, I won't say anything to anybody about what we saw today. Do you all agree? Then swear to it."

Others: "I swear!" [They engage in a four-way handshake.]

Loren: "I can go to the library tomorrow."

Betty: "Me too."

Jeanine: "I can."

Marti: "I can't. I have summer school in the morning and swimming practice in the afternoon. But we can all meet at our house after dinner to go over what you find out. "

Loren: "What if I have to watch Petey?"

[Loud groans]

Marti: "Bring him along, I'll let him play with my Nintendo set until we're finished. He won't care what we're talking about."

Everyone agreed and Marti pulled into the lower-middle class neighborhood where the Simpsons lived. Loren and Betty Sue got out. As Marti and Jeanine took off, Betty Sue said she was too scared to stay home by herself. Loren asked her friend if she could stay overnight and then got permission from her mother. Betty Sue went home for her white nightie and toothbrush, not pausing for long in her own dark house. Wanda told her to call her mother at the Red Arrow Café and Dauphine okayed the stay.

Wanda and Lanky noticed the girls did not talk much or eat a lot or even fuss at Petey at the dinner table. Petey made faces but no one looked at him. He ate his supper quietly. Wanda saw Loren shoot significant looks to Betty Sue during dinner, and both girls excused themselves early. Normally they would be full of news about a shopping trip to Brownsville, not letting anyone else talk at all.

"Lanky," Wanda said later, "what's wrong with those two?" Lanky shrugged his shoulders and put a last piece of potato and meatloaf into his mouth.

"Beats me. Maybe boy trouble."

Loren lay next to Betty Sue in bed that night. Betty Sue's eyes were closed but Loren figured she was faking being asleep.

"Betty Sue?"

"What?" came the low reply, almost whispered.

"It's not that this dead girl thing is just exciting in an unusual way...."

"What do you mean?"

"I mean, I just realized something a moment ago while laying here."

"Like what, Loren?"

"I just realized I'll never, ever be the same after this. I think this really means something."

"Then I'm afraid."

"Me too."

Both girls listened to the cicadas for hours, not moving at all.

XXI Sister Thompson's Radio Revival Hour

Zillah and her mother Amy sat in Amy's tattered living room. Zillah stared out the window. She was thinking of Otto, the Los Cocos butler. He was unlike anyone else she had ever met, both severe and yet kind at the same time. She marveled at the irony of his life story and wondered why he wept when he talked of his twelve years in a coma.

"Why would he want to be awake during the War? All that killing and hating—he should be happy he slept through his young years. I sure wish I'd slept through mine."

Zillah also wished Amy would go to bed so she could go back to Los Cocos and her pretty room. Amy sat next to the hearth, wearing a dirty red cotton shawl and a necklace of rhinestones that twinkled in the setting sun. The rhinestones were the first things she ever owned which had no practical purpose.

"These here rhinestones are sacred," she said. "God must have gave them to me." She gave the room a quick, affirmative nod, as if to convince it of her notion.

Zillah turned away. She would not tell Amy again that the necklace came from Goodwill, and before that, K-Mart. An old dog wandered in from the rickety front porch of Amy's house. Amy saw him and jumped up to get a pan of leftovers for the skinny, mangy hound that had come in unannounced yesterday from the highway. Maybe the dog had spent many years in a Mexican ejido; maybe he had been the hunting dog of a Monterrey businessman whose hounds had a habit of escaping. Amy thought the dog was a "hound of heaven" because she had heard about that too on Sister Thompson's radio show on Station XERK. Zillah was just thinking about packing her paper bag to go home when the familiar organ solo of Sister Thompson's radio show came on the air. Amy, beginning to doze after petting the dog, suddenly woke up and fiddled with the radio dial. It was too late for Zillah to leave.

MY BELOVED FRIENDS, the radio preacheress orated. The organ played a furtive chord. I KNOW THAT MANY OF YOU ARE LIVING IN SIN (amens from the background) AND YOU JUST CAN'T PUT THE PARTS OF YOUR LIFE TOGETHER (amen) (Organ chord) OR YOU'RE FAR, FAR FROM HOME. (yeah!) AND YOU MISS YOUR LOVED ONES (Zillah stepped to the other room and motioned back to Amy that she was going out to use the privy. Amy, smiling, nodded). WELL, WHAT CAN YOU DO? (Don't know! amen!) WHAT CAN YOU DO? (Zillah shrugged, said "beats me"). WHO CAN YOU TURN TO FOR SUPPORT? WHO CAN MAKE YOU FEEL LIKE YOU'RE ALIVE AGAIN WHEN YOU HAVE GAVE UP ALL HOPE? (Amy yelled "Jesus!") (organ chord) (Shouts) (Amen!)

Suddenly, though, it was not funny any more. Zillah realized she did not have anyone to lean on, except Amy and maybe Otto or Elena Muñoz...pretty slim pickings in a busy world where all too often people somehow don't give a damn. Amy was certainly a fool, but at least she had something to live for: Sister Thompson's weekly encouragement and blessing. Zillah began to wonder if it really was bad to lean on something, though. She had leaned many times before and fallen on hard ground.

When Zillah came back in, the radio show was off the air. She was happy because it had become cool where she sat in the yard among the whispering banana plants, waiting for the show to be over. Amy was asleep in her chair, the dog had gone, and Zillah had to prepare the old woman for sleep. She had a hard time getting Amy up, undressed and into the bed. Sister Thompson's radio show had always excited Amy, but now the exhaustion was becoming dangerous to the old woman's health.

"Sister Thompson going to kill my momma if she ain't careful," muttered Zillah, tugging up the old bedspread over the length of Amy's bed. Amy was sound asleep, a smile graven on her old face. Zillah leaned down and gave her a peck on the forehead. She knew Amy would be completely senile soon and probably would not know her daughter before long. It all seemed so futile sometimes.

Zillah walked back to Los Cocos in the evening air. She walked past Barry Madden, who was coming from Los Cocos where he had been studying the landscape and grounds. He still wanted to get in there. He said nothing to Zillah; he did not know she was a Los Cocos employee. Zillah hurried to get back to her room, barely giving Barry a glance. A few moments later a cold shudder passed through her body—a heavy sense of foreboding clung to her like the light perspiration on her lip and brow from the clammy evening air. She had to tend to Amy again tomorrow, so what could possibly happen? The dying sun went behind a cloud. Zillah felt something she had not felt in twenty years. A sense of expectation.

Elena Muñoz was in the living room staring at the gargoyle on a corner of a pier table. She was lost in thought. Popol Vuh could not get her attention though he tried flying about squawking and even pooting on furniture. Elena was thinking about nothing important. Her mind ran over a few business items: new tux for Otto? new rubber skunk for Kuon? (Kuon, lying at her feet, looks up in surprise. Can he read minds, Elena wonders.) Shrugging, she gets out of her chair and goes to her room. A demanding need to sleep passes over her. She flops on the bed and later dreams:

She was a grown woman still, but back again with her parents who were both alive. They were all at a party, people laughing, carrying tall drinks, and sitting comfortably on sofas. Mariachi music outside played softly until trumpets began to blare.

El Lobito, her father, stood up slowly and walked to the door. Elena felt panic rising. "Oh my God," she thought. "He's going to die now." Somewhere in the background Elena heard the music fade and cease to a portentous silence. Her mother pointed to her father and in a croaking voice said to her, "Follow him." Elena had no choice but to go after him. He went to the old black car. Elena cried out but was impelled to follow. She reached for the car door handle, expecting to see her father with half his head blown off, smiling and asking her to join him in the hearse-like auto. But when she opened the door, her father sat in the back seat looking happy and smiling like a fragile rose. Elena said, "Daddy, are you alive again? I can't believe it! I've missed you so much, daddy, I...."

El Lobito shushed her by putting his index finger over her mouth. His hand was warm.

"Yes, baby. I'm alive again, but only for now. There's something I have to say to you, darling, so listen. Tomorrow night something is going to happen and I want you to be prepared."

"But Daddy, what–"

"Just listen because I don't have much time. Remember–tomorrow night, about 9 o'clock."

And he faded from the car. Elena watched him vanish into thin air. She woke up in a sweat.

Her daddy! Hale and hearty! Not dead! And what did he say? Tomorrow night at nine?

XXII Working on a Mystery. Barry Visits.

The girls were finally going to meet at Marti's house. Jeanine had been to the library and she walked into the den carrying books, sweat plastering down her curly blonde hair. So far, only Jeanine and Marti were there. The books Jeanine carried were about ghosts, ESP, and other mysteries. The big ones were past issues of the *Palmyra Sun*, the local paper that published until 1980 when competition from the Corpus Christi and Brownsville papers made the *Sun* set forever. It was really no loss to the community; word got around well enough by mouth for most things. Marti asked her why she got such old edition books.

"Well, the Allemeist girl looked like someone from the 1950's. I knew that because I've seen pictures of Janie when she was in high school. They wore hair and clothes sort of like that. And I remember the way everyone looked in "Grease" at the movies—you know, that whole fifties scene."

"Oh yeah," said Marti, her eyes lighting up. Just then her mother walked into the den. Marti told her they were working on a local civics project for school next year. Suspicious, her mother inquired deeper.

"We have to see how the city government has changed since, uh, 1951," was Marti's explanation.

Since Marti's parents had moved to Palmyra in 1962, her mother had no interest in the town's past political arrangements. The woman lifted an empty tea glass from the table and said, "How many times do I have to tell you to use a coaster?" to no one in particular. Then, reluctantly somehow, she left. There were edition books of the *Sun* for every year, but there was no index. They would have to go through every issue. Soon afterwards, Betty Sue and Loren came over (without Petey, thank God), and the four girls leaned over the yellowing newspapers bound into book form and studied them as closely as old monks in their scriptoria. With four girls, it was much easier to cover more time; still, they did not seem to be getting anywhere. They were already up to January 1959 when it was time to split up and go home.

Loren: "What will we say we've been doing?"

Marti: "We'll say we've been playing Crazy Eights and talking about boys. They'll believe that."

Jeanine: "I'll leave the other books here, Marti. We can read them tomorrow."

The girls made plans to come to Marti's again the next night. Betty Sue had a date, so Loren walked home by herself. It was about a mile and a half, but the road was safe and no one would bother her.

Her footsteps echoed off the pavement behind her as she stepped onto the lane. The setting sun put a gleam on a cactus and the tops of some tall raintrees in someone's yard. It was certainly a beautiful warm evening, though Loren's thoughts chased each other, diaphanous wisps in a mental graveyard. Would she and the others find something amazing like "ALLEMEIST GIRL KILLED IN TRAGIC ACCIDENT!"? Such appeared not to be the case. And she had other problems. What was she going to do for a summer job? She could not hang around the house, and putting up with Petey all summer would be a pain in the neck. She still needed to talk to Betty Sue about Dauphine's possibly hiring her, but she just had not gotten around to it. Allemeist, Allemeist. A-L-L-E-.... She wondered how it was pronounced.

Dauphine Candor was getting ready for the dinner rush but was annoyed at the little setbacks at the Red Arrow Café. First, Barry Madden had been in to talk with her again, much to the pleasure of the perverted goons in the kitchen. Mr. Rossi had come in one minute before closing time the night before, so the night cook could not shut down the kitchen. Then the dish washer bitched because he could not finish for having to wait on the cook. It was, all around, one of the worst nights ever in her experience with the restaurant business. Barry Madden's visits were bad enough. Why was he paying her so much attention? Like a little electrical playlet currently showing in her skull, Dauphine replayed the mental movie again, trying to find meaning in an apparently meaningless conversation. Was there a layer of meaning in what Barry said that she did not understand? She imagined the Red Arrow as it always looked early in the morning: sleepy-eyed summer people with sunburned, fussy three-year-olds; loudmouth teenagers sitting in the sunny booths and teasing the girls in their group or cracking jokes about odd-looking passersby; the smell of coffee and bacon and doughnuts, the porcelain clatter and clang of stoneware plates hitting each other in the kitchen. And then he comes. Barry comes. A few heads turn. Barry is still handsome, and middle-aged women eye him appraisingly, discreetly. A killer.

Barry looked at Dauphine sheepishly, showing deference.

"Good morning, Dauphine."

She let him call her by her first name because her name tag said it, and she had to wear it every day. Despite herself, Dauphine felt a slight rush of pleasure at hearing his voice. Everything about him irritated her: his walking clothes, his unshaven face, his obviously phony bashfulness in front of her despite his well-known reputation. And yet, his presence had its good sides too, not the least of which was a warm masculine interest in her opinions and conversation. Dauphine was not so sure it was a real interest or just a means to an end, but for the moment she did not care.

"Good morning, Barry," she said, trying to sound too busy to give him the proverbial time of day. She threw the little breakfast menu in front of him as if it were a Frisbee, but at the same time she smiled to let him know she was teasing. He immediately grinned back, beaming so hard that his ears moved up. She went about her business, filling a water glass and getting silverware. One of the kitchen creeps stuck his head into the dining room and looked at Dauphine knowingly. She ignored him after sending him an icy, flashing stare.

"I haven't been here for a while," said Barry.

"That's right, where've you been?"

"Oh, around. I've been trying to find a job here in town. Things look pretty bad all over, though, and it's been rough. But I'll find something soon. I'm not too worried about it yet."

Dauphine wanted to ask him more in the way of personal questions but she hesitated to do it for fear that he would ask her things about herself he had no business knowing—at least for now.

"I need a place to live," said Barry, "because I'm tired of moving around."

Dauphine wiped off the butter pan counter as she thought of Barry's words. How could he need a place to live? He inherited a house here in town. And what did any of this have to do with finding a job? What was this man up to?

XXIII Unpleasant Memories

Mary Ann Banks had a headache due to the noisy air conditioner in the window behind her. Business had been good lately; she was making all kinds of retirement home sales up and down the coast. She thought about buying a new car but could not decide between a foreign or domestic auto. After considering the pros and cons, she was surprised to find she had a painful nagging headache, and the martini at lunch with a prospective buyer had not helped matters. She leaned back in her chair and fell asleep. The same dream that haunted her for years returned with all its nasty familiarity. Mary Ann was doomed to relive her husband's death in dreams of surprising regularity—about once every three weeks.

It always ran the same way: Out the window a thunderstorm's rage swirled in ever-quieting eddies around the skyduster palms, leaving puddles of water around the bottom of each tree. Mary Ann struck dumb and insensate by her husband's heart attack, sat like a wooden marionette looking with knothole eyes through the plate glass window. An old man smoking a cigarette and reading a brightly-colored issue of Life sat in the beige waiting room chair across from her. His occasional, wondering glance asked, "What are you doing here?" though he did not speak.

The smells of alcohol and death hid each other intermittently as nurses breezed through the swinging doors that led to the bowels of the hospital. Mary Ann felt a twinge of nausea when a kind old lady with a flower on her collar came up to her and gave her a towel. The lady spoke about the bad weather and told her she was sure that Mary Ann's husband would be all right. The woman smiled constantly when she talked and Mary Ann responded by smiling back mechanically. But her head was stuffed with cotton; she could not understand what the old lady was talking about. Mercifully, the old woman sensed her intrusion, and after a few more niceties she took Mary Ann's wet towel and went to another part of the waiting room.

Mary Ann was surprised at her own lack of emotion. Here she was in a hospital, it was a few days before Christmas, and she herself was waiting...for what? She knew Bob was dead when she laid eyes on him, but she hoped that maybe, just maybe she was wrong. He had complained of a headache and gone upstairs to bed early. When she came up later he was pale and his skin was very cold. A widow. She was a widow. It was so hard to believe. Did she have to wear black? The absurd question seemed as reasonable as any other did for the moment.

"I want to sit here all day—forever, in fact," she said to herself. "I'm dry, I'm not feeling anything bad, and it's quiet." The old man watched her talk to herself, then was summoned by a nurse to the admissions desk. She droned on and on about a box on the admission form that he had forgotten to fill out. A nurse came through the door a few minutes later.

"Mrs. Banks, would you please follow me?" She was not smiling. She turned on her brisk, rubbery white heels and went back through the swinging doors, detaining it for Mary Ann. Confused and numb, Mary Ann was conscious only of the weight of her purse on her shoulder as she walked through.

The doctor knew all the right things to say, and his tact and brevity comforted Mary Ann. Bob, she was told forthrightly and gently, was dead. He had died at home. The doctor gave her some Valiums and mild sleeping pills. While Mary Ann waited in the anteroom with the nurse, the doctor phoned Wanda Murphy, her friend across town, and told her to come get Mrs. Banks. Wanda's husband Lanky came to the front of the hospital in his green Ford station wagon. Little puffs of exhaust came out of its tailpipe. Lanky looked embarrassed.

"I don't know what to say, Mary Ann. He was a good friend. I just don't know what else to say about Bob than that."

"I think it's a wonderful thing to say, Lanky. Can we go home right now? I'm so tired, so tired."

The ride back to Palmyra was uneventful after the wild ride at 90 to 100 mph the night before. Mary Ann had not ever driven that fast in her life, but she hoped getting to the hospital coronary unit in Brownsville would save her husband's life. It had not. And the drive back to Palmyra had been a strange, quiet journey, past all speech, past all reckoning. The lightning had flashed, the rain poured, the thunder rocked—all the night before. She with her dead husband lying on the backseat of the car where she had dragged him. There had been no time to call anyone but the police, who had escorted her in her high-speed flight down the rain-slicked highway. And now the sun was out and there was nothing to do but listen to the radio and look out the side window at the fields and trees and patches of deserted land.

Mary Ann woke up and tilted her chair back to its working position. She put her head on the desk blotter.

XXIV The Los Cocos Group. Brenda Says Goddammit.

Later in the evening the four girls started to think about getting together again at Marti's house. Only Marti had a home big enough to keep out snoopy siblings and parents, and in her den they could scan the

Sun back-issues and talk about their strategies. Loren had made it home early enough the day before, so there was no problem with her being punished and having to stay home with Petey. The girls had not called each other yet, however. There was still time to do a few chores.

Kuon sat on the Los Cocos seaside porch and casually watched seagulls dive and dip for food. Kuon always wished he could catch a bird to eat, but they proved too fast for him. Popol Vuh squeezed through a jalousie and flew down to where Kuon lay appreciating the thalassic wonders of the Gulf. Popol Vuh was smoking a Winston Otto had given him, and he plopped down in front of Kuon's nose. The old toucan eyed the dog and deliberately blocked his view of the water. Kuon growled and rolled over on his back, his massive legs and paws splayed in the air during a yawn-and-stretch, backscratching exercise. Kuon would not have minded taking a snap at Popol Vuh, but the bird was clever and fast and could always get away. So the two pets lived in an uneasy camaraderie based more on mutual respect than on affection.

Popol Vuh felt ignored and angry and he spit out his cigarette butt. Kuon was not in a playing mood and something had to be done about it. Space music came from the house where Elena was playing with her Yamaha synthesizer.

Elena harbored and nurtured dreams of becoming a retro surf music star even though she knew she was too old for it. The name of her band was going to be Francisco Bizarro, a corruption of the name of the man who conquered Peru and killed the Inca emperor Atahuallpa in 1533. Elena thought it appropriate that Atahuallpa converted to Christianity as the Spaniards garroted him for his country's gold. As his face turned purple and his eyes bulged, the conquistadors prayed for his soul. After all, no gold was attached to that.

All in a day's work.

So, what better name for a band? Elena knew her band would never get started but she liked to think about it anyway. And the word *bizarro* in Spanish means "brave."

She next turned on the ondes martenot, an electronic music instrument that provided outer-space sounds for fifties' sci-fi movies. Its bilious, tinny vibrato keened over the sloping yard of the estate. Kuon hated the ondes martenot. It hurt his ears.

Meanwhile, Popol Vuh was trying to rile Kuon. He turned his beak to the left and right, eyeing the huge hound in front of him. Kuon yawned, showing a fence of white fangs on the red porch of his mouth. Popol Vuh regarded this natural bridgework with feigned disinterest; a direct assault would be impossible. Thinking to give up his mission, the old toucan turned and gave the dog a curt flip of his black tail. Then he saw Kuon's rubber skunk abandoned about three feet from the reclining mutt. A chink in the armor?

It was after dinner but not many people came to the Tropicala that evening. Two drunks and Brenda, the girl who ran a local laundry and dry cleaners and was a regular, sat at a table near the lifted wall. There was only a fitful breeze. Ed listened to all three of them speak conspiratorially about someone else even though he could not make out the whole conversation. Brenda flicked her cigarette into the sombrero-shaped ashtray. She said, "All I know is, goddamn the whole goddamn mess. That's all I know."

Ed grinned and laughed to himself. Brenda was certainly a talker and had an opinion on everything from politics to religion to local union troubles. Her answer to every controversy was a curt *goddammit* and a flick of her cigarette.

Ed finished slicing lemons and limes and then got out the plastic container of margarita salt. He shook some of it into the salter-bowl and then checked his supply of clean glasses.

Running a bar is no easy life. He had to know when to be understanding and when to be firm, when to tease and when to leave customers alone. Ed sighed. He had other problems as well. Crooked barbacks. Dishonest waitresses. Fights. Weirdos. One wimpy-looking salesman came in every three months or so and walked immediately into the woman's restroom. He had caught Brenda once on the toilet and was treated to a stentorian goddammit. For some reason he enjoyed seeing women in bathrooms. After hearing a scream (or curse, in this case) the salesman would run out to the parking lot, evidently satisfied with what he had seen.

Then down Hwy 77 to the next bar, no doubt. And from then on, Brenda latched the bathroom door behind her when she went in.

Ed glanced at the slowly revolving Coors clock that showed a moving mountain stream in the background. It was nearly 7:30 and still no more customers. Edna Parker, his pianist and friend, chose to walk in the door at that moment. She smiled with her whole wrinkled face. She loved the sea and sun, and their mutual three-way kiss had left her an old-looking woman even though she was only forty-nine. She sidled up to the bar and Ed poured her a light gin-and-tonic. It was her only drink most evenings since she had to keep her wits about her to play the piano.

"Hello, Ed," said Ed Fernandez, teasing Edna for their similarity in names.

"Hello, Ed," she responded. Ed asked her once why she wanted to be a pianist at a piano bar when she had a whole summer to be with her husband and kids.

"You just answered your own question, kiddo," said Edna. She liked to call him kiddo.

Edna tugged at her white, short summer culottes and retied the string tie on her purple, peasant-cotton blouse. Ed caught a glimpse of a gold chain around her neck. She always wore discreet but beautiful rings, usually diamonds or emeralds. She looked out of place here, a woman of position slumming in a dingy little South Texas bar. But Edna was genuinely fond of her job and usually had a brandy snifter full of dollar bills by the end of the evening. Then, after three months of such evenings, she and her family would leave for their uppercrust life in Houston, where Mr. Parker was really Dr. Parker—a heart specialist of national reputation. Edna then did charity work, played bridge, went to PTA meetings, worked out at the spa, and ate chicken salad sandwiches for nine months until it was time to pack the Mercedes and head for the Valley again.

Edna and her three children—Chuck, Danny, and Howie—always came to their South Sand Island condo on June first and left on August thirty-first. The father joined them by private plane when he could. Edna loved him but did not want to be around him too much because he took away from her piano practice time. She also wrote original music, just for the Tropicala patrons. It was an odd life, but a good and happy one for Edna. The only thing that worried her was Chuck's withdrawal from life, his gradual pulling-away from friends and school and social activities—all for his new passion: astronomy. Edna began to wonder if his eye was attached permanently to the lens of his reflecting telescope.

"It's a phase," she told herself. "He'll grow out of it soon." But when? He was seventeen. "A phase of what? the Moon?" Edna stared at the back of Ed's head as he was busy at the cash register counting out the night's till.

"Ed," she asked.

"What, honey?"

"Kiddo, do you realize that I've never asked you any personal questions? And we've been friends all this time."

"Oh Jesus. Fire away." Ed threw his hands up in mock despair.

"You told me when I applied for this job that you were divorced. What was your wife like?" asked Edna.

"She was a pretty little girl I knew in high school. When I got back from the service I was convinced I was in love with Guadalupe--I called her Lupita; everybody did."

"Was she Mexican?"

"No—born in Crystal City about the same time as me."

"What happened? If you don't mind talking about it."

"No, I don't mind. I used to, though. Jesus, we were real young and I wanted the *solar*, you know? A family house in suburban Brownsville, a step over the border into the mother country."

"And?" asked Edna because Ed's attention began to wander.

"Lupita and I were happy for about a year and a half. Then my mind started working on something else."

"What!" cried Edna. "You mean you started cheating on her?"

"Oh no," Ed laughed quietly. "I mean, my brain started wandering. After about a year of struggling to get and keep a job, I started staying up at night just to hear the freight trains pass. I wanted to see the world. I didn't do that too much in the army, just saw a few bases in the South—nothing special. I got restless. Lupita still loved me, though. She was a good woman. We didn't have kids. Maybe that would've made a difference."

"It probably would've," offered Enda.

"Yeah, maybe. But you know something else, Edna?" he squinted under the black light and looked at the pianist intently. "I never got a chance to be alone. Lupita never let me just sit and think. It was always do this, do that....my brains never got a chance to rest. `Let's go visit my mother, let's go visit your mother, let's go to the store, let's visit the neighbors—'." Ed hit his forehead with the heel of his hand. "She made me want to do, want to live every minute like it was the last minute on earth. Then one day I thought to myself, `This is good but it's not for me,' and I left her."

"I'm sorry," said Edna, genuinely meaning it.

"No, don't apologize for anything," he said. "There's nothing to apologize for when two people find out they got two different kinds of life in them. She couldn't understand my way and I couldn't live hers. But the split was OK, we're still on talking terms. No hard feelings. And Lupita's remarried."

"What about you?"

"Remarry? I'm thinking about that. I'd like to, but I have to be sure of one thing."

"What's that?" asked Edna.

"It has to be a woman who can love other stuff besides me. And one who can travel at the drop of a hat--or the picking up of one."

Just then Brenda and the two men laughed at a private joke they were sharing.

"Goddammit!" went the cheery, beery voice of Brenda around the room. The two men turned around. They were Lanky Murphy and Barry Madden.

XXV Domestic Grief and Hangovers

The summer moon began to shine over Palmyra, and the wind began to blow warm over the coastal town but cool at the beach. Janie Norworthy had had a bad day, and her husband Lenny was saying something about the spinach. She turned her face to him, irritated at the interruption in the train of her thoughts. Jeanine, who had come over for dinner, suddenly had a stricken look on her face. She knew what was coming. Janie had hoped to talk with her about her educational plans to find out what her goals were, and if she could, to steer her away from the humanities. She was nonplussed when Jeanine told her she had to go to Marti's house that evening. Here Janie had gone to a lot of trouble, and her little sister decided to bug out after the evening meal.

Lenny was saying that he did not like the boiled egg slices in the spinach. The children placidly picked at their food. Jeanine seemed lost in thought. And Lenny kept talking about spinach. From nowhere, it seemed later, fury swallowed the heart and mind of Janie Norworthy, and something went off like a bomb in her head. No tears, no crying—that was not her style. Carried on a tide of anger, Janie was almost afraid of the sound of her voice, a rasping shriek seeking a vulnerable spot on the person of her husband.

"Who cares what you want, you stupid bastard!" The words coming out of her mouth of their own accord like a spasm of desire. Jeanine stared at her with saucer eyes, the children turned around and cranked up for crying, Lenny looked at her as if she were an alien from Neptune. She threw her plate like a flying saucer across the room." I hate your guts, you utter moron! I must have been crazy to marry you! What did I ever see in you?" And with that she stalked out of the house and into her car.

Jeanine was embarrassed for Lenny. There he sat stunned with disbelief.

"What did I say?" he asked Jeanine. She could feel herself blushing. She took the children out of their highchairs, then turned to Lenny.

"I think I better go now," she said quickly and flew out the screen door before Lenny could say anything.

Someone got Brenda home all right, apparently, because she was not sitting at the table when Barry got back from the bathroom. Lanky was so drunk his eyes were glazed and crossed. Barry knew that he himself was not in better shape. It was clear: Lanky had not drunk this much since his college days in New Orleans, at the Seven Seas Bar. He wondered for a moment if Lanky was dead. He was catatonically still, staring ahead, with a stupidly sagging face. Barry spoke to him.

"Lanky? Lank, you alive? Hey, wake up."

"Yeah, I'm okay. Where you been?"

"Bathroom."

"Oh (burp)." Lanky put his fist on his mouth and yawned. "Gee, I didn't know I could still drink like this."

Barry laughed at him and gently said, "You can't."

He helped Lanky find his hat and led him by the arm to the door. Barry had long experience helping friends out of bars, as well as being helped out of bars himself. Ed Fernandez noticed and thought they should not be attempting to drive back to town. The Tropicala needed a bouncer/waiter/bartender. Could Ed have found the right man for the job? He was sort of familiar too. A moth flew in front of a black light tube, agog at the moony purple glow. What was left of Edna's gin and tonic glowed metallic blue-green as its ice cubes melted. In the truck, weaving homeward outside:

"Had a nice time, Barry. Brenda was funny. We shouldn't be driving...."

"Curses a lot, don't she?"

"Only says 'goddammit', nothing else," said Lanky, then adding, "Hey, I got someone for...for you to meet."

"Yeah? Who? I don't know if I trust your fixups. I haven't seen you for years."

"It was funny we run into each other today after all these years, and you walking down the street like you own it."

"Yeah, you old pistol, it's been a long time, ain't it?"

Barry paused and turned his wobbly head to Lanky. Landscape went by. One of them was driving, Barry thought. But who? The he realized his hands were in his lap and he could hear a truck engine rumbling. Lanky was driving, much to Barry's relief.

'God, I'm going to feel like hell tomorrow' ran through Barry's head. Lanky said, "What were we talking about?"

"You were going to fix me up."

"Oh yeah, her name is Dauphine, you'll lo...love her." "What? Who? You know I have been trying to get up the nerve to ask her out for a week now! And you're gonna ask her for me? Great!" Barry let out a drunken whoop.

Lanky stopped the truck.

"Uh-oh, I think...I think I'm gonna be sick..."

XXVI Expectation

Though it was just dark, it seemed to the two men that it was past midnight. Lanky was miserable for the rest of the trip home. Barry drove for him.

"Barry," he began suddenly, "I'm looking for something, you know? I gotta nice family and we have a lot of fun together and all. And yet I'm still looking for something, you know?" Glancing at the form hunched down in the seat next to him. "Yes, I do. I do know what you mean."

"Why am I dissatisfied then? I should be happy if I got everything. I don't think about this all the time...Just once in a while, though—....

"No one goes through life with everything they want," Barry answered quietly.

"You're right, sure. But I think there's going to be an answer for me soon. And then I'll know what it is that'll make me happy. I don't know when. But I have a feeling it's going to be soon."

XXVII More Sorrow

Two hours earlier, Mrs. Tikhonov had brushed small bits of potting soil from her hands and pulled off the green Sears garden gloves. She was trying to mulch some golden raintrees she moved from the north side of her house two years ago. Even today's small effort left her exhausted and the evening's balmy wind had not helped the way she thought it would. Pasha was inside, watching the TV set. Silvery light patches, she could see through the window, danced over his glasses, his face and chest. Yelena pulled herself up first on one foot, then the other. She hobbled over to the chaise lounge and sat down slowly. Every muscle ached as she poured herself a glass of water from the lime-green plastic pitcher with Mickeys, Donalds, and Plutos on it. She wiped her brow and thought about her garden, her home, her life. The wind grew stronger.

"Look how these things grow here!" she said aloud to no one at all. "And I love the smell of the dirt and the warm air and the way the clouds gather to the east, in castles so high they look like fortresses on cliffs. This isn't like Russia at all," said Yelena to

herself. "It isn't like Berlin or Paris or New York. I have found happiness, I have found contentment here. I know Pavel has found the same things. We can go no farther down any road." Old visions of greatcoats, sleighbells, and onion-dome churches passed through her mind. For a moment she could hear the soft guitars, see the glass of claret before her at the Astoria in St. Petersburg . . .
A strong gust of wind moved things in the yard. Her patio chimes rang.

She took another sip of water, her thoughts turning to an old heartbreak, her grandson Valerian who had left so unfortunately, so unexpectedly many years ago, after the tragedy that had changed him. It was so hard to lose a daughter-in-law in a kidnapping incident. She was never found again. Valerian was broken after that. He drifted to New Orleans, then Memphis, then disappeared in Chicago. So far away! So unhappy a young man! And now he would have been forty-one—a young, vigorous age! The family could assume only that he was dead, and Yelena prayed every night for the souls of her blond-haired, blue-eyed Valerian and his wife. She was sure of one thing. Her grandson would never have left to go so far away on his own. She knew the truth: gypsies drugged him, threw him in the trunk of an old car and took him away, hoping for ransom. But when they found the Tikhonovs poor, they killed him. That was the only explanation that made sense. She glanced up to see Pavel looking at the television. She heard rattling behind her—the jingle-ringle of a chain-link fence being moved.

Two gypsies with daggers clenched in their teeth were sneaking towards her, crouched down and with sneers on their twisted faces. In horror she sat up to call Pavel.

"Pa...!" was all that came out of her mouth before she grasped her chest, leaned forward trying to breathe, then rattled her throat. The old eyes saw the last of her garden. Where else can Mrs. Tikhonov go? Is there another place on earth?

Pavel found her later, draped oddly on her chaise lounge. Two large pieces of cardboard had blown into the yard. Where had they come from? The look of terror on his wife's face had been undeniable.... Could this cardboard have had anything to do with it?

XXVIII Inspiration for Amy

Amy Mortcap had finished watching "Family Follies" on TV and waited quietly for thirty minutes until Sister Thompson's Radio Revival Hour came on her little portable Sony. During the interval she usually prayed or tried to do some darning or green bean snapping.

She tugged at her white turban and wondered if Zillah's day off was today, tomorrow, or the next day. Slowly, Amy's world was shrinking; she daily lost some bits of information that once made her what she was—a strong woman, a proud woman of faith. Amy knew she was dying, but she hated to die in her ugly little shack, under the horse-head lamp. She looked at the open can of pork and beans in front of her. It was the best she could do, now that she was too old to stand in the kitchen, cooking like a young woman with a family to feed.

'I'm hungry,' she said to herself. She knew no human ear was listening. Reaching over to her radio, she flipped the on switch and tried to find XERK by sound alone. It was not easy. There were many Country-and-Western and Mexican stations, all competing for gritty AM-radio space. Finding her station, Amy waited for the familiar organ chord-roll that announced Sister Thompson's show. Amy went to the kitchen to get a drink of water, and by the time she got back the program had already started. She sat down nice and slow, actually falling the last two inches with a soft grunt of effort. A little cloud of dust rose from the chair's back.

MY BELOVED FRIENDS, began Sister Thompson, I WANT TO TELL YOU SOMETHING VERY, VERY SERIOUS TONIGHT.

There was a pregnant silence, a sigh of anticipation.

I HAVE BROADCASTED FROM THIS HERE RADIO STATION FOR SEVEN YEARS COME THIS AUGUST.

Amy said, "Amen!"

THIS SERIOUS THING I HAVE GOT TO TELL YOU ABOUT IS I WON'T BE ON THE AIR ANYMORE. Amy's weathered face was expressionless. DUE TO FINANCIAL PROBLEMS I AM FORCED TO DROP THIS SOUL-SAVING LIFE-RENEWING WORK. IT HASN'T BEEN EASY, MY

FRIENDS. YOUR CARDS AND LETTERS OF ENCOURAGEMENT HAS BEEN A BLESSING TRULY.

Amy's face sagged slowly, her head wagging in disbelief. The can of pork and beans fell out of her lap and onto the floor. A young pullet on the front stoop saw it and came in to peck at it.

Amy always wanted to write Sister Thompson a letter just like the other listeners but she never could: she did not know how to read and write. The program dragged on but the old woman caught only the last few words of the show:

AND FOR THE LAST TIME, FRIENDS, I SPEAK TO YOU AS SISTER THOMPSON IN BROADCAST AROUND THE STATE OF TEXAS. DO THIS FOR THE LORD AND FOR SISTER THOMPSON—GO OUT INTO THE WORLD AND BE SOMEONE'S MOTHER. IT DON'T MAKE NO DIFFERENCE TO THEM IF YOU ARE A MAN OR A WOMAN OR BOY OR GIRL. YOU NEED TO FIND BODIES AND SOULS TO TAKE CARE OF OR YOU WILL SURELY DIE. AS I SAY GOODBYE, I TELL YOU ONCE AGAIN THIS IS MY LAST SHOW. GO OUT INTO THE WORLD AND BE SOMEBODY'S MOTHER. THEY NEED YOU TODAY. AMEN AND AMEN....GOODBYE, BELOVED FRIENDS, AND GO IN THE LIGHT OF GOD, WHO IS FATHER AND MOTHER OF ALL PEOPLE, LIVING OR DEAD.

Amy sat in her chair for a few minutes. The station crackled with static, now empty of programs.

"I so lonely," she said. The pullet looked up and studied her, then went back to its eating.

She got out of her chair and went to the door, looking at her chickens, her banana trees, her withering space in the world. Then she hobbled into her room, filled a suitcase with a few personal items, and waited until dawn. Amy knew what she had to do. "I gonna do what Sister Thompson say. I gonna be somebody else mama now. Zillah don't need me no more." She wanted to spend her few remaining years on earth doing what she knew she must do.

Her many children met several years later, discussing what had happened to their mother. They were humiliated by reports of her vagrant behavior and ragged appearance. Thinking to commit her to an asylum, they had combed the highways of Texas and

Louisiana trying to find where Amy had gone. One hot summer day, one of Zillah's brothers, Abner, pulled into a Lake Charles, Louisiana, Seven-Eleven store. He asked the attendant if she had seen a very old woman walking along the highway. The manager in the back overheard the conversation and came out with his eyes fixed on Abner.

"She not only passed by, mister, she came in here passing out a bunch of fruitcake leaflets about being everybody's mother. She said she was going from convenience store to convenience store in the whole world to tell the people what the Lord told her to say. Now, I am a religious man myself, but I don't go in for...." Abner interrupted.

"Mister, do you have one of those flyers? I'd like to see it."

"Yeah, as a matter of fact I do," said the manager, "just in case there was some trouble with the cops." He opened his grimy little desk in the back and came out with the flyer. Abner ran his eyes over it quickly. In bright red capitals it proclaimed:

I'M YOUR MOTHER.
THE LORD SENT ME TO HELP
YOU ANY WAY I CAN.
AMY, DISCIPLE OF HEAVEN.

Abner turned back to the parking lot. He glanced to the east, almost wishing he could see Amy tottering down the road, tearing bits of paper from an old bag to pass the time as she walked and sweated her way towards who knows where. Abner went back to Texas and gathered the family together to tell them the news.

And Amy herself?

She was smart enough to get off and stay off the interstate, spending nights by the roadside in shacks or churches or mobile homes where religious people would have her. Occasionally she thought about Zillah as she looked into dark woods on her way along the Gulf Coast. No one bothered her. Even though an old lady, she seemed utterly harmless and so poor that she was not worth robbing. Once a young black man in Mobile stopped her.

"What you got in that bag?" he said, snatching it from her. All he saw was some dirty clothes and printed leaflets. Seeing nothing of monetary value in the bag, he threw it on the ground and continued on his way. Amy picked them up patiently and kept walking, her arms burdened by the pink and red flyers holding her message to the world.

XXIX Domestic Grief

Elena was drinking gin and tonics. It was exactly 9 PM when Elena closed her writing desk and reached up to turn off a lamp in the shape of the planet Saturn, one of her prized possessions. She had been writing a letter to her agent in Costa Rica, telling him she thought Popol Vuh would be returning to his country at least one more winter. She sighed and reached behind her to scratch the nape of her neck.

A terrible din came into the house from the patio—a tremendous barking and growling and squawking and talking. Kuon, she saw, was leaping in the air. He snapped and snapped at two black shapes in the air above him. His tooth-filled muzzle closed and opened like boxcar couplers. One of the black shapes was Popol Vuh. He was trying desperately to maintain his altitude and hold Kuon's rubber skunk in his bill at the same time. The old bird was drifting into the patio door, which Elena quickly opened.

"Give me that!" she cried, and snatched the rubber skunk from midair—only the toucan was still attached. Popol Vuh was slung shot across the room. He landed on top of an Old Dutch etagere, and knocked down several seashell displays and a "Visit Florida" conch lamp spray-coated with red glitter.

Kuon was not exactly sleeping through the escapade; he made several more lunges for his skunk as the bird drifted sideways and down before Elena had grabbed it. In one last frantic effort, the German shepherd leaped into the air and flew toward his beloved mistress. Unable to make a mid-flight correction, Kuon sent Elena spinning into the etagere where the unconscious bird already lay sprawled with his beak wedged into a nautilus shell. Everything fell on Elena as Zillah and Otto ran from opposite directions to see what was causing the commotion.

"Himmel!" said Otto.

"Jesus!" said Zillah.

Kuon had his skunk again and held it defensively in his mouth and under his paw. But his attention was broken when he saw Elena's fuzzy-slippered feet sticking out from a pile of old seashells. Fearing reprisal, the massive dog yipped and fled through the patio door, and out into the night. Zillah and Otto tried to revive Elena but she was out cold, knocked unconscious.

And again she saw her father.

XXX El Lobito Finally Speaks

El Lobito was looking at the eastern horizon as the sun rose. He was wearing his old white summer suit and the almost-opaque sunglasses he always wore in life when the sun was too bright for his sensitive eyes. Elena spoke to her father.

"Daddy, it's you. You said you were coming back and now here you are. What do you have to tell me about, Daddy? You said before that it was very important."

"Elena, mi hijita, I am here just one more time to tell you something I feel you need to know. Sad your mother couldn't be here. Her spirit didn't want to return, even for a little time. But that doesn't matter. You'll see her before too long yourself. You aren't young anymore, daughter."

Elena shuddered at his words. They were true. Perhaps twenty years separated her and death.

"Well, then, father, tell me what you have to tell me."

El Lobito removed his glasses, and in place of eyes there were points of light, with rays radiating in all directions.

"Then hear me, daughter! Your fate does not lie in this place. You must find the twelve people who will make themselves known to you. You'll know them when you see them."

Elena tried to interrupt with questions.

"Don't say anything, girl!" he shouted. Elena sat respectfully at his side as he continued to speak, squinting at the terrible light in his eyes. A mist was forming around his head. At this, a greater urgency passed into his voice.

"You will know the twelve when you see them, and when you are gathered you will leave this place, and leave it forever. You may never return to Los Cocos, but the others may return if they choose to. Don't try to interrupt me! I have almost no time left."

Elena wiped the corner of her eye. Then her secret feelings all these years had been true: she was destined to leave Palmyra, just as she suspected. It was one reason why she never really wanted to be involved too deeply with the locals, and somehow she had known all these years. El Lobito paused momentarily, then continued.

"And where will you go? You must go the land of Altun Ha, far to the southeast."

"Where?" she asked.

"To the land of Altun Ha. After spending a night on the main pyramid, you will face the sea at dawn. There a wonderful revelation awaits you, and then you will know YOUR DUTY TO YOURSELF."

El Lobito began to fade, and Elena jumped up at the first ray of dream-dawn's light filled her eye Elena screamed frantically,

"WHERE IS ALTUN HA?"

"ALTUN HA?"

"ALTUN HA?"

"ALTUN HA?"

"Altun Ha? Altun Ha?"

"Vot iss she trying to say, Zillah?"

"Beats me," said the maid.

Otto scratched his baldhead and absentmindedly patted Kuon's back. The dog had come back in several minutes before, with a sheepish, apologetic look on his face. The dog scanned Elena's face anxiously as she came out of her faint.

"QUICK!!" shouted Elena suddenly.

"Ach!" shouted Otto.

"Eeek!" screamed Zillah, who let go of Elena and fell backwards. Kuon barked and Popol Vuh squawked a muffled sound as he worked his beak loose from the nautilus shell. Elena shocked them all.

"Quick! Get a pencil, Zillah, and write this down. Are you ready? Well, hurry please!"

Elena was concentrating so hard that she did not even raise herself from the floor. She lay looking at the ceiling, her gray-brown eyes somewhat glazed by her confusion and the blow to the head. She gave the maid the number 12 and the words "Altun Ha." Zillah did not spell it correctly but that did not matter. Elena finally got up and went to the sofa. Otto and Zillah looked at her with amazement. Elena had always been strange, but this last incident was the strangest of all. Elena looked at them hovering over her head.

"Don't worry about me," she said. "I'm fine. I have some thinking to do, so you two can go about your business." She smiled warmly at them as they left. The room moved uneasily as Elena tried to sit up. She was slightly nauseated from the bump on her head, but her thinking had never been clearer. First things first, she thought. I have to find out where Altun Ha is. And she knew someone in town who might know. The Muñoz family realtor, Mary Ann Banks, mentioned once to Raul Muñoz that she had a woman on her staff who knew about ancient civilizations. The name Altun Ha might be known to her. The southeast her father referred to could not have meant the Egyptian pyramids since they were actually to the northeast from where Elena lived in South Texas. That left Latin America. It was late but Elena knew what she had to do. Packing now, then the research. She flew up the stairs, her sandals clattering on the shiny marble steps.

XXXI The Murphy's' Scheme

"You WHAT?" shouted Wanda.

"So who cares?" said Lanky. "What difference does it make?" he hung his head.

"It makes plenty! Jesus, Lanky! Dauphine is our friend, and you want to match her up with Barry Madden? Don't you remember his reputation? Christ, how could you do this?"

"Well, honey, I didn't think you'd get so put out over nothing! It's just a date and Dauphine can certainly take care of herself. The way you carry on, you'd think I was the preacher marrying them or something." Petey ran in.

"Mama, Loren isn't here. I can't find her." Wanda nervously smoothed the tousled hair on Petey's head.

"That's OK, darling. Loren is spending the night at Marti's. They're having a slumber party." Petey and Lanky rolled their eyes upward in mock pain. Pity Marti's family! Listening to that giggling all night long.

Wanda took a sip from her cup and turned her attention back to Lanky. She showed a forced calm.

"And so when is this big date you set up for Dauphine?" she asked, glancing over the rim of the cup.

"Tomorrow night," said Lanky.

"Well, that'll give me some time—not a lot—to help Dauphine pick out a dress and do her hair." Wanda's eyes focused out beyond Lanky's head, as if she were trying to visualize Dauphine's appearance in several dresses and hairdos. Lanky began staring at a spot outside the breakfast room window. Wanda nodded.

"Yes, I hope this date doesn't turn out to be a mistake."

XXXII Research

Scene: Marti's basement

Situation: The four cruising teens are getting restless looking through the back issues of the *Sun*. Jeanine picks up her coke and flips a page quickly. Betty Sue absentmindedly stuffs potato chips in her mouth. Marti and Loren comment on the old clothing advertisements while they look for anything about the ghost. The girls are seated on the floor around a large coffee table.

Jeanine: "Hand me the other half of that sandwich, will you, Marti? Thanks."
Marti: "It has to be here somewhere. I know what I—what we felt. We weren't wrong, were we? Oh, look at this dress. Can you believe somebody would actually wear that?"
Loren: "No. But why does it seem like so long ago? It was just a few days ago that we went to Brownsville."
Jeanine: "I know what you mean. I feel the same way. There's something kinda spooky about all this dead girl business. Do you think it's right to...to disturb the dead?"
Betty: "What do you mean, dummy? It's them that disturbed us! We were minding our own business when we passed through that part of the road."
Loren: "Well, let's go up to 1963. It can't be any later than that—not unless Allemeist was some weirdo who didn't keep up with fashions. Like I said before, this may be crazy. We probably won't get any in...."
Jeanine: "Loren? What are you staring at? [Other girls look up, almost frightened] Loren? LOREN? Answer me!!"

Loren: "Look. Oh my God, look at this. Oh look at it!" passing the volume over to Betty Sue and Jeanine; Marti runs around to the other side to read]"
Marti: [reading aloud]

"HIGHWAY DEATH
August 20, 1959. Kenedy County police headquarters and Texas State Highway Patrol in Kingsville report the accidental death of Karen Allemeister, 17, of Palmyra. Details of the accident have been gathered from eye-witnesses who claim that Miss Allemeister fell from the back of a pickup truck into the path of an oncoming car driven by Edward Fernandez, 23, of Brownsville."
"I think he's the man who owns the Tropicala."

[Marti breaks off here, unable to make a big effort to stop shaking]
Betty: [gently] "Marti, do you want me to finish reading?"
Marti: "No, thanks. I think I can finish."

"Allemeister was returning home from a picnic date with a boyfriend from Palymra when she accepted a lift from Otto Scheinke, a new employee of the Muñoz family. No charges have been filed against Scheinke or Fernandez, pending autopsy report. Her guardian, Mrs. Sarah Jerralds of 422 Tooley Blvd., Palmyra, survives Miss Allemeister. Interment will be at 4:30 Friday, August 24 at Seaview Gardens Cemetery. Classmates of Miss Allemeister are asked to attend."

The four girls looked at each other in dazed wonder. Marti glanced at her watch.

"Let's get in the car and go back," she said. "We can talk in the car." The girls had to sneak out the high basement window.

XXXIII What Future?

Janie Norworthy grew tired of driving up and down Tooley Blvd. Her anger passed but now the dawning realization of what she had said to her husband, and even in front of her sister, left her feeling ashamed and guilty. She pulled into a small store parking lot and bought a pack of cigarettes. She had not smoked for five years—or was it six?—but she needed a smoke now. The little convenience store was packed with cans, produce, Fritos in small packages, magazines, liquor, limp celery, dairy products. Janie asked the fat, watery-eyed lady behind the counter for a pack of Winstons. It was the same brand that Otto and Popol Vuh smoked; however, Janie was of course unaware of the coincidence of their preferences. She paid for the cigarettes, a can of beer, and a candy bar. As she walked out the door, an old feeling of affection for Lenny, her husband, came over her. She pushed the feeling back inside. She had outgrown him, she told herself. He was a good man, a kind man, but what future could they have together? What future?

A voice stilled by years of training called up from the recessed of her mind. She opened the car door and got in. The voice asked, What future? What future? What kind of future were you wanting in the first place?

She slammed the door, turned and craned her neck to see out the back window, then roared off down Tooley as the summer people began to congregate in the front of bars, nightclubs, restaurants, the Tetrapylon Game Parlor, and the Red Arrow Café. Dauphine Candor was serving coffee to Mr. Rossi and trying to smile, without much success. Amy Mortcap would put her first religious leaflet in the same convenience store the next day. It would be handwritten on a piece of paper by person or persons unknown. Amy did not know how to write.

Janie, not being there that day, did not care. She was cruising down Tooley. How odd! She had not done this since she and her friends were in high school. She remembered those days–she remembered when she, Karen, and Wanda used to drive around looking for excitement and boys on a Friday or Saturday night. Wanda had Lanky, even then, but she would go along sometimes just to be a good sport. Janie was coming up on 422 Tooley. This is where Karen used to live with Mrs. Jerralds. Janie felt loneliness, an old ache she had not felt for years. Oh yes, her dead friend Karen. What times they had had. How funny Karen had always been!

This beer is making me maudlin. I hate beer!

Janie never talked about her friendship with Karen after the girl's death. Her parents knew she had been disturbed deeply by the death because the two had been like sisters, but Janie never showed any emotion—either receiving the news of her friend's death, attending the burial, or living on afterwards. She never again spoke of Karen to family or friends.

Janie white-knuckled the steering wheel. She kept driving down Tooley until, before she knew it, she was out of town. The turnoff to the main highway veered to the right, the Rise and Los Cocos to the left. Janie passed the ramshackle Mortcap house. She passed Zillah who was taking the long road to Los Cocos and looking squarely at her path ahead. Then she continued on until she reached the top of the rise. Glancing to the south, she could see trucks from Norias and Armstrong delivering King Ranch goods to the rest of America. Cars filled with working 'sin papeles' hastened back to the border. Janie at that moment decided to go to Mexico for a few days. It would be nice to get away and do some exploring. She turned to get back in her car, but standing in her way was a huge growling German shepherd. Janie stood very still as the dog began to bark and growl intermittently. A black shape fluttered from palm tree to palm in the year beyond the fence. Perhaps a bat? Janie could see the shape out of the corner of her eye. She dared not move while the bristling dog stood just five feet away. What a night this was!

Mary Ann Banks could not sleep. She thought about going to the office to tie up some loose ends. That not being a good idea, she went instead to the fridge and got a piece of cheese. Flopping down the hall in her raggedy cloth slippers, coffee-stained and faded and marvelously comfortable, she addressed her mind to some of the issues in her secretly owned philosophy books. This evening's chapter dealt with the nature of truth. The more she read, the more she began to think that philosophy now depends heavily on science. But there were still realms of thought where science was not supposed to go and did not even want to go. The nature of truth, as far as anyone cared, is odd but not completely unknowable. Most valid knowledge can arrive in several ways, but our culture has generally recognized two: revelation and knowledge obtained through observation. The first way Mary Ann had no use for. Revelation meant nothing to her insofar as the Bible goes. Much of it, to her thinking, was provincial and inaccurate. She could dismiss the Bible, on the whole. But revelation completely? Revelation in some other form?

Getting back, she kicked off her sandals and got in bed, then thought better of it and went to the bathroom. Three minutes later she emerged from the bathroom and covered herself with the sheet. Pensively poking the last morsel of snack between her jaws, Mary Ann admitted to herself that the notion of revelation held an attraction for her; it was so much easier and more dramatic than learning by the scientific method. Would it not have been wonderful if some "bright Being" had appeared to Socrates or Plato and his group, explaining what the future would hold, exposing to them the faulty premises they sometimes built their opinions on? Or, if it were possible, what if that same Being had appeared to a twenty-year-old Christ?

Mary Ann felt a slight pain in a twingy nerve in her back and turned over to her normal, on-the-stomach sleeping position. Maybe it is time for a new kind of revelation. What kinds of things would we learn from it? Where would it come from? How would it change us? Have I put the cat out?

Mary Ann Banks, with the discipline typical of all of us, had turned her thoughts to her cat, a car battery that needed replacing, several small-parcel land deals in Sarita and a stray thought or two for her dead husband. He had been dead for so long that Mary Ann almost thought of him as always having been dead. Sleep, deep and sound, overtook her.

XXXIV Sneaking Out

It was very late when the four cruising teens left Palmyra and headed south through fields of ripening milo and groves of oranges. For once, the radio was off and the girls did little talking. The eerie feeling that Betty Sue and Loren got the night of the discovery of Karen Allemeister was returning with a startling, powerful intensity. Jeanine felt the hairs at the base of her neck rise as she considered Karen's clammy presence and the world beyond the grave. Being from Texas, three of the girls had no doubt of the existence of God, but since they had been raised in more or less prosperous American homes, their experience of death was limited to faraway deaths of great-aunts, premature infants belonging to grown cousins, and the like. Actual death with all its implications seemed a bad joke perpetrated by television to frighten them. They did not know it, but one of them was afraid of the death principle itself, which had snuffed out Karen so completely, so conclusively, so unfairly and at so similar an age to theirs. Marti kept squirming in the driver's seat. These thoughts were on her mind, just as they were on Jeanine's and Betty Sue's minds. Loren let the warm wind buffet her face. Her window was the only one open. Her hair, tossed in a blonde angry torrent around her head, continually beat at her cheeks and temples. She too felt the approach and triumph of death but was relieved to know that at least something came after the procession was over. In its own way, the forms and essences of life continued past the grave—something that Loren had secretly doubted since late childhood. She had also doubted the very existence of a universal intelligence. At Christmas and Easter her childhood self and her love of God revived, but after the cultural heritage and the holidays went their ways, the old nagging doubt began again. Loren of course would never discuss her doubts with anyone. They seemed perverse and absurd in the face of so much popular opinion, and yet....

But here, here where she lived in Palmyra, a young girl who had not experienced love and the mysteries of adult life felt suddenly reassured, intrigued, and wiser in the vicarious embrace of sober Death. She still was not certain of God's existence, but at least something did happen after people died.

The girls continued their lonely nighttime trek southward. Coming down from a small hill, they passed the clump of live oaks and headed a little farther down the road.

Then the radio came on by itself.

Marti screamed and the others followed suit. Loren was shocked out of her daydream and tried to turn off the AM-FM Motorola radio, but the knob turned itself again. Marti's eyes bugged out and she nearly drove off the highway before feeling the gravel on the road's shoulder and applying the brakes. Plumes of dust followed out into the darkness behind them.

The windows rolled down by themselves, the window cranks spinning wildly. The girls tried to roll the windows up, squealing in terror. The radio static cleared and suddenly Sister Thompson's radio show came on for some seconds, soon followed by Connie Francis singing "Who's Sorry Now?" No one noticed in all the panic, Betty Sue grabbed Loren and screamed.

"I was afraid something like this—"

"Let's get out of—!"

"I'm scared, I want to go—!"

"Let go of my arm—!"

"Let's get out of this—!" Then no radio, then stillness. Then no wind. A glow before the hood of the car. And then, the apparition.

XXXV Isolation Ends

Elena inspected her front lawn filled with royal palms. They chattered in the night breeze, the stars overhead brillianted like frozen gems; Kuon and Popol Vuh raced in a zigzag pattern over the small open area among the throngs of tropical foliage. Lushly colored flowers—orchids, begonias, bird of paradise, jasmine, gardenias, jacaranda and malinche—threw fragrances into the night air like a distracted old woman. Suddenly Kuon raced to the front gate, leaping the low fence in one jump.

Elena raised her head from the glass of chilled white wine she was drinking. Her white gown, diaphanous in the light air currents, flowed behind her as she made her curious way after Kuon. Popol Vuh hid in his sneaky toucan ways, flying clumsily from one palm thatch to another. Elena looked quickly back at her odd house. The jalousies of the third floor were lit, but the exterior paints had faded in the moonlight. From a first story window she saw the gleam of black lights in the den and saw Otto's round head as he washed pans after dinner. Zillah was in her room, probably watching TV. The sea beyond the house flowed like moonlit mercury.

Following Kuon's track, she was concerned that he might attack someone beyond the gate. She would have to retrieve him soon or there might be trouble—something she did not want, now that she knew what the future held. Peering through the iron bars, she saw a young lady in dark blue slacks and light cotton blouse poised against the hood of her beige '80 Citation, her eyes pinned to the big dog blocking her way to the car door. Janie second-guessed the dog and walked slowly around the front of the car to get to the passenger side.

"Hello," said Elena, from behind a tree. She identified herself and named Kuon as her guard. Janie thought the woman had to be either fascinating or crazy or possibly both. Somehow the face was familiar. Maybe she had seen it before she went to college. Anyway, the dog backed off and it was time to speak.

"Hello, I'm Janie Norworthy. I stopped up here to look at the view, and the dog—"

"Oh don't mind Kuon," Elena said, her short, salt-and-pepper gray hair lying still in the thick silence. "The only thing he's ever bitten is a rubber skunk." It was a lie but it seemed appropriate to make the girl feel better. Janie looked up at the stars and then thought of something else to say.

"I work for Banks' Realty. Didn't they handle your account years ago?" Elena ignored the question and came from behind the tree. She stared at Janie and cocked her head.

"Where were you going?" Elena asked.

"I...uh...I—I was going to Mexico. I just had a fight with my husband." (Why am I telling this woman these things?) Elena's eyes opened more.

"Do you know about Mexico?"

"Yes," said Janie, feeling growing discomfort.

"You do? Then where is Altun Ha? I have to find out where Altun Ha is." Elena ran to the front gate. For a moment Janie thought the older woman was running away. She let Kuon back into the yard, where Otto's burly voice carried a message: "Ku-on! Din-ner!" To which a stange black shape, with wings, also responded. It was time for an avian repast as well, and perhaps if he was lucky, a cigarette. Elena shut the gate and drew closer to Janie who was sitting on the hood of her car.

"Altun Ha? I'm not sure, but...."

"Be sure! Be sure!" said Elena.

"Let me check my books. It's been a long time."

"Get back here soon."

"No, wait. I just remembered, and I am certain. Altun Ha is in Belize."

"British Honduras?" Elena's plane had landed there once.

"No, it's called Belize now." Janie explained where Altun Ha was—about an hour north of the largest city in Belize, Belize City. (What else?) It was the old colonial capital. The new capital was called Belmopan, she thought.

"And that's where Altun Ha is?" asked Elena.

"Yes." Janie noticed it was getting cool.

"Have you ever been there?" asked Elena, grabbing her arm and staring into Janie's face.

"No, I'm sorry, I haven't. Why is it so important?"

"It just is." Elena did not think she wanted to tell Janie the truth yet. Elena looked around nervously. She wished she was in her house and in her bed. She asked Janie if she would like to get out of the night air. Janie said she had nowhere else to go and would be happy to take her offer. They had a small snifter of brandy each while Janie sat agog at the spacey splendors of the Los Cocos living room: spare stucco walls, galaxies painted on them, an entire wall of glass, a niche with a statue of Tezcatlipoca, and beyond it, the Pleiades, sisters shrouded in star mist. They stayed up talking about themselves and their lives until three. Janie was then led down a brown and beige hall to a very cool, comfortable guestroom. Her last thoughts before she went to sleep were of Lenny, her children, and Karen Allemeister. Exhaustion pulled her under, at last.

XXXVI Dauphine Refuses to Primp Too Much, and a Surprise on a Date

"It's a late date, Wanda," she said. "How many times I got to tell you that?"

Wanda stood behind Dauphine, helping her put the finishing touches to her hair. Wanda wished Dauphine would dye her hair brown the way it used to be. Dauphine would have none of it.

"I'm not sixteen, Wanda. I'm not going to try to look that way. It's okay, I'm going to look fine. The way you're worrying, you'd think this was your date."

Dauphine's neighbor pshawed and laughed, throwing the brush on the cluttered vanity. Bottles of perfume that Dauphine had never used sat there. Most were cheap little bottles given as obligatory gifts from reluctant, half-known nephews and nieces. The good ones were from Betty Sue, who was now supposed to be spending the night at Marti's. Dauphine made a move to stand up.

"Stop!" yelled Wanda. "You can't get up now. I'm not through combing out the back."

"I thought I'd better call Marti's house to check on Betty Sue. Are you sure Marti's parents are there? I don't want any of those football boys over there tonight. There's been talk of a lot of drinking going around the high school."

"Do you think Loren or Betty Sue would do something like that?" Dauphine cocked an eyebrow and looked knowingly at Wanda.

"I guess we're in no position to talk. Remember what we did on Sixteenth Street in our senior year? Ow, you're pulling my hair!"

Barry showed up shortly after nine, just as he was supposed to. He affected a breezy, chatty air. Wanda wondered if he'd been drinking, but after a while she saw it was a defense. My God, she thought, this man is scared to death. He escorted Dauphine to the car and opened the door. His car newly washed both inside and out, looked better than it ever had. The nearest good restaurant was in Raymondville (a Mexican one), but a nice little Italian place in Harlingen was just about as close and had a bit more atmosphere. Mosquitoes were out, for some reason, and Dauphine felt herself perspiring as she took his hand to fit herself in the passenger seat. She noted happily how polished Barry's manners were; despite his nervous silences, he had an innate sense of decorum that at other times he had, unfortunately, chosen to suppress.

The air conditioning was cool, the radio was not too loud, and Barry got in the car, beside her. He smelled of pleasant shaving lotion.

"Dauphine," he said. "Look, it's been awhile for me, and I don't—"

"Don't sweat it, Barry," she laughed her voice as high and happy as a girl's. "I could tell you about some dates I've had that.. Whew!" She wiped her brow and glanced heavenward. Barry grinned and took off the emergency brake.

Betty Sue's mouth hung open. Loren was just staring, taking in every second, wanting to remember everything she saw and felt. Marti sat at the driver's seat, her eyes covered and mouth whimpering; Jeanine lay with her head resting against the back of the seat. She was so afraid that she went limp the moment the apparition appeared, and she could not raise her head.

They all recognized the form in front of them as it came nearer to the car from a dark little arroyo.

Loren opened her door and got out. Marti started to reach after her and almost screamed but it was too late. Loren was more stunned than frightened. The apparition floated in a sea of beautiful Neptunian voices.

"I know you. You're Karen Allemeister, aren't you?"

"Yes," said the apparition, even though its mouth did not move. Loren noticed that the apparition was much thinner, more attenuated than the school picture the girls had found in the accident report column of the *Sun*. Much, much thinner. But still that beautiful placid face. Loren was nonplussed but felt compassion for Karen, her truncated young life.

"What is it, Karen?" said Loren. "Do you want to talk to us? Why did you stop us on the highway? You could've had anyone." Loren spoke in a tiny, almost whispery little voice.

"No," said the apparition."Only you could see me."

Marti took her hands down and looked at Loren and the apparition speaking. "Ask her what she wants!" said Marti, frightened. Loren ignored her and asked, "Are you a ghost?"

"Why did you come here?"

"I haven't left here for twenty-four years."

"No, I meant why? Why did you want us here?"

The spirit turned away and began to hurry off. Loren begged it not to go. As the apparition began to fade, it faced her and said:

"Bring me Barry Madden."

The date began well. Barry opened Dauphine's car door and led her into the restaurant. Immediately Dauphine's nostrils were assailed by spicy tomato smells. The occasional clack-clacking of plates from the kitchen competed with the soft conversations of diners at their tables. A stencil of the port of Naples was on the wall. Each table bore a paper napkin dispenser, cracker basket, citronella candle, and menus with pictures of gondolas and statues in them. Dauphine smiled to see these wonderful things.

"I have not been happy in years," she said to herself under her breath, "but I'm happy tonight." Barry noticed how her eyes shone in reflection of the candle. He lit a cigarette during dinner, and gazing at a print of the Duke of Urbino, realized he had fallen, ever so calmly, in love with Mrs. Candor. Dauphine was not exactly sure what she felt, but she was willing not to ask any questions for now. Barry was lulling her defenses most effectively. The violinist played a gypsy piece, dripping with longing, in A minor. The musician circled behind Dauphine's chair. She was embarrassed at all the attention the violin player showed her.

"Don't look that way," said Barry.

"Oh, I don't know. It's just sort of—I don't know—sort of icky."

"Dauphine? Don't you believe in the romance of it all?" Barry posited lightly.

She looked him squarely in the eye, her own filled with vague remonstrances, joys, sorrows, regrets.

"Romance is a beautiful lie," she said.

"There are many other lies in this world."

"Some are harmless; others aren't."

Barry looked at his plate for a moment. He decided to change the subject.

"Dauphine," he asked slowly, "why didn't you go to college?"

"I was young and in love and I thought I knew everything I needed to know."

"You didn't?" Dauphine took a sip of water while he waited for an answer. She looked at him again.

"I knew everything but the blindness of my own heart."

"And what happened then?"

"I don't have to answer. You can see the story of my life." He looked around the room and saw a familiar face. Brenda and a date were sitting in a corner. Barry heard a soft, carefree Goddammit from across the room.

"Lasagna's good, isn't it?" said Barry to Dauphine.

"Yes, it is. I appreciate you doing this. I've never eaten here before." (What does he really want?)

"I guess you don't get out that much." (Does her daughter take up too much of her time?)

"Well, I have to work and take care of my daughter." (God, don't let him be the kind that wants the young ones.) After dinner they decided to drive down to Brownsville for dancing and then thought better of it. It was very late. They decided to have drinks at the Tropicala since the manager would be having Edna Parker at the piano there. And between her sets there would be the best jukebox in town. So why not? Barry aimed the nose of his car northward towards the towns Rudolph, Norias, and Palmyra. He felt better and more important than he had in years. This night was special that was for sure. He hadn't given his seduction plans any thought. He was just happy for the companionship. They talked seriously again.

"We were talking about college earlier," Dauphine said as she self-consciously patted her bouffant hairdo to shape it after crushing it against the headrest. "Did you finish?"

Barry felt real shame for the first time he could remember. "Uh, no." He offered nothing else.

"How come, Barry?" Barry usually had a cock-and-bull story he saved for this embarrassing question, but somehow it did not matter anymore.

"I partied and drank too much and ran around a lot," he said.

"Do you think it's all that important anyway, Barry?"

"No, but I hate to start things without finishing them. It's a point of honor, I guess."

"I guess you weren't very honorable, then?" asked Dauphine, her face deadpan.

"Yeah, I guess you're right. But look. I got it figured this way: I know what I want out of life, and school wasn't going to help me get it. At least not back then."

"There's something else, though, isn't there?" Barry felt a stab of apprehension. Dauphine put her arm around his shoulder and patted him.

"You've forgotten that I was in Palymra then, too, Barry—even if only to stay with my Aunt Louise. I remember seeing you and hearing about you. You were quite a beauty then, you know."

Barry laughed. No one ever called him a beauty before.

"And I remember Karen," she said quietly.

XXXVII Some Quiet Reflections of a German

It was 2 AM. At last the dog and bird were asleep. Dreaming about chasing something, Kuon growled and paddled his feet in the air. Otto knew from his reading that when people sleep they become more or less paralyzed, no matter what they dream about. This paralysis is wise because if our ancestors had dreamed and moved at the same time, they would have fallen out of their arboreal beds and into the very maw of night. Or perhaps the jaws of a leopard. Dogs, on the other hand, are hunters and possess to a lesser degree the nighttime paralysis found in humans. This, Otto knew, was why Kuon's legs windmilled in the air as he slept on his back near the Harvest Gold washer/dryer combination. Popol Vuh snored and snorted gracelessly, a victim of oversmoking and overeating.

Otto's thoughts turned to the lady who visited Los Cocos this evening. It was the first time in many years someone had visited. Repairmen and deliverymen came and went, and Raul and his family occasionally came by on afternoons. But never just friends. It was because Miss Muñoz really had no friends although she had many admirers in town--people who had figured out she was the secret job-getter or hospital bill-payer. If these same admirers had bothered to call at Los Cocos, they would had left wondering what was missing. Something had not been right, principally because Miss Muñoz loved people but she had difficulty dealing with individuals. But of course no visitors ever came to Los Cocos anyway. Otto noticed that Miss Muñoz had a way of staring at strangers as if they had grown wings--or sprouted a tail or a halo. She was used to seeing Otto, Zillah, the animals and her brothers' families. Anyone else might as well have come from a gas planet in Andromeda.

"Ach," said Otto to himself as he hit his shoulder on a laundry shelf. "Now maybe tings vill change around here." Little did he suspect how much would be changing in the next few days. Otto reflected a little more before leaving the washroom. What an odd life he had had. This was a good place to be, though. He did not have his own family but people here needed him to survive, and that made him feel appreciated and wanted. More and more he thought about retirement. Yes, the Muñoz plan was quite generous so money would not be much of a problem. But where to retire? Otto did not know many people in town, and no one shared his concerns and worries but Zillah. In a vaguely conceived way, he know he would have to stay near Zillah. She was his only steady companion and workmate. He felt a brotherly affection toward her even if he did not understand why she sat in her room so much or why she took such a jaundiced view of life. But when they talked in the morning over coffee, after breakfast dishes were washed, she would smile and joke and occasionally tease Otto about his blue eyes or gray hair. Then she would jokingly complain about all the work she had to do that day.

Zillah had not liked the dog at first, but now if he wandered into the room she would reach up from her dusting and affectionately tug on his ear or scratch his head. And Popol Vuh? The toucan already knew several African-American dialect words by sound (since toucans can speak) and would often ride on the vacuum cleaner, unruffled by the noise, as Zillah pulled it from room to room. Zillah would occasionally sit in her room and give the toucan a cigarette, and then sing to him. The toucan always cocked his head and puffed thoughtfully. In the background a soap opera hummed on the TV. Zillah sang soft, sweet, low.

Otto got ready for bed about 3:30. Something had seemed different about this night, and he could not fathom it. Los Cocos had its first guest in years, but even that was not the source of Otto's restlessness. He shrugged as he put his head on the white pillowcase. Whatever it was would wait until tomorrow.

XXXVIII Tickler of the Ivories at the Piano

Edna Parker was exhausted, and for a moment the front door of her beach house on the south part of Sand Island would not open. The walk home has been refreshing after she had been in the Tropicala's smoke-filled atmosphere. Although it was only one AM at the time, Ed had sent her home. Edna complained of an incoming headache and decided to bug out early. It was a slow night and Ed could always crank up the jukebox. As she walked southward on the beach a safe walk since the island was small–she glanced up at the stars and immediately thought of Chuck, her mystery boy, her problem child, and one of her greatest delights. "Obsessed with the stars," she sighed, mentioning Chuck's inability to face life on earth. The other two presented no special problems; they were easy in their recognition of life around themselves, accepting with childish artlessness the ups and downs of everyday life. But Chuck? He presented an altogether different set of problems. She opened the door and there he was, reading a book at the dinner table–so absorbed he had not heard her come in. She put her keys on the mantle and took off her wrap, a small blue rebozo she bought last year in Torreon on vacation.

Up at this hour, she thought. Who could understand him? Nurture him? Sometimes it seemed utterly beyond her understanding why he reacted to life the way he did, why such a lovely boy should tune out everything but his monomaniacal (was it that bad?) thing about astronomy. From being an active, involved teen of fifteen he had become an introverted loner, rarely leaving the house with his friends and then only for a few hours at a time. One friend had told her nobody wanted to talk with Chuck anymore because all he wanted to talk about was space. Alarmed, Edna decided to ask him, in an offhand way, why he thought so much about the stars when there were so many other matters to catch his attention: schoolwork, friends, dates, cars—the retinue of invariables of an adolescent's life. His reply?

"Mom, how big is the universe?"

"As far as I know, uh, it's limitless, goes on forever. What does that have to do with—"

"And how big is the earth?" He stated. "I mean by comparison."

"Well, by comparison it's very, very small."

"Do you think it's smart to spend so much time thinking about an insignificant pebble in the universe?"

"I never thought about it that way," she said, "but what about the universe inside you?"

He had turned away and said nothing. She knew her strategy would not work a second time.

Chuck's father wanted to handle the problem in typical Texas style—confrontation, explosion, argument, and understanding. Something good might come of it. Dr. Parker also wanted to take away his telescope and books but Edna had nixed his suggestion. It seemed his only contact with humanity had come through the use of the telescope. He was constantly writing other amateur astronomers and talking to them long-distance. He always paid for his calls by mowing lawns or doing other occasional work for neighbors who sadly remembered the sleepy, cheerful character he had been instead of the intense young man he was now.

Edna walked up to him and he looked up at her and smiled. He was reading something, no doubt an astronomy book. To her surprise it was not. It was a book about beach ecology. At least it was a start. Every sorrow, if overcome at all, is overcome slowly.

XXXIX Barry Explains

Barry realized that for the first time in years he was talking about Karen Allemeister. So many things about her had faded her voice, the way she walked, the beauty of her lips. But she was his "first" and he had been hers. Nothing about her body would he ever forget, even the little hollow at the base of her neck in front, where she had a small mole. Dauphine did not pry; she just sat in on a monologue she had been invited to listen to. She knew by the way she held the small lace handkerchief in her hand that she was falling in love. She always held her thumbs inside her fist when she felt it was going to happen. She looked at her hands often as she listened. Dauphine felt that maybe Barry was interested in her more than just casually. She was not sure, so she would have to watch her step until she was. That was all there was to it. So easy. Like falling off a log.

"And after Karen died...I don't know, Dauphine. I just didn't care." He expected the usual platitudes:

Yes, it's a shame she died—

One so young—

Wasn't it for the best—

He did not get them. Instead, Dauphine asked, "Barry, did you think about killing yourself?"

"Yes," he answered. "All the time."

"Why didn't you do it?"

"I thought I had so much to look forward to; it didn't seem right to end it all."

"You really loved her, didn't you? I know that sounds overused—you pretty much worshipped her?"

"Yeah. She was a goddess who adored me right back."

"Barry, you never really did get over it. You're dying right now for her. I mean really dying."

"Yes. I've wanted to die for twenty-one years now."

"Oh, Barry," said Dauphine. She tried to see off into the distance, turning her head out the side window.

They drove on in silence, listening to the hum of tires against the blacktop highway. After twenty miles Dauphine spoke. "It's so beautiful tonight, Barry. I—" the car lurched violently forward, then snapped to an abrupt stop. Dauphine's head and shoulders flew forward and she hit her head against the dash. The car motor raced furiously but the movement slowed and stopped. Dauphine felt the car slow down but was afraid to raise her head. A sharp pain on her face and in her neck made it hard to lift her head. Had they had a wreck?

Almost as if by choice she decided, "I want to pass out," but something stopped her. She realized Barry was trying to pull her back. He was shouting that he did not know what the matter was, he was so sorry, and what happened? Dauphine opened her eyes to see a car in front of them. And there in the backseat of the other car she saw Loren and her daughter! What? She really wanted to pass out now. Something was very wrong here. What were the girls doing out at this hour? Marti's mother w-was supposed to—supposed to be....

Loren looked at Betty Sue.

"He's right behind us!" Loren squealed.

"What are we gonna do?" said Betty Sue. "My mom's with him. Oh no!" Betty Sue put her head against the window and sobbed.

Barry got out of his car and headed for the four teens' car. He did not know who they were but he was going to tell them their prank—whatever it was—was not funny. They'd hurt someone.

As he strode over, a burst of wind shoved him over the trunk of Marti's car. The wind howled over the prairie and put grit in Barry's eye. But there was light. Were his carlights on?
It was something else. The wind called his name, a gust from the mouth of darkness, a starless plainsong of agony.

And there stood Karen.

And Barry rose as the wind ceased.

"At last, Barry," Karen said in a voice like dust.

Suddenly, back in Los Cocos, Janie sat up in bed. "Huh?" she said. Her brow was sweaty. She lay down again and patted her face with a Kleenex. And Mary Ann was dreaming about her dead husband and the drive to Brownsville along the same road.

And on that same Highway 77, Yelena Tikhonov would be brought to her gravesite in Norias tomorrow.

And Popol Vuh rubbed his beak on a corner pole of his cage. Kuon gave his rubber skunk a few chews in his sleep.

And Elena Muñoz scratched a spot on her left ear.

And Amy Mortcap was sleeping in a culvert in Florida and scratched the same spot as Elena.

And Barry could not speak.

"Barry, don't look at me like that. It's Karen, it's me."

"You're dead," was all Barry could say.

Karen studied him for a few seconds with her irisless black eyes, then answered.

"I'm sure that's true. You can look at me and see that."

"What do you want?" Barry said just a little too loud. Loren shifted her head to hear each speaker as if she were listening to a conversation among friends in the halls of Palmyra High.

"I wanted to see you again, Barry. No, don't look away. Why are you angry with me?"

Barry could not lie."You died, you ruined my life, you twisted my future and my feelings. I never got over you, Karen. Even dead you're trying to screw up my life."

"You think I chose this?" she said. "You could have come home with me instead of going to visit some of your football buddies! I might have been alive now." The wind tossed and fretted.

"I loved you so much," said Barry, looking dazed and exhausted.

"I've waited all this time to hear that, Barry. At the very moment it happened, I told myself 'This can't be! I can't die!' but I did. Nothing worked out, Barry. Nothing worked out."

"Don't touch me," said Barry as she neared, his eyes shining with horror.

"I've touched you all these years, Barry, and I couldn't die completely without seeing you. I couldn't give up and leave here."

"You've waited to find me all these years? Why didn't you just appear in my room at school or at home? Why did you let all these years pass?"

"I couldn't leave; I'm tied here."

"Go away, Karen. This is more than I can bear." Barry wept softly.

"I will go but I have a few words to say. I want you to know a few things. First, I want to tell you that I loved you too. The years have changed you but I am ageless. You can be happy at least about that. And my years here were not a waste or even sad. I watched the cars that passed and looked at the people in them. I have learned so much about people. And I watched the turn of the seasons and the course of life and death. It's odd, Barry, but I enjoyed it. Don't cry over me. It won't do any good now."

"What will happen now? Where—"

"Where will I go? Because I have seen you at last I can leave now. Come to me, one last time. I won't hurt you. I want to say goodbye." She put her diaphanous arms about him. Adamantine droplets glistened down her cheeks. She had not said where she was going.

"Your skin is warm!" she sobbed, and let go. "Barry, if you honor anything we were, you must learn to live. Be kind to everyone. Life is so short, and so many people have so much love to give. I had so much to give you, but now I can never give it. I am utterly beyond you forever. Goodbye, my tired sweetheart." She moved apart from him.

"Goodbye, Karen," he answered, staring at her fading image as it dispersed like mist at some distant dawn. "Karen, will you leave this place now?"

"Yes," came the faint answer.

"Where will you go?" He ran after the almost invisible image.

No answer.

XL Next Day

Dauphine was still home in bed. Betty Sue and Loren had taken sedatives supplied by a neighbor who was a nurse. They were awake now only six hours later. Even though it was eleven o'clock in the morning, a dewy sweetness was in the air, as if the sunrise in its dreams could not face any reality but the pleasant, watery sigh of that night's passing. Loren and Betty Sue did not look at each other or talk while Wanda fixed them coffee and began to talk to them at the breakfast table.

"Well, no one was hurt. And now I guess I understand why you girls did what you did—Loren, I'm not going to give you a punishment. But I will tell you this: I wish you'd trusted me enough to tell me about your experience. I could've helped you."

"Mrs. Murphy," said Betty Sue flatly, still weary from the sedative that merely slowed her down yet would not make her sleep. "What could you have done?"

"I grew up with Karen Allemeister, that's what I could've done. I could've told you all about her."

Loren and Betty sat up and listened carefully, their mouths slack.

"I never thought about her and you being the same age, but I guess you are," said Loren.

"We went through high school together, honey. And Jeanine's sister Janie was one of our friends. We used to drive around town to look for excitement, same as you girls do."

"But Mama, how did you know we do that?" asked Loren. Betty Sue blushed.

"Don't be such a fool, honey," laughed Wanda, and then she took a drag from her cigarette. It was a Winston. "All teenage girls do that. We certainly did, every time we didn't have dates or just felt like getting together...."

Loren interrupted.

"Please, Mom, tell us about her, anything that you can remember"

Wanda told the girls about the first few weeks of school when Karen had come to live at Mrs. Jerrald's house. Then she recounted the romance between Barry and Karen, and ended her story with more details of the young girl's death. What emerged from the story was a tale, dark around its fringes, of a confused yet beautifully robust and popular girl coming from another city under unknown circumstances. According to Wanda, Karen never wanted to talk about her previous life and ignored even pointed questions put to her about it. Wanda thought that maybe Karen had confided in Barry, but she was not sure. That was all in the past now.

After a few more questions, the girls began to yawn, and Loren got Betty Sue dressed and walked her home.

When she got back, Loren felt that her life was changing. She was tired of death, tired of Barry, tired of Karen. She wanted something productive to do this summer. Life really was short, she realized. It was time to get on with it. And her summer vacation. Betty Sue felt the same urge. She wanted to throw herself into something—a job, a boyfriend, school—just something. Neither girl realized that there might be few times that the four of them would be together again. The forces of modern life would break their fellowship into a thousand shards, and the plasma of bond between them would attenuate itself slowly into nothingness. Reunions, if they come, would always be happy. That at least is a pleasant residue given by the past.

Barry woke in his own bed. For a moment the memory of what had happened the night before did not occur to him. Then in one slapdash brainwave it all came back—all the fear and hurt and eerie surprise of Karen's presence.

"Oh my God, what happened to Dauphine?" he said aloud, poking through his own memory to see if he could remember the rest of the night's events: Dauphine unconscious on the backseat? Some teenage girl driving his car while he stared off into space? Being in shock? Then a hospital—the Palmyra Kenedy County Hospital? Then someone drove him home. Yes. Wanda? Old Wanda Benson? Yes? She married Lanky Murphy. Then a pill, then oblivion. Barry got out of bed and realized he felt great. He planned to walk to the hospital. It was not all that far anyway.

Elena Muñoz woke up clutching her stuffed sweet potato. It was a gift from one of her dead husband's old friends in Louisiana who grew sweet potatoes for a living. The stuffed sweet potato was fuzzy and two feet long. Over her head hung a mobile of the solar system. A breeze from the open portal of her bedroom wall sent Mars crashing into the much larger Jupiter. Elena considered the consequences of such a disaster in the real solar system. Would the climate change? Would we see the palms of Toronto? The mangoes of Kamchatka? The glaciers of Amazonia?

Janie awoke down the hall. She had a slight hangover—no pain, just that cottony feeling in the sinuses and a twinge here and there. She removed the gown that Zillah had given her and took a blazing hot shower before putting her clothes back on. Someone had laundered them during the night, and even her shoes had been polished.

When Janie came out of the room and stepped into the den, she saw Elena on the phone. Elena acknowledged her presence with a wave and a smile, and kept talking to someone. Janie sat down in an overstuffed chair and thought about eating. Her stomach grumbled just as a raggedy toucan flew by her and landed on a potted dracaena. He turned his beady eye toward her, his banana-boat beak aflame in the ll:00 morning light. Otto came in with a tray of Cornflakes and milk and a soft-boiled egg. A boattail grackle screeched repeatedly out in the front yard.

"Yes.... I'm sure, yes, Raul," said Elena. "I'll clear it all up later. No. I'm fine. Don't worry, will you? I know what I'm doing. Yes! How many times did I tell you? I'm getting a big Winnebago touring camper. I can't tell you why; it's a secret. Yes, other people are coming. No, you don't know them. Just make the purchases—and trust me!" Elena hung up the phone.

Though the two women had stayed up talking the night away, they never got around to talking about what Elena really had on her mind. Janie sensed greater need and urgency in the older woman's looks.

"Miss Muñoz, is something wrong?" Janie asked as she cracked open the egg.

"No, Janie, but there's something I have to tell you. You know you don't want to go home—at least not just yet. I have some chores to attend to on the grounds here and in town. I may seem crazy to a lot of people but—" Janie opened her mouth to protest, even though she knew Elena was right. Elena held up her hand in demand for silence.

"--That's beside the point now. I have something I have to do. I have to go to Altun Ha. You just heard me talking to my brother. He's taking care of the details for me. He'll do as I say because he understands me. I have to go to Altun Ha in—was it Belize? —Because. ...(Elena hesitated and looked out at the sea, shading her eyes with her tanned hand) my father came to me and told me to go there. He didn't say what, but I expect something wonderful to reveal itself to me there." Janie could not be restrained.

"Why," she asked, "did your father ask you to go there? And why is that so important a request?" The younger woman took a sip of her hot tea.

"It's unusual and important because my father has been dead far longer than you've been alive." Elena put on her thin-slit sunglasses. They made her feel like a space mariner.

Oh no, thought Janie. She really is crazy.

Elena continued, "Just hear me out; then make up your own mind. He told me to take some other people with me to see this place, the new country." Elena did not add that they were all to stay in Belize. That was something she hoped they would decide on their own later. "And when we arrive at Altun Ha I am to climb the pyramid before dawn and wait for the sunrise. I know, I just know I'm going to learn something important there."

"What kind of important thing?"

"If I knew what it was, I wouldn't have to go."

Janie shook her head as she looked at her cereal bowl. Zillah came into the room, dusted Maya pottery and hummed an Otis Redding song. She was thinking about Amy Mortcap, her obsessed mother, out on the highway. (Worrying about Amy was something she did best while singing to herself.)

"It sounds crazy to me, I'm sorry," said Janie. "I can't go."

"I'm willing to pay for everything, including the expenses of the other ten people. I have about $3 million at my disposal. I can do everything—including sending everyone home—for much less than that."

"That's fine, but what about my job, my family?" Janie Norworthy was clearly weakening but putting up a brave front.

"Bring them or leave them. It's your odyssey, your opportunity. If they come, it'll be theirs, too."

"But we can't just pick up and—" protested Janie.

"Why not? I'm offering you a chance to do some research and help me organize what must come."

"But what about the house, the yard, the neighbors, the—"

"If you love those things more than adventure, then you'd better stay. And you'll be as angry as ever and bitter and unhappy if you don't give yourself this chance."

"What chance? What do I get out of this?" Janie fairly shouted.

"Maybe what you've been looking for. Maybe we're looking for the same thing. People are pretty much alike everywhere. They need the same things."

"But is it safe to go there? I've heard there's trouble in El Salvador and Guatemala, and—"

"You decide. I have to go now. Otto will help you out to the patio. Have a glass of Texsun and think about what I'm saying." Elena left, utterly fearless at the prospect of leaving Los Cocos, Palmyra, the United States. She was fearless but she did wonder if she was doing the right thing. If it were all her imagination then she would lose some money. That's all. But was there enough motive for her leaving? Somewhere, in the jungle, in her brain, she heard the tones of the bass flute—a mist rolled over Lubantuun, Xunantunich, ruins to the south—the wind blew off the Caribbean and the frigate birds waited suspended in air. And then? And then? And then she was sure.

XLI Listing and Wooing

PEOPLE TO TAKE WITH ME was what the top of the sheet said. Underneath that was the name "Janie N." written in Elena's scrawl. Not a very imposing list, but it was a start. The summer had begun in earnest now and it was time for Elena to begin her search. She did not know anyone in town well enough to ask, and certainly her brothers would never go, even if they worried about her safety. They were not that kind of people, and besides they had their own families to worry about. Even Raul, the understanding one, was mystified, as usual, by her behavior.

Afternoon clouds scudded past the shore and contemplated serious rain when they hit land. They gathered over the coast. Popol Vuh, always sensitive to changes in air pressure, flew down from his third floor perch and in through a special plastic port Otto made for him. Elena was propping her head on her chin, absentmindedly clicking and unclicking her blue Papermate pen. Kuon was chasing birds off the front lawn, most of whom landed back on the ground after he ran past. Popol Vuh glanced around the room for the rubber skunk, but it was not around.

"You bad toucan!" said Elena in mock anger. "You just keep trying to tease Kuon. He'll get you one day if you aren't careful."

"Skronk," was Popol Vuh's reply, and afterwards he chewed his cud as only toucans do.

"You're disgusting," said Elena. "I should have bought a cockatoo."

Zillah came into the room and began shutting windows to keep the rain out when it came down in sheets, as it always did this time of year. Elena enjoyed the ozoney window-breath for a few more moments, then picked up her phone. She called Janie's room, which was to the rear of the mansion.

"Janie. Are you awake?"

"Yes, what can I do for you?"

"You need to help me find eleven other people. I don't know anyone here, not really."

"You know more of them than you think, at least by reputation."

Elena was mystified. What could Janie possibly mean?

"Are you taking the maid and the butler?"

Elena was delighted. Of course! Zillah and Otto! That made three people so far, not including herself. Elena asked Janie, who was resting through the hottest part of the day, to come to dinner at 5:30 if it was convenient. Janie said she would be glad to. That gave Elena three hours to handle Zillah and Otto.

"And so that's what I'll be doing. You may go with me or stay. I don't want it to affect your employment here, except that Raul may let you go rather than keep staff in the house. Either of you can retire and stay here in town. You have pensions." Otto and Zillah looked at each other questioningly. Kuon barked to be let in out of the rain. Elena said, "I'll let him in. You two sit down and talk it over." Otto and Zillah talked for about fifteen minutes then came into the next room to see Elena look up expectantly.

"We want to go," said Zillah, "but I got to check up on my mama an' my brother every once in a while. Is that okay?" Elena nodded and said she would pay for the phone calls. Otto had no reservations at all about going.

"I am bored, vould like to zee new places," he said. "I slept too much, ditten get to zee de vorld like I should." He hesitated, then spoke again.

"But vat about dog und bird?"

"They'll go with us, of course," exclaimed Elena, surprised that anyone would even think about a separation. Zillah and Otto both smiled and said they could be ready to go with an hour's notice. Elena felt a tear at their loyalty as the three of them toasted each other with vodka martinis. The rain roared outside. Popol Vuh pooted. Kuon shook water from his coat all through the den as he sought his beloved toy. The German shepherd knew that a vast change was in the air, a change far more permanent than the ephemeral tropical shower pelting the roof at that very moment.

XLII What the Girls are Up To and Lanky's Revelation

The collection process was long and difficult, but here is what happened:

Since the four cruising teens disbanded after their adventure on the highway (more by mutual agreement than parental intervention) the girls went their separate ways: Jeanine helped Lenny watch the kids by babysitting at her parents' house. She was confused and disturbed over Janie's disappearance. She occupied her time watching daytime TV and playing with her sister's children. She stayed on the phone trying to get Marti or Loren to come over, but there was no time for visiting until school started.

Betty Sue was only fourteen and a half so she could not work, as such. She took jobs mowing lawns for people Dauphine knew and babysitting for the few people on her street who had children. On Friday nights she had a few movie dates in town, and she met a high school junior from another part of town. His name was Randall and he got to use his father's yellow Porsche whenever he wanted to. Randall said his father was thinking about giving the car to him when he graduated next year. It was not true, but Betty Sue did not mind as long as she was having fun.

Marti's parents saw to it that she spent the rest of her summer being a counselor at a children's day camp in San Benito. It was a long drive, but her parents wanted her to have something constructive to do. "No more reading the paper or chasing down ghosts all night," they said. They got no argument from Marti. In her spare time she swam in the family pool and played tennis at her father's country club on the western outskirts of town. Bored out of her skull....

Loren's summer took a strange turn. She took to walking down to the lagoon by herself. She wanted to think about high school and her young life's direction. Besides, things at home were not that great. Even Petey seemed cowed by the ominous atmosphere in the Murphy house. Lanky was drunk every other night. When Wanda tried to talk to him about what bothered him, he left the room or started a shouting argument. The couple was clearly spoiling for a big fight, and Loren did not want to be around for it. Her mother looked haggard as she sat at the breakfast table, her eyes with dark half-circles under them, staring out the kitchen window, thinking about how little coffee was left in the canister.

Loren left early for her walk. She thought about taking Petey with her, but he was already outside. Probably playing with his friends the next street over. Funny how sometimes she really liked being with Petey, hugging him or putting an arm around him. Just when she thought he would embarrass her to death in front of her friends, she would suddenly think, who are these people to me? Petey is my brother—much more important than any friends I might have just now. Then she would feel ashamed at her insensitivity to him, thinking Petey's feelings were hurt by her constant carping rejection; her continual, petty correction of every little mistake he made in dress, speech, and table manners. Loren's eyes watered as she thought about her meanness and cruelty. And at that very moment at home Petey was stealing her share of Coke and her snack cake! And laughing about it!

Loren continued walking toward the lagoon. Maybe she would cross to Sand Island to see if, among the blaring small Japanese radios and tanning bodies, she could make friends and pretend she was from Corpus Christi or Houston, and not a Palmyra hick-townie. Funny, she and her friends had not even been to the beach yet this year. It was too soon after school let out, and then there was the Karen Allemeister thing and—

She soon found herself looking at the morning sea, bright with the eastern sun still not far from the horizon, sitting like a mandala on show for a warm eternity. Not far down the beach she saw a boy about her age looking at a book. He glanced up at her and then abruptly looked down again. Loren examined the waves coming in. Should she bother to say hello? He looked nice enough. Maybe a little skinny.

"Hello," she said tentatively. "I'm Loren Murphy."

"Hi," he said. "I'm Chuck Parker."

An awkward silence followed then the first tentative conversation. Chuck was reading an astronomy book, as usual. Loren started asking him questions about it. Occasionally they stopped talking and faced the endless, endless sea.

Wanda's sixth sense about her children's presence was not operating. They were not in the house. Okay then, Mister. If this is what you want.... She walked into the den and stood in front of the television show Lanky was watching, then turned to cut it off. Lanky started to protest but she interrupted.

"Now what the hell's going on here, and what the hell is wrong with you? You've been moping around here for days acting mean and gloomy and I'm goddamn sick of it, if you want to know."

Lanky, sick to his stomach with emotion, looked momentarily out the side window, then snapped back.

"There ain't nothing wrong with me so shut up and get out of my way. I'm sick to death of you always bitching at me!"

Wanda decided that her confrontation tactics were not working. Still sounding angry, she softened somewhat.

"Look, whatever's bothering you is something we can work out. We've always been able to work things out some way."

"Okay! Okay!" shouted Lanky. "You want to know what's bothering me? You really want to know? I'm sick and tired of never having anything. We're not getting anywhere, we're only losing ground. I want to get nice things for you, to hold a good enough job so we can have extras. Extras that mean a lot, not to us, but to kids. Look at what Marti's parents give her! Why can't I do that for my daughter? She's just starting to grow up. Why can't she have advantages? We can't send her or Petey to college, we can't set them up in business, and chances are good I won't even be employed next month!"

So. It finally came out. Lanky's delivery company was not doing well. Lanky had also neglected to tell Wanda that at times he felt his family were leeches, vampires, parasitical creatures who robbed him of his youth, his education, his desire to travel. And yet he knew he had chosen his fate—and then—by his own volition. It was childish to feel this way, he knew, but now the host creature was drying up—what would his little leeches do? Lanky was afraid, not angry.

Wanda was not completely surprised. Lanky had mentioned before in broad hints that things were not going well.

"It's my fault," she said gently. "I should've known something was wrong at work but I decided not to pay attention. I had other things on my mind." Lanky then spoke his mind completely.

"I'm just restless. I'm tired of doing what I do. I want a change, something new. I just don't know what. I was talking to old Barry. ."

"Barry Madden?" asked Wanda.

"Yeah, Barry Madden. He said he had the same feeling sometimes. But he wasn't encouraging me—don't get me wrong. He was trying to tell me that all men get to feeling that way sometimes."

"Some women too," said Wanda.

"Really? Well, that settles it. We've got to start looking for something new. I wonder what we can do."

"How much time do we have left at your job?" Wanda asked, preparing herself for the worst.

"About three weeks, for certain. Maybe a little more."

"Let's start looking around, then. We may have to leave Palmyra. Or we can try to get through to Raul Muñoz. Maybe Crazy Elena has some work."

"It's worth a try."

And Lanky went to the phone.

By the end of the day, and through various stratagems, Elena had these people sitting in her den at Los Cocos: Janie, Lanky, Wanda, Otto, Zillah, Petey (Loren had not come home until late and she was tired). All considered, they were now seven, including Loren who would probably go where her parents went. As the group talked softly among themselves over the soft space music in the background, Elena entered and, in her orchid print muumuu, addressed the curious crowd. Janie Norworthy had tried to explain, but there had not been enough time to cover background and details.

Elena was uneasy having so many people in her house, but she knew she had to talk to them and get to know them well in the next few days. They all might be living close together for the rest of their lives. Elena felt she was addressing a bizarre convention of some kind, a ragtag compilation of humans at loose ends, making do, being on hold. She spoke in a low, quiet voice.

"You all know who I am and I know who you are, so we can skip the introductions. Although I have never spoken to some of you, I know about your jobs and the basic outlines of your lives. I guess I'll know a lot more in the coming weeks, and you'll know a lot more about me too. Let's not get into the past here.

What I'm offering you all is a piece of the future, a chance to change your lives, or take a break from them temporarily to see where you want to go next. I'm offering this opportunity free of charge for you, all expenses paid. All I ask is that you stay with me for two weeks as I make the journey I have to make. I see so many questions on your faces, so first let me make a few announcements and then I'll answer questions and fill in background—not necessarily in that order."

A little laughter passed through the room. Elena continued, "First, we are only seven people. I need twelve, including myself. If you know anyone here in town who would like this chance for a new experience, I urge you to call that person and let him know."

"Second, the large Winnebago camper I ordered is on its way from Houston. It will be here by tomorrow and is a completely self-contained unit. You can come to Los Cocos again tomorrow to look it over." Kuon was barking at all the strange cars in the driveway. Popol Vuh was nowhere to be found.

"Third," continued Elena, "is my motive, which I think we should get right out in the open immediately." The group leaned forward perceptibly. Elena Muñoz cleared her voice and continued. She knew she could tell only just so much of her motives. Telling any more—telling the whole truth—would frighten them away. "Where I'm going is Belize. It used to be British Honduras. It's now an independent, English-speaking country in Central America. I have some personal, uh, business to take care of, and I also want to get away to do some thinking. If I find what I'm looking for, I'll stay there. And I'll pay the airfare of anyone who wants to return to the US. Once again, I'll pay all expenses getting there. When we get to Belize City, you can either stay with the caravan or go your own way. What happens after that is up to the weather and to the Fates and to you."

Where is all the indecision, the uncertainty that one might expect to find in the voice and demeanor of Elena Muñoz? Whither the usual lack of fortitude? Elena herself could not figure it out. It was not even cocktail hour yet.

"Now," she said, "are there any questions?"

"Yeah," said Lanky. "Are you into some religious thing? We don't want to get involved with some Jim Jones/Guyana kook. I don't mean to poke my nose in your business; I just want to be sure."

"And you should be sure you want to do this," smiled Elena. "Rest assured: I have no religious convictions whatsoever. Come to think of it, I don't have many convictions at all, other than the belief that I'd rather not hurt anybody."

Wanda spoke. "What about our house? Our kids' schooling? Our relatives? What will we tell people?"

Janie interrupted here. "Wanda, let me tell you something. If you stop to explain to everyone, you'll never get on the road; it's summer vacation now and there won't be any school; if you feel you can't extricate yourself from your community, then you shouldn't go. It's that simple. It's that complicated."

If the time had been any more than two weeks, Elena was sure that other questions would have come up. Why us? Why twelve? Why Belize? Why now? But she saw suspicion on her travelers' faces, a look that showed confusion. Things were happening so fast to people like Wanda and Lanky that they had not even begun to think of questions or consequences. They would be spending a long summer vacation among people they did not know. When and if they got back, Palmyra would be there and so would the schools, the churches, the stores, the friends. And yet Wanda only dimly suspected that her journey would be a turning point as well. She lay awake in bed that night trying to think of all the necessary details. Lanky breathed deeply next to her. The cool-ice moon looked curiously at sleeping earth below. Wanda, like her daughter some time ago, thought: "Nothing will ever be the same after this."

She heard footsteps out in the hall. Petey was walking in his sleep again, no doubt. But when she saw the light on in the shabby den she knew someone was awake. Petey was looking in an atlas. He held up a map that showed vast bodies of water in the lower-left and upper-right corners. An irregular, lumpy strip of land curved lazily from left down to right. He was pointing to one of the lumps.

"Is this Belize?" he said. Wanda realized he was sleepwalking anyway. Wanda asked herself what she was doing to her family.

XLIII The Epic Catalogue

More could be said about each man or woman in Palmyra who decided to go with Elena Muñoz to her new world. Like her, they did not know exactly why they were going, but a sense of unquiet moved them all, restlessness that only a new situation can calm. Some of them worried that a new place was not the answer, that they were fools to try anything new at their ages.

Mary Ann got involved over the next week and her great fear was that she would somehow have to give up her past if she left Palmyra, somehow drop the memory of her late husband. It was an action she both dreaded and sometimes secretly longed for.

Barry Madden, on the other hand, had an opposite fear. He was afraid that just The Going was more important than The Destination, and then he would be wandering the globe at a time when he wanted to feel he really belonged somewhere specific on the face of this planet. To make things short, here is a list of the people who decided to go: (1) Elena, (2) Janie, (3) Wanda, (4) Lanky, (5) Petey, (6) Loren, (7) Mary Ann, (8) Barry, (9) Dauphine, (10) Zillah, (11) Otto, and (12) Chuck Parker. Chuck got to go because Loren had to go, and Edna thought it would be an interesting two weeks for Chuck. Over the course of a few days, Chuck seemed to come out of his shell and smile around Loren. Rather than have him risk a lapse into his old state, Edna let him go with his new girlfriend when she found out that Loren's entire family was going. She inquired no further into any circumstances.

And of course, the toucan and the dog got to go, after Elena made all kind of fussy, elaborate preparations for their comfort and care.

Two bathrooms, five bedrooms, and many other facilities lay aboard Elena's wondrous Winnebago. She crammed the imposing mode of transportation full of food, emergency medical supplies, books, musical instruments, language books, and spare parts for every contingency. The liquor cabinets were stocked too. Elena was taking no chances on being left boozeless in the wilds of Mexico.

Every day became a chafing, irritatingly endless list of needs and delays. It is not easy to organize twelve people whose lives are dissimilar.

A lesson lay in this for Elena. She sat one quiet evening after dark in her jalousie room. It was well, she thought, that the group intended to be together only two weeks. Aside from that time, they'd have three or four days on the road—possibly five? —To reach their destination. The return trip, the same. Other thoughts occupied her as well; they were not organizational thoughts, just questions on the validity of what she was doing. If she had not had her money, no one would have even considered coming with her. It was not so much what she was doing that impressed them as it was the way she was going about it. First class all the way for private travel. So what if they were impressed with surface comforts? Comfort is comfort. It will not stop her or them from becoming what they want to become or doing what they want to do.

A sleepy croak from outside the window betrayed the nearby presence of Popol Vuh in a stunted frangipani bush. The sea air was so cool. Elena ran a hand through her gray hair and took a sip of Coke out of her University of Texas alumni plastic glass. She toyed with a fan from a Chinese fan palm sitting next to her desk.

But what was she trying to do? Elena said to herself that she had been alive for fifty-some years. There was nothing in life she had not seen, read, or at least heard about–with the exception of Belize. But what did she expect from her morning on the pyramid of Altun Ha? A suspicion was rising in her every day that she was going crazy. A real loca. Like her mother? Elena shuddered. The possibility of her being insane has seriously entered her mind for the first time. Poor Mama, wandering around in the garden in her nightgown, calling out for El Lobito. Oh the fear, the fear. Why should I leave this place? I love my home. I don't want to leave it! I have plenty of money and enough to keep me busy. Why should I chance giving up everything for what was in a dream? Maybe I am crazy. I have to think! I have to think!

Elena pulled herself out of her chair and took the exterior spiral staircase to the roof of the jalousie room. There stood Zillah holding a plate with a sandwich on it. In her other hand she held a red hibiscus flower. Zillah's black skin shone like tar in the evening light.

"I want you to have this flower," she said. The moon was behind her head. Elena wanted to ask why but she seemed to know almost immediately, without asking. Zillah did not know how to smile. She had never had to, never had much reason to. She did not smile this time either. But she did look at Elena straight in the eyes. Zillah's were still dark but just hinting of going gray-blue, the washed-out color of old age. More noises in the front yard, birds setting in for the night. The millionairess waited for her maid to speak.

"I can't wait to leave. When we going?"

Elena—who could smile—did.

XLIV Various Encounters

"Do you want popcorn?"

"Yeah. I'll get it. You go get us some seats."

"All right."

Loren walked to the exact middle of the theater. The cartoon, starring Chilly Willie, had already begun. Chuck was buying popcorn at the snack stand in the lobby of the Viscount Movie Theater. Loren wished this moment would never end: here she was with her first serious love, alone at a movie with him, just two days before going off on a romantic adventure with him. No, other people would be there, including her parents and Petey. But she knew that most of her attention would be placed on Chuck--helping him study his astronomy books, collect plants, discuss things with him. He was so easy to talk to and be with. He did not have to show off or make out every second. At some times she thought of his almost as just a friend, but their kissing sessions had grown more and more intense lately. They had even dabbled in sex, much to Loren's guilty feelings afterward.

It bothered her that she could feel such powerful emotions and could be possessed so completely by them, carried aloft on a whirlwind of passion she was sure no one else could understand.

Wanda was not the kind to try to control her. Wanda knew that Loren was a good girl—better yet, a smart one—and could take care of herself; however, the older woman told her daughter not to do everything for Chuck.

"I like Chuck, honey. Don't get me wrong."

"Then what is it? What's bothering you?"

"I'm just telling you this for your own good. Don't disappear completely inside his world. Remember that you're a separate person, not some arm or leg on him. You have to have your own life too."

"Why, mom?" She asked curtly. "You don't have a life separate from Dad."

"I regret," said Wanda, with a sigh, "that I made my husband and family my whole life."

"Mama!" said Loren, shocked out of her reverie of loving subservience to Chuck, and genuinely pained at her mother's perversity.

"I mean it. You're in love now and you don't believe me. But you'll remember this talk and you'll thank me one day." And Loren did not believe it. Only Chuck was in her life now. He returned with the popcorn. Reel one of the movie began, and Chuck put his arm around her and kissed her neck just below the ear.

Mary Ann Banks and Dauphine were talking at Dauphine's house. Wanda and Lanky would have come over for a talk, but they had gone to Odessa to visit Wanda's aunt June who was ninety and probably would not make it to ninety-one. They would be back tomorrow, and then the group would soon begin their journey. Mary Ann and Dauphine wondered if everyone else was as excited as they were.

Mary Ann thought Dauphine would be more at ease in her own home, so Mary Ann had come over to talk with Dauphine at the waitress's house. Despite their closeness in age, Mary Ann seemed much older than Dauphine. Mary Ann tilted her squarish eyeglasses back on her ski-jump nose.

"Let's get down to brass tacks and talk turkey," said the real estate begum. "What are you going to do with Betty Sue?"

Dauphine looked as confident as someone about to make a prepared statement to the press.

"Mary Ann, I'm going to leave her with my sister in Odessa. School's out and she can't work, so I don't see any hassle with her staying there. And her boyfriend can make that drive in his fancy car, so I don't see there's going to be any trouble or problem."

Both women were school acquaintances in the past, never friends. Mary Ann's parents were educated and Dauphine's were not. And they both lived in different sections of town—those sections marked not so much by distance, house size, color or even race as by invisible plasma of "yes-money" and "less-money." The distinction was important to the teenaged Mary Ann, but the woman speaking did not consider their social caste important now. She and Dauphine were talking for a different reason. They needed to compare notes on the upcoming voyage of land discovery and their impressions of their fellow pilgrims.

Since Palmyra is a small town, almost everyone knows everyone else's business, so there was not much that the women could tell each other. Mary Ann found out about Lanky's financial problems. Dauphine found out more about Janie Norworthy. She knew Janie in the past but was not familiar with this highly educated attractive blonde whose abandonment of her husband she did not approve of. But approving or disapproving did not matter much to Dauphine; she wanted to know what Janie (and Mary Ann herself) wanted from this trip.

"Honey," said Mary Ann, "don't you have something stronger than this coffee? Let's you and me drink some sherry or wine." Dauphine just happened to have a bottle of Aliança white, and she opened the chilled emerald bottle, half in celebration of the trip and half in response to what amounted to a direct order from a more commanding personality than her own. The dry, cold wine gurgled into the stemware and Dauphine resumed her seat. She also made a mental note to end this conversation early enough to take a shower before work. She politely reminded Mary Ann of her employment obligations, and Mary Ann smiled and said she would be leaving soon anyway—and could she offer Dauphine a lift on her way to work? The waitress accepted graciously and tugged out her housecoat hem expectantly. And Barry was coming over tonight, too. Complications! Troubles!

"So, let's take the bull by the horns and wake up and smell the coffee. Why are you going to Belize with the rest of us?"

Dauphine wondered what she meant by "us," since she was better known among the others than Mary Ann was. But Mary Ann's other ways were so winning that Dauphine decided to answer as frankly as she could.

"I want to be something other than a waitress and I want to be with Barry. I can't reform him. That, I know. But I can show him he is loved and needed by someone. Someone who'll put up with many things as long as they aren't abuse. I'm forty years old now. Do you have any idea what that means? Any idea? Of course you do, Mary Ann; but look at my case. I haven't had a successful business. I haven't had a successful marriage, either."

"Weren't you and Mr. Candor together for, oh, ten years? That sounds pretty successful to me," offered Mrs. Banks.

"Yes, but it wasn't a lifetime. And I am not prepared to start my life over because I have responsibilities to Betty Sue."

"What do you mean by 'start my life over'?" asked Mary Ann.

"I'm not ready to educate myself to start a career now. I don't know if I could begin all over at my age. I want to depend on Barry," said Dauphine, "and I want him to depend on me."

"You know what I think? I think you ought to steer a middle course here. I don't know what's wrong or right, but I think your best bet is to make yourself ready for both contingencies—a life in the tropics or a return to Texas; a career of your own or dependency on Barry. Either choice exposes you to risk. They get you coming and going!"

"Mary Ann, all that chance talk sounds so much better to me than boredom. I'm just ready for some new challenges. And this new country presents so many! I've done some research. They need people desperately to teach school, grow crops, run cattle farms guard the borders, repair machinery—the choices are endless. But you probably don't want to listen to me. I'm just a housewife who's never done anything but keep kids, carpets, pets, and clothes clean."

"Is that how you justified your existence?" demanded Mary Ann.

"Why should I have to justify myself to anyone?" asked Dauphine politely.

After a few awkward moments, Mary Ann smiled and said, "Good. Then quit apologizing for being what you are. Plenty of things are less important than keeping kids. But what do you want out of this trip? I have my doubts about Elena's sanity, but even if she is crazy, she has a reputation for kindness, as you well know. No one hates or even fears her despite the fact that she nearly owns this town. For years she has been known to treat everyone—all people—alike, from the poorest to the Kings themselves. And they all treat her the same way: they love her. But what I mean is, I think I understand her motives whether she knows what they are or not. But what about you, Dauphine? What do you want to get out of this trip?"

"Besides having a place where Barry and I can have something real together, away from our pasts here, I have a few things I want to do. More wine?"

"Sure. What else do you want to do?"

"I've always wanted a beautiful garden—a garden of tropical plants, with their huge leaves and brilliant flowers glimmering in the sun. I've tried doing that in Palmyra, and it works for a while, but there's always a freeze and everything dies. Oh you know, about once every five years or so, I lose my plants. I just want to go to a place where things will never die, where there will be no more winters; I want to go to a place where I can grow my plants and live in peace with my neighbors—other people who understand and see things the way I do."

"Is that all?" asked Mary Ann.

"Yes, for now. I hope other things will occur to me when I'm there."

"That's what Elena's hoping for."

"And you just said she's crazy."

"Crazy like a fox," said Mary Ann.

"What do you mean by that?" asked Dauphine.

"Oh nothing. Her motives seem clear and innocent to me. Maybe they are. I just wish I understood more."

"It's hard to explain when you're not sure of things."

"I know. You don't need to tell me. I don't know why I'm going either."

Petey did not want to visit his Aunt June. She was old and wrinkled and ugly and her hair smelled like peanut butter. She could not always remember his name. He had pitched such a fit that Lanky had decided to let him stay with Dauphine. But right now he was just south of town, walking on Tooley towards Los Cocos. He passed the southmost clapboards, the liquor billboards, the highway cut-off signs, the hill where Los Cocos was, the Rise. He put his little brown head over the fence. Ranks and ranks of royal palms, their stalks like concrete pillars, gleamed with their lustrous dark-green pinnate fronds in the two p.m. sunlight. He saw a dog approaching and backed away from the fence. The dog attacked the fence as though he wanted to eat it as a snack before attacking the boy. Petey knew he was safe for the moment. He crossed his arms in front of him.

"You stupid dog," he said to Kuon. "I'm not bothering you so just shut up."

Kuon, outraged at his speech, began snarling and barking again. It was too far from the house for Otto to hear, and Zillah was at Mrs. Mortcap's house dividing up the few not-worthless possessions in Amy's house. So no one paid attention to Kuon's warnings. Out of the second-floor flexport flew a floppy black figure towards the unsuspecting youngster.

"Go away!" said the toucan. "Get the hell out of here!" Petey reached down and picked up a small stone. He threw it at the toucan as hard as he could. He missed the bird but popped Kuon on the flank near his hindquarters. The German shepherd yipped and cried, running away from the gate. The boy looked on in amazement as the toucan landed on the fence next to him. Popol Vuh tilted his head and studied Petey.

"Get lost, boy," said the bird.

"Drop dead, toucan," said Petey, and he turned to walk home. Elena came out of the house where she was poring over the last delivery manifests that day. Frightened, she looked at the boy in her yard tentatively, tilting her head in a strangely toucanine way.

"Do I know you?" she asked softly.

"Yeah," said Petey. "Why are you taking us away from here?" To Elena he looked angry, so she decided to talk to him like an adult.

"I have some personal business to attend to in Belize. No one's forcing you to go—or are you so dependent on your parents that you can't survive without them?" Her tone was not sarcastic. Petey was embarrassed and turned red.

"Get lost, boy," said the bird.

"I could stay with somebody else if I wanted to, but I don't want to."

"Then why does your parents' trip with me disturb you?"

"What do you want with them? Why don't you run off with some man and live in that new place? Why take those other people and my parents?"

Petey's words stung her deeply. She had not considered her enterprise disruptive. And as for being a woman? The thought had crossed her mind only vaguely in the past ten years. Her life had been celibate for what seemed an eternity. Chastity had become the necessary order of things. Had it taken an ill-mannered boy to wake her up to herself?

She answered Petey. "This trip is for two weeks. As for the other part, no man particularly wants me. I can't help it if men are sometimes stupid. Does that answer your question?"

Petey seemed satisfied with the answer but still looked suspicious. Narrow brown eyes studied her. Then he ran down the road. Elena's face was burning. She could not delay the trip much longer; the emotional drain was getting to be too much.

XLV Goodbye to Texas

Wanda and Lanky were on the road home from Odessa. It was 100 degrees all the way, the summer heat now no longer a shimmering caress, but instead a heartless torturer who numbed the eyes and robbed the body of its will to breathe. They had taken Lanky's truck (no air conditioning) hoping they could travel mainly at night, but force of habit made them drive during the day. Wanda was not just hot, she was genuinely in fear for her life.

"Babe," she said, trying to sound offhand. "Can we stop for a bite to eat?"

"Sure. Next town's forty miles though." Off in the distance she saw a farmhouse baking its tin roof in the sun.

By six o'clock temperatures has dropped, and the rest of the trip back to Palmyra consisted of miles and miles of mesquite bushes and cactus giving way to oaks, fields, and, eventually, eucalyptus trees. Power lines by the side of the highway threw their crosspieces in different directions as you looked down the center point where sky, grass, highway, and power line meet. Huge clouds rolled inland from the Gulf, bathing the normally semiarid land with mists and storms and towers of brilliant white. The twisty ahuehuete trees, as the Mexicans call them, shimmered green in the setting sun; lines of tall, tall *Washingtonian* palms sat like fuzzy hatpins stuck point-down into the earth. Produce vendors, selling citrus and watermelons in lumpy pyramids, turned on yellow porch lights, which attracted moths. A group of Mexican boys wearing black slacks sat on the hood of a '54 Plymouth by the side of the road, drinking beer and grinning, deep in conversation. One of them kept an eye out for cops.

Wanda sighed over and over. They were leaving all of it: weekends (only rarely) at South Padre Island, beer and shrimp on Sand Island, her friends, her neighbors, her garden. All of it. And as an experiment to see what she was living for. How odd, she thought, that she and Dauphine were such good friends, and yet– and yet her needs and Dauphine's were so different. Dauphine had her own reasons for going; she wanted to join with Barry, to make a life with Barry in some kind of permanent, more-or-less happy arrangement. Wanda's needs were as yet not completely known to her, but she would eventually have to look into the smoking mirror of her own wants. Though she would have denied it, Wanda wanted to prepare for a life alone, an inner place where even Lanky could not go, where even the cried of Loren and Petey could not penetrate. It is a secret, it is the preparation for thought and rest, it is the herald and proper introduction to a good life and a serene letting-go.

Wanda needs to be alone, thought Lanky, not even suspecting that he knew her better than she knew herself.

Were there to be pyramids for Wanda? An awaiting of the sun?

She caught a quick glimpse through the salt cedars beach and salt flats and water as they exited the highway and rolled down Tooley Boulevard.

"Dauphine to join, me to pull away," she said softly in the bathroom of the gas station outside of Norias. They were almost home.

And although a fog was lifting for Wanda, confusion grew for Barry. Despite his best intentions he had become royally, luxuriantly drunk. He might go to the café to see Dauphine, or he might not. It was certainly up to him. Anyway she would be taking her vacation time starting tomorrow. Her boss wanted her to take off only a week, but Dauphine had insisted on the usual time. He threatened (indirectly, as always) to fire her but she knew it was all bluff. But Barry was sitting behind the Tetrapylon Video Game Parlor, propped against a milk can and drinking Four Roses.

The manager's dogs barked in his right ear. They did not want Barry in the alley. "This trip is for the birds," said Barry to himself. "I must be crazy to even think about going to it. I ought to have my head examined. I ought to…." and he decided it was too hard to talk. He went home and lay down in bed. To no one again he said, "The day after tomorrow's the day." He fell into a dreamless, misty, fogbound sleep bordered with silvery, gracefully shaped rain creatures. Though surprised at their beauty in his sleep, he knew they were insubstantial. A newspaper blew into the alley and a car bearing Mary Ann Banks passed by at a slow crawl.

Mary Ann was in her own thoughtful mood. She almost ran a stoplight before coming to a skidding halt, her body metronoming back and forth in the front seat. At least she had not hit anything. The rest of the trip home was uneventful; the real action was in her head: her dead husband's memory was talking to her.

"Why do you want to go there? We never had any business there." "What difference does that make? You know I still love you and always will. Surely I'm not betraying you by—"

"But you are. We never did this. We didn't go off to new places together."

"I'm still alive. You're dead."

"You killed me by not getting me to the hospital on time."

"That won't work anymore. I'm guiltless and you're just a memory now. I was everything to you and bent backwards for you all the time, when I really wanted to kill you sometimes. You could be pretty selfish, you know."

"I don't see that this has any bearing—"

"It doesn't matter what you see because I, Mr. Banks, am going to Belize."

Silence.

Victory?

Jeanine was watching the Norworthy children all the time now. Lenny had little attention for them now that he had to hold down two jobs. His frustration grew every day, and he wished to lash out at the woman who had given him these burdens. Perversely, Lenny began to punish Jeanine for what her sister had done, although he knew that without Jeanine he would have much less chance of making ends meet. Her mother did not like Jeanine's being there all day, but she thought the assignment would last only as long as Janie was gone, or until school began again. Jeanine was withdrawing from her friends. She sat a lot in the Norworthy TV room in the den of the house, as if waiting for instructions of some kind. Nothing ever happened. Jeanine could stand less and less to look at the everyday world. Abruptly she found herself in a world minus her sister and her friends, and the four cruising teenagers seemed a dream long past. At one point in the summer not long after the caravan left for Belize, Betty Sue received the following letter:

Dear Betty Sue,

I almost never get to see you anymore and none of our other friends too. I can't figure out what's happening with this trip to Latin America and nobody asked me. I heard you weren't going so I thought I would write. I guess you chose not to go. I never got the choice. You need to call me at Janie's (under Norworthy in the book) or come over some afternoon or evening. I feel so left out of everything.

Love, Jeanine

Betty Sue felt sorry for Jeanine and did come over, but she was not prepared for the strength of Jeanine's overwhelming loneliness and sense of abandonment. Betty Sue felt guilty for ignoring her, but her new life with a new boyfriend seemed the smartest, safest course to pursue for the present. Summers are strange, she thought. It is almost as though people stop progressing for three months and become suspended in the heat.

On the evening before the company was to leave on their journey, Ed Fernandez opened the Tropicala as usual. If rumors were true, the crazy bunch leaving with Muñoz were leaving tomorrow. He poured himself a cola and wondered if he would like to go. Just then, Brenda stumbled in the front door. Her new fuchsia wedgies always caught on the doorsill.

"Goddamn it," she said casually, and walked into the bar. Edna came in a few minutes later and the three of them started talking.

Ed was surprised to find out that Chuck, Edna's oldest, was going with the "crazy caravan" as it was being called around town. Edna explained why Elena would do what she planned to do, but Ed and Brenda were unconvinced.

"It just isn't right," said Brenda.

"People just don't do those things," said Ed. After giving a few more details, Edna sort of changed their thinking. At best the caravan seemed a waste of time and money; at worst it had sinister overtones. However, Edna was optimistic. She described the changes in Chuck, and Ed and Brenda shrugged. Ed looked at his watch. No one had come in and it was almost 7:30. He and Brenda went to town for a hamburger before the night crowd came in. Edna minded the store for the time being. And the sun went down for the last time in Palmyra for the Crazy Caravan.

XLVI The Adventure

A. ***Dwarf palmetto:*** *found in wet places from Florida to Texas, north to coast of North Carolina. Second hardiest of Western Hemisphere palms. Palmate (fanshaped) leaves, stalkless.*

Elena Muñoz, her graying hair tucked under a red bandanna, made one last run around the Winnebago before climbing up to the driver's seat. She would let Otto and Mr. Murphy drive much of the way, but she herself wanted to drive out of Palmyra.

Hesitation and doubt were thrown aside, at least temporarily. The rising sun, just roaring up out of the flat Eastern horizon of the Gulf, perched momentarily to light the world before beginning its heavenly trip. Elena had gathered her troupe of malcontents at three o'clock that morning. She gave them a briefing about itineraries, where they would be at certain times, when they could call home if they needed to, how they could be reached by relatives with messages. Elena did not want relatives of her voyagers to interfere with the trip, but she knew that trying to keep them apart would cause even more trouble. When she plied them with coffee at 3:30, they sat puff-eyed and cotton-headed and listened to her words.

"You can go back at any time. I told you I'd see to it. But don't inconvenience your fellow travelers or me. If you have to come back here, wait until we get to the next city before asking me about paying your passage. Now, do you all agree to that provision?"

"Yes," they said nonchalantly, as if promising to brush their teeth after every meal.

Loren and Chuck sat in the compartment immediately behind the driver's area in a sort of "sitting room" where passengers could look at each other or swivel their chairs to see the passing show. Behind the sitting room lay the bathrooms, kitchen, a general sitting area arranged in rows of seats like a bus but with game tables and reading areas here and there among the seats. Beyond this large room lay the dark, cool, and silent sleeping quarters. Soundproofed and air conditioned against people noise, engine noise, and sunlight. A large corner of the sleep area contained strange compartments. In the last section--which was convertible into a solarium--were Popol Vuh and Kuon, the bird in a large cage hanging from the ceiling's metal spine, the dog loose, rolling on his back and, doubtless, chewing his rubber skunk which Petey Simpson has christened "Squeaky." Squeaky, the object of so many affectionate chomps and nips, had begun to show his age in tatters on his tail and head. Elena eyed the squeeze toy disapprovingly and tossed it on the lawn. Knowing that dogs don't like too much change, she had made a special trip into town to supply the anxious dog with a newer Squeaky.

Tampico was the first stop for the exhausted travelers. Elena pulled into a large motel parking lot outside the city and near the airport. She gathered her travelers into the general meeting room. The grayish polarized windows cast an eerie light over Barry's tired face. He was still recovering from his hangover, but surprisingly he was the only traveler who expressed interest in exploring the area.

So this is how the trip started. The Murphys, minus Loren, went back to sleep after breakfast. Mary Ann and Dauphine talked over some research into land sales in Belize. Dauphine learned that she could buy up to nine acres of rural land, or a half acre of city land without having to submit a development plan to the central government in Belmopan, the nation's capital which was far inland from the old capital, Belize City. Janie Norworthy was dozing off in a reclining chair in the big room. Otto and Zillah were cleaning the breakfast dishes. Zillah was in a good mood even though she was worried about her mother. Otto did not care about anything. He was happy to indulge his ancient wanderlust again. They enjoyed the novelty of washing plates in a sink, just like the old days. Otto scratched his white head and whistled the tune to "Du, du, licht mir im herzen." The flat pan of South Texas rolled swiftly by. Barry Madden pressed his temples and moaned in his sleeping room.

At 8:00 they were at the Mexican border. Elena had stopped a few times on the way to get gasoline, air for the tires, (which she put in by herself) and to make checks on her Winnebago's systems. The U.S. customs officials waved her over and there was a major traffic jam, with much cursing behind the caravan in Spanish and English. Elena woke up her charges and they identified themselves. It looked like a dope-smuggling operation to some of the border guards, but the whole thing would be too obvious if it were. They checked out the police records of some of the group but found nothing. The Mexican customs officials told Elena that she must return with all electrical equipment--TV's, mixers, and so forth--on her camper. A few other details passed uneventfully, and the Winnebago pulled through the morning-bright streets of Matamoros, and on southward to the gut of Mexico. Elena paid a bribe of $150 at the 15-mile checkpoint inside Mexico. Everyone was satisfied with the speedy service at the checkpoint. The life of Mexico between Matamoros and Tampico is like a held breath between the subtropics and the tropics. The countryside is flat except for some oddly shaped mountains off to the right. Sadly, the sea is never visible from the road. It is a land of green, hot temperatures, milo fields, cotton farms now abandoned. It looks like a mirror image of its sister land, South Texas, but with a greater mysteriousness, a greater sense of pause. The only place worth noting in this Latin Rub' al Khali is a large orange concrete ball by the side of the road. A line circles the top half of the globe. A sign says TROPICO DE CANCER and bang! Suddenly you are in the tropics. On June 21 of every year, the sun is directly over that orange ball. For our caravan the sun had retreated past that point, headed south again. But Elena would soon repass the zenith in her van's careen to the interior of Mexico. Now for Tampico.

"You can either sleep or go for a walk. If you go into town, it would be a good idea not to go by yourself. Try to travel always in twos at least until we reach our destination. And who speaks Spanish here besides me?"

Wanda's hand went up. She said she studied it in high school and occasionally had to talk with Mexican tradesmen. She added, "I don't know enough to hold a conversation, though."

Barry wished Ed Fernandez were there; he spoke Spanish like a native. Otto raised his hand. He spoke a broken but quite serviceable Spanish.

The trailer doors whooshed open and Petey was the first to jump out. Three well-dressed little Mexican children looked at him as if he were a Martian. He looked at them and said, "Hello." They continued to stare, not knowing what to say. Behind them a traveler's palm waved like a fan-shaped banana. The motel lawn was intensely green, almost painful to Petey's eyes. Frangipani bushes, now growing confidently in the tropics, threw their pink and white blossoms' perfume all over the grounds. One of the children ran forward and took Petey's hand. They wanted him to play. Petey looked behind him, half in fear and half to ask for permission to play. Lanky came down the trailer steps with Wanda holding his right hand.

"Yes," Wanda said without asking questions.

"Just don't go too far."

When the four children got to the motel playground, the Mexicans tried to ask Petey where he was from and where he was going in such a huge bus. They kept pointing to the trailer and shrugging their shoulders. One of them, a boy about Petey's age, drew a rough map of the U.S. and Mexico. As an afterthought he added Central America. Then he gently pulled Petey's finger to the map and pointed at the bus at the same time.

"Oh!" said Petey, stopping himself from scratching his brown, curly hair. "I came from here," he said, "and I'm going here." He drew a line down the coast of Mexico and added more to the vestigial Yucatan the boy drew. The children looked at each other, and then the boy, evidently knowledgeable of geography, said in Spanish, "Belice." Petey said, "Belize, yes! I mean sì sì!" Then Petey pointed to himself and said his name, but the others said their names so rapidly that he could not distinguish their unusual first names from their surnames: Ioladia, Guadalupita, and Efrencito. The children pointed to a man in black swim trunks reading a paper at the pool, and a woman with brassy red hair crocheting in her lounge chair. These were probably the children's parents, Petey thought. The father glanced up from his newspaper, tugged down his sunglasses, and came over to the children who were playing in the light of the rapidly setting sun. The Mexican children ran to him, rubbing their hands on his back or his knee and looked back at Petey with an oddly proprietary fog in their eyes, as if to say, "You may have a big trailer but you don't have this daddy" The man smiled at Petey and spoke to him in English.

"Where are you from, boy?" said the father.

Petey said, "Palmyra, Texas, mister. We're going to Belize. My name's Petey Murphy."

"Well, Petey, you'd better go back to your van because it will be dark soon. My children have to eat dinner now, no?"

"OK. We had some fun anyway."

"Petey," the man said as Petey turned to go, "tell your driver that sometimes it takes hours to cross the ferry at the Panuco River, about three or four miles from here. But once they get beyond the river, there will be few problems with the road. And Petey—be careful." He gave Petey one last look with his greenish eyes and replaced his sunglasses. He then turned away.

Petey felt chills run down his back. Why did the man say that?

At that moment Lanky and Wanda returned from their walk around the motel grounds. The name of the motel was the Posada de Tampico. Elena got permission to use the back parking lot to set the RV for the night. To her surprise she had driven the entire first day, and she was stone-tired. Lanky and Wanda lay together in their sleeping compartment looking at some children in rags washing autos in a nearby parking lot. Petey wondered why the man had told him to be careful. The rest of the party was already asleep, dead to the pleasures and pains of life.

Elena was up at dawn, fiddling and futzing in the kitchen. Wanda and Dauphine walked arm-in-arm around the grounds, talking about the next two weeks and what was in store. Then they went to the motel restaurant to get a cup of coffee and chat the way they always did at home.

Lanky and Barry had a wrestling match with Petey and Chuck, while Loren looked on and laughed. She watched Chuck with opened eyes, studying this boy who evidently was not used to touching other people. He was getting better every day.

Otto and Zillah were busy taking Kuon for a walk and cleaning Popol Vuh's cage, respectively. Popol Vuh was angry at his confinement and Zillah let him fly around the solarium until Kuon came back. Kuon eyed the bird hungrily until his food was brought to him.

Everyone in Crazy Caravan marveled at the newness, the pleasure of just starting a long vacation. The sun shone bright and the sea breeze was still cool with its seven o'clock marine breath.

Elena came to the general sitting room with a huge tray of Bloody Marys, replete with hot sauce and celery.

"Bloody Marys for all grownups," she called. The dog barked and the bird squawked as feet thudded into the room. The children were offered fruit juices. Wanda and Dauphine came back after their gossip session in the restaurant. Everyone was laughing and joking.

"I wonder what the poor folks are doing," joked Lanky. "I think they havin' Bloody Marys," answered Zillah, trying to smile.

B. ***Trachycarpus fortunei:*** *native of Eastern Asia, very hardy palm. Has burlap-like outer bark, palmate leaves. Found generally in U.S. south of the 33rd parallel and along southeastern coast. Requires more moisture and cooler climate than American West. Also known as the Windmill palm, it grows from eight to twenty feet tall at maturity. Usually arranged in groups of threes for maximum landscaping effect Safe to l0 degrees F.*

The ferry ride did take three hours. All the auto passengers, particularly the Americans, were outraged at the amazing inefficiency of the ferryboats. The Mexican themselves, usually long on patience, grew angry at the incredibly stupid delays and problems. One boat—the only one out of three in service—got stuck on a sandbar and had to be tugged loose. The ferries were not being repaired because the government had plans to build a bridge between Tampico and Ciudad Madero. According to local governmental ways of thinking, the ferries therefore no longer needed maintenance.

Barry and Dauphine played spades with Loren and Chuck. Although their age differences was great, it was plain that they were the only pairs of lovers on the trip, and it was amusing to Barry to see the teenagers as younger reflections of himself and Dauphine. Already he and Chuck had had some private talks together. Chuck seemed nervous around Barry at first but now he was warming up to the man. Dauphine and Loren were not as close. Dauphine felt strange about taking one of her daughter's friends into confidence, but she was motherly and friendly at the same time. A difficult juggling act, but the only one Dauphine felt comfortable with.

The next night was spent in the seaside town of Tuxpan even though it was only a few hours from Tampico. There were problems with the exhaust system, which Elena wanted cleared up immediately. The town was a picture postcard of Mexico—a blue-water canal, pleasant marketplace, white houses with red Mexican tile roofs, and a beautiful, uncluttered beach. Everyone was happy that, if the trailer had to break down, it chose to break down here.

After lunch Otto and Zillah took out lawn chairs and watched the sun move overhead. Then Otto suggested they go to the mercado.

"What's a mercado?" asked Zillah.

"A marketplace where you can buy all sorts of interesting things," answered Otto. They went.

Zilllah was amazed at all the color, noise, and stink of the marketplace. Piles and piles of pears, nopal cactus blades, mangoes, and bananas sat under the brightly colored canopies or tarpaper shacks. The smells of strong, strong coffee and pungent fruit and meat permeated the market's plaza. Little children, wearing clothes that seemed to come from the Sears or Penney's but without shoes, ran through the cooler concrete market nearby, rather than sit with their mothers and fathers in the sun-heated atrium. A Mexican record shop painted in wild stripes of hot pink and purple blared forth music redolent of hot, sexy jungle nights-conga drums, flutes, and guitars. The sun died away and thick, darkish blue storm clouds rolled into Tuxpan from the Gulf. The intense greens, purples, blues, pinks, yellows, and reds of the buildings in the market reinforced the cacophony of the record shop and the afternoon sky itself.

Zillah had bought a huge red and green scarf and wrapped it around her head to keep the sun off. The music made her tap her feet, then, for the first time she could recall, move gradually into a rhapsodic dance, waving her scarf in the growing freshets of wind. The market and Otto stood openmouthed as Zillah jumped and tossed like a maenad to the music, and Otto wished his legs would allow him to join in. Several Totonac women started to dance in their stalls. Little children gyrated and screamed, little brown hands stole a watermelon and someone pursued, parakeets chartreuse and blue and white squeaked in large rattan cages. A fat man carrying a stalk of bananas danced like a marionette.

The record finally stopped, but Zillah's eyes were still on fire. She looked at Otto and his mouth was hanging open. She said, "I never going home again. Never."

The frantic fire for dance that inspired the market died as soon as the first gusts of sheeted rain hit the steaming stone roof of the market building. Huastec Indians wrapped their babies in the rebozos as the temperature got cooler. Hernan Cortés himself could have seen them sitting like stone goddesses beneath the dripping atrium cornices, safe from the rain. The tic-tac-tacking of a scribe's typewriter made a staccato tattoo, embroidering the giant claps of thunder. Zillah walked home in the rain. She stalked proudly down the paved avenue near where the gutters flowed with furiously muddy water. Otto walked behind her, studying the shapes of the buildings and trees around him.

"I really am a bomb ready to go off," Zillah thought. "I on fire."

She and Otto had something close to a spiritual experience that day, but things were different for Chuck and Loren. They sat with the others during the storm under the RV's vast awning, a collapsible extension that made a porch for the air conditioning—weary caravaners. The first bloom of their infatuation had not faded. Chuck could not sleep at night. He thought of the sumptuous beauty of Loren, her trusting, intelligent eyes, her laughing mouth. And those kisses! As they left Texas on the first leg of the trip, he said to her," All those jokes about somebody's kisses being like wine or honey are true. Your kisses really are like that."

She answered, trying to think of some way to quip, to lessen the compliment of his words. Her lips were not like honey or wine, she thought. Obviously, his were. Her breath was a combo of Listermint and Crest. Her lips were by Yardley. All prosaic to her. But her god, her star-obsessed love? He was the original beauty. She was surprised he could not see the truth. So passed another one of their misunderstandings that eventually was a cause for delight in conversation. As lovers they were explorers of realms they could not yet understand—each other.

As the rain pounded on the awning, Mary Ann and Elena got into a discussion about Modern Life. This would be the beginning of many such discussions. At first the others were nonplused by Elena's genuine insights or Mary Ann's command of philosophical ideas, albeit couched occasionally in hackneyed phrases. Barry was interested and listened, but Lanky, Wanda, and Dauphine were skeptical about the worth of the discussions.

"I guess this kind of argument is okay," said Dauphine, "but it's all just a bunch of words. If they don't lead to anything, what's the use of them?"

Barry said, "You have to start somewhere. Words let you argue things out first, then decide what to do—or not to do." Everyone was getting into a talkative mood despite the violence of the storm.

But all Chuck could do was look at the perfection of Loren's face, her movements, and her body. And everything she owned—the books she read, a stuffed animal, an old board game—all these took on unearthly meaning to him, as if they were hints of some ecstatic knowledge that, if he learned it, would catapult him like a meteor beyond the drab of the world, beyond death, beyond time. Only then could he join his stars in a sort of roaring perfection, a sense of kinetic Empire among the silver dots dancing unseen now above their heads. But Loren?

She, on the other hand, had terrestrial feelings, lived in bewilderment. She scratched her forehead, puzzled, before turning out the overhead in her sleeping compartment every night. Bewilderment showed itself in several ways. For one thing, Loren could not understand why he was someone different every time she looked at him. Every kind of light, every mood he had brought to her someone new. Chuck was Chuck, no matter. But what were these chameleon tints and shades that always revealed a new facet on a known diamond? Why did she walk around the block back home and always see someone who had his nose, or his hair, or even his glasses, and see that person as a usurper of something special and hers alone? Or why, as they lay together in clumsy embrace, did she feel the tenseness and pleasure of his heartbeat, his way of seeking her eyes, speaking the codex of her fears and desires?

She glanced up at him now, as Mary Ann and Elena were talking. She felt her pulse rate quicken not because she felt love, but because he seemed to look right through her.

"It's my opinion," said Mary Ann, "that the quality of American life has decayed in the last twenty years. We have all become isolated from each other. Just look—first came the radios and family members didn't play games or talk to each other any more. Then with TVs they didn't even look at each other, let alone listen! Then if that wasn't enough, air conditioning cut off one family from the next." She aimed her remarks at the rest of the group, "Do you remember when our kids were little? We all used to sit on the front porch to cool off after dinner. We'd see our neighbors and go visit them, or they'd visit us. The children played tag under the streetlights or just sat and talked with each other. But walk down the street now. What do you see? Houses humming like refrigerators, people cut off from each other and their neighbors; there's no sense of caring about other people or even having anything to do with them, period!"

Elena pondered what Mary Ann was saying. Lanky was nodding in agreement. The others watched Mary Ann as she continued, hanging onto her words.

"And now look! There are computers everywhere. I don't have anything against them but I'm sure if they're part of the solution or just another way of cutting down on human contact even more. Occasionally business people like my husband and me would have to go to seminars or conventions or regional meetings of one sort or another. We got to know other people and made friends with colleagues in other states. But now they have teleconferencing, tele-this and compu-that. And why? Why is the human contact cut down so much, why is there less and less of it every year?"

The participants eagerly offered their ideas.

"Because there are so many kooks these days," said Wanda. "You don't know who to trust anymore. There are political and religious kooks and sex kooks and people who just want to hurt you in order to get rid of their own meanness feelings. I don't know why."

Barry added, "It's hard for most folks to trust anymore because people move around too much. Can you imagine living in a small village with all your aunts, uncles, cousins, nephews, and nieces? Can you imagine seeing your grandchildren any damn time you wanted, because they live just down the street? Who lives like that anymore? We are separated from the one group of people we should look to for our sense of security. And they aren't there. What kind of society is that?"

Petey looked from person to person as the discussion continued. He had Kuon on a leash now; Otto saw to it that the boy and dog became friends. To make sure of Kuon's safety, however, Otto had tied the other end of Kuon's chain to the underframe of the van. Petey was only sort of pretending to restrain the beast. No one noticed how proud he was.

Janie stood up and added an extra ice cube to her tea. She turned, faced the group, and spoke with a near hiss in her voice. Her green eyes flashed and her teeth were bared in controlled anger.

"What makes you people assume that more contact is a good thing? You've been watching too many soap operas. Wake up! Forget diet shows! Forget your moronic TV stations! They're teaching you garbage anyway. Life isn't like that; it's best when it's a struggle to know, not just survive. The merest rat can survive. How do you measure out your lives? It's hard to tell. You don't seem to value anything but the shallowest of emotions and entertainment. Maybe you could stand a little more isolation, a little more time away from paperback romances and grocery store scandal rags. Maybe you ought to develop your minds instead of asking for a world that can never be again. My God, what makes you assume even that other people are necessary to your existence?"

Everyone was stunned, particularly Mary Ann. The hardness of Janie's argument made Wanda answer. "We all know you're the educated one, Janie. You don't need to tell us your accomplishments because every man and woman you know in this...uh...back in Palmyra admired you for your degrees and grades. And I never thought I'd say it, let alone think it, but I agree with just about everything you say. Except the part about human contact. Maybe you're different from me, but I learn so much more about life from my children and..."

"Oh come on, don't hand me that domestic bliss crap," said Janie, wrenching her arm in front of her, as if wiping away Wanda's idea.

"Now hear me out. It's my turn," said Wanda, holding her hands up as if to stop the traffic of words among everyone else.

"I'm not going to get personal here because it isn't right, but I do want to say, Janie, that the human contact aspect of life is valuable if the contacts are satisfying to you." Janie opened her mouth but Wanda stopped her. "Not because they're something special, but because they're part of learning about the world as a whole. People are a large part of our world. If you say you want to know things, then other people must be known and known intimately. But that's just for me and people like me. You may be constructed differently, and now you're doing what you've always wanted to do. I'm not trying to say that you have to be like everyone else."

"That's good," said Janie, "but what I meant was that most Americans, at least women, are relationship slaves. Men have never been, not if they didn't want to be." Barry spoke, turning from looking at Dauphine.

"I know what you mean, Janie. I've been by myself for years. It's just that your perspective changes when you find somebody you really trust. Then the relationship isn't slavery."

Janie looked off into the rain thoughtfully. She sat down in the green plastic and aluminum lawn chair.

"I know you're probably right, but it's just that my marriage taught me some things...."

And Elena added, "What marriage doesn't?"

Until Otto and Zillah returned, with plastic sheets over their heads to keep out the rain, the rest of Crazy Caravan thought about the conversation. Elena suddenly realized she was lucky that she lived in the same town as her brothers, how good it was that they had not left for Chicago or Houston or Dallas. It was sad that families had to break up and go their separate ways. And, ultimately, for what? for jobs, for a way to earn a living. Are there no ways for families to earn livings together except in farming?

Pleasant reminiscences aside, Elena felt the need to meditate over her father's message. Some might have called it praying. As she sat watching the storm's waning intensity, she looked within herself, trying to address the spirit of her father, as she had done for years, and especially since his mystical appearance earlier in the summer. After hearing Otto and Zillah's story about the marketplace, Elena went into the van and padded across the mint-blue carpet to her room and shut the door. She pulled out a red notebook. It had no writing on the front to tell it was a diary, but that is what Elena decided it was.

August 10

Today we pulled into Tuxpan and I am confused.

And that was all she could think of to write.

C. *Sabal palmetto:* *common genus of palm native to New World, state tree of Florida and SouthCarolina. White to gray trunk. Hardiness similar to T. fortunei. Can stand great extremes of cold, heat, and drought; also tolerant of light salt spray. Fan-shaped leaves, tall straight trunk, sometimes reaching thirty to thirty-five feet. Small berry-like fruits in autumn. Retains old leaves.*

The next day passed almost without incident. Calm seemed to sit among the group, though Petey, Loren, and Chuck oohed and aahed at the growing lushness of the countryside. At a Pemex station in Veracruz, a boy about fifteen years old and wearing a Dallas Cowboys football jersey told Elena that a great drought had blanched and wrinkled the face of Mexico, that it had not rained in the highlands for a year in some places. But the jungle about them-and by now it truly was jungle-seemed to belie the boy's words. Sometimes in the distance, he said, you could see the gigantic volcano Citlaltépetl, or "Star Mountain" as it was described by the Aztecs. Now it was known by the more prosaic name of Orizaba. Closer, the mountains, low and soft and green, hid the highway like a black rope coiled among their vibrant flanks, almost daring the elephantine van to thread its course.

Lanky drove well here. He was distracted by the breathtaking greenness of the banana and pineapple and coffee plantations that quilted themselves along with patches of riotous jungle thick with trees and vines and flowers the size of melons. Lanky felt an odd elation in the cab of the van; this place in Mexico was definitely not his "run." But he was happy to be helping to be making sure that Elena's trip and theirs was a success. He, like the others, was just starting to grope for what he wanted out of this trip. He had no clear feelings about it at all except for the dissatisfaction he felt back home and the hope that Belize might offer something different. He leaned his skinny frame over the driver's wheel and rubbed his eyes to get the sleep out of them.

There was something else vague about his feelings: Wanda seemed to be pulling away from him, ever so slightly, almost completely unnoticeably. Only some inner voice told him this—the same voice that suggests paranoia when we do not know all the facts or lose our perspective. On the surface, Wanda was the same as ever, maybe even more attentive and pleasant. But that was just it. Why would she go completely out of her way to please him when she usually did not? Another hint lay in her eyes—eyes that seemed to show greater and greater distances in their depths when she thought he was not looking at her. Those distances, that cool alienation which confused him, also frightened him.

And there was one more thing: he did not like the growing togetherness of Loren and Chuck. He did not have to admonish Loren yet, but he had always been able to show his disapproval through silences, changes in facial colors or expression, or movements.

He reached for the radio and got a Mexican station playing lively "musica tropical". Lanky snapped his fingers like a teenager and saw sign after sign saying NO REBASE—NO REBASE—NO REBASE. No passing! No passing! His mind returned to his marital problem. There was nothing to be done now; he would have to wait out the next few weeks to see what the future held for both of them.

"How come Dad's mad at you?" Petey asked Loren as they pulled out of Tuxpan.

"He's not mad at me, dummy," she replied, too hastily. She knew he was beginning to show his signs when she and Chuck were holding hands or walking down the road or beach without the others.

"Most fathers must be like this about their daughters," Lanky thought. Perhaps they are.

The next day passed quietly as well. The motor home stopped in Coatzacoalcos, a city lying nearly at the bottom of the Gulf of Mexico. There seemed to be more money here, more houses and better roads. The dark green jungle—supremely, self-confidently lord of everything but the gulf of blue-green water to the north—sat like a Maya chieftain surveying a watery kingdom. There was an odd slant of light in Coatzacoalcos, a strange purple-violet to the sunset that confused Barry and Dauphine, who felt edgy and went for a walk.

Downtown was not far from the hotel grounds where the motor home was staying, so Barry and Dauphine decided to explore. At first they chatted about their houses back home and speculated on the condition the neighbors had left them in. Barry's brow sagged as he thought of the pet he had allowed to die so long ago due to his negligence and excess. That could have been fifty years ago—or never, he thought.

Downtown was lit up with colored lights and lanterns, and trumpets blared over the tops of squarish concrete buildings. The air was very still. Marimbas cooed very softly from the *zócalo,* or town square. The two lovers quickened their footsteps, Dauphine regaining temporarily the youthful vigor that her daughter always showed. She ran before Barry and laughed, as if trying to lose him in the thickening crowd of black, shiny heads. The music was lively and engaging, and some couples were dancing on the zócalo walkways. Some of the girls wore traditional, long flounced skirts and flowers on their heads. Car horns blared in the night as friends met friends in the plaza, teenagers laughing or smoking Baronet cigarettes amid a cacophony that bothered or inspired none. Barry and Dauphine held their hands over their ears and found an empty bench. The crowds abruptly broke and separated on either side of the street. Barry craned to see what would make the crowd dissolve so quickly. A line of pickup trucks and old panel trucks garlanded with flowers came riding around the square, honking their horns. Girls riding in the backs of the trucks waved to the crowds and threw flowers and trinkets. Barry took Dauphine's willing hand and ran to the front of the cathedral to get a better view. Suddenly all the girls jumped from the back of the truck and ran to Barry, who through his camera viewfinder was surprised to see them coming after him. Half-delighted, half-uneasy, he let the girls push and cajole and tease him onto the pickup truck. They giggled incessantly, pelted Barry with flowers, and made him dance with them to the approving guffaws of the locals.

Then, inside the truck, Barry saw the smashed pink bicycle with red streamers hanging from its handlebars.

A howl of horror rose over the zócalo.

Mary Ann had wanted to take a walk through the countryside or even downtown, but she could tell Barry and Dauphine had wanted to be by themselves. It was not a verbal message, or even gestural. It was almost chemical. Their togetherness reminded her of her dead husband. How many times had they excluded other people so they could be alone? So this is what it felt like. It was not a pleasant reality but it made its own biological sense.

Heading out of town was out of the question. Night was coming fast. And Mary Ann did not want to tail Barry and Dauphine, so she wandered around the motel and its grounds. Dinner had been delayed due to some confusion between Zillah and Otto, and so it would be dark before the meal was ready. According to a sign she had seen when Lanky had pulled in, this was the Hotel Gireye. It was clean, spare, and low.

Mary Ann washed her face and set out at a brisk pace. She walked the length of the Winnebago and saw a faint blue light from the rear. Elena was sitting on top of the solarium compartment with a pitcher of some clear drink. The German shepherd was sitting next to her, looking down impassively at Mary Ann, his tongue moving with his panting. Elena was staring at the stars just now beginning to shine as the tropical night began to fall quickly. She did not see Mary Ann. The real estate maven began to wonder what profundities were going through Elena's mind. Someone who contemplates the heavens that way must be plumbing vast, impenetrable depths of probable truth.

Actually, Elena was thinking, "Hm. This dog needs a bath. And the bird needs to get out some. Now, should I buy some fresh fruit here, or should I wait until we get to Villahermosa? We've been on the road for three days...or is it four? We have a long bridge to cross tomorrow. Then we'll be in the Yucatan. At last."

Mary Ann continued her walk to the edge of the motel property. She put her hands on her hips and sighed as the roar of night insects crescendoed. She heard footsteps behind her and turned around. A man with graying hair and sports clothes came up to her and bowed, sweat beading his forehead. He said something

Spanish, and Mary Ann answered "No comprendo," her only handy Spanish phrase. The man said, "I am sorry. I did not know. You have seen a tennis ball?"

"No, I just got here."

"I see. I must rejoin my friends," he said politely, and ran back to the lighted court. He took a few running steps and turned to smile at her briefly. Mary Ann felt something she had not felt in years—elation, infatuation, and lust. Her husband's shade did not hover over her, she was free from his influence for the moment. Viewing the dark of the highway with distaste, she turned to the lighted courts where someone important—or someone she wanted to be important—was playing. O bright world!

The sink was clogged:

"Ain't doin' that," said Zillah who sat on the kitchen floor with an aluminum pot on her lap. "Ain't," she repeated, like a mark of terminal punctuation. Otto's face was getting red.

"Gott damn it, Tzillah! You vill do diss!"

"Ain't got to, and don't cuss me."

"Vot you vant me to do? I got to change a filter and flush der system!"

"It stink bad, and I don't got to."

Otto threw his monkey wrench on the kitchen floor and stomped with weak old legs around the room. His face was like an angry peach. Chuck and Loren ran to the kitchen, somehow expecting to see a group of gold-toothed bandidos robbing the kitchen. Their actual disappointment registered in their droopy, if questioning faces.

"Get OUT!" shouted Otto. Zillah sat impassively like a cast-iron Buddha frozen to a temple floor. She did not see Otto yelling at the two curious teenagers and thought he was addressing her.

"Ain't got to," she repeated. "This my kitchen too."

Loren ran out of the motor home to a bench near the old swimming pool. A little tree frog had fallen in and was swimming casually in the lighted water, unaware as yet that there was no escape. She thought she was too sensitive and wiped her eyes. Letting that old fool hurt her feelings, yelling at her that way. No in call for that! Chuck came out of the shadows and called softly to her. For once she wanted to be alone and did not answer. He practically stumbled over her.

"Why didn't you answer me?" he said.

"I just want to be alone a few minutes."

"Well, you could've said so."

"I didn't know I had to tell you everything I do."

Chuck found that there was a rent in the gauzy fabric of love he had woven for himself. His anger and hurt grew and rather than say something he would regret later he stalked off into the night. Loren waited until he was out of earshot, then wept.

Meanwhile, Elena had gotten drunker than she meant to. Her head buzzed merrily and the stars gleamed and popped like flashbulbs in the woozy cosmos above her. She realized something, though. Doors were slamming. People were making ugly noises. Shouting. She glanced to her left and downward. Lanky and Wanda nearly ran out of the RV. Elena's head bobbed like a fishing cork as she tried to hear the conversation, but she needed to pee and the dog was getting fidgety. Normally she would have left so as not to hear a private argument, but alcohol had cloven her sensibilities. Through the still air she heard Wanda speak first.

"You never told me that before. Why? How come?"

"It never seemed important!" shouted Lanky, shrugging his shoulders as if trying to make a raving maniac understand him. Wanda hated that patronizing gesture. It reminded her of her father's way of dismissing her existence when she showed any legitimate emotion. He always passed her off as some kind of Unstable Female, an ill tempered, idiot girl who could be cajoled with a doll or chocolates or, later, with a new dress.

"Damn! You men are all alike!" she said, punching him in the shoulder.

"What did I say?" asked Lanky, shrugging his shoulders again. Wanda grew more and more angry.

"Why didn't you tell me you had a crush on Karen Allemeister? You never told me! I thought you trusted me!"

"What difference does it make, honey? She's been dead for years. I didn't say I was obsessed with her; I just said—"

"I know what you said! Don't try to weasel out of what you said!"

Elena rapidly lost interest. It sounded like TV. She opened the hatch to go into the solarium. Kuon pushed past her to get to his long-missed rubber skunk, and Elena rolled matter-of-factly off the top of the solarium, just catching herself by one arm on the remains of a luggage rack bar. The jolt should have wrenched her arm out of its socket, but she hung there, passively satisfied that she was not arguing with anyone, like a dizzy orangutan trying to decide which way was up or down. She gave up trying to figure it out and let go. Her feet hit the ground heavily, but she landed upright. And just in time to see a black figure emerge from the open solarium hatch and flap its wings in a salute to escape.

"Oh, it's you," smiled Elena, and waved. "Bye!"

When Dauphine came in she looked like a banshee with her sweaty hair standing up in wild tufts all over her head. Barry had been sedated but was still mumbling. She and two Mexican men threw him in bed. Kuon was howling at the moon or perhaps at Popol Vuh's empty cage. Elena was sitting in the driving compartment in utter darkness, the little dashboard fan blowing weekly in her face. She was trying to maintain her high by taking weak drinks. In a moment of boredom and sorrow, she fiddled around in her purse for Kleenex but found instead a slip of paper bearing a faint telephone number. The paper was yellowed and old but the handwriting was definitely her own. Now whose number could this be? She scratched her head and poured herself another drink. Idle curiosity turned to real curiosity. She simply could not place the number. She read it slowly to the overseas operator so as not to slur her words. The phone rang. Elena tapped her toe on the floor and snare-drummed her fingers on the dash. Finally a man's voice answered hello.

"Who's this?" asked Elena.

"Who are you?" asked the man.

"It doesn't matter; just listen, OK?" The man said nothing but "Do I know you?" and paused for a reply. Elena decided to trust what's-his-name.

"Listen," she said. "I've brought a lot of people with me on a wild goose chase through Mexico."

"What?" he interrupted.

"You heard me," she continued. "Everyone's arguing and fighting, and now my pet toucan's flown away."

"Lady, if this is some kind of joke, I—"

"It's not a joke," she said. "I'm in deadly earnest. Mister, tell me I'm doing the right thing. I have a lot of people fighting here. What have I done? What should I do?"

"Lady, are you some kind of weirdo?"

"Just listen to me, will you?"

"Do you live around here? I don't like—"

"Oh forget it. I just wanted you to tell me what to do."

The man she called was Ed Fernandez. Somehow the number had found its way to her purse when Chuck came aboard Crazy Caravan, probably taken verbally from Chuck as a way to reach his mother at the bar in an emergency. The call was answered, of course, by Ed. Edna was not in and had not told him she might get phone calls from Mexico. Thus Ed did not yet know the source of the call, just as Elena was ignorant of its destination.

"No one can tell you what to do, lady," Ed offered, now beginning to suspect who the caller was. "You can always come home."

"Nope, can't do that. Not home yet. Home's in Belize." Ed was now sure of the call. Elena said she was going to hang up now.

"Only one last thing," she mumbled. "I'm so scared and lonely and unsure of this whole thing." Ed kept his conversational tone.

"So, what else is new with the human race, lady?"

"Yeah. You're right. Goodbye." She hung up.

The van was not moving when Janie woke up the next morning. Scattered textbooks on the Toltec-Maya ruins of Yucatan lay at her feet with boxes of tissues and scattered articles of clothing. Janie had been untouched by last evening's brouhaha. She got up, took a quick shower (plenty of hot water, no noise!) and looked around the van. What she saw left her open-mouthed.
Zillah was sleeping on the kitchen floor, aluminum pot in her lap and head perched on a low stool. The sink was still stopped up. Lanky was asleep on the kitchen bar. Wanda was missing. Dauphine and Barry lay together very uncomfortably on a short sofa in the sitting area. Loren was locked in her room, Chuck in his. Mary Ann was not to be found, and neither was the bird. Otto was

outside in the white morning light trying to figure out the drain. Janie ran to the driver's compartment and found Elena snoring in the driver's seat, the little fan breezing her face like the lick of a devoted puppy.

"Damn it all!" Janie shouted and pulled Elena out of the chair, dragging her to her room. Elena looked around and said her arm hurt, then passed out again. Barry and Dauphine got up and stretched then waited for Janie to come back through. She snapped orders at them and they obeyed. Nobody expected differently.

"You get the plunger and undo the kitchen drain. Barry, you go wake everyone but Elena up."

Petey came out and rubbed his eyes.

"Mama and Daddy were fighting last night," he cried. Janie took him by the shoulder and gently turned him around.

"Yes, but nothing's wrong now. Would you do me a big favor, honey? Good. Go outside and look in the trees around this motel. See if you can find the bird. He got out last night. Would you do that?"

When he nodded, she patted his cheek and sent him to get dressed. She told Barry to see if he could help Otto, who had no mechanical sense at all. She stopped them one last time.

"Tell everyone but Elena there will be a general meeting thirty minutes from now. The ones who are missing can be filled in later. " It was soon found out that Wanda had slept with Loren, so she was accounted for. Mary Ann came in later, looking embarrassed but happy. People were cleaning up everywhere and she was afraid that the van's departing had been held up because of her. Janie was just getting ready for the meeting but she still had a big brush and bucket of soapy water in her hands.

"Mary Ann! It's you. Good. Come in. Meeting's getting started." Everyone but Petey and Elena were there.

"Okay, you people. I don't have any idea what happened here last night, but I'm surprised at all of you. Elena is back there, sleeping off a drunk, probably because she was overwhelmed with the responsibilities of making this journey. If you can't be civil to one another, at least try to for her sake. Remember that all of you (and that includes me) are getting this trip for nothing. Too bad for us that so far we're too stupid or lazy or irresponsible to get anything from it. That may be true of you, but it's not true of me. I know what I want, and I want you to find what you're looking for. But you're not going to take it from me! So we're going to be on the road in thirty minutes. And I hope you're ready to go by then." She threw her brush into the bucket and stalked inside. The members of the caravan looked at each other then continued working.

When the van lurched forward, Elena woke with a start and looked around her. For a pleasant moment she thought she was back at Los Cocos, looking toward the sea through a bunch of ramrod-straight royal palms with their white, almost cement-looking stems and feathery dark green fronds. But why was Los Cocos moving? Then it all came back to her—the fights, the rage, the fear in Dauphine's eyes, the bird flying—the bird! Elena rose from her bed but fell back again, reeling with gin-induced nausea and a previous day filled with exhausting situations. Oh, my Popol Vuh. Flown away to the jungle not knowing how to survive on his own! Elena wept effortlessly into her pillow.

Petey played a solitary Monopoly game (no one else had time) on the floor of Wanda's room while she talked with Dauphine. Now that the van was moving and there was little for them to do, the two friends escaped with their full coffee mugs (cleaned by a less recalcitrant Zillah) into a haven to exchange information.

"Everything was fine until then. It was like we were having a romantic Mexican vacation or something, you know?" said Dauphine.

"That's really a funny coincidence, though—same bike, same color, same streamers. I wonder if the bike was the same year's model as Karen's bike?"

"I guess we'll never know."

"Sounds like a nightmare come to life," said Wanda abstractedly. "So what happened here? Looks like there was some trouble last night over this way." Wanda's face clouded. She told her friend about Lanky's admission about Karen the night before. When she cried, Dauphine looked at her and said, "What on earth are you crying for? So what if he had a crush on Karen at one time? She's dead and besides, she was never any competition for you! Most boys liked Karen with their glands, not their hearts. You reacted too strong, I think."

Wanda was stung by Dauphine's words, but coming from her, they had the ring of truth about them. Wanda thought that maybe a wedge was being driven between her and her husband. How could she apologize to him? What would she do? After considering a number of alternatives, she decided simply to say she was sorry.

Mary Ann closed her paperback on dialectics. Oh, last night! It had happened so fast, no time to think or weigh options or even decides right from wrong. He had taken her. The tennis player, whose name had gone in one ear and out the other, had simply and unequivocally taken her.

She sighed and took another sip of grapefruit juice. Lucky for her, no one had noticed her absence or simply had not paid attention to it. She had been lucky. No one had said a word to her about the night before.

I wonder what Epicurus would have said, she thought. Would he have approved of it? Or was it simply hedonism? As if an iron gate fell in front of an open passageway, all thought in her head on the matter abruptly ceased. Her reaction the night before had been instinctual, unavoidably sexual. Very little was said. The trip to the little cabaña had taken five minutes. Thirty minutes later, and after explosive, passionate pleasure, she had found herself on the highway, walking back to the hotel without a thought in her brain. Then his little white Fiat pulled up beside her and he had laughed at her. She had laughed in return and jumped in. How had she forgotten how sex was? How could anyone forget? The single-mindedness, the course of the blood in its inevitability. There was no hand wringing, no evil dreams. Only the relief of unhitched breathing and the incredible living silk of someone else's skin. He could have been a rapist. He could have been a gigolo or even some kind of maniac. He was not. And it did not matter. Only the pleasure of that moment had mattered, and it was almost as good as thinking.

A pothole in the road made her look up. The Yucatan was flat, flat was the Louisiana of her early childhood. Somehow she sensed they were going inland. A rickety sign said "Macuspana l46 km." Some chickens pecked by the side of the road. An old Indian woman with a baby wrapped in a dirty pink cotton blanket glanced up and saw the van. Her eyes and Mary Ann's met against the backdrop of low jungle.

Then Mary Ann knew something. The woman's sweat and pain in carrying her grandchild in the steamy weather was something. Somewhere, sometime, that old woman had had her own moment "in the cabaña." The only free pleasure she would enjoy intensely! And now, years later, she carried the result of the result down a tarry black highway. Mary Ann craned her neck to look back. The grandmother was still watching her with some hostility, it seemed. The ex-real estate woman said aloud, "It doesn't really matter, does it? It wasn't right, it wasn't wrong. I had an experience." True experience, like Mary Ann at this moment, is mute. One last voice: Dead husband, are you there? No answer.

Petey and Loren disagreed over the correct location of one of Petey's Parcheesi men. Loren said it was here. Petey disavowed her claim, saying it was there. Loren was sad over her fight with Chuck the night before. She hit Petey a glancing blow against the forehead, and he turned and punched her arm. Wanda came in and warned both of them about waking up Elena.

"If you can't play like human beings I'll take that board away!" Slam. She left. Loren looked at Petey with poisonous hatred, a heat strong through its own quick passing.

"Who wants to play this stupid damn game anyhow?" She left Petey by himself. Petey rubbed his forehead—now bright red—and wished he were home. His little dirty fingers picked up the wooden tokens.

D. ***Phoenix canariensis:*** *also known as the Canary Island date palm, an ornamental. Common throughout Southern Europe and Deep South, P. canariensis bears inedible fruit unlike its relative, the common date palm, P. dactylifera. The Canary Island date palm is hardy to 20 degrees F and is prized for its glossy dark-green pinnate fronds and thick trunk.*

Elena put on a zebra print muumuu and held the enema bag, now filled with ice water, on her head like a native on safari. Her eyes felt like two red beacons glowing in the early afternoon light. If she had blinked them alternately, she would have resembled a railroad-crossing signal. The worst of the hangover was done with, however, and now there were other matters to attend to. She took out her journal and paused, pencil eraser in mouth, before continuing.

August l5

"Raging hangover. Beginning to doubt my own sanity for this and other reasons. Popol Vuh escaped because of me, no effort made to find him. I feel terrible today. Where is my pyramid? Oh, 'mi Lobito', why don't you reassure me? I'm frightened!"

And so she was, but the van was moving: someone must have been driving. For once she decided to let the others worry with details. She could not face realities today. Petey knocked gently on her door, which she opened slowly.

"Do you want any Pepto-Bismol or something? Mama told me to ask you." Elena was ashamed of her disheveled hair, her rosy eyes.

"No, Petey, thank you. How is Kuon? Is he eating?" Elena asked this question because the vicious German shepherd usually quit eating for two days or so after Popol Vuh was shipped to Costa Rica for the winter.

"Sure," was the treble reply. "Bird's eatin' too."

Elena was slow to react. For a moment she thought the boy was making a very cruel joke. But his face was guileless. No smirk.

"You mean the bird is back in his cage?" asked the heiress, her bangle-bracelets chiming as she pulled the enema bag off her head. Her own shouting throbbed at her temples.

"Sure thing," said Petey. "I thought you knew." Elena hugged the enema bag, then Petey, then the smiley-face pillow Betty Sue had given Loren for the trip. With a few steps she was in the solarium dancing around with Kuon, who was happy to see her even though he did not know the reason for this special midday attention. She batted Popol Vuh's cage and made the old bird flop angrily in the air. He spat and skronked and squawked as Elena continued to dance around the small room, which smelled of musty dog pelt, feces, very slight diesel fumes, and dog food. She then asked Petey for the details of the recapture, and Petey did so, telling her that he had found Popol Vuh asleep on a low limb of a young ceiba tree on the Hotel Gireye grounds. A piece of mosquito net had ended the bird's short freedom.

So, maybe El Lobito was right? Maybe she would reach her destination, and all would at last prosper? She made her adieux to the animals, then returned to her room to add the good news to her diary:

> Wanda and Barry will find their own selves!
> Janie will find a lost city!
> Mary Ann will find the meaning of life!
> Chuck and Loren will find each other!
> And I will finally know what my duty to myself IS!

Many miles from Elena's dancing gyrations, Palmyrans continued their lives as they had always done. One of Petey's friends was playing ball in the street and got hit by a car. It broke his leg. Everyone signed the cast.

Betty Sue enjoyed some of her new freedom but she was worried about her mother. Maybe she had made a mistake going off with Barry. But Betty Sue was still dating the Porsche boy although she was getting tired of his jealousy. She was also worried about Jeanine, who seemed at a loss without her older sister. But that was not all. Jeanine's behavior had been pretty weird lately. Phone calls late at night, waking up Betty Sue's aunt and causing a lot of questions, tears and fears over the telephone. Compassion, Betty Sue knew, was not one of her strengths. She decided to write Marti and ask her what to do. A lavender envelope arrived seven days later from her friend, expressing sadness at Jeanine's problem but offering no real help.

"I never did understand Jeanine much," she wrote. "She was always Loren's friend. I'll talk to her and see what I can do."

Pavel Tikhonov tended his little garden with decorous if inexpressible sadness. Without his wife he wanted to die. Settling his accounts and preparing for that soon-to-arrive day gave him a feeling of accomplishment. He suffered a restlessness that called for the end of things that, somehow, refused to come.

Brenda and Ed were sharing a beer at three AM in the Tropicala. The fan palms rustled and clattered like a boneyard in the night wind. The neon lights hummed softly as they attracted insects.

"Yeah, she really called me. Can you believe that?" Ed asked.

"What did Edna say? Is she worried?"

"I didn't tell her. I figured Muñoz was on a toot. No harm."

"No harm, my ass! You better tell her everything that happened. Her goddamn baby's on that trip, you know."

"Sure, but I don't think there's trouble."

"You're the Boss," said Brenda, losing interest.

"Brenda? What are you doing next Monday night?"

"Who wants to know?" she said, flicking her cigarette.

"Me."

Janie and Mary Ann lounged in the general sitting room for some minutes before they became aware of each other's presence. Janie made a bland observation about the weather, and Mary Ann was not slow on the uptake. After a few preliminaries she began to tell Janie about the night before. Communication never had seemed so important as it did now.

"It was all over before I knew it. Then I decided to spend the rest of the night with him. A little voice in my head kept saying, `Of course this is right. Of course I'm going to do it.'"

The old Mary Ann would never have told anyone, and here she was, telling her own employee. It did not seem to matter now. To her surprise—or maybe it was not so surprising—Janie was sympathetic and seemed to understand what she had gone through. Mary Ann unconsciously closed the red leather copy of Rousseau's "Confessions" and put it on her lap. There was an air of confidential serenity between them.

"It was the same way with me and Lenny," said Janie quietly. "We slept together on our third date. I was the aggressive one. Lenny wanted to wait until we were at least engaged. I found that charming."

"Janie," asked the older woman, "do you miss your children? I wanted to ask that before but for some reason I think I can today. " Janie's face blanched slightly.

"Yes," she conceded, "I do miss them—especially at quiet times like this. I guess everybody back at the office thinks I'm a monster."

"Probably not. I don't think they understand you too well."

"Do you?"

Their talk gradually turned to the paleoastronomy of the Maya in the Petén during the classical period. Janie said that she was formulating a hypothesis about some of the codices, still undeciphered, that lay in a New York private collection. If her hypothesis were borne out by research, a lot of the inscriptions in stone would finally be deciphered. The utterances of ages long past fascinated both of them. Mary Ann was learning more and more about her destination. Belize was no longer a simple, unknown place she was going; it became a state of mind that required a detachment from the past and a growing respect for the powers of ideas. She had sensed this potential before, but her job kept her thinking in the here and now, crippling her movement towards growth and forcing her to spend her mental energies elsewhere. No doubt this expense would be canceled forever. Now she had an entrance to the world of thought. She envisioned it as a crystalline structure encasing the earth itself, which, even with its sweat and stupidity and death is the fount of all ideas. And Belize, she finally realized, was where that structure would display itself at last. This, then, was to be her, Mary Ann Bank's, revelation. She was to see the meaning of a red hibiscus against yellow grass, the six blue-greens of the Bay, the rumble of precious jade rivers, of nephrite waves, of staghorn coral. Six blue stars were to shine overhead.... And a line from earth to moon to Venus to beyond.... She shook her head, grasped her throat. A vast empty sky and empty ocean both stretched before her, a warm infinity, cool wind. Her face reddened.

"What's wrong?" Janie asked.

"Let me tell you—.... There's only a hint...of it..."

"Tell me what?" She could not speak. It is wordless in its anticipation, a star coming to Earth. It is a sense of oneness and awe. The ocean heaves.

"Mary Ann. What's the matter! Let me go get Dauphine!" Janie hurried out. Mary Ann murmured quietly: Ecstasy, ecstasy.

Soon a violent rainstorm rent and sacked the dark-green jungle. Petey and Loren looked at the huge lianas hanging from the tropical oaks, so similar to the oaks back home and yet as tall as cathedral columns. The sky turned almost black and Lanky was obligated to pull the van off the highway as soon as he could find a place.

There were not many people in this part of Campeche. The Mayas could be seen in little villages, their ancient homes. However, in other places the twentieth century intruded. The van stopped at hot-pink, stucco, squarish building with a roof border of white decorative bricks that said REFACCIONES BARDENA 24-18-07. The rain was so hard that the pink stucco seemed to drain away into the roadside swamps. A fat Indian man wearing a white guayabera shirt and dress slacks stood under a corrugated tin front porch. There was nothing to do but wait for the end of the deluge.

Lanky and Barry were sharing conversation and beer in the driver's compartment.

"Hey, this reminds me of the last time we were drinking and driving," Barry chuckled.

"God, don't remind me. I was drunk on my ass," moaned the truck driver.

"Yeah, that was some night. I'll never forget Brenda."

By and by, Barry got around to telling Lanky what had happened in Coatzacoalcos. Lanky, of course, had heard most of the details but he wanted to know why Barry had reacted the way he did. The two men were fast becoming companions, easy pals awash in a sea of women and children. They had similar interests but their backgrounds and experiences made them very different people. Barry said that the real surprise about that night in Coatzacoalcos was not the bike itself, but that it was the last thing in the world he expected to see at that particular moment. Lanky laughed, but Barry touched his shoulder.

"You weren't there that night out on the highway. I can't tell you how many things from way back hit me all at once. I hadn't seen that bike for twenty years, and wham! There it was, and all those girls from the Coatzacoalcos zócalo sort of showing it to me. It looked almost like a trap, like they were waiting for me to show up downtown so they could play a cruel joke on me. You know what I mean?"

Lanky dropped the small grin he generally had on his face when talking with others. "No, I don't understand it, but I know you all saw something out there. Barry, don't hold it inside you,

you know? Try to see it like the accident it was. Those girls couldn't know about Karen. How could they know?"

"She was pregnant," Barry said irrelevantly.

"Uh. What did you say?" Lanky choked on a swig of brew.

"She was pregnant. Karen was pregnant." Lanky sat speechless. Howler monkeys hooted and screeched through the noise-canopy of insects. The storm abated swiftly and then regrouped over the Gulf, but it had left Crazy Caravan.

"Why are you telling me this?" asked Lanky.

"So is Dauphine."

"Jesus Christ, Barry." Lanky started the truck and pulled two more beers out of the cooler. They toasted Elena.

Amy Mortcap had probably reached the point of no return. She would not have recognized Zillah even if she saw her again. And she could just barely remember where she was from, recalling more clearly than anything else the bananas in her yard and the horse-head lampshade with the burnt spot in it. And that was about all she remembered except for her mission in life as described on the now-defunct Sister Thompson's Radio Revival Hour. Amy was steadily growing physically healthier. Her body responded almost magically to the constant walking and talking that her mission of motherhood demanded. In Two Egg, Florida, she stopped in a white folks trailer court and knocked on the door of a modest little trailer. A fat white man about forty and wearing a torn undershirt opened the door a few inches.

"Whaddya want?" he asked. Amy was going to go through her usual routine about Sister Thompson's mission and so on. But this time she decided to do something else.

"You called about de maid?" she said.

"Yeah, but that was about a month ago. What kept you? And ain't you just a little old?"

A miracle! The man really had called a domestic service. Sister Thompson had been right; God was moving in his mysteries. She found someone to be a mother for, and he had already requested a maid.

"I old, honey, but not too old to take care of yo place here. Easy for me. You jus' watch." He barred her way into the trailer.

"And what do you want me to pay? I told 'em not to send somebody who wanted a lotta money. How much, before I let you in?"

"Ain't nothing you have to pay, honey."

"Huh?"

"Ah sez you don't gotta pay."

He narrowed his eyes and put his fists on his hammy waist. "Is this for real, old lady? You ain't settin' me up for no robbery, are ya?"

"No suh. Um-um. Not me. You just feed me and give me a bed to sleep in and I do fine. Just fine."

The living room reeked of beer and gunmetal and urine. A large color TV was tuned to a pro football game. A wall hanging made of velvet depicted a forest scene replete with deer. A bullet hole and its burn passed through the deer's head. Another wall tapestry showed dogs of various breeds playing cards and smoking cigars. Curtains over the sink were torn and their bottoms dirty where half-clean hands were hastily wiped.

"Are you sure you don't want no money?"

"Just enought to get cleaning things and a few washrags, honey. "

"Don't call me honey."

"Whatcho name?"

"Just call me Boss for now. Lemme show ya your room. Hope you don't mind it's dirty. I s'pose you're old enough to live here and people won't talk."

"It perfick, hon...Boss."

Amy lay down for a few minutes before getting up. Her first job while Mr. Boss went to work was to clean her own room, which had urine-soaked cardboard boxes in it. Kitty litter was everywhere. Boss had kept a cat in here. The room stank as only a catroom can stink. After corralling the cleaning bucket and Spic `n' Span, Amy moved through the rest of the trailer. She took down the curtains and ran their grimy gauze through the washing machine, along with some sheets, pillowcases, and clothes. She set small table upright and vacuumed up spilled ashtrays, all exhaling old, dead cigarette fumes. This made her nearly gag, and she opened the door and all the windows. A sweet breeze carried off some of the odors; and, Amy thought, a good cleaning would do the rest. She was very tired but felt vaguely satisfied.

The days of late summer passed, and Amy began to rehang low curtains and get down to hard floor scrubbing. Every afternoon she took a break to listen for Sister Thompson's radio show but of course it was never on. Having made Boss help her clean things higher than she could reach, and having nothing else to do in the trailer, she turned her attention to the exterior windows and to Boss's yard itself. She planted sunflowers and little patches of bananas and umbrella grass. She put out tomatoes and collard greens and hoped the tomatoes would get at least big enough to make green tomato pickles. Amy did not know anything about climate, but she knew she was far north of where she used to live.

There might be a difference in the seasons by the time late fall rolled in. Boss, who first sat and watched her comical bending and groaning, soon had to show her what to do and how to do it. A man who never had a garden suddenly became more expert than she herself, a woman who was old almost before Boss had even first heard of gardens. Amy knew that gardens were necessary for a happy life, and she let him have his way. Boss began to lose weight and dress in clean clothes more often. Amy could not cook but she did make salads and put on pots of beans of greens occasionally. Boss, on the other hand, began to eat fewer TV dinners and worried about Amy's health. These changes were slow, not happening overnight, as might seem from this brief description; certainly Boss was slow to trust Amy with his home and possessions. When he got suspicious of her he would accuse her of things he knew she could not have done. For his efforts he always got an utterly blank face, his sure sign that Amy was not lying. She ignored his accusations as though they were less than nothing, a hole in the air.

Their conversations were not long. Amy had almost no interests in common with Boss, and she did not understand his political views or his relationships. Both of which seemed to have an underlying feeling of violence, of retribution, of a man living as a beast among other men, with no laughter or tears or soft music. Boss had women, Amy knew. But she never saw any of them and Boss never discussed his personal life with her—his girlfriends, where he came from, and even what he did for a living. He once gave her a phone number "at work", he said, "in case you need to get a-holt of me during a emergency." It was all just as well with Amy. She did not want Boss to know anything about her either.

And she never saw any of his bills or correspondence or anything that would identify him. And Amy in her own craziness simply did not care.

Crazy Caravan pulled into Xpuhil, a small Maya town in the middle of the Yucatan Peninsula. To the west lay Mexico and the Gulf. To the north lay Merida. To the south lay the jungles of Guatemala. And, to the east, lay Belize. Elena was excited. She tossed and turned in her bed that night, trying to stop her mind from thinking about details. Some people had to call home. Others had to have minor medical attention. Zillah and Otto were barely speaking to each other. Popol Vuh seemed to be slowing down a little more every day, a raggedy black clock running out of ticks an tocks. Elena had a feeling she was racing against time, but there were no real reasons for her to feel that way. They were on schedule more or less. The tension in her back and sides and in her head was growing. Her body was telling her that it wanted to be alone, completely alone. It was impossible here, but she would have to do it soon or risk a nervous prostration—an ailment she had not had since Raul's children once came to spend a weekend with her while their parents went out of town.

She could take no more. She reached for the light over her bed, then opened a hidden compartment near the bed and took out her journal.

August l6, ll:30 p.m.

"Trip is nearing end but adventure is just beginning. Can't sleep, have to consider all needs and alternatives if something goes wrong. In Xpuhil tonight. Rather spooky."

The town was little more than a church, a small café, a Pemex gas station, and a dim collection of houses and huts fading off into the moonlight. Beyond lay open fields of mud and stubble interspersed with tall foliage. Stars scraped across the sky overhead, diamonds rubbing over a sheet of complacent velvet. Elena turned out her light and lay down her pencil and fell asleep.

Meanwhile, however, there was a small group in the general sitting room, all in their nightclothes and robes. Although in the jungle, the van's air conditioning capacity made the inhabitants feel quite cool. They were used to seeing each other dressed this way. The men and Janie had gone out earlier to talk to the locals, but they had not been friendly to rich foreigners, principally because they had never seen such a camper before. When allowed to board it and look around, they became much friendlier and even invited Janie and Otto to drink with them. It was mild beer served in a big pottery bowl, which was passed from hand to hand.

But now the village was slowly going to sleep, and the caravan was newly bathed and prepared for sleep. With all the recent excitement, however, several seekers of fate had not succeeded in sleeping. They were Petey, Chuck, Loren, Janie, Otto, Mary Ann, and Zillah. At first a card game was proposed but the atmosphere was so congenial that they eventually decided to tell stories instead. Though it was late, they were determined to tell something that they had heard about or had experienced.

"Who's going first?" asked Mary Ann, who adjusted her glasses because her face cream kept letting them slip down her nose.

"Let's go from youngest to oldest!" said Petey, but was overruled by Mary Ann and Zillah, the two oldest who did not care to reveal their ages. Since Petey had a story ready anyway, they let him go first. And these are the stories of a night in Xpuhil:

Petey's Story

"Well, see there was this man, you know, and he only wanted to do one thing. What he wanted to do was be someone special. He didn't have anything special going for him, either- no looks, he couldn't do anything, no money, no nothing. All he wanted to do, like, was be remembered by the world as somebody really special. He was always frustrated because he couldn't find anything to make him stand out in a crowd. He was even average height. He went around constantly goofed up in his head because he was afraid there was nothing one-of-a-kind you could say about him."

Then one day he woke up and decided that since he wasn't special he may as well end it all. And that's just what he decided to do. There was no lake or ocean near he lived so he decided to throw himself in a stream. He went to the stream and got ready to jump in. What he saw surprised him. There was a girl's face looking back at his, where his face was supposed to be. Now, that really surprised him and he reached up to his face to see if his beard was still there. It was. The reflection was from a lady in another world who was thinking about killing herself because she was unhappy in her world too.

"All of the sudden both of them figured if they could be with the other one in a new world, life might be worth living again. So they reached into the water at the same time and touched each other's hands. The man was so happy he jumped right smack into the water and went under. After a few moments he could breathe air again and he took a big noseful of it. Then looking behind him, he saw the girl in the water once again. Only now she was in his old world, while he? He looked up suddenly, not knowing what to expect. Then he saw the place around him was a beautiful jungle full of ferns and parrots and stuff."

Loren interrupted. "That's the stupidest story I've heard in ages," she said, but the adults frowned. Even Chuck did. And that hurt her worst of all, even though they had made up earlier. Things between them were still a little tense after Coatzacoalcos.

Mary Ann seemed genuinely interested.

"So, Petey," she asked, the heel of her hand under her chin, the fingers anxiously twitching in her mouth. She had a passion for stories. "What happened with the man?"

"I don't know," he said, "but I can make up an ending."

"Please do," said Janie, though it was clear she was manufacturing enthusiasm. Petey cleared his throat histrionically and his eyes sparkled with all the attention he was getting.

"Well," he said, "the man decided he'd better keep what he had instead of risk it again with that girl. And he walked off into the jungle that no one else on this world had ever seen."

Janie said, "That's a beautiful story. And it points up something. There are so many choices to be made, and we all have to make them blindly. We don't know what the outcome will be."

Mary Ann added, "But are we completely blind? Surely there is some guide to what will probably work out for the best."

"Just common sense," said Zillah, "and nothing else."

"My turn!" announced Janie. "I have a story ready now."

Janie's Story

"This story is embarrassing, but it's funny anyway. When I was a sophomore in college I fell in love with a first year graduate student who had been on digs in Guatemala and Honduras. He was like a god to me. And though at the time I thought I loved him for his mind, it's plain that his looks and sex appeal helped his case. I followed him worshipfully, taking in all he said about his experiences out in the field. He was also well educated in other things I knew so little about like music, art, history, and poetry. Poor little me, I was completely agog at his every move, his every idea. Now that I look back I see how superficial his knowledge really was. Because he arrived at it so effortlessly it was hardly worth the knowing, and he never studied anything in depth, always satisfied to take his professor's word for every conclusion. But I'm straying from the subject.

To my complete surprise he asked me one Friday to go with him to the local student bar. Since I had a way of following him anyhow, it seemed only courteous that he'd ask. But I saw it only as a step away from a proposal of marriage. We drank beer far into the night and talked of everything we thought or felt. He walked me to the dorm at two a.m., and even though it was cold and rainy I could swear it was like a balmy spring evening. Well, you know how it goes: I asked myself, `Is he going to kiss me? Is he going to kiss me?' I dreaded he would. Then I dreaded he wouldn't. He'd probably seen what was left of the pimple on my nose and now found me glitteringly repulsive. People passed us giggling. All during this time we were talking about the shape of the pyramid of the Magician at Uxmal. I was so drunk I could barely follow what he was saying, but he was lit up too so no one was the wiser. At the door of the dorm he shook my hand and said goodbye, then on second thought gave me a peck on the cheek.

Somehow it didn't feel the way I thought it would feel. His lips were chapped. He turned to go and glanced down at my feet, then left, mustering all the self-control he had. My slip was down around my ankles. Sticks and leaves were caught up in it, and it had apparently fallen out during the walk back across the quad. Talk about total humiliation! My whole world and self-image were shattered. I could see no way of excusing myself or explaining, but I must've unfastened it somehow on one of my frequent trips to the bathroom during our intellectual beer bust. And yet with all the embarrassment of it, I couldn't help laughing at my own ludicrousness as I talked about shape vs. function in Mayan pyramids about which I knew next to nothing anyway. Me, with an undergarment trailing behind, gathering acorns, leaves, and twigs like an overzealous squirrel." Everybody was laughing as Janie covered her own eyes with her hands, smiling at her own gaffe.

Chuck looked around at that moment to ask Petey a question, but the boy had fallen asleep on the sofa against the window. Chuck gently picked him up and took him to bed, returning quickly to listen to more stories. Mary Ann noticed Otto in the corner. He was quietly cutting celery and potatoes for potato salad.

"Otto, why don't you give us a story?" He looked surprised at first but then wiped his hands on a kitchen towel and looked at the roof as if he could find the missing part of his life there.

"I'll tell you vat de day vass like vhen I vass knocked out." Everyone was interested in Otto because he rarely spoke at all, let alone talked about himself. And the twelve-year coma he suffered was fascinating to everyone present except Zillah, who had heard the tale before. Otto rubbed his chin and put his bowl on the counter.

Otto's Story

"It vas in 1933. In December. I vas quite young den, a student preparing to enter de university in Leipzig—a fine school, you know. Anyvay, I had been at home vit Mama und Papa dat day, listening to de radio und helping Mama get ready for Christmas. She used to bake a lot of cookies und other things so good from de kitchen. Ve had a little telephone in de parlor und I callt my girl Liesl to see if she vanted to go skating. She said yes and ve vent to de municipal rink de vay ve alvays did. No one vass dere, so ve began to practice our promenade—you know, vit de hands held zo—und skated und skated for vat seemt hours. I remember Liesl vore a black skirt und had a muff for de hands dat vass vhite rabbit fur."

"Now, vhat happent next, I am not sure. It is so hazy after all dese years. I saw two brown shirt boys about my age enter de rink. Dey vould chenerally leaf you alone if you vere not a Jew, but dese boys vere drunk. One pincht Liesl from behindt und I turned to fight, but someone else hit me on de stomach. Probably other brownshirt boy. My head hit de ice very very hard. Und I vake up an olt man vit crooket limbs und no teeth und no parents und no Liesl und no Deutschland but rubble. I asked de doctor to let me die but it vass too late for dat, und I vas afraid of suicide. Vhen I got out of de hospital I decided to go to America to start over."

"Why did the brownshirts pick on you?" asked Loren. "It's not fair!"

"I aks myself dat kvestion for years, not to kind answer. I ask Gott for answer und vait for his reply. Dere is none. I figure, dere iss no Gott after all. Und if no Gott, den no mean reason for tings, ja? Vas somethink dat had to happen, und maybe it save my life. But to sleep for tvelve years iss long, long time."

Mary Ann asked, "What is the first thing you said when you woke up?"

"I tink I ask for a drink of vater. But my voice did not vork at first. I had to make sign language. Und I remember vaking up once during the var, or I think it vas during the var. But I went under again. Maybe I just dreamt it all."

Everyone was getting sleepy. Even the moon itself seemed tired as it reached the horizon. As if at a signal, the storytellers rose to go to bed, stopping only to make polite goodnights and to agree to another session tomorrow. And tomorrow, Zillah said, we will be in Belize.

E. ***Syagrus romanzoffiana:*** *common name is Queen's palm or, in the trade as "Cocos plumosa." Has very long, dark-green pinnate frond and a very straight, grayish trunk. Feathery fronds sometimes break in high winds and will bronze at 25 degrees F. Few exist above the 30th parallel in the Eastern U.S. or Texas.*

Like Moses on the borders of Canaan, Elena was given to pausing reflection that morning in Xpuhil before the van finally reached its longed-for destination. For surely the residents of Crazy Caravan were growing morose or restless, according to their lights. Kuon actually had snapped at Elena when she got too close to the rubber skunk, whose head was nearly chewed off by a dog no longer in love with the idea of traveling. When she leashed Kuon for a walk that morning soon after dawn, several well-meaning

Indians offered her wads of colorful pesos for the dog. She was flattered, thinking the Indians impressed with her animal husbandry and canine grooming. However, they wished to spit Kuon and eat him, dog being favorite meat of the local tribe. Elena had eaten dog as a child once and had enjoyed it, but the idea of eating Kuon seemed little less monstrous than pedophagia, the same affliction suffered by the misguided and perverse witch of "Hansel und Gretel." Her frangipani print muumuu snapping in the breeze like the flag of a nation gone color-mad, she re-boarded the van and made arrangements to leave immediately. Somewhere in the back of her mind lurked the suspicion that, given the chance, these natives might also be tempted to dine on toucans.

Now that the van lurched forward into the new, fresh-cool morning, Elena felt a stab of guilt and shame. Not only had she thought the worst of the natives, but she had also made no effort to meet, get to know, or visit any of the Mexicans, who were also members of La Raza like herself. She then realized to her chagrin that none of the Caravan had made an effort to get to know their host nation. She was determined that, in Belize at least, they would get to know the local people, invite them to their van and accept reciprocal courtesies. The trip home through Mexico would give the others a chance to meet people from south of the border; and since she intended to let them use the van if they drove it back for her, she thought she could induce Chuck or Petey or Barry to strike up friendships with the Mexicans.

On reflection, though, she realized that her little band of people had an excuse for their limited access—their time schedule. Never had they spent more than one night in any place, and the itinerary had been an emotional and social burden to all of them. And yet, of course, the time limits had had to be followed. Besides the animals, for example, there was mounting evidence of trouble between the members of the Crazy Caravan. Mary Ann had acted differently since the group had left Coatzacoalcos. She sighed a great deal and left her reading to stare out windows. Petey was beginning to tease the dog simply for something to do. Loren and Chuck were back together but with a strangely chilling circumspectness. Maybe the youngsters were seeing each other as humans, not lovers, for the first time. And yet they seemed to be getting closer by the day despite their discovery—or perhaps because of it.

"And me?" thought Elena, "What's going to happen to me?" Waves of nostalgia for her old Los Cocos hit her. And yet now it was gone from her forever. It could never be reclaimed as her haven of seclusion. Those days were sadly over for her. She had dreamed the night before that she was on a patio, looking out over the Gulf. Her dog suddenly barked as if he did not know her. She turned around to reassure him and saw in her sleep the beloved front of the house with its thick thatches of palms and the austere little Japanese gardens that she had made from shells and pebbles. The house had been so quiet in her dream, so restful and secure and beautiful and mysteriously special with its galleries, walkways, gardens, and cracker-box shape. And most of all, her beautiful jalousie porch with its myriad plants and sea view! What a loss!

But beginning and eventually canceling her nostalgia was her anticipation that finally, and for her alone, something extraordinary would be happening in the next few days. She felt she would be introduced to some kind of secret, like an Eleusinian mystery initiation, which would change her for the rest of her life. Now no time for sorrow, now no time for regrets. What's done is done....

Dauphine looked at herself in the mirror and said the exact same thing to herself. She was in her forties, unmarried, and pregnant by a man who was probably an alcoholic and certainly poor husband material. Sure, Barry had his charms. Who didn't have at least some? But his mental instability made him seem like a mistake to Dauphine, a woman who realized this would probably be one of her last chances to get a husband to provide security for herself and Betty Sue. And now that she was pregnant, a third party entered the picture. With that thought she vomited into the toilet until she dry-heaved. Goddamn pregnancy. She was too old for this madness....

And just four hours later, the van came to Ciudad Chetumal and entered the customs area on the border of Belize. The van was searched for illegal sale items because the Mexican peso, recently devaluated, made Mexican purchases more attractive to Belizean shoppers who dutifully boarded buses to shop in Chetumal. The Mexican border guards began demanding high mordidas and managed to destroy the confidence of the Belizean shoppers. News of the border guards' greed arrived in Mexico City but, of course, the Mexican government had done nothing. Elena was prepared to expect a request for a substantial bribe, but word of her van's destination had not gone through the usual channels. The bribe network was weakest from Tamaulipas to Quintana Roo (Chetumal's state), so the guards let the van pass with very little of the take they could usually expect. After the guards had filed out of the swooshing van doors Barry started the rumbling motors which puttered over to the Belize side. Further questions from Belize immigration officials confirmed the fact that everyone but Miss Muñoz was visiting for probably two weeks. Elena was summoned to a back room where a very black man with a smile rose and welcomed her to Belize. He explained the nation's immigration laws and suggested Elena contact an attorney about real estate, investment laws, and other matters. He gave her a pamphlet describing government services and regulations, then released her to join her friends, who themselves had already been checked out.

"We're here, we're here!" shouted Mary Ann and Petey. Wanda cried. Lanky and Janie and Barry toasted each other with a Sprite. Chuck and Loren kissed. Kuon barked and Popol Vuh skronked. Otto and Zillah danced in a circle.

Elena scanned the horizon of her new nation. This was no vacation for her. The flat jungle stretched out in all directions but there was a smell like sea air in the breeze. Hm. A breeze of Belize. A little poem. Somehow appropriate. Elena prayed for guidance as the van made it sway south, on the narrow but paved highway, towards Belize City, some 60 miles away.

The van took up most of the highway south through Corozal, the northernmost province, and passed fields of sugarcane, bananas, and swampy lowlands. Occasional patches of thick jungle encroached on the narrow road, and around just about every bend lay an old house on stilts for protection against floods, snakes, and sometimes intruders. The houses had red tin roofs, white or brightly colored clapboard sides, and long green shutters. More prosperous groups of houses had window treatments with jalousies similar to Elena's. The little town of Corozal itself was the first settlement of any size they passed through. Corozal had vivid gardens and a small marketplace. Then came Orange Walk, where there was suddenly much more a feeling of Englishness. All the towns and waysides could be explored one day, of course, but now Elena was tired and wanted to sleep anywhere but in the van. She longed for the caravan to get to Belize City. Before long, an irregular slash of blue-green jade hacked its way through the jungle. Wild figs and mangroves, their roots gnarled into fantastic Gothic buttresses, lined this riverbank now visible from the road. The sea air, heavy and thick with humid heat, was pushed into the air system of the van and intoxicated the whole group.

The van went over a small bridge and found itself on the outskirts of Belize City, the former colonial capital and still the largest town in the entire nation of 200,000 people. In Belize City the houses grew bigger and some of them shabbier, but they never lost their distinctive shape or their projection of a casually comfortable attitude. Elena learned much from looking at Belizean houses. They were object lessons in intelligent design and a tribute to the love of convenience and informality in the Belizean spirit.

The amazing part of Belize City was its heterogeneous society. All races and nationalities blended to form completely new ethnic strains. The Maya, Caribs, Europeans, Lebanese, Africans, and Mexicans all contributed to the genetic pool. Cinnamon-skinned little girls with gray eyes and ringleted hair played tag in their green Catholic uniforms. A man black as coal, his eyes almost yellow-green, stood at a corner, uneasily eyeing a group of "base boys"— unemployed young men who had nothing to do but harass passersby. The black man relaxed visibly, it seemed to Elena, when the base boys caught sight of the van. They shouted obscenities and looked in the street for rocks but found nothing to throw but two Belikin beer bottles. The very black man walked discreetly away, pretending to rub his English chin and nose to hide his frightened expression.

Tiny little shops with open Mexican style entrances ran a sort of hothouse competition with each other, selling papayas, cabbages, used children's clothing, trinkets, T-shirts on a clothesline. Cheap little bars and eateries dotted the area near the Swing Bridge, the central focus of Belize City life, along with the marketplace and the city square. Bougainvillea tossed its crepe-papery purples and reds with abandon in private gardens under the tall, stately coconut palms.

Ah, coconut palms thought Elena. At last, at last. They're swaying tops tossed gently in the afternoon wind, their orange-yellow coconuts sitting still near the bases of the kelly-green fronds. Squat little defenses of oleander and croton marked off more prosperous yards. Picket fences showed boundaries, so unlike Mexican concrete fences with their protective bristle of broken glass bottles along the top. And then, the Marine Parade, the waterfront street of the Foreshore, and the Bay of Belize.

Day 1

The Crazy Caravan pulled to its final stop with a last squeak of a rear brake. The van tilted to the right with the weight of the passengers, who were all looking and pointing at the different shades of water in the Caribbean. Wanda, usually quiet and unassuming, called the entire group into the sitting room.

"I know some of us are not very religious, so maybe you can just wish for luck. But I want to thank God that we got here well and happy, that no one became sick or was lost. I want to ask God to protect us for the next two weeks and to give us the guidance we need."

"Amen," said everyone.

Elena unbowed her head and stepped forward. She explained that she had some remarks to make as soon as Mary Ann read the housing plans for the near future. Taking care of hotel reservations had been her responsibility since Tampico, when Elena became too nervous to handle the stress any longer. The real estate maven/philosopher lifted her voice, using words and phrases even more mysteriously free of clichés. Everyone noticed. She told the group about their rooms and the meal plans they could choose from. Then they could go their separate ways; however, on Day 15 they had to assemble at the Belize airport in Ladyville, about eleven miles from Belize City. There were at present no questions, and Petey was fidgeting and restless to get out of the van.

Elena stepped forward and cleared her throat.

"I'm talking to you now, not as your leader or benefactor, but as your friend. This trip and my life before it have taught me a few things. I'd like to tell you some of my thoughts."

She paused and put her hand high on the large sitting room window, leaning absentmindedly on the thick glass structure.

"First, you must know one thing: there's no guarantee that you'll get anything from this trip. You all came with me because you found something intolerable in your lives. I don't include the three children, of course, and I don't include Otto and Zillah. They certainly have their own reasons for coming, but I think their loyalty had motivated them more than any personal need. I'm thankful for that. And I hope Chuck, Loren, and Petey find lifelong meaning in what they experience here. But here's what I really want to talk about: my reason for coming. These last few days I have been frightened of this task I have undertaken—the safety of all of you. Now I set you free and cut the reins of my control as well as of my protection. I have a vigil to attend. The prospect of it doesn't frighten me, but I have to do it mostly by myself. Any of you my stay in the van, the hotel, or anywhere you please. I suggest you call members of your families back home and let them know you're safe. Then go on about whatever business you wish. We will be together tonight for maybe the last time."

"What do you mean?" gasped Dauphine, leaning on Barry's arm. Shock flew around the room; an almost frightened look appeared on Chuck's and Loren's faces.

"What I mean," Elena said, "is that I must stay in Belize forever. It's now my home. All of you will be flying back home instead of driving back. The tickets have already been bought and can be picked up before flight time at the TACA counter at the airport."

A chorus of "and you didn't tell us that" was let loose in the room, but Elena cut them short with an impatient wave of her hand.

"I couldn't tell you about my reasons because I thought they were my private business and because I thought you'd find my motives ridiculous. I'd still rather not discuss them, but I have to live up to a promise I made to myself. If I live up to this promise I stand to learn strange and wonderful things. If I don't, I will have lost nothing but time and some money."

The look of curiosity on their faces made her want to tell them of her vision of her dead father, but she knew they would think her crazy. Mary Ann, lying in her own bed some weeks earlier, had been right about something: everyone wants a revelation of some kind.

All people want insights that will dramatically change their lives. It does happen, of course, but only to a rare few: Buddha, Christ, Mohammed, Julian the Apostate, Teresa of Avila, and all the nameless millions upon millions of souls who in circumstances of wretchedness or weakness, disease or health, youth or senescence, saw something they could not explain but that changed their lives forever. For a caveman the vision was simple, a shooting star that exploded in a flash of light as it struck the atmosphere. He was the only one who had seen; he was the only one who could interpret and spread his magic tale of experience beyond the ordinary. For the ancient Greek the experience might have been the first flush of ecstasy in a Dionysian rite or the release, the hymnal gorgeousness of chants to Aphrodite. For later ages, different kinds of visions.

Chuck and Petey took Kuon for a walk around the block. The boys and the German shepherd jumped on the sea wall and ran along it as far as they could, the old clapboard houses of Belize City to their left, the alexandrite-blue Caribbean to their right. They were all happy for reasons they did not understand. Chuck felt a profound familiarity with the city, an eerie sense that he had been there before but had never known it until now, almost as if he had lived another life here. Meanwhile, Kuon pulled them past a Chinese restaurant that overlooked the sea, a city park lined with benches and copper plants and oleander. The sea wall gave out, so they circled through a neighborhood to get back to the hotel a different way from the way they had come.

Flamboyant trees, their orange-red tops on fire, suddenly showed themselves between tall crackerbox old houses with large verandas and breadfruit trees. A sign said Gabourel Lane. A group of boys tried to sell them a lottery ticket of some kind, but Kuon growled menacingly. The black boys said nothing more and continued down the street before beginning to sing a rhythmical song. Chuck and Petey could not make out the words. After a short time they made it to the hotels street and continued on their way, grateful to be heading back towards something familiar. The dense lushness of tropical foliage and the charm of the almost European-looking neighborhood were too much to take in at once.

Nearing the hotel, the trio saw another small boy waving a newspaper in the air. "Amándala, Amándala!" he cried, piping his high voice as he strolled towards Albert Street and the business district. A bunch of old yellow Chevy taxis and equally old drivers parked at the Ft. George entrance waiting for fares in the afternoon sun. A woodcarver sat near the entranceway, selling carvings of conchs and fish in zericote wood. A fat woman in a purple dress walked down the street with a basket of mammee apples on her head. She wore a white bandanna in her hair and pink house slippers on her feet. Overhead, the frigate birds sat motionless in the air, waiting for gulls to catch fish so the frigates could steal them away.

Wanda and Lanky were having a Belikin in the hotel beer bar. The other caravaners were clustered, with various drinks in hand, around the salt-water swimming pool. Wanda was thinking she had not really talked with Lanky for a long time. They communicated in grunts or with sex or a few words when necessary. The last time they had expressed any feeling between themselves had been the busy night in Coatzacoalcos. It is sad, Wanda thought, that is the only way we have of talking to each other.

Lanky loved the rich sea breeze blowing through the bar windows. Someone next door was playing a piano in the cocktail bar.

"This reminds me of that night at Los Cocos," said Lanky, "the first night we thought about coming here. Tomorrow's going to be an exciting day...do I look for work or just take it all in?"

Wanda thought about it for a minute and then answered by touching the warm back of his big hand.

"You know what I'm remembering right now?" she said, ignoring his question. "I'm thinking about the time you took me all the way to Matamoros for dinner when we were kids. Now look how far we've come for two beers apiece." Lanky laughed. Wanda needed him tonight. She knew they would make love. Lanky would be as ardent as ever. He would feel her heart beat as he lay next to her. He would think the beating was a sign of her arousal. She would cling to him with a fierceness born not of passion or lust or any pleasant memory of their songlike love for all these years; she would take him the way she did because, despite all her present longings, she knew she was going to leave him. But for what? For what? For what? The echo in the brain chided her.

Jeanine Atwell came home late every night for the last month before school started. Her parents worried about her because she seemed to be withdrawing from her friends and spending every day watching Lenny's kids.

"First of all," she said in her own defense, "Lenny is stuck with those children and can't afford a babysitter." Her eyes flashed angrily at her parents, who sat across the breakfast table from her. They held their coffee cups suspended between mouth and table, unable to believe the fire in their daughter's voice. "And second, you'll notice that I don't even have any friends left. They have all been hustled out of town by one thing or another."

Jeanine's parents seemed momentarily cowed into submission by her outburst, but they were not the kind to let her be sassy. The backlash began. Her father, a successful part time carpenter and civil servant with the Texas Department of Highways, stood up and said, "Listen here, young lady. Now you just put a civil tongue in your head...."

Ten minutes later Jeanine was flying out the front door on her way to Lenny's.

Her obsession with mothering Lenny's children had really begun to worry her parents, but they thought the first day of school would change her and bring her back to herself.

Even Jeanine herself had begun to notice changes in the mirror. She almost never went out now. Her face went pale and gaunt, the cheekbones pushing outward from her once rounded face. The wavy dirty-blonde hair was the same; the green-blue eyes were the same. But she looked like a girl considering a light case of anorexia before going on to something else. Eating was not a problem, however. She sat in front of the TV and ate popcorn or washed dishes in the sink. She enjoyed watching her sister's children playing like savages in the well-shaded backyard filled with golden rain trees and delicate avocado bushes. Jeanine occasionally thought she was moving into her sister's place and felt a little guilty.

But why feel guilty? Janie threw her family and husband away.

It was not her business to take over; Lenny would have to make his own arrangements. (He's so alone and hurt—I just can't leave him now, not now with the kids and everything)

Jeanine told herself that this vicarious motherhood was good practice for the future. Even her parents had said so for the first two weeks. But now they did not like the looks of it, particularly when Jeanine came home after Lenny should have been through with dinner. Her parents asked her casually what she and Lenny talked about after she had cooked supper every day and sat down to eat with him and his children.

"Oh, stuff," she had said. "He asks me about my friends like Marti and Betty Sue—not that there's much to say about them any more. Then we talk about Janie and then what's going on in town, and—"

"What do you say about Janie?" they asked.

"We just wonder about what went wrong."

"Do you think it's right for you to talk about your sister that way?"

"Sure. Lenny's family, isn't he? There's nothing I know about Janie that he doesn't know."

Just the same, they added, they wanted her to tell Lenny to find a housekeeper because school would start before too long. They also told her to pass the word on to Lenny to come over next weekend for dinner, if Friday night was okay. It seemed that Jeanine's parents wanted to talk to him.

Betty Sue sat on the front porch of her aunt's house, rocking in a big white rocking chair and listening to an approaching thunderstorm still so far away she could see its entire boundaries. Tiny lightning bolts, looking like sparks, traveled from the flat slate-blue bottom of the storm cloud to the newly cooled earth below. A small breeze began to toss the dry grass in the front yard devoid of trees and fronting the two-lane blacktop highway just beyond a grassy drainage ditch. Betty Sue's heart was on fire. She was not getting along with her aunt; she missed talking with Dauphine and telling her mother about her life. The summer's activities, which at one time promised to yield many interesting mother-daughter conversations, were sighing at sunset and winding down.

Occasionally in South Texas there is a hint of things farther north—a breath of cool air, pumpkins carved as jack o' lanterns, Christmas lights and tinsel on the streetlights in the Harlingen business district. But for most of the year it was difficult for this part of the United States to think of itself as not a part of Mexico.

And no such hints of other worlds reached the young girl who sat sweltering on the hot front porch of her aunt's rackety-tack white house. The earth and sun here seemed to go mad with heat and dust, as if the desert out west were marching relentlessly eastward toward the innocent Valley communities. Betty Sue took another sip of her Dr. Pepper and composed a letter to her mother, who had called her twice during the trip—once from Tuxpan and again in Coatzacoalcos. Both connections had been poor and the conversations frustrating and fruitless.

Dear Mom,

I'm sorry the last phone call was so fuzzy, just like the other one. The phones in Mexico must not be very good. I wish you would come home. I'm not doing so good at Auntie's house, she's not used to kids anymore so please come home and get me. I don't know if you will get this in time but if you do, please come home soon. Am sitting on Auntie's porch looking far over a plain at a thunderstorm. Makes me want to crawl in bed and sleep. I hope you and Barry are having a nice time with the other people. I want you to know that it's OK with me if you like him. I think he's cute for an old man.

Betty Sue

P.S. I remembered my toothbrush on this trip. Haven't heard from Marti. Say hi to Loren for me. Miss her, too!

Day 2

While Elena prepared herself for her ordeal and Betty Sue rocked comfortably on her aunt's front porch, momentous things were happening back at the trailer park in Two Egg, Florida. Amy Mortcap had managed to take over Boss's life completely. She told him whom to date. She told him how to dress and she repaired the buttons and rips in his salvageable clothing.

Boss was much happier but he still would not tell Amy his name.

"Cain't bear to work for no man wif no name. No sah. I sure would try to find out who I workin' for. Sister Thompson she'd want me to know. The Lawd'd want me to know."

And then Amy did something she would not normally do. She opened a desk drawer in Boss's room and found a bill from the electric company. So that was his name, she thought. It sounded familiar but she did not know where she had heard it. The blue and white envelope said "William Gandy Candor" and gave an address. Amy put the bill back in the drawer and felt ashamed at what she had done. She went to the kitchen to wash the old breakfast dishes and feed some scraps to a stray cat. Amy prayed for forgiveness and kept looking for a sign that God had answered her prayer. Was Mr. Candor the man she was to be the mother of? Would he let her mother him?

Otto and Zillah also washed and dried the last plates. Otto fixed a pan of dog food and carried it through the length of the van. No one noticed him as he went past, an air of destination and purpose making him all but invisible to the other residents, who of course had other things on their minds. Otto opened the door to the solarium and found Kuon chewing busily on his rubber skunk, now a headless apparition of frayed latex with a black tail, white stripe. In the roomy cage above Kuon's canine head, Popol Vuh was trying to master the secrets of the cage door—first with his beak, then that availing nothing, his claws. The large yellow, blue-green and black beak made it look as though a small bird were trying to pry open a door with a plastic banana.

"Shtop dat," said Otto casually. "Leaf der cage alone." He gave the toucan's beak a thwack using his middle finger and thumb. The toucan protested immediately, flopping over and over in the cage in petulant anger. Otto noted this with some alarm since it meant that something was wrong with the bird's sense of uprightness. Perhaps a veterinarian would have to be called in later, but for now it was good enough that the bird was merely hungry. He even smoked a cigarette after dinner. Kuon occasionally rolled his big predatory eyes up at the toucan and chewed his skunk in domestic docility. Only God knows, thought Otto, what violence that dog plans for this bird. Popol Vuh became increasingly restless after feeding and smoking. Kuon ate half his dinner and stopped. There was a feeling Otto had not expected so soon. The time had come for the members of the group to go their separate ways. Before long, he knew, he would have to decide what he would do with his remaining years.

Day 3

"I agree completely," said Lenny as he wiped his mouth with the napkin. Jeanine's parents relaxed visibly.

"I'm worried about her myself, Mom. She doesn't do anything but take care of the kids and me. Sure, I appreciate it, but it's like she feels guilty or something for what her sister did. Unless it's...."

An unspoken message passed between Lenny Norworthy and Jeanine's parents, Mr. and Mrs. Atwell. They looked at Jeanine playing with the children through the picture window.

Mrs. Atwell spoke," You don't think she may...uh...have started to feel something for you?"

"I'm not the smartest man in the world, but I can usually see that sort of thing. I haven't seen it in her eyes or expression. "

"We don't know quite what to make of it. Her friends' going away was hard on her. She's too shy to mix with the summer people. Most of the parents around here tend to discourage that anyway. "

"Yeah, Janie's told me that."

"So, Lenny, what do you think we should do to handle this problem?"

"For now, I sure can use the help, but I think if she came three days a week it'll buy me more time to find a hired replacement. And thanks for the offer to take the kids yourselves. I think it would just upset them, though. I have to talk with their mother. I have to find Janie and ask her what she wants for the future. I sure can't go on living this way. I wish I knew what to do. I wish I knew what to do." Mrs. Atwell touched his shoulder.

Chuck and Loren walked along the sea wall. It was close to sunset. They were talking about Elena. "What do you think it's all about?" he said. "I don't know," said Loren," but I wonder...if somebody dead appeared to her. I wonder if—"

"What do you mean? For God's sake!" said Chuck, waving his forearm in dismissal. "How can that be true? The dead don't talk to us; they don't—"

He suddenly remembered Loren's description of what had happened to her and three other girls on a South Texas highway in the dark of night. She resumed, unaware that her experience had been momentarily doubted.

"I wonder if her mother or father appeared to her—or maybe her husband. But what is her vigil all about? Why did she have to come here?"

Chuck reached around her shoulder, resting his wrist on her shoulder blade. He leaned down to kiss her only to find she had turned in the opposite direction and was almost running back to the van. Was she angry again? He asked himself. Lately there had been so many little flare-ups. Loren ran until she reached the door of the trailer. To Chuck she did not seem angry; it must have been something else. He got on his stomach on the sea wall and began to look into the water for conch shells. If she were mad he would let her cool off. Love could wait a while—the universe was there in front of him, engrossing to him as usual.

Loren was far from angry. She ran into the trailer and burst into Elena's room—a place she had spent many hours with the millionairess gossiping about men, doing petit point, discussing their beliefs and preferences. The white door flew open, and there lay Elena in a heap of old terry cloth robes, underwear, and unsorted muumuus. She was asleep. Elena slept the sleep of the near dead, and even with Elena's stony repose Loren felt driven to wake her. She poked the women in the elbow and patted her forehead.

Elena finally woke with a start. A brief look of annoyance, then concern passed over her face.

"Is something wrong?" whispered Elena.

Loren stared at her intently, the look similar to a snake's dull eye fixed on his prey.

"You saw somebody dead, didn't you?" It was less a question than a statement. Elena searched the girl's face and rolled onto her back and stared at the ceiling for a few moments. Elena looked pained.

"Yes. It was my father."

"It's happened to me, too."

"That's right.... I almost forgot. Loren? How did it feel?"

Loren put her head on Elena's stomach. The older woman absentmindedly reached down and stroked the girl's silky blonde head, like a mother helping a daughter through a bad delivery.

"Before we saw it I thought it had something to do with the most important thing in the world, like it was a way of explaining everything. But when it actually happened I didn't get that feeling. I just felt like I was being shown something deliberately, you know? Like someone was trying to clue me in on what we, people, are really like and what we're here for. For a moment I thought I saw and understood. Then the feeling faded away. I couldn't hold it."

"I know what you mean," said Elena. "I know what you mean exactly."

"I'm going with you to the vigil," said Loren.

"Okay," said the elder—and there was no more discussion about it. The sun burned a hole in the 3:00 PM sky. All light seemed arched in a vault over Belize, over the place just beyond the horizon, Altun Ha. The frigate birds were silent; the gulls were noisy.

Barry and Dauphine discussed the future. That was all they seemed to do.

"Let's get married, here and now," said Barry.

"I'd rather wait until we get home," said Dauphine. Barry took a deep breath.

"Lanky knows. I told him." Dauphine looked shocked momentarily but then sighed.

"I guess it doesn't matter, Barry."

"He didn't smirk," Barry reassured, holding his hands up in a suppliant gesture.

"Hon, at my age do you think I really care if a man smirks at me? You don't blush at forty."

"Forty-one."

"Bastard."

She laughed and pulled his ear.

A few moments of staring out to sea passed. The saltwater swimming pool of the Ft. George beckoned, but neither of them had the energy to swim. Coconut palms cast bony shadows over the pool. Dauphine got out of her lounge chair and walked through the hotel garden filled with white and pink frangipani.

"I wish we could grow these back home, they—" Barry interrupted:

"Do you want to go home? Look how beautiful this place is. And do you know the biggest entrepreneur here is an American? We should be able to make a living here. We'll get Betty Sue sent down. She'll love it."

"No," said Dauphine. "It's pretty here but I don't want to be an exile. I want to go home and let the baby grow up an American. I want Betty Sue to have her old friends and to grow up with them."

"I want to stay," said Barry. "I don't have anything to go back there for."

"What about me?"

"Of course you'd be worth going back for. You'd be worth staying for, too. Just think about it for a few days, even though I know you've made up your mind. Try to see things through my eyes. I've seen them through yours, you know."

It was now near sunset. Loren left Elena's room and went to the observation room at the end of the van. She looked out the glass enclosure and scratched behind Kuon's ear. Kuon responded by constantly sending his long pink tongue up to his nose and jerking his right leg in a pseudo-scratch response. Looking to her right, Loren saw Chuck, Petey, and a small black Belizean boy squatting near a picket fence surrounded by oleanders. They were picking the flowers and leaves off the bush. Loren felt a surge of concern for some reason she did not understand. There was something about the long, green leaves, the white flowers. The white flowers. Something about them. She decided to walk over to where the boys were. Kuon barked to be taken out. Loren took the time to get his leash. She wished she could see Betty Sue.

After Loren had left, Elena cried for a few minutes. Wiping her face with a wrinkled yellow Kleenex from a travel-pak dispenser, she picked up a few things to put in her suitcase. Loren would have to take what she herself wanted to bring. Elena packed a change of clothes, her toothbrush, some toucan food, and new rubber skunk (a surprise for Kuon), and a few tins of prepared food. As an afterthought she also packed her camera. After all, she thought, tomorrow is the most important day of my life. I will not only know what my duty to myself is; I will also know why I was born and what the meaning of my life is supposed to be. One question can not be answered without the rest of them being answered automatically. Tomorrow is a real red-letter day, a watershed, a landmark.

But the under-voice that also spoke to her was the voice of doubt and fear. The under-voice told her that there was nothing worse than what would actually happen: It would be okay to be bitten by a poisonous snake. It would be okay to be lost in the jungle at night. It would be okay to be raped and robbed by the guide on the way back into town. It would even be okay to be stabbed or shot by the occasional nuts who prowl all the highways of this world. These disasters she could live with, or die with—if that were the case. The worst thing that could happen, the under-voice told her, is nothing at all. Nothing. Nothing. No dead father. No vision, no revelation. No statement of duties, nothing made clear.

"Please God," said Elena, falling to her knees in her room. "Anything but nothing. Anything but nothing...." The under-voice was mocking. It knew that Elena was a spoiled, selfish old bitch. With all her money she did not deserve enlightenment. She deserved discomfort and struggle, just like all the rest of her passengers and ninety-five percent of the rest of the world. "And here you are," said the under-voice, "spending more of your money trying to find crap. What you're looking for is crap. You have made a fool of yourself."

During this torture she continued to pack. Only one corner of her ondes martenot remained visible in its special leather holder.

"The under-voice is cruel. The under-voice is part of me," she whispered.

Mary Ann sat by the poolside as the sun went down. She had a piece of hotel stationery in her hands. It had a green Mayan logo letterhead. It was airmail stationery. Near the top she wrote these words:

WHY I'M UPSET

It always helped her to make a list of reasons for being upset. Usually the lists were clearer than discussions about her state of disquiet, the reason being that she spoke mainly in cliches when under stress. She used to tell Janie, "If I've told you once, I've told you a thousand times, we've got to take the bull by the horns to find a way to pull the wool over our competitors' eyes and give them the slip. Sales are scarcer than hens' teeth. And wishes won't pay the rent, so let's face the music." And so on.

WHY I'M UPSET

1. I want to be with Arturo in Coatzacoalcos. (He was not a friend. He was a lover.)

2. I'm afraid that Elena is going to get something spiritual out of this trip that I won't.

3. I'm afraid of drinking the water here—although there's no reason to feel that way.

4. Janie is acting strangely lately. Very restless. Have caught her crying in spare moments when her nose was out of her art and archaeology books.

5. I'm also upset that when I just get everything figured out, I'll have to die for something stupid like slipping on a banana peel or walking between parked cars.

6. There's no refuge anywhere on earth, and no one has time to explain or even ask what things in life mean.

7. My real estate business has probably collapsed.

8. People think I'm ignorant. But that's not all. I'm inadequate as well. I try to keep it a secret. Everybody knows anyway.

9. I'm afraid to even think of what the future holds for me. I don't have faith in anything.

10. My sinus ailment is acting up again.

Mary Ann sighed. At last, all fears objectified, stated, given utterance and official status, even if not given relative value. Sinuses and the problems of human existence crowded into one quagmire of personal miseries. Maybe the Buddha was right. Maybe she was making herself miserable with her wants. She wanted sex, she wanted money, she wanted refuge from life, she wanted meaning, she wanted excitement. Wouldn't it have been easier to be a quiet widow in a dark house, with nothing to do but seek reassurance from television evangelists, live on Social Security checks, and play bingo at the Community Center every Friday night with women twenty years older than she? Perhaps to watch the photo portrait of her dead spouse gather dusts while she waited for her children to visit?

Mary Ann had seen this, too, and she had seen it far too often among women a little older than she was. They were castoffs, relicts for whom there were no room and no mercy. The mantle of decades sits on their shoulders. One day they will rise, she thought, and turn over this world. Then Mary Ann closed the stationery folder. Kuon howled out in the lane. Mary Ann drifted into sleep.

At the same time Mary Ann perused her list, Chuck, Petey, and the Belizean boy looked for a toad under the oleander bush. No one seemed able to find it. Chuck noticed Petey, who suddenly stiffened and fell on his side. A small green (or was it brown?) snake bolted out of the bushes and away from the shore. For a few moments Chuck thought Petey had eaten an oleander leaf or put an oleander stick into his mouth. But there were no signs of that. Chuck looked for the snake, but he had disappeared into a clump of grass near a doctor's signpost. It was lucky that Chuck saw the sign. His young friend Petey was near death before ten minutes passed.

Chuck was too frightened to cry. He carried the drooping Petey across the yard and into the doctor's house. With all the perversity of nature, fate turned against them. The doctor was not at home.

The whole van was alarmed. Otto came in search of the boys to get them to come to dinner, but his annoyance at having to find them turned to horror when he saw Chuck running down the street, his eyes bottomless with shock. He babbled as Otto snatched the boy from his arms.

"Oh Jesus. Jesus what's happening what's happening I think it was a snake I think oh God it was...."

Otto backhanded Chuck, sending the boy's glasses into the ditch. Otto shook Chuck by the arms, Petey thrown hastily over his right shoulder.

"Vat vas it? Don't be stupid now. Vat did dis?" He slapped Chuck again. The Belizean boy ran up with the doctor's housekeeper, who had told the boys the doctor was not home. They had run off before she could tell them she would call an ambulance. She told Otto she expected medical help any moment. The German butler who had been lucky enough to sleep through World War II no longer felt lucky. He spun and ran to the van, telling the housekeeper to send the ambulance to him. The housekeeper did not understand and began following Otto, shouting. Meanwhile, Chuck had come to. He told the lady what Otto had said. Since the van and house were within sight of each other, there would be little delay. The housekeeper waited outside her house to point the ambulance drivers in the right direction.

Elena jolted out of her reverie. Her door cracked the paneling behind it as she flung it open quickly, responding to Janie and Zillah's screams. Otto yanked at Petey's shirt until the little buttons flew off. Petey was a brittle piece of bony ivory tossed onto a Formica counter. He had stopped breathing.

Lanky and Wanda were not around the van. They were wandering through Tropical Park, a residential area of Belize City. They looked at the flaming purple and red bougainvilleas, the royal palms with trunks like concrete pilings, their green wicks a prelude to a verdant, pinnate fire. They turned a corner and walked up a curving street with front yard gardens on all sides. They continued to talk about what they might do in Belize. A parrot flew overhead.

A chill passed through Wanda, as if the sun had gone behind a cloud. It was very warm, but the cold sensation she felt was distinct. She thought, for a moment, that the chill was the first manifestation of her plan to leave Lanky. The next few months would be painful, even dangerous. She did not know how strongly her husband would react to her announcement. And then the endless questions: "Why? Is there somebody else? When he knew damn well there was not anyone else. What did I do wrong? What about Loren and Petey?" And so forth, just a few drops in a sea of pain. The chill was maybe a foretaste of a sensation that she, Wanda Murphy, had never known, the delicious sensation of complete aloneness. Yet she feared that state's stern requirements and hardships. She even knew that it would not last forever, that one day she would have to find someone else or come back to Lanky. Or she would have to give him up forever in the face of a discontent that had no name. She wanted not truth, like Mary Ann or Elena Muñoz. Wanda wanted destiny, a sense of connection with the earth and the rest of the universe in whatever way she could have it. It never occurred to her that she might keep Lanky and her ambition at the same time. The two seemed mutually exclusive to her.

They walked back to the main road and took a stray cab back to the van.

Their dead son looked at them with sightless eyes from the top of the Formica counter. But dead only for a while. His breathing was restored in gagging fits. The snake was a common jungle viper, rarely seen in town. Chuck's description of the snake led to its identification and the use of an antivenin. The boy's life was saved. Wanda and Lanky sat in their room, struck dumb by the surprises of death, and then life again. The drain of too heavy emotions in too short a space exhausted them. They followed the ambulance to the small white hospital downtown. Petey was confined for the rest of the day, and his parents sat with him overnight.

Elena's response to Petey's situation was curious. Instead of making a headlong, frantic rush to find help, she had barked orders to everyone in the room: "Open that window, shut the door, flag down the cops, call a cab." Her be-muumuued arm and pointed finger changed direction like a polychrome weather vane. After the crisis was over, Janie collapsed on a sofa and cried until Zillah came over to her and fearfully, tentatively patted her on the head; Zillah acted as though she wished she could pat the woman on the head from across the room, but such was not possible. Janie buried her face in a red pillow and wept more than anyone had ever seen her do before. Otto brought the toucan into the room for exercise. It flew from lamp to lamp and finally landed on the back of the sofa where Janie Norworthy's head lay. He turned his head sideways and eyed her beadily. "SKRONK," he said in the way of toucan encouragement. To no avail.

Otto asked himself why Janie was acting so strangely, particularly since she had not given Petey a thought since the beginning of the trip—except to berate him for being noisy. Now she was inconsolable. Why? Asked Otto of himself.

Petey was dozing off in his white hospital bed in the white room of the squarish white building. A ceiling fan turned over his head and he saw it momentarily before he fell deep into sleep.

In a dream, he was looking into a pool of water in woods he had never seen before. There was no wind, no sound. Instead of his own face, he saw the face and green eyes of the man in the motel back in Tampico, the man who had told him to be careful on his trip. He had green eyes, green like the snake who had bitten him.

Suddenly a snake with huge fangs burst up through the water's surface and flew at Petey, latching onto his throat. As the snake pulled him down to the water, it turned into an arm. Elena's arm.

Ed Fernandez and Brenda were talking at the Tropicala. It was three in the morning, and it was quiet everywhere except for the roaring of the crickets of Cigüeña Lagoon and the whoosh of noncommittal stars overhead.

Edna Parker and they had discussed the Crazy Caravan and the various reports that had seeped through from relatives. Edna was happy to get a call from her boy Chuck that evening, but his voice had sounded frantic, hyped, as if he had taken amphetamines and was screeching through seven levels of metabolic change. Edna was fidgeting with her coaster, her hands trembling for most of the evening. Ed had taken her off the piano. He plugged in the jukebox. He asked if she wanted to go home, but she said no; she needed to keep busy. And it was not even *her* baby hurt, her once-introverted stargazing child. But it could have been. It could have, even though it was Petey. And so far from home.

After closing at two, Ed fixed a round of drinks for both women and sat with them. Brenda knew what had happened. She tried to change the subject. Edna could only look down at her own lap, but the alcohol started working and she seemed less rigid, her eyes taking quick glances around the dim bar.

Brenda said:

"And the old man left, just like that," and she snapped her fingers.

"Where'd he go?" asked Ed, drawing a puff from his cigarette. "To New Orleans. They got some kind of old folks home for Russians that live here in the States. Goddamn it. The craziest goddamn thing I ever saw."

Ed added, "Would you stay if it was your wife?" Brenda shook her head.

"No, I guess I wouldn't after all."

"What are you talking about?" asked Edna.

"The old couple near here, near the Lagoon."

"Yes, what about them?"

"She died," said Brenda.

"What happened?"

"Heart attack," said Ed.

"They were very, very old," said Edna. "What did the old man decide to do?"

"He packed a bag and left for New Orleans," said Brenda. "They have a place he can live there. The Russian church provides it."

"My God. How sad to be so old," said Edna, who got up and walked down to the end of the island without even saying goodbye.

Brenda and Ed sat together. She looked up at him and squinted for a moment, almost as if to pass judgment on him.

"Ed. Hold me. I'm scared."

Not long after Ed held Brenda in his arms—perhaps two or three hours after—the sun's lip touched the green and gray horizon of the Caribbean. It was still mostly dark, a neutral wash of morning mist obscuring colors more than they would normally.

Elena Muñoz, a wealthy woman in her fifties, awoke with a start, her brown eyes flashing in the overhead reading light, her gray hair shining in tousled tufts. She took a long stretch, yawned, scratched her left side. The hot water poured into the shower stall, instantly enveloping her in soothing steam. The pleasant relaxation of sleep wore off quickly; even as she stood in the shower the plans and worries came back to her with painful familiarity. Crying softly, she shampooed her hair, finished soaping herself, and rinsed in the warm tap water. She wished she could stay there all day, never going to the pyramid, planning her trip back to Los Cocos. And she could, she knew. She could simply take her things and sit in the airport lobby until the next plane to Miami, Houston, or New Orleans arrived. It was not so difficult. No one would care.

"Damn," she said softly. "What the hell am I afraid of? You'd think I was going to my first confession or getting married. Why am I acting this way? I should be happy to know what I'm going to know."

She consciously silenced the under-voice that then was trying to speak of dark things, betrayals, foolish faiths and the gullible idiots who believed them. Janie came to mind. She did not believe in Elena's mission. Poor sad woman! Nothing to believe in, nothing to wait for. "I am really blessed among all people. Tonight I'll find out impossible thing. The Unknowable. My duty. Of all things!"

She got out of the shower and dressed slowly, putting on a large red silk muumuu that had huge red hibiscuses on a yellow field. A light spray of cologne at the wrist and neck, then out to the dining room. There everyone stood looking at her, even Wanda and Lanky, who knew Petey was out of danger and that Elena was facing another sort of danger.

Zillah was the first to move to Elena.

"I want you to have dis," she said, and opened her brown fist to show a tiny little kewpie doll. "It's for good luck. It don't work too good for me, but mebbe for you."

With the other hand she put a white frangipani blossom behind Elena's left ear and a red hibiscus behind the other. She whispered to Elena that, whatever she was looking for today, Zillah hoped she would find it, and maybe tell the rest of them if it was not a secret. Elena realized then that Zillah was much more than she seemed to be. She had figured out what Elena's mission was, even without being told. The maid knew the dangers of this mission, just as do all people who have suffered secret tragedies of one sort or another. Elena kissed her and turned to the others. Otto wept while handing her a brown paper sack with Elena's favorite sandwiches in it. At the bottom of the sack she saw a Ho-Ho and a fresh mango. Elena was touched to see his kindness made manifest, this man who had had such an odd and difficult life, literally waking up in a new world at a time when he should have already lived his best years. She pulled him close and said, "Otto, you will soon know what I learn from my vigil. Maybe I'll be able to help you make sense of things. ..." Otto answered yes.

The others gave little mementos or puzzle books since they knew Elena was leaving early, long before any shadow lengthened into a tropical dusk.

The guide's white station wagon waited in front of the hotel. The man selling carved mahogany dolphins and other trinkets watched her get in the car. A very dark young man carried a covered cage and led a large dog to the car. Even the little teenage girl who ran the T-shirt shack near the hotel came out to see what the commotion was. Soon tiring of standing in the sun, she went back to her electric fan and radio.

The bird cage sat in the back seat with Elena, who normally would have sat in the front seat with the guide and asked him questions. But the bird gave her an excuse for not talking to anyone. Elena had a floppy green sun hat perched on her head. The ridiculous piece of millinery could not decide whether it was meant to be a chapeau or a piece of military camouflage. Blotched with sweat as well as brown spots, the hat bore three large white plastic daisies on the front. Mary Ann had said she had brought it especially for Elena's vigil, and Elena was happy to have it although it made her look like an herb garden from the neck up. Loren sat, as if stunned, in the front seat.

The dog did not like the heat. He jammed his big hot black nose through the inch worth of rolled down window in the rear of the car. Maneuvering to get air, the German shepherd trampled Elena's little suitcase and bag of lunch prepared by her once-comatose Teutonic butler. Dog hair floated in the air, and the bird got scared at the unusual noises. Popol Vuh fluttered wildly and Elena began to worry that in his frail old age he really might hurt himself. However, as soon as the air conditioning came on and the car began to roll, Popol Vuh settled on his perch and dozed off. Kuon stopped whining and settled down.

Elena recalled the conversation with the minister of government she had requested an interview with in the Government House in Belize City.

"Miss Muñoz, government have no trouble granting your request but they do need to know certain matters. You know of course that this is not Mexico, and the offer of a 'consideration' of any kind would make my ministry fodder and me for the opposition party. All I need, madam, is a statement of your intent."

"Minister Randolph, I've already explained the situation to the Prime Minister and members of his cabinet. They expressed no hesitancy in granting my permit. Why do you want to stop me now?"

"I'll fill out the rest of the permit for you, Miss Muñoz. I'll leave the "Reason for Permit" blank open. Would you please write in the words that best express the reason for your overnight stay at Altun Ha? I'm sorry, I can't grant the permit without complete documentation first."

Elena picked up the pen and saw the minister rub his brown chin while he looked at her. He is barely old enough to shave, she told herself as he rubbed his chin, almost surprised to feel there was a beard there. He wore a white shirt and black pants and brown shoes. His round Maya face was still damp from the heat outside and the nervousness he felt dealing with a wealthy American eccentric. In a way, she was pleased to know he took his job seriously. There was a very small processing fee, paid to a bursar in the front office. Elena was surprised that a nation of 200,000 had an opposition party, especially one that relished the role of watchdog. Asking a brisk young man in the office, she found that the controlling party of Belize had been the PUP, or People's United Party. According to the young man, they had been in control of the country long before independence from Britain in September 1981. The young man continued talking with Elena as he escorted her outside. The opposition party, now in power, was called the UDP, or United Democratic Party. The UDP favored foreign private investment and a more favorable business climate. Both parties had their strengths and weaknesses, and each was just beginning to experience a real political awakening that the British were no problem anymore, that centuries of independence and service to the nation lay before them.

But that had been the second day of her stay in Belize City. It seemed a thousand years ago as she headed towards the jungle past Ladyville.

The narrow highway bore to the right some distance down the road. There was a few farms and patchy spots of cleared land. Sometimes there were metal warehouses containing small businesses, most of them just getting established. A sign indicated Belmopan to the left, and the driver, Mr. Cargill, turned right into a smaller paved road that seemed just big enough for one car. How two could pass was beyond Elena's reasoning, but then, she had her mind on different matters. They passed groves of coconut, small Mennonite farms freshly painted and oddly reminiscent of some Pennsylvania spreads and extremely thick jungle choked with philodendron and tall hardwoods.

They passed farmhouses on stilts, their fronts shaded by mango or cashew trees. Papayas grew in ratty little gardens dominated by perhaps a truck on cinder blocks or a rusted 1957 Chevy station wagon. Small legions of parrots flew overhead, their colors undistinguishable due to the failing afternoon light.

The guide drove over the bouncy road that led to the entrance of the Altun Ha restoration. Although still early in the morning, the day was growing hotter and became worse by fits as the sun passed behind huge white water-laden Caribbean clouds. Elena could see why this place was sacred to the sky god. Though the sea was not far, it lay just at the horizon granted by the top of the huge pyramid of Kinich Ahau. The silver band of the sea tantalized Elena, as if by seeing the Caribbean she would somehow feel less alien.

In any case, there was an odd sensation assailing her: she was in a kind of Los Cocos, a very ancient and unforgiving Los Cocos just a little too far from the open ocean. But it did not matter to her. She knew that within one day she would accomplish the thing she had come for. What happened after that was up to whatever—if anything—controlled her destiny.

A sense of relief, with a breeze, swept her, drying the nervous perspiration under her arms and pushing her iron hair back over her hairline. She opened the car door and grabbed her little suitcase in one hand, the birdcage in another. Kuon barked and clawed at the window to get out, but Elena hardly heard him. Her eyes were fixed on the top of the pyramid and the void beyond. The sight was nothing she expected. There was no profound stillness, no stench of time-obsessed Mayan centuries. There was only breeze and a feeling of newness, of expectation.

The guide, a quiet intelligent young man from the city, asked the caretaker when the park closed, since Elena had made it clear she wanted to stay all day and all night. The fat little caretaker with a gold star in his front tooth scratched his forehead and looked at Cargill quizzically.

"What man, you don't know?"

"Know what, Ramos?" replied the guide.

"She stay the whole night. Got government permit and all."

"Odd lady. She say for what in that permit?"

"No. Minister he say it's OK though."

The guide paused to eye the top of the pyramid, haloed by the silvery-yellow rays of the sun. A sudden eeriness made him shiver.

"I should leave them. She don't need me till tomorrow...if then. I wish I could figure out what she's doing."

"Hey, Cargill, maybe you don't want to know, eh?" The two men laughed their uneasiness at the sight before them dissipating along with night mist still stuck in green packets of shade. As Mr. Cargill lurched back into his car, he caught another tantalized Elena, as if by seeing the Caribbean she would somehow feel less alien.

In any case, there was an odd sensation assailing her: she was in a kind of Los Cocos, a very ancient and unforgiving Los Cocos just a little too far from the open ocean. But it did not matter to her. She knew that within one day she would accomplish the thing she had come for. What happened after that was up to whatever—if anything—controlled her destiny.

A sense of relief, with a breeze, swept her, drying the nervous perspiration under her arms and pushing her iron hair back over her hairline. She opened the car door and grabbed her little suitcase in one hand, the birdcage in another. Kuon barked and clawed at the window to get out, but Elena hardly heard him. Her eyes were fixed on the top of the pyramid and the void beyond. The sight was nothing she expected. There was no profound stillness, no stench of time-obsessed Mayan centuries. There was only breeze and a feeling of newness, of expectation.

The guide, a quiet intelligent young man from the city, asked the caretaker when the park closed, since Elena had made it clear she wanted to stay all day and all night. The fat little caretaker with a gold star in his front tooth scratched his forehead and looked at Cargill quizzically.

"What man, you don't know?"

"Know what, Ramos?" replied the guide.

"She stay the whole night. Got government permit and all."

"Odd lady. She say for what in that permit?"

"No. Minister he say it's OK though."

The guide paused to eye the top of the pyramid, haloed by the silvery-yellow rays of the sun. A sudden eeriness made him shiver.

"I should leave them. She don't need me till tomorrow...if then. I wish I could figure out what she's doing."

"Hey, Cargill, maybe you don't want to know, eh?" The two men laughed their uneasiness at the sight before them dissipating along with night mist still stuck in green packets of shade. As Mr. Cargill lurched back into his car, he caught another look at Elena, an absurd bundle of waving muumuu and hat, carrying assorted paper bags and cases and a birdcage and a trailing dog. The unsteady figure pushed her way along the path, through the ancient courtyards and over a slight rise. Behind her, a young blonde girl, Loren, carried a few boxes and carefully followed in Elena's footsteps over the grassy path while her mouth hung open at the green intensity of the jungle near her.

As she reached the base of the pyramid, Elena stopped to put down her suitcase. The crest of the pyramid thrust brutally, proudly above the foliage on either side. The sun sat atop the pyramid like an unrelenting idol. Elena began to climb. The pyramid was very steep, and each step hurt her thigh muscles. But with each step she felt a pleasant eeriness, that feeling which makes your hair stand on end, but not, somehow, out of fear. She was surrounded by a sudden momentousness, both feeling it and radiating it at once. Something pushed outward from her chest. It was her heart complaining at the strain, yet it was also an adrenaline-thrill provided by the circumstance at hand. The caretaker swigged from his Coke bottle, then stopped, noting the bizarre dignity with which she mounted the tall trapezoidal structure sticking its brown-gray head above the forest canopy.

When the phone rang, Sheriff Monahan of Jackson County, Florida, was asleep with his feet propped up on his desk. It was all right, though, since he was not on duty; he had fallen asleep only while doing some odds and ends of paperwork. The phone's jangling was like a nuthouse patient screaming for Thorazine at 2 a.m. After he picked up the phone and rubbed his eyes, Sheriff Monahan's face grew ashen, and what might have started out as a smile turned to a stony stare at the courthouse wall in front of him. He picked up his gun and holster, put them around his waist, put on his dark shades, and left the office. He passed several of the ARRIVE ALIVE signs vandalized from the interstate and stacked for removal outside the building. Barbarians, these young kids. What'll become of them?

The call was from Two Egg, about five miles from the county seat of Marianna. After getting preliminary statements, the sheriff prepared a written report on the situation in Two Egg.

"AN ELDERLY BLACK FEMALE, APPROXIMATELY EIGHTY YEARS OLD, NO EXTERNAL SIGNS OF FOUL PLAY, WAS FOUND DEAD IN THE SERENOA LAGOON

TRAILER VILLAGE AT 6:15 p.m., AUGUST 30, 1984, BY OFFICER JOHN B. TUBBOTTS. DECEASED WAS FOUND IN THE MOBILE HOME OF WILLIAM G. CANDOR, 45, OF TWO EGG. APPARENT TIME OF DEATH WAS 5:45 p.m. CANDOR CLAIMED THAT HE FOUND THE BODY, MRS. AMY MORTCAP (EMPLOYED AS HOUSEKEEPER TO MR. CANDOR) ON HIS RETURN FROM WORK."

The report went on to speculate on the Candor alibi, and evidence seemed to preclude foul play.

But the truth was somewhat different. Candor had come in, said hello to his housekeeper, and gone to his room. Moments later he burst out of the back of the trailer, carrying a baseball bat and screaming threats. Amy knew he had discovered her snooping and she tried to dissuade him from hitting her. She lifted her wrinkled arms like sticks helpless in the wind, saying, "Please don't hit me, Mr.Candor, please don't, please don't." All the while he moved toward her, blood-hate in his eyes, cursing and swinging the bat inches from her head.

"Please don't hit me. I'm your mother, Sister Thompson told me to. Don't...back home in Palmyra I left home to find you. I had to find you an' I did, now don't...." Suddenly she stood up straight, almost as if she were not afraid of him any more. He saw a puzzled look in her face and backed off. Maybe she'd been putting hexes on him, maybe....

Standing straight up, Amy looked so surprised, almost as though she had never seen this place, or William Gandy Candor, or even heard of Sister Thompson. She turned from William and looked out the trailer window, her eyes glazed. And she fell over the breakfast table, dead.

At that very moment, Amy Mortcap's middle aged-daughter was in Belize, far away. She was eating a bowl of cornflakes and bananas and milk. She listened to a local group, the Lord Rhaburn Combo, playing reggae music on Radio Belize. The song was called "Bad Card." While she ate, Zillah toyed with a red hibiscus. It had become her favorite flower. A group of dirty Rastafarians waved at her as they walked down the Marine Parade on the way to the Baron Bliss lighthouse at the tip of the point. She wanted never to leave this place. It intrigued her. She did not like some of the people but she liked the idea of living in a city built up from a swamp by rum bottles and mahogany chips. It seems liquor and wood had lifted the city from the sea. And the Belizeans? They did not seem to care. Home is home. Zillah thought about her poor mother for a moment. She was so frail and alone. Zillah felt sorry for her, but it was getting so bad that at the end Amy did not often recognize her. And Zillah had a destiny of her own to fulfill.

Amy therefore died unmourned, though back home there would have been many to mourn her for her loving selflessness. Amy was stupid in many ways but she had never purposefully done harm to anybody. That alone classed her with an intellectual elite, the artistic few, the knowers of the heart's darker secrets.

And yet even more had happened between Mr. Candor and Amy Mortcap.

Candor put up his baseball bat and looked at the corpse. She had said "Palmyra." Who was she? She had finally told her boss her name some weeks ago, so at least he knew that. But Palmyra? Her accent had been familiar—perhaps that was why he had trusted her as fast as he had.

After the interview with the sheriff and a Jackson County detective, Candor was released but warned not to leave the state since he could consider himself somewhat under suspicion. Candor did not mind; he assented to the sheriff's demands, his big right hand thrust into his blue jean pockets. He ran his left hand through his thinning iron-gray hair, the same color of his long-unseen wife's. For something had clicked in his head. He wanted to go to Palmyra, he wanted to see his daughter. He wanted to see his wife's face when he turned up back in town. Mr. Candor had lived too long by his wits to pass up an opportunity presented by his black maid. Was Amy a spy, sent to see if she could provide evidence of desertion? Certainly, Candor guessed, it could not be mere coincidence that sent the woman to Two Egg. It had to be part of a larger plan conceived and executed by Dauphine. A plan to get what Candor had, maybe. He could not be sure–there were a thousand questions in his mind. He went to the bathroom, packed his shaving kit, his toothpaste, several changes of clothes. And on his way to the bathroom he checked himself in mid-path, returning to the chest of drawers and pulling out a .357 Magnum he had bought three years ago when a friend of his had gotten him interested in pistol shooting, hunting, and gun collections. He wanted to bring the gun, though the reason why was still buried somewhere in his head. And he left Florida, headed west. ARRIVE ALIVE, the signs going out of Marianna said. He would arrive in Palmyra alive. He would find out what Dauphine was up to. "Won't she be surprised to see me?" he told himself. Her spy failed. Maybe he would get his daughter back. Maybe Betty Sue was tired of living with a waitress. At least he could give her a better home. He scratched a brutal face atop a brutal body. Somebody's going to get it. Somebody's going to pay for all my years of failure. His black car hurtled westward through western Florida.

The afternoon hours found Elena resting calmly, if not comfortably, atop the pyramid of the sky god. Loren sat talking with her for two hours, but when the sun got very hot Loren explored the other pyramids—all unrestored—and the shady paths leading into the jungle. She could not believe the huge philodendrons growing up the trees or the massive Orbignya palms, some covered with strangler figs. The growth of the jungle seemed random, chaotic, but extremely powerful—smooth barks, buttressed roots, delicate high canopies blotting the blue-yellow tropical sun. The heat was somewhat less choking than the heat of summer in Palmyra, and Loren noticed that there were few insects.

But what most occupied her thoughts was Chuck. Loren had to shake her head to clear out all the surprise. Just a few weeks ago she had been a young teenage girl, cruising around with her friends and enjoying her young life. Now here she was, in the middle of the jungle in a country she had never heard of before, keeping company with a woman who was the town crazy. She had taken on, as well, the pleasures and responsibilities of a love, her boyfriend who was both boy and man, friend and stranger, gregarious and loner. To see herself in the mirror of her romance was to see a fragmented image made even more unstable by her parents' needs and the pressure of the trip. Buying a Coke from the caretaker, Loren sat in a little hut-like pavilion. She soon felt the need to sleep, and the caretaker did not mind when he found her asleep on a long picnic table. He chuckled and covered his mouth when he saw her. Even worries about love would never stop Loren Murphy from getting her sleep. Meanwhile, Elena looked out to sea, played her 'ondes martenot' softly, and checked to see that the toucan was cool in his covered cage. The dog soon tired of sitting in the sun. He went to one of the vaulted priests' rooms on a lower level of the pyramid. Solid masonry, they were amazingly cool even on this hot tropical day.

Elena was hot and tired herself. This day's initial oddness, beauty, and even the beginning of ecstasy–had all faded in the light of full day. She began to feel a little stupid, then worse. The undervoice began to whisper deadly, logical words to her. It called her a spoiled food and a lunatic of the worst kind. Elena put the ondes martenot back in its case. Everything she believed in, her arts and crafts, her love of the night sky, all these abandoned her in that cruel one PM sky. She looked about herself, seeing the absurdity of her life and works stripped naked by a self-loathing so breathtaking, so categorical, that almost nothing light or happy could squeak through. The gates of Reason were slammed shut as an anxiety ice-cold and lonely came over her. She looked around to find Loren and was surprised to feel glad the girl was asleep. The self-hatred continued unabated. The undervoice rose to a higher pitch.

"You stupid bitch. Just a few more years, then you die all alone. You're weird, you're useless, and what good has your life been to anyone? All your money and your stupid house in outback Texas have been of no importance to anyone. You've thrown your life away."

Elena edged closer to the eastern end of the pyramid. It was unrestored, and jagged rocks lay far below. She spoke softly, wiping the sweat from her brow.

"If I throw myself headfirst down this cliff I can knock my brains out. Then this pain will be over with at last. I'm so tired of it all. I'm so tired of this struggle. If I just stand up and fall forward I can knock my brains out on those rocks down there."

Small lizards and vines crisscrossed the rough boulders below. A vague stench rose from them, as though vermin had died and were rotting quietly, just out of view.

Elena would have killed herself except that she was so tired and had eaten almost no breakfast. She was not even sure she could stand up. The pain of her anxiety and depression solidified into numbness by three o'clock. She continued staring eastward at the bright rim of the Caribbean. This is the throne of obsidian, this is the horror of horrors... What if nothing happens? What if? What if? No one knows how much suffering there is here. No one knows...no one knows...no one....

Chuck sat with Petey for the rest of the evening. Petey did not want to be read to. He did not want to discuss stars or astronomy or racing cars—his secret passion. He wanted to talk to Chuck about his sister. Somehow the words came easily. He glanced up at Chuck from a comic book in his lap.

"Do you love my sister?" he asked. Chuck tried to laugh the question off, but Petey's gaze did not soften.

"Yeah, I love her. What's it to you, squirt?"

"Will you marry her?"

"You sure have a lot of snoopy questions." Petey reached out and took Chuck's arm. Chuck was very surprised at the intensity in the young boy's face.

"You have to be good to Loren. You have to make sure...."

"Make sure what?" asked Chuck softly

"Make sure she never gets hurt by anyone. You have to take care of her."

Chuck gradually stopped grinning. Petey's words went through him. The little boy with dark brown hair and pale skin did not let Chuck's arm go. He had found out some things since nearly dying. There was something that Loren should fear. He felt it somehow.

Something.

The nurse came in at that moment and told Chuck to go away. The boy was getting too upset and was still too weak for agitation of any kind. Chuck, too tired and bewildered to argue, returned to the caravan. He arrived at the precise moment that the sun touched the western horizon. Night fell very quickly.

Elena's spirits began slowly to lift, and by the full dark her expectations began to rise. If nothing else, the punishing undervoice had ceased its cruel chatter, the feeling of blank futility leaving her as one, then two, then many stars appeared. The moon was slightly larger than a sliver, though not by much. It moved very high in the sky, spreading its faint light on the trees and other pyramid mounds near her. The Caribbean wind began to blow once more and allowed Elena to remove her floppy hat. Popol Vuh began to complain about dinner, and Kuon also left the priests' room to check out the food situation. She dutifully fed them and felt hungry herself, but when she tried to put the food to her mouth, she felt nauseated. Something inside her head told her this was a time to do without, a time to deny herself. She closed the bag of food and looked at the stars while scratching Kuon's neck. A shower of meteorites flew overhead occasionally. The temperature dropped to the high sixties as Elena began to drift into sleep. Hunger and emotional exhaustion pressed her to the pyramid's surface and held her there, covered by nothing but a small tarpaulin. Loren awoke with a start and ran to the pyramid. Kuon could not see her and barked, waking Elena temporarily. She told the girl to find a safe place to sleep on the pyramid, and since the only safe place was where Elena was, Loren pulled herself up the steep, narrow steps and lay near Elena. She too fell asleep again before too many hours passed. The night was deep and dark and still but for the soft keening of the wind and the jungle was silent except for the steady chirr of crickets and wild animal calls. The fall into sleep was uncompromised. Their heads turned to rock despite their wish to stay awake.

Day 4: APOTHEOSIS

Elena squirmed on the uncomfortable paving stones at the apex of the pyramid. The morning was cold. Loren slept soundly, rarely moving. Elena could see her lying still, breathing easily, and she did not feel so lonely any more. Elena looked at her digital travel clock. A thrill of surprise passed through her. It was 4:30 AM, almost dawn. She felt a little giddy, almost cheerful. Even if nothing happened, at least this trial would be over. But then she reconsidered.

It had to happen!

Elena went to the priests' room to urinate and came back shivering to get under the cover. Maybe, she thought, maybe nothing will happen. Then I can go back to....

"Elena!"

(No, no, this can't be. Yes, it is real!)

"Elena."

She heard her father's voice. It was no longer small. It sounded strong, a clarion from across the galaxy.

"Father! Is it you? I'm here, just as you told me to be!" Loren did not wake.

"Elena my daughter." A large circle of golden light appeared in the sky above her head. It coalesced and became the human image of her father.

"You've come, Elenita, mi hija." His black hair was blowing in the night wind, his eyes were points of light again, radiating in rays. He floated in air. Elena opened her mouth to speak but nothing came out.

"First, Elena, open the cage door."

Elena looked surprised but then did what the spectra said. Popol Vuh stuck his big banana beak out suspiciously. He rattled it on the bars like a prisoner with a tin cup. He then flew out of the cage.

"Now let the dog go."

Elena complied.

"Throw away the rest of your possessions."

She did, tossing them down the face of the pyramid. The caretaker heard a slight noise, then went back to sleep.

The specter of her father lifted her in a whirlwind; her muumuu flapped like a flag snapping on the open ocean. The rays from his eyes met her gaze.

Elena spoke with her father about many things. Then she found herself looking at the entire band of stars from a vantagepoint she could not determine. The pyramid was a dot below her.

"Look, daughter."

Far, far to the south, flashes of light roared up into the sky. When their beacons burned low, she saw vast ships moving, streaming from the earth's atmosphere into space. Another voice, not her father's spoke.

"THIS IS YOUR DUTY TO YOURSELF: YOU ARE TO MAKE THIS VISION COME TRUE. THERE IS MUCH THAT CAN SAVE THIS WORLD FROM ITSELF. BUT ONLY IF MANY LEAVE CAN THE WORLD CONTINUE. A NEW CARAVAN WAITS FOR YOU. YOU MUST BEGIN TO PREPARE FOR IT—"

Elena still could not speak. But she felt questions rise in her heart.

"YOU MUST PREPARE HERE. THIS LAND HAS ALL THAT IS NEEDED. IT SHALL BE A CROSSROADS ONE DAY, A GEM AMONG ALL LANDS. YOU AND OTHERS MUST MAKE IT A LENS TO THE STARS—"

Elena felt herself beginning to descend. Soon the top of the pyramid came into view. Her possessions were smashed. Her beloved pets were gone. Loren was yet asleep. And Elena was in ecstasy. And still the voice returned.

"ADOPT A HUNDRED CHILDREN. TRAIN THEM IN A SCHOOL IN A COMPOUND DEVOTED TO RESEARCH. THEY ARE THE ADVANCE GUARD. THEY WILL LEAVE THE WORLD SOMEDAY. LOVE THEM AND CARE FOR THEM. PREPARE THEM FOR WORK HERE AS WELL AS FOR THE STARS. ALL THIS IS YOUR DUTY. THERE IS NOTHING ELSE. THERE NEVER HAS BEEN—"

"Who are you?" Elena managed to whisper.

Of course, there was no answer.

Her bare feet touched the pyramid top. Thousands of voices sang languorously, mysteriously from blue and green stars. The immensity of the cosmos yawned before her. Its endlessness, its endlessness; only to embrace it! Embrace it! Embrace it like embracing the wind.... She fell into a dreamless slumber. Dawn caressed her but did not wake her. She smiled in her sleep.

Popol Vuh liked the jungle.

Kuon found a new home with a childless Mennonite couple. He still had his rubber skunk.

Mary Ann paced her room. It was dawn, and she knew that Elena would return soon. She could not wait to hear what Elena had to say. There was a knock at the door. It was Janie, who had finally finished all her preliminary studies and was now ready to go exploring in the jungles.

"I'll be leaving soon—just need to get a few more supplies. Thought I'd say goodbye."

"Sit down," said Mary Ann. "There's no rush. I know you want to wait until Elena gets back anyway. And say, you were pretty upset about Petey there today, weren't you?"

"Yes. He reminded me of my children, so helpless in the face of trouble."

"Why are you telling me this?" She reached for her hotplate and put on some water for instant coffee.

"I really miss my children. I'm so torn inside. I don't know what to do. Seeing Petey made me remember how children are. I want to make this expedition but I want to see my kids too."

Mary Ann fiddled with the hotplate and some plastic cups.

"Janie, I've about had it with you," she shouted, throwing a mixing spoon on the small table. "Go on your expedition. Just do it and stop mealy-mouthing your stupid guilts. You've temporarily thrown your family away, and it's just too damn bad for them and you, isn't it?"

Janie looked hurt. She cringed. Mary Ann continued.

"When you're finished doing what you want to do, call home and ask if you can come back. If Lenny says yes, then you've gotten away with everything. Lucky you. If he says no, you can't come back. *Finis*. He couldn't stop you from seeing your children in any case, thought I can't understand why you'd want to see them again after you'd left them. So let's just cut the crap, OK? I'm not in the mood for your handwringing. You intellectualize everything, then want everybody to feel sorry for you when some hurt comes your way."

Janie knew her former boss was right, and the truth stung her hard. She pulled herself together and bought her supplies. She lined up anthropologists from Cornell and art historians from the University of Mexico and the University of the West Indies, all in the amazingly short time of two weeks. But of course that was later. She still was curious enough about Elena to wonder what happened to her.

So it was that Janie had passed a crisis point. That still left the other members of Crazy Caravan. Lanky and Wanda? Barry and Dauphine? Zillah and Otto? Petey, Chuck, and Loren? Mary Ann? The bird and the dog were already taken care of. The young

Mennonite couple learned quickly never to touch the beloved rubber skunk. The toucan found a hole in a giant jungle tree. A tiny treefrog looked at the toucan, the toucan looked at the treefrog. It was plain that Winston cigarettes would be difficult to find in the jungle. Popol Vuh took to chewing on a twig.

XLVII Life Resumes, Elena Returns

They all were sure Elena was crazy. Barry and Dauphine stared at the ceiling. Lanky and Wanda shook their heads in disbelief. Petey, back in the Winnebago, was in bed. Loren and Chuck were intrigued, especially since Loren had gone through the experience herself. She did not tell him she had been asleep at the time. She wanted to believe it all was true, and saying she was awake seemed to make it feel more like truth. Chuck never questioned her participation in the mystic conflation of events on the pile of Kinich Ahau. And during the questioning, Loren nodded as if to agree with and corroborate everything that Elena said.

Elena told her story. Lanky was still not sure if Elena was one of those Jim Jones types, but he looked at her as if to ask, "What is all of this to me?" Janie was dumbfounded and felt that, in some small way, she had known what Elena's experience was going to be. Of course, there was no logical way she could have known—but everything that had happened to Elena sounded familiar, like an old, old tune stored in the mind's backroom and then dragged out for some occasion. Otto and Zillah wondered what the next weird step of their employment would entail.

"So, that's what happened," said Elena, calmly clapping her hands in front of her. "I officially consider this caravan closed. I'm leaving the van tonight. I intend to sell it after it carries you back to the States. That is, those of you who choose to return. I have a lot to do, and in surprisingly little time."

She checked into the Chateau Caribbean, a hotel overlooking the sea from Marine Parade. The cables and phone calls like blue sparks flew from her room for the rest of the day. The others, minus Janie who had left to find scholars for an excavation or exploration, scratched their heads in wonderment.

"Well, what are we going to do?" said Barry. Everyone looked at everyone else. Who was staying? Who was returning?

The painful emotional pulls were postponed when Elena threw a lobster banquet for them at the Chateau Caribbean that evening. Janie returned happily after a day of telephone recruiting which yielded some luck. After the dinner had started, Elena came out of her room and offered a toast. The early night outside was violet, the candles bright orange.

"To our little group. May you all find what I found today." After the toast she explained what happened later that day. She had called lawyers, contractors, Raul her brother, real estate agents, various politicians owing her favors, connections with NASA. She also called the Minister of Immigration and promptly arranged to be a resident alien, with an eye to becoming a citizen of Belize. It was a necessary step, she was told, to start a private school. Nothing else could be done that day. and the lobster party was feted with tubs of rock lobsters, all steamed to perfection and served with butter or various sauces.

Though at first confused and upset about what the future held for them, the others in the caravan asked Elena if she would hold off selling the Winnebago until they could explore a little more or complete chores of one kind or another. Elena said yes, she would give them two full weeks to make their plans. Elena invited along a tall, serious-looking real estate agent that looked a little like a silvered version of a movie star. He was from America originally. He sold Elena a small-unnamed caye about twenty-five miles from the Belizean shore. Elena planned to make her home there, and she let nothing stop her from getting the land. There were several hotels interested in the property but she had outbid them. The man showed slides with aerial views. The caye was much like Sand Island at home.

"Tomorrow," she said, "I'm going to several orphanages in this country and Guatemala and Mexico. The paperwork will take several months, I'm sure, but I intend to take custody of at least one hundred poor children, as I told you I would."

Lanky noticed a glow in her eyes that he had never seen before. The personality was the same except for a new self-confidence where before there had been only confusion, insecurity, and searching.

As Elena listened to the agent describe the island, she said a small prayer to her father's spirit. She asked for his guidance in all things—the school, the research, and especially (as her happy eyes swept the room) in choosing wise people to stay with her. Otto and Zillah would stay, but who among the others? It was a question which would have to be answered soon.

The night wore on; yachts with softly glowing lights bobbed in the bay in front of the Chateau Caribbean. Elena, as always, sat in front of the windows and let the warm evening wind fill her lungs. The stars came out again, and she felt the same ecstasy as from the night before: the ceaseless surge of the ocean which hinted at a thousand philosophies, a million possibilities. And yet she realized that here she was, for the last time, with her beloved friends. Though only barely acquainted in some ways they had gone through many experiences together. And among the rest of themselves, she knew, there were new secrets and new relationships of trust and affection. Some were pulling apart, others were coming together—the fate of all things in the material universe, and probably every other kind of universe as well.

The talk and hilarity waned at about ten o'clock, and Elena made one last toast. Wanda and Barry had tears in their eyes. They held hands. Dauphine cried on Lanky's shoulder. Mary Ann and Janie stood on either side of Elena with their arms around her waist and shoulders. Chuck and Loren held Wanda's hands. Otto and Zillah tried to comfort Barry and ended up patting his head and telling him it was all right. They had been through much, yet most of them had not found what they were looking for. Elena reminded them they still had a week of their journey left and that many things could still happen to them. She then told them she would be leaving in the morning. She asked them to consider staying with her on her island home if they felt their destinations lay with her. She asked them to think about her experience. There are so many things to live for, she explained. Her space research was just one of them.

Mary Ann left the others to themselves to puzzle out their next steps. She followed Elena into the corridor. Elena turned around and smiled. "Do you want to see me?" she said.

"Yes. I need to talk with you about something very important."

"Come in, then," said Elena, and opened the door.

Mary Ann looked at Elena's room for a few minutes, framing her questions mentally while Elena changed to a nightgown.

"What you told us isn't enough," said Mary Ann abruptly.

"About what, Mary Ann?"

"About what happened on the pyramid."

"I've told you everything I know, everything I can remember."

"But it's not enough! I have to see a pattern in it. I have to understand it. One thing, though: I really believe you, I really believe it all happened. I just don't understand what the words mean. What they mean to me and to everybody everywhere. Do you understand?"

"I think so," said Elena, who sat on the corner of the bed and began to talk enthusiastically. She tried to help Mary Ann draw conclusions from the message at the pyramid of Kinich Ahau, the Sky God of the Classical Era of the Maya.

"First of all, my vision and the voices that spoke to me weren't for everybody. They were meant for my guidance, my destiny. I know that you're looking for wisdom and a good life, and I know you think I can tell you something extra. Why, Mary Ann Banks? Are you my Ananda, my St. Paul? Will you record everything I tell you so that future generations can remember? Isn't it certain that anything I say will be misunderstood and misapplied and eventually distorted? I'm no Jesus or any other religious figure. All that can be said for me is that something very strange happened to me." Mary Ann then spoke.

"You didn't get any feeling for—or thoughts about, uh, ultimate questions?"

"Like what?" asked Elena

"Like why are we here? What is the universe really like? Is there a god? What is it like? Is there life after death?" Elena looked at Mary Ann silently for a few moments.

No twenty seconds of silence ever in May Ann's life were as important as these. She hungered to know so many things.

"I'll tell you what I did learn from the experience that I didn't know before. Commit it to your memory, Mary Ann, but please never tell anyone. I won't have my vision dragged through the mud. Eventually others will realize I'm right, but I don't want an unhappy life trying to maintain an impossible privacy. Even an island can't protect me from the mass of humanity wanting some reassurance. But here's what I think is the answer to your list of questions. One of them I have no doubts about: the dead do survive. I don't have any proof other than what I felt."

"Where do we go after death?"

"Some go to a vast void somewhere. It's like the central point on a record: it doesn't move. They can stay there as long as they want. Then they can come back to earth as another person. Others stay around, like Karen Allemeister or my father, for instance."

"Who sends the dead ones back?" asked Mary Ann.

"No one sends them, anymore than one sends an acorn to the ground or a fish downstream. It just happens."

"But why? Why do things happen this way and not some other way?"

"Who knows? Maybe at other times different things happen to dead people. All essences or material things in the universe behave the same way in that they come into existence, they pass from existence, then they come into a new existence again. And one day, after I die, I'll live again too."

"Does it ever come to an end?" asked Mary Ann.

"You seem to think it tiresome to be born and reborn. I don't see why. There's no effort in it at all for you. Next question was, uh, what the purpose of it all is. I'm not sure, but I got the feeling that 'purpose' exists only in our minds, not anywhere else in creation. We can only find purpose, to satisfy ourselves, by experiencing and doing. There is no substitute for either of them."

"Are you sure about all of this?" asked Mary Ann.

"No," answered the millionairess.

"Did any of this ever occur to you before—you know, like, on your own?"

"Sure. Some of it," answered Elena, "but I'm not completely sure I'm right. I talked with my father just a little before the other voice began, and...."

"Who was the other voice?"

"I don't know. It seemed vaster somehow."

"Could it be God?"

"No. I can't see why it should be. Maybe it's one of the dead who hasn't been permitted to join the others. But how am I supposed to know?"

"If it wasn't God, then is there a god?"

"I couldn't say, Mary Ann," said Elena picking up a night cream jar and began unscrewing the lid. Cleansers, perfumes, and hand lotions poured out of an old handbag onto the bed. It was obvious Elena was anxious to go to sleep, but Mary Ann insisted on more talk.

"One last question, if that's OK with you."

"Shoot," said Elena.

"What does all your news about space have to do with these ultimate questions?"

"I can answer that. Get up off the bed and pull me up too. I'm tired."

Elena held on to Mary Ann's hand and pulled her gently to the window. Mary Ann could swear she heard a faraway anthem. The night between the stars was raven-black, comforting and indecipherable. The moon's silvery glow reassured her from the upper left corner of the window.

"Look at that out there, Mary Ann. Look at the immensity of it all. And you know what? We are aware of almost none of it. How stupid and blind we must be to think we know anything about universal laws or eternally true principles. What utter nonsense from our tribes we bring with us into the future! We're like cavemen trying to start a rocket with a flint blade. The range of thought, which we thought possible, is completely incorrect. It is really much larger. We're like earthworms conferring degrees on one another while the real world waits just over our head, past the sod. My father and the voice wanted to tell me this much: don't waste your time talking about life and death. Getting to the near universe is only a first step in one of thousands, or even millions, and when we take that millionth step, we will still be JUST STARTING.... Can I go to bed now? I'm tired. Hmm. This muumuu stinks." Elena took it to the bathroom and washed it in the sink. Mary Ann stayed at the window trying to digest Elena's words. This woman who had just told her some of the secrets of the secrets of the universe was humming "April Love" and evidently enjoying herself as she tried to squeeze air bubbles out of her wet muumuu.

XLVII Three Scenes and a Tale

It was eight in the evening. After hanging around the Tetrapylon Game Parlor on Tooley Boulevard for about an hour, "Boss" Candor decided to have a beer. He drove past the Murphy house and then saw his old home. It had changed a lot. The bitch had planted a few trees and flowers. Big deal. The whole house was not as neat as his trailer, but he had conveniently forgotten its condition before Amy came and adopted him. He knocked on the door just in case Betty Sue was there. Getting her back would be easy if Dauphine was gone.

But no luck. Nobody home.

Candor roared back down Tooley and pulled up in front of the Red Arrow. He clutched the steering wheel and squinted to see if he could make out the form of his ex-wife serving coffee or smiling at customers. He got out of the car and pressed his nose against the plate glass window. She was not there.

A waitress. Big deal. The little tramp.

Candor forgot his own frequent unemployed stints, but it did not matter to him at the moment. Dauphine's co-worker Frieda was wiping down a counter, her back to the window. Candor cursed and left. He jumped in his old black Chevrolet Impala and headed out towards the causeway and that old bar on Sand Island. Ha! Wouldn't Ed Fernandez be surprised to see him after all these years? He and Ed had been friends at one time, but William Candor suspected that Ed would not even recognize him now. So much had changed, now that he knew what the score was. He knew how the waitress bitch had made his life a misery. He knew the score. He didn't want to hurt her but he did want his daughter back. He knew the score. And if he acted real nice, he knew he could get Ed to tell him where his ex-wife and daughter were. It shouldn't be hard to do. He was clever, he knew. He knew the score. He knew the score. He knew the score. He knew.

At midnight he left the Tropicala drunk. He had learned a lot of things that night. Ed and Brenda, now lovers, recognized old Bill Candor right away. Ed was a little suspicious at first, even behind the grin of recognition the eyes were questioning: What are you doing back here? Candor claimed to be in South Texas on business. He said he was working in a Mobile shipyard. Hard work but he liked it, he said. They had chatted a few minutes more, then he asked where Dauphine and Betty Sue were. He seemed jovial enough to Ed, but a little warning bell went off in the bartender's head. Something about William was just Not Right. He could not decide what it was-the eyes, maybe, or the clothes. Ed knew that Betty Sue was supposed to be coming home soon from her aunt's home in Odessa. Dauphine was safe, of course, because she was in another country-and one that most people had never heard of, to boot. He decided to tell William. William would never go there.

"Oh, yeah," Ed admitted casually. "She and some other people from town went to Belize." He had to explain where it was and why the Winnebago had left. It was clear to Candor that Ed did not know the whole story but the facts were clear enough. The damn tramp had taken off with some rich people in a Winnebago. Traveling like a first-class bitch. He could teach her a lesson when he got down there. She was getting too big for her britches. Hanging around with rich folks, drinking rich folks' bourbon and feeling air conditioning on her sweaty bitch neck. Ha. Some fun. That bitch would pay and pay. And pay.

Elena kissed each of her friends goodbye. She lined them up in front of the van at dawn and whispered in one of each set of ears. No one ever found out what was said to the others. It did not matter. The message was private. Zillah was visibly upset. That maddeningly impassive, almost stupidly sphinx-like expression was rent and thrown away. Zillah's protection from pain had been tossed out like so much garbage.

"I'm gonna miss you!" she sniffled. Elena patted her back in an embrace.

"You can do just fine while I'm gone, Zillah! I know it!" she said bravely. The black woman was not convinced, but she knew she would have to succeed anyway. Some would go, some would stay. Elena addressed the full group for the last time as the airport cab arrived in front of the hotel.

"I've got to leave now. I'll be back in two weeks. The construction of the compound on the caye should be well underway a month from now. Otto, remember to sell the van, and make sure that everyone returning gets where they want to go. I wish I had time to ask all of you to remain with me, but I know you want to make your own choices. I hope to see many of you. Remember that you can live here. You can find meaning here. But it's in the doing. It's in the experience. It's not the place-but what a place this country is. I'll be back in two weeks."

The wind, warm already, ran down the dusty streets of Belize City. The sun was strong, but rainclouds to the east were coming in swiftly. The earth almost sighed in anticipation of cool and rain. And Elena got into a cab headed towards the airport in Ladyville just as the first big drops of rain began to splatter the van's huge awning.

The caravaners were quiet. Otto was reminded of the way Zillah had danced back in Mexico. Mary Ann led the way into the living area. No one felt much like talking, but they wanted to see one another, feel assured by their mutual presence.

Only Petey spoke when he was brought back from the hospital. Mary Ann was in a brown study, and Barry and Dauphine helped Otto with dinner. Zillah disappeared into her room. Petey said, "We've got to start deciding," the exact words everyone was thinking but nobody dared to say.

"Honey, let's not today. We'll all talk about it tomorrow." The sky grew darker and darker until about ll:00, and the rain fell in writhing gusts. The storm season was approaching, and it soon would be necessary to start making decisions.

After a mainly silent dinner punctuated by a few questions to Petey about his doctor and the hospital, the table was cleared and the group entered the sitting room.

Lanky thought, "We'll never be here together again."

Wanda thought, "So this is the beginning of the end."

Janie came back from an expedition organizational meeting and excitedly told the group about recent finds in the Petén of Guatemala, the lowlands bordering Belize on the west, a vast hot jungle crawling with swamps and insects and terrifying remains of Mayan cities. She also spoke of a dig in the north of the Belize. The site was called Cerro, and within its confines lay the remains of one of the earliest Mayan cities ever.

Loren sighed and tried to imagine herself a Mayan priest atop a pyramid to a Chac or Kinich Ahau. She alone among them knew what it meant to make a vigil. Just looking at those huge stars whirling in the heavens was enough to make her believe in anything.

At that moment, Loren's mind awoke.She reached over to Chuck speechlessly and tugged his shirt, as if in pain, as if in horror. She pulled him by the hand outside the trailer. She now saw how the heavens moved; she now thirsted to know more about the cosmos. A divine sensation within her, or perhaps from outside her-had placed a spark in her mind, tindered by love, engulfed by the impulse of silver stars in her blonde hair and the reflection of the Pleiades in her eyes.

"Loren?" Chuck said, almost in fear. Something had happened to Loren. He watched the tears course her face, lining its soft young contours. He pulled her close, thinking she was afraid of something, maybe their future. He knew it had occurred to Loren that one of them might stay in Belize and the other might return to Texas. A soft tropical night brought the murmur of lapping water over the waterfront of Marine Parade. A small sailing boat, its name and registration unreadable in the night, moved up and down, up and down, rocking its crew to sleep above the night-purple waters of the bay. Loren was beyond talking.

She would enjoy the recklessness of youth a little more, but her concerns were now changed. In the space of a few moments she felt her world yanked from under her. Gone was the self-confident high school student, blithe in her ignorance and self-absorption. Gone was the girl whose main concerns were her reputation, her popularity, and her academic achievement. Those things no longer seemed to matter, swept aside by a sudden appreciation of the enormity of choices to make. However, it was a mood that did not, could not last long in the mind of a young girl. Soon she was herself again, laughing and teasing with Petey. But something underneath the surface was forever altered.

Later, Mary Ann called the group together for iced tea. Petey reminded her that she had not told a story in Xpuhil. It was, the dark-curled boy reminded her, her turn.

"Oh Petey, these people don't want to hear me make up a story. We all have things on our minds," she said. But everyone protested. Zillah spoke loudest.

"Let's put off thinking about tomorrow. Come on and tell a story." Everyone agreed, even though it was getting late. Petey was asleep not long after Mary Ann began because his medicine had a soporific effect on him. He was later sorry he had not heard all of Mary Ann's story.

Mary Ann was in agony. She could not decide what to say. Should she tell something about her real estate business? She certainly had a lot of funny stores to tell. Maybe she could make my story about something from her reading of the *Critique of Pure Reason*. A decision had to be made, and she set herself to the task.

Everyone got comfortable as Otto lit a large candle and placed it on a table in the middle of the room. There were no sounds but the quiet hum of the air conditioner and carloads of Belizean teenagers laughing and making noise outside the trailer. The Winnebago had begun to attract attention soon after it arrived in town. There had been no trouble, however. Most simply wanted to see the giant van. As night drew on, even the noise of cars faded and ceased.

Mary Ann's Story

"There were three brothers who lived in a faraway land. They lived with their mother and father in great wealth and family happiness. Time passed, and one day the eldest brother announced to his brothers and parents that it was now time for him to make his way in the world. He packed a few belongings and set out into the world to find adventure and fortune. His father and mother wrung their hands and consoled each other with touches, leaning their gray heads against each other and meaning over the loss of their eldest.

The second son, seeing his parents' pain, decided to live in the same village that he had grown up in. They were able to see him every day, and they found great comfort in the son's presence. However, the second son was forever longing to see new lands and new mountaintops the way the eldest brother did. Eagerly he sought word of his elder brother, his exploits and adventures on the roads of the world. The second son found out from traders that his brother longed to come home but had grown accustomed to his vagabond life and found it too difficult to change. He thought the next meadow, the next curve in the forest path, the next grotto would bring him fame and fortune.

One brother, then, languished for the comforts of home and family; the second brother yearned for the life of an adventurer.

Seeing this created a problem for the youngest son. He scratched his young head and tried to make sense of what he saw. He saw his eldest brother chasing a dream without worldly substance, a shadow passing over the land, rootless and unknown—yet learning of great wars and loves and wonderful kingdoms in foreign lands. The youngest son also saw his second brother, secure in his homeland and beloved in his village. Yet he knew his second brother to be unhappy, sitting home day after day, waiting to hear news of a world that soon would become impossible for him to even dream of seeing.

So what could the youngest son do, since neither course of life could possibly satisfy him for long, neither the going nor the staying? It would not be possible simply to travel for a few years, then return home. He knew that, once made, his decision would probably mark the course of the rest of his life. He thought for many days and then came to an answer."

"How can there be an answer?" interrupted Lanky. "It's a dilemma. If he goes, he's unhappy. If he stays, he's unhappy. How can there be a solution?" Zillah and Chuck leaned forward, ready to hear the answer. Mary Ann continued.

"The youngest son decided what to do. He enchained his parents and second brother, seeing to it they were not in pain and well fed despite their confinement. He sold the house and all its belongings and put his parents and brother in a caravan. When they saw their home receding in the distance, the parents wept bitterly for their past and their homestead. They could not understand the cruelty of the youngest son, and he did not try to explain himself, remaining deaf to their cries of 'Why? Why' The second brother did not cry, but soon he faced forward to see where the caravan led. He asked the youngest brother where he was taking them, thinking he meant to leave his family to die in some forsaken place so that he could claim all they owned, disinheriting his brothers and eliminating his old parents. But the youngest son, barely a man, answered their questions at the end of the day near a campfire that shone almost blue in the dark.

'I am taking you to our eldest brother,' he said, for of us he was the wisest. He suffers, he learns, he knows the stones of the earth. In bringing ourselves to him, I add love to experience. And so the youngest son solved his problem: he did not leave his family, nor did he stay, nor did he allow his eldest brother to wander alone through the world. When the brother was found there was a happy reunion and the parents forgot most of the sorrow of their leave-taking, now that their family had been reunited for what would be their eternal travels. Later the sons took wives, and many descendants of the old parents sought the ends of the earth in the same spirit."

"What a story, Mary Ann," said Barry. "Where'd you get it?"

"I made it up. Just now. Don't know how I did it, but the subject has been on my mind lately." She sat down again, partly embarrassed over her tale, but all the caravaners had understood it. Chuck spoke, "I guess we'd better get some sleep. We'll probably be leaving here in the morning." Wordlessly, they all nodded and left to get some sleep. The next day would see the fracture of their circle of friends.

Just as they left to prepare for bed, the radiophone rang. Zillah answered. It was Elena, who was now in Guatemala City. She had not accomplished much yet, but one minister had been impressed with her money. She felt sure that some headway on the adoptions would come soon. Everyone was cheered to find Elena well, but they were exhausted from a full day.

William Candor already had a TACA airline ticket in his pocket. It was for Belize City, ETA 11:50 local time. Candor patted his chest pocket to feel the reassuring rectangle of papers. He slept inside his black car in a grimy, deserted Houston parking lot. Tomorrow at 10:00 in the morning he would board Flight 110 for Belize City.

He'd see what Dauphine was doing. In the weird light of 4:00 a.m. he planned his new life. He would find Dauphine and his daughter and he would make things right. He would show them. He would show everyone what a real winner does. No fruity old broad and a group of geeks would make decisions for him. No sirree. No sirree bob.

It was also in the wee hours in Belize City. Wanda could not sleep, Chuck could not sleep, Lanky could not even lull himself into a pre-sleep daze.

XLIX José Ah

Elena Muñoz, heiress to millions soon to be used in ways she'd never have expected, will soon pass temporarily from our story. She is gathering the paperwork and hiring lawyers to adopt children in Latin America. The case of one child in particular, José Virreina Ah, a Mayan boy from the Department of the Petén, Guatemala, will serve as an example. He is eight years old.

José's mother died after the birth of his younger brother and youngest sister. In all, he had seven siblings, two of whom had already died before their mother. José had known nothing but hunger all his life, but housing was cheaply made and the family owned the land on which their hut stood. The jungle offered much in the way of bananas, papayas, and other fruit, but José's growing body needed much more protein than he could get from the fruit, beans, tomatoes, and corn that made up his daily diet. His hunger, even after a meal, never quite allowed him rest. Though by nature a happy, lively boy, José suffered from internal parasites and a rather brutal upbringing by his confused father. Mr. Ah perhaps would have made an excellent father, but Guatemalan life could not teach him how to be a mother as well. Worsening unemployment and a bad crop pushed Mr. Ah into a level of frustration that can lead only to family violence. One evening, José came home too late from his shabby little church school. His after-school chores were not done, and his father began to beat him. Even while dodging his father's blows, José could smell the rum on his father's breath. More than fear José felt the new sensation of disgust. His father had begun drinking with friends to pass the time. Now, all the man had was time, and he chose to pass it in the companionship of men who also found themselves unemployed and disenfranchised in a world they could not understand. Just enough of a glimmer of awareness told them they were condemned to a life of meaninglessly persistent poverty, a chalky tastelessness made more bitter by their refusal to learn to read, or to go to the city to learn a trade, or even to pay lip service to the idea that a better world might lie away from their father's patchy acres of infertile soil.

José's father literally kicked him out of the house and told him to live in the forest. José cried but not for long. In his childish way he had known what was coming, and his leaving would mean more food for his little sister and brother. He walked to the priest's house and explained. The priest told him to sleep on one of the pews of the old church and that he would talk to Mr. Ah in the morning. José saw no help for his situation and left the church even before the village's roosters began to crow. He would walk to Guatemala City and find work—whatever work an eight-year-old could find.

And there, standing on a street corner looking at the crash wreck of a '49 Chevy sedan and a '63 Chevy coupe, Elena Muñoz saw the boy. He was desperately skinny, his red shirt stiff with filth, snot, and dried sweat. He had just stolen a tin of shoe polish. Now all he had to find was a soft rag and he would be able to polish shoes a little closer to the business district. The tips might keep him in food. He could sleep in dark places, even though it was often very cool at night.

She called him over with a smile on her face. An hour later- and after a meal and some ice cream-she asked the boy about his family. Some days later, Mr. Ah woke to find lawyers knocking at his door. They offered him 14,000 quetzals for eleven years' custody of his son. He took the money and said he would gladly give permanent custody to the rich Mexican-American lady, doing with his son what she would. The lawyers said "That's fine with us" in broken Spanish and returned some time later with revised papers giving permanent custody to the rich Lady. Mr. Ah was very drunk and red-eyed by now; he cursed the lawyers, his son José, and his fate in this imperfect world. And he signed the document. Elena later reflected on how amazingly powerful her money made her. Elena looked at the ragamuffin sleeping on her hotel suite couch. He was wearing comfortable new clothes, his belly full. And only God knows, she wondered, what is in his head. Two weeks later when she finally returned to Belize, José Ah would be the first of the *sky children*, the children of Kinich Ahau, to go to the caye that has no name.

L Together and Apart

Bus tours can be fun if you are in the mood for them. They are cheap, the company can be nice, and there are always the memories of shared excitement later. Sick and tired of the RV and ghosts and the meaning-of-it-all and arguments between each other, Barry and Dauphine decided to take a bus trip to Dangriga, in the wetter southern part of the country. Dangriga had once been called Stann Creek. It got its start as a loading point for shipments of mahogany back when Belize was British Honduras and when the only way to make a living was by swinging a big axe at big trees. A curious race of people, the Garifuna, lives nearby. The men and women of Garifuna speak different languages. Men are therefore bilingual through learning first their mother's tongue and then later the language of men. Barry wanted to ask the bus driver how women communicated with men. The bus driver, a rather dull man, said, "by talking." Barry and Dauphine laughed to each other as rows of questioning ceibas and coconut palms watched them pass. The bus was crowded with just about every kind and color of person. The roar of the diesel motor sounded more like a machine gun with a stuck trigger, and a mixture of Carib, Spanish, and English shouts filled the air. At first the couple had wanted to take along a picnic lunch, but they decided to throw caution away and sample the local restaurants.

Barry was not sure, but he thought his woman, Dauphine Candor, was beginning to show. Her belly had not so much rounded as it had simply lost its shapely concavity and seemed poised on the question "What's here?" Overeating? Lack of exercise? Age? Perhaps a baby? And at her age, with a grown daughter! Of course, her changing body gave Barry a few opportunities for teasing, but as time went on he teased less and less. Maybe it was the danger of a woman's pregnancy in her forties. Maybe it was Barry's fear that he would drink too much, that he would not take care of his wife (wife?) and child. Maybe he refused to face his own age, his own failures in youth. In any case, some of the Belizean women spoke kindly to Dauphine over the racket from the motor and a group of rowdies in the back of the bus. A loudmouth girl wearing a yellow dress and listening to a big radio-type player blaring reggae music and was whooping and laughing with a group of teenagers a little younger than she was. The bus driver made no move to quiet her though she was screaming at the top of her voice–and obviously drunk from the moment she boarded. Both Barry and Dauphine were later happy to get off the bus and away from her.

They found a boxlike little beach hotel of white clapboard and cinder block and checked in. After unpacking, they went out to the beach chaises and Dauphine watched Barry as he fought with the waves. In a curious way she realized he was a ruined man. From the sternum up, he could have passed for a man in his early thirties except for a little gray at the temples. The skin around his eyes was not even particularly wrinkled. But from the top of the belly down he was definitely a man in his forties—overweight, a paunch. Of course it did not matter to her. She loved him anyway. But in his heyday, she knew he had been a real beauty. With that thought she drifted into sleep while an azure wind slipped through the salty mangroves and rattled palm fronds, like bones.

Barry came out of the water laughing until he saw Dauphine dozing. In that lucid moment—a moment unlike many passed with his hand on the neck of a bottle of Four Roses—Barry Madden decided that he wanted to stay in this new country, to make a life here no matter how difficult and unpleasant things might be at first. He would find work, he would sell his house in Texas and throw his lot in with other American expatriates. He could start a business, maybe, something that would make him independent financially again and yet would give jobs to other people of the country. Maybe he could be a part of Elena's project. She had asked them to stay, after all. His thoughts drifted over the first cataract of sleep. The afternoon sun must have been hot, but he and Dauphine were cool in the shade. Then he too was asleep. There was always time for argument later.

Mary Ann headed north, accidentally passing the turn-off to Altun Ha, which she wanted to visit but did not think she had time for. Turning her rented car around, she visited the site that had meant so much to her wealthy friend.

Her mind was set to feel nothing. She almost defied Altun Ha to do anything to her or for her. She went through the ceremonial plaza; it left her cold. Then she saw the pyramid of Kinich Ahau. It sent a shiver through her, almost something like recognition of a familiar but long-lost memento. The lower staircase rose to a platform. The platform contained the priests' rooms; then came the main staircase jutting up to the sky. Atop the pyramid was a block of stone big enough to sit on, and there Mary Ann put her behind to catch her breath and rest her legs. In the distance she saw a British Harrier jet and heard the calls of monkeys and birds.

Maybe it was the time of day, but she was not too impressed. Maybe it was the busload of tourists from America who kept shouting, snapping gum and photos, and demanding soft drinks. Mary Ann wished them to hell.

"I told you I wanted to go to Jamaica, but no! It had to be here! Well I'm hot and tired and...."

"Gimme it, gimme the cam'ra! Mama, Jimmy won't gimme the..." Mary Ann was ashamed of her countrymen.

An hour wore on but Mary Ann felt nothing more inspirational than her primary frisson. How could she have had a revelation there among all those loud tourists, Coke bottles waving in their hands? But then, why not? Why should not there be a revelation at any time of day? So it was that Mary Ann likened the effect to the way a medium always insists on dim light and a point of focus like a candle. Why not call the dead back at a hockey game? Why should the atmosphere be so important? She carefully climbed down the pyramid, reaching behind her back to steady her descent on the steepest staircase she had ever seen. She got in her car and continued her drive to Corozal. So, it was not for Mary Ann Banks to have a revelation like Elena's, even though Mary Ann wanted such a revelation much more than Elena had wanted one. Elena had desperately wanted to find out her duty to herself. But it was for Mary Ann to wish that a revelation would tell her why things are the way they are, and not some other way. Maybe it is too much to ask of a spirit who appears to people. Maybe spirits want you to accept what they say, without any backtalk.

"Well," Mary Ann said aloud to herself, "so much for revelation and spirits. I'll have to learn what is and what isn't by figuring it out myself." She found the North-South Highway and turned left to catch the way to Corozal.

About forty miles down the road, and as she sat sweating in her white linen pants and cotton shirt, she saw a young Latin man standing almost casually with his thumb out, as if it hurt his pride to be hitchhiking. Mary Ann laughed at his comical hauteur and transparent posturing. Just a glance at his clothing (torn khaki slacks with a red-buttoned shirt) his clouded eyes and even the slight forward tilt of his head–all these told her it was his first hitch-hike. I am too young to be doing this, he probably was thinking, but Mary Ann could not read his thoughts. From him emanated also a slight hint of violence, however faint. The potential was there, but buried under a form of youth still childish in its basic limn. He was at most seventeen or eighteen years old, and a small seventeen at that. Mary Ann stopped, though she could think of at least seven reasons to keep going. Here she was in a foreign land, driving a rented car she was responsible for, picking up a boy she had never seen before and who could possibly have buddies in the forest who might shoot her or blow the air out of her tires. They could all descend upon her. But she stopped anyway. The young man smiled and trotted to the car. She looked at his leaning-down face framed in the passenger window. He spoke perfect English though he seemed somehow hesitant to speak at all.

"I'm going north," he said.

"Where to up north?" she said.

"I need to go to Corozal."

"Hop in, I can use the company," she said. After three miles he turned the gun on her.

LI Boss Arrives, Janie Heads West

Due to an odd tailwind the TACA flight from Houston arrived early in Belize City at ll:47. Boss Candor looked around just long enough to disapprove of the tiny airport. A cab driver took him into Belize City and he checked into the Ft. George. At the front desk he learned about the Winnebago's location just down the street. Otto was sweeping around the van's awning when Candor came by. He could not be sure how much the German knew about him, but if he wanted to find his wife and daughter, he knew he had better pretend to be friendly. Candor introduced himself with a big Texas grin and an iron handshake. Otto grimaced in pain. Twelve years of sleep never do much for chiral anatomy, and Candor did not help the situation with his bludgeoning grip. After introducing himself, Candor tried to make small talk about the size of the trailer and Mrs.Muñoz's wealth. One of Otto's eyebrows lifted. A tone of suspicion took residence in his voice, and his usual resonance became flat and thin. He kept trying to ask Candor what he wanted, but Candor continued to make observations on the weather and, of course, Otto's accent.

"Yeah, I recognize your voice," Candor said. "You was mixed up in that little gal's death back in Palmyra. Everybody knowed it was a accident, don't worry. It was a real shame, musta been hard on you, too, huh?"

A few moments.

"Vat do you vant?" Otto repeated, staring into the cloudy, violent eyes of William Candor. The butler had seen that same look on the faces of the brown shirts who pushed him down onto the ice fifty years ago. The eyes accompanied a mouth set like a cobra trying to smile.

"Mrs. Candor is in Dangriga now, south of here. I don't know der hotel. Excuse me please. I must vork now." Candor was put off by the butler's refusal to give more information. He asked if she had brought a teenage girl with her, and if there had been a companion. Otto finished sweeping and turned to walk into the trailer, ignoring Candor's questions. As he mounted the little steps, the butler's arm was yanked behind him and he was thrown onto the ground. His head hit a piece of concrete from the old sea wall that Hurricane Hattie destroyed back in 1960. As he passed out he wondered how long he would sleep this time. It was cool under the Winnebago, and he could almost forget the buzzing, stinging pain in his head. He saw Boss Candor's running feet down the Marine Parade. Lanky came out of the trailer just as Otto passed out. He heard Lanky shout to him but all he wanted to do was sleep. The shouts turned to meaningless roars, and Otto felt himself being dragged from his resting spot under the trailer. He felt dried blood congealing on his forehead. He said, "Villiam Candor" to Lanky almost as an afterthought. Then he was unconscious for a whole day.

Janie Norsworthy traveled farther and farther inland. Several great mounds like green apparitions dotted the flat central-

Yucatan plain. Her archeological group, mostly members of Southern and Western U.S. universities, were a companionable collection of writers, professors, photographers, and other art specialists like Janie herself. And the conversations at night around the campfire, or in rented huts in tiny villages, made her feel once more the call of her profession, her life's effort. Soon the craziness of the caravan, the mental struggle to decide to leave her family—all these faded with the passage of several weeks. More was happening besides, more than the art historian might have bargained for. Emil Kavanaugh, a colleague from Vanderbilt, was paying more and more attention to Janie, sometimes to the point of intruding on her conversations with others. He was always supportive and helpful; his advice, pragmatic and worldly. And she could not find fault with him as a researcher, a Mayan specialist, or as a man. Two things caused her consternation, however. He was married. Janie considered herself a liberated woman but her recent split with Lenny left her more in a mood for aloneness than the pain and readjustment of a new love affair. Janie was just waking up after years of mental stagnation, and she was determined to complete her studies while still in the jungle, then pursue a position in a field that is still vastly overcrowded. She considered, momentarily, stringing Dr. Kavanaugh along to see if he could get her an instructor's job at Vanderbilt. But the effort seemed unworthy of her, nor could she devote her time and planning to become an effective tease. She decided she would be one of the crowd, a "team-spirit," a sort of "agent libre," free of the usual encumbrances of adult society.

Like Diana, she would chastely lead, or follow, her group of travelers in the jungle. This was her final decision on the matter, and she turned her attention to other details. And one night, Dr. Villas's wife Susan reported the words of an old Petén woman she had talked with in the marketplace of a small village nearby. The old woman was brewing an unidentifiable tea over a flat little fire. She said that when she was a girl, her father had traveled about one hundred fifty miles to the southwest. There, not far from the Mexican highlands, her father had brought a group of English bromeliad and orchid traders, and the little girl had been brought along as a helper to her father. She had enjoyed the trip simply to see other places and other customs, but she had not been prepared for the massive stone monuments and mounds she had seen not far from their camp.

It was rainy and her father was not interested. He did not mention the girl's discovery to the English traders for fear that they would disturb spirits that should be sleeping forever.

"I shrugged and then forgot it,"' the old woman had said, amazed at Susan Villas's opened eyes. "No one seemed interested in what a young girl had to say. And my father warned me against repeating the story. He told me that one day he would lead explorers to my lost city. He would make a lot of money, and we would all have enough to eat and something left over besides. So naturally I told no one. Only now Father is dead and I could not lead an expedition if I wanted to."

"You should've seen the look on my face. It must've been rich," laughed Susan. "I calmly asked this woman if she'd make me a little map of her city's location, just out of curiosity," I said. And she drew me a map right then and there. I gave her some food and came back just before dark. I was so excited I forgot to buy any fresh fruit or vegetables in the mercado. That's why we're eating out of cans tonight. But who cares?"

Janie and the others hastily made plans to find the old woman's lost city. It was probably a ceremonial center if it existed at all, but the lead was worth following since no new sites for exploration in Belize, Guatemala, or Mexico had turned up since the pre-Classic Cuello site materialized in northern Belize, not really too far from Altun Ha. Janie's group flew to Mexico's southernmost state of Chiapas, landing in the capital, Tuxtla Gutierrez. There they arranged for guides, settled grant disputes with university officials back home who wanted to know who Janie Norworthy was, and hired porters and assistants for the trek to the lower jungles. Janie knew that something momentous would happen on this trip. Somehow this great ceremonial center, like so many others, waited to be rediscovered after centuries of abandonment. Would it be Classic Maya or Toltec-Maya? There was no way to tell without looking, and the old woman had not told her enough. Her answer awaited her two days to the east by highway, and one on foot to the site the old woman claimed lay filled with stele, carven objects of various stones, tattered remains of buildings long covered with brilliant cloaks of bougainvillea and sinuous strangler fig.

LII Palmyra the Old

Lenny Norworthy wiped his hands on a kitchen towel as he watched his sister-in-law walk home. It was not far, so driving Jeanine was not necessary. She had just finished helping him with the evening pots and pans, those things which you can neither put in the automatic dishwasher nor leave for later when you feel more like scraping cooked-on food. Jeanine had shown him how to leave water in a pot overnight to soften burnt-on food so it would be easier to clean out the next day.

"The only thing you have to remember," she had said, "is you have to put the lid on the pot so roaches can't get in it. If the pan had something sweet in it like chocolate it's better to put the pan in the refrigerator to keep it away from hungry pests."

Lenny knew none of these things before, but with Jeanine's help he was painfully, slowly learning to care for himself and his children. He could wield an iron, cook different kinds of food, and even change a diaper now. He also understood why his wife had been restless with her domestic routine. But then Janie had always been smarter than he ever had been.

But surely she must miss us...if not me, then her children, he thought, putting his wedding band back on. Jeanine was going back to school tomorrow and could not help him as much anymore. And Jeanine herself could not stop talking about how her friends Marti and Betty Sue had come back to town and how she had missed them all desperately during the long, lonely dust-days of July and August. She had not seen them yet due to one delay or another, but she knew she would see them in school tomorrow. Jeanine passed through a crisis of loneliness that summer and was forever changed by her experience. It made her less dependent on the good wishes of her friends, less concerned with pleasing them at her own expense. But in the old way, she longed to giggle with them, discuss boys and clothes and TV shows with her friends. Her biggest sorrow was that Loren would not be sharing in the fun. To Jeanine, Loren was dead. Loren had made no effort to write or call or even send postcards. Jeanine was also miffed by the fact that

Loren and Betty Sue had gotten boyfriends this summer. She had not. She hoped desperately that Marti had shared the same fate. Misery loves company. Misery demands company.

Betty Sue and Marti unpacked their bags the moment they got upstairs in Marti's room. They compared goodies. Marti had bought a lot of boots, belts, and blouses in a store near the place she had worked. Long summer days with no TV had started Marti's reading habit as well. A bunch of tattered romances with names like *Love's Flaming Desire, La Chingada Natchez Kingdom* fell like autumn leaves from her overnight bag.

Betty Sue had gone crazy with her aunt's nagging, and she could not wait to get out of Odessa. They had fought several times during the summer, so much that Betty Sue did something she had not done since her eleventh year; She cried. One good side to visiting her mother's sister was that the woman had no daughters and always enjoyed going shopping with Betty Sue at the mall. Betty's lanky frame and black hair looked fashionable, and her aunt had bought her several pairs of designer jeans, sandals, blouses, and even more embroidered Mexican dresses, all of which she loved for their bright colors and intricate, fancywork designs. The girls spent thirty bright minutes comparing summer loot. As excitement waned (along with promises to exchange clothes often), the girls' conversation turned to boys, school, and other friends.

"Do you think Stanley Burgen and Loretta the Hog are still dating after all this time?" said Betty Sue.

"Ewww! Don't even talk about it, it's so gross! If those two got married they could open their own sideshow of geeks! Ewww, I can't stand it!"

Betty Sue paused, then spoke.

"Have you heard from Loren or Jeanine?" Marti said that she had received weekly letters from Jeanine despite the fact that Marti had not answered most of them. In fact, Marti was glad her parents had sent her out of town for the summer; she herself had needed the rest and distance from the Allemeister thing. At first Marti had bad dreams while away at camp. She often woke with a start and a sudden gasping for air. In the dreams she would be driving, but before she turned around to talk to her cruising friends, she would feel the crunch of metal under the wheels and hear the scream of Karen Allemeister as she was run over. Then she would turn to the others for help, but they would be corpses sitting beside her or in the back seat–Jeanine, Loren, and Betty Sue, their heads lolling at obscenely impossible angles.

Sometimes Marti woke up screaming, but her bunkmate got her calmed down quickly after Marti explained the situation. Her bunkmate, a sophisticated girl from Conroe brushed her long blonde hair as Marti explained what had happened to her on that dark night on a Texas highway. Not only sympathetic, her bunkmate actually stopped combing her hair and listened, rapt at Marti's story of love beyond the grave. The girl was not sure she believed the olive-skinned tennis-type in front of her, but the dreams did explain the occasional screams and frequent noises Marti made at night. Marti became a sort of camp celebrity overnight. It was because, as Betty Sue put it, "People respect experience."

The girls made plans for a happy reunion with Jeanine at school the next day. They all promised to meet in the cafeteria for lunch if they got different home room assignments. And what a glorious year it would be! They were all going to be seniors! But wasn't it sad to start the year without Loren? They agreed the next day, over hot dogs and beans on the green plates and maroon trays, that they would even have been happy to see Petey. But not all that much. Ewww!

It is noon on Sand Island. The gulls fight over some old bait dumped by a passing fishing boat. Shouts in Spanish and Vietnamese could be heard over the bay and onto the white-sand offshore island that was popular with people from all the state, and even visitors from as far away as Canada would try to bargain for a few winter weeks in the condos that were first built by Banks Realty, Inc.

The fishing-boat noises and the squawking of Gulf gulls—like white flies around fish—joined to capture Ed and Brenda's attention. Brenda still ran the laundry and dry cleaning service but she was in the Tropicala more and more often. Edna Parker grew increasingly annoyed with Brenda and her "goddamns" until she realized that the young woman had a crush on Ed. Edna was ashamed of the way she had treated Brenda through most of the summer. She apologized this way one evening near closing time:

"Brenda, I'm sorry I snapped at you sometimes this summer. You see, I'm worried about my boy and...."

"You don't need to apologize, Mrs. Parker. And I think you understand why I'm here now, don't you?"

"Yes I do, Brenda. And I think it's wonderful. I have to go back to Houston in a few days. Let's get to be good friends," asked Edna.

"Only one thing would make me happier," Brenda gave an idiotic grin.

"I know, I know," Edna smiled and sighed. "He'll come around. Don't give up just yet."

"I won't," Brenda said, her eyes glistening either with moisture or determination. Edna could not tell which.

Ed was in the stockroom-taking inventory of his bottles. He counted the unopened cases. He lined up the Pinch bottles, the Chivas Regal bottles, the Stolichnaya bottles. The overhead light cast ghostly glass-reflection shapes around the tiny room. Pretty soon the electricity would be cut off. Pretty soon he would be forced to sell the bar to someone who would abandon the building to the elements, preferring one day to sell the expensive land to a wealthy housebuilder or condominium contractor. And it would be a sad loss for the love life of the community. Almost every love affair that started in Palmyra High or the Red Arrow Café or even the Tetrapylon Game Parlor eventually ended up in the Tropicala. The entrancing neon lights would glow red and green. The lifting wall brought in the sea air. The jukebox and Edna played everything there was to hear.

But that was going to be over soon. Soon the Tropicala would have to close. The summer rush, which usually paid for most of the year's expenses, had been lighter than usual. Several student bars had opened in Harlingen, drawing away the nightclubbing crowd. Now only the regulars could make it to the Tropicala, and that was no longer enough since the Crazy Caravan had taken away most of Ed's business. It was especially hard on Ed because he was getting used to having Brenda around. He talked with her every spare moment he could instead of chatting with the regulars all night long. Brenda usually sat with the regulars anyway, and soon Ed began to listen to her opinions and ideas. Sometimes the regulars and Brenda would even end up arguing politics with Ed, who though a good man, seemed to be blind to everything but

Hispanic issues. Brenda laughed at him sometimes, but usually she defended his ideas.

Brenda also began to change clothes before coming to the Tropicala after work. She began to wear soft-looking blouses and shorts, and on Friday nights a skirt or dress. Brenda had had to work like a man all her young life, but she knew what Ed liked and she studied how to please him. She even tried to clean up her speech. She did fine on everything except the imprecations ascribed to the Deity. One fault, Ed Fernandez had decided, was not too bad.

But the Tropicala was going to close and there was nothing anyone could do about it. He notified the Banks Real Estate agency of his intention to sell. Mary Ann would have been happy to hear of his decision, but she had her own problems at the moment, real estate being the last thing on her mind. How sad, Ed thought. No more sea breeze, no jukebox, no happy inspired drinkers. An institution was passing, and it was taking his livelihood with it.

LIII Too Much, Too Fast

Even the lush tropical splendor of Dangriga had not been enough. Barry and Dauphine had gone to Placentia Point to another hotel. An argument was brewing, had been brewing for two days now. Like the Caribbean, so calm and blue, the words and touches between the lovers had the sham of calm. But it was then the beginning of the hurricane season, and the sun baked the ocean, making it gasp its moisture out to the wind and sky. Far off in the eastern Atlantic near Africa, little collections of thunderstorms questioned each other, "Who will rise to be the Monster? We can't play without a Monster." And then the storm would spin itself into a heat-frenzy, growing larger and large, its eye pressure lower and lower, the winds wound up like a colossal gray top. And on September first, when her daughter was starting her senior year of high school, pregnant Dauphine Candor began arguing with Barry Madden. The pitch of their voices rose six notes, then eight. Guests in rooms next to theirs began to complain to the desk.

The desk clerk knocked on their door. He begged them to stop arguing. Dauphine suddenly appeared at the door and stalked past the dapper little man in a red guayabera shirt. She said, "Excuse me" and walked out to the beach, her face crimson from anger and embarrassment. Barry followed shouting and gesticulating as if trying to show the world something wonderful that it just would not see.

"Who are you, anyway? You come traipsing into my life, take it over, then tell my daughter and me where we're going to live. I just want to know where the hell you get off doing that," said Dauphine.

"Geez, why do you get so defensive? I'm just trying to give you some logical reasons why we should stay here. You make it sound like I'm trying to ram it down your throat or something." Barry watched her pull her white caftan robe more tightly around her shoulders. The wind lifted her hair. He marveled at how young she looked, the color high in her cheeks. She turned and walked to the sea, her bare feet kicking out pinches of sand behind her. "Women! Goddammit! There's no reasoning with them, there's no talking with them, there's no..."

"He thinks he knows everything, the stupid bastard, she thought. Wow. College dropout. Big deal. I should have known better. Why was I so stupid? Why am I here?"

"It's just like talking to a doorknob. I may as well be talking to a doorknob. You want to know why you hate this place? I'll tell you why! You're a Texas hick! You've never been anywhere but Palmyra and you'll never put up with any other place! As far as I'm concerned, you can shove goddamn Palmyra and your penny-ante waitress job because you're not really fit to do a whole lot more."

Dauphine quietly passed from pique to anger, to a burning, silent rage. She stared him squarely in the face.

"What make you so special that I'd want to live with you anyway? You drunk! You, you LOSER!"

Barry hesitated on the brink of attacking her, but even in the heat of his own wrath he found no spot in his being that would allow him to strike Dauphine. But he wanted desperately to hurt her with words, to cut her self-esteem to a nub. No words would come forth. Everything about her that could be said was also true of himself, and he chose not to give her the advantage she would certainly press. He decided to lie.

"Lanky told me all about you. Don't think I don't know! He told me all about your little flings. Salesmen? Ha!"

"At least they work for a living, Loser."

"...as insurance men and realtors and plumbers and who else, Dauphine? Who else did you sleep with?"

"...not your goddamn business. Good God, I'm glad I found out about you in time! And Lanky would never say those things about me!"

An hour later found Dauphine still in a high rage, on a bus back to Belize City. She tapped her sandal impatiently as she listened to a Mexican mother of three fuss and fume over her children. The whining and movement in the seat behind Dauphine nearly drove her crazy. The fat woman in her rebozo seemed unable to get all three children to shut up and sleep. The bus slowed down for the stop in Dangriga, and Dauphine welcomed the chance to get away from the woman and find a new seat. Her stomach was acid-filled and nervous, and she decided to get a Coke in the station. At a grimy little porcelain-topped Cart Blanca table in the station sat a familiar-looking man with a beard. His stare ate through her shoulder, not only undressing her mentally but somehow probing her soul and mind as well. It was the look of someone who had known her a long time. And during one huge thud of her heart, she grew faint and terrified, for she suddenly pieced out the crazy eyes, the shoulders, and even the familiar belly.

He winked at her, shook a beer bottle like a school bell in his hand. She dropped her purse. William Candor was offering her a beer and a bite of his sandwich.

"Just drive, woman, and shut up," the young man shouted. He took a pull on a white Caribbean rum bottle with a picture of a cassowary on the front.

Mary Ann was trying to make herself think, to force herself to assess her situation and think of all the alternatives. If it were to be just rape, she would be lucky. Add robbery and matters still would be bearable: the credit cards replaceable, the traveler's checks ditto. But what if he's planning to murder me? the cloudiness in her mind, the inability to think or plan, passed after half an hour and Mary Ann began to consider her situation. She wished she had not left the hotel or the van that morning. She would have given up her business and her home just to find the passenger seat next to her empty, with nothing pointed at her head but the air conditioned breeze passing over her burning brow. She wanted to speak but was afraid of angering her kidnapper.

"Where are you from?" she asked nervously.

"Mind the road, bitch. Don't need no talking from you."

However, her assailant began eventually to talk about himself anyway, telling her about his unemployment problem, his home life, his school days at St. John's College. He told her it was the best school in Belize, and it had been a shame the school had been removed from Belize City and taken to the capital Belmopan. They continued driving for what seemed like hours though the sun overhead had moved very little. Mary Ann finally had enough.

"What are you planning to do to me?" she asked, staring him in the face. He shifted his eyes away.

"Don't know yet. Turn off up there where you see the dirt road," he said, waving his gun to the side as casually as one would indicate with a pencil. Mary Ann hated to turn. Whatever chances she had would disappear once she left the relative busyness of the two-lane blacktop, but she could not see an easy way out.

"What if I just let..."

"Turn now," he said, and they drove down a two-track dirt road that was free of ruts and seemed to be used often. The road occasionally lightened as the jungle cleared on either side to show a little farm or guinea hen enclosure. Small shacks with green, roundish mango trees near the chicken yard graced the view to one side, and there was thick, foreboding jungle on the other.

"See that house?" the man said. "I want you to stop there." What appeared to be a large child's clubhouse, by American standards, was here a home. An old black man with white hair came stooping out of the low door, wearing a white T-shirt and sandals. The young man hopped out of the car as soon as Mary Ann cut the motor, and he ran to talk with the old man. Mary Ann considered wildly for a moment the possibility of starting the car and, leaving the car in reverse, making a run for the dirt road she had just turned off. But there was no chance of escape. The moment she cranked the engine would be the moment he turned and aimed his gun at her. She decided to wait. At least she was still sitting in her car. The old man seemed to be arguing with the younger one, shaking his finger and shouting words Mary Ann could not hear. "If only I could start the engine, if only I could back out of here in time," she said to herself aloud. All manner of schemes flew through her head, but nothing seemed to buy her enough time to think.

It was too late anyway. They were both heading toward her car.

LIV Happy to See You?

"I can tell you're not too happy to see me," he said casually, as if talking to a lunching co-worker. He quickly told her he would make it all up to her, they would start again somewhere else in Texas or Florida, there was no reason for them to be apart any more. Boss Candor picked his front teeth with a toothpick.

"I make a good living. I'm over my middle-age crazies. You'll see. Everything will be fine. And where's my daughter?" Dauphine still could not speak.

Meanwhile, Mary Ann tried to smile but the strain was too much. She stared at her captors as if wanting for them to sing her a little tune. My God, let it be over quickly, she thought.

"Get out of the car," said the old man. His eyes did not seem cruel or crazed with drugs, so Mary Ann complied. The old man pointed to the shack he had just left.
"You want me to go in there?" she said, swallowing audibly.

"I'm not going to hurt you, lady. Please." She walked over the grassless swept front yard, looking a wildy left and right with darting eye hoping to spot as escape route. None was there for her. The shack was dark except for a postcard-size window. Under its feeble light sat a table and two chairs. She suddenly felt very wealthy, vulnerable, North American.

"Through my young friend's stupidity, you've managed to stumble onto our operation here. That's really unfortunate." He spoke like a midwestern professor, not a poor Belizean farmer.

"What? What operation? I haven't seen a thing, mister. I just want to go back to Belize City, get on a plane, and leave this place. I'm not exposing anyone."

"I wish I could believe you," he said, shaking his gray head. Mary Ann wondered what he was talking about. The younger man stood fixed in the doorway. Mary Ann decided to speak.

"Look, I don't know what you're driving at. I haven't seen anything, anything at all. I'm willing to forget all this if you just let me go."

"I know you haven't meant us any harm, but we have to protect out operation." He began to explain what the operation was, despite her deliberate attempt not to listen. Something occurred to Mary Ann in a moment of brilliance, of a sort of final translucence. Of course the details would be what she had expected already. Of course they grew coca and ganja for Rastafarians. The huge profits from street sale in Brazil and the U.S. and Canada were funding the back-to-Africa movement–buying land, handling legal details, gathering the people for an almost-Biblical migration. And here lay the moment of elucidation for Mary Ann: she had seen nothing, heard nothing since the young man had pulled the gun on her. An irony–weren't all things so? The elucidation, the transcendent fact she had sought all these years lay in the faces of these two strange men. That fact? Mankind is ravening beasts, almost limitless in their search for moronic violence. Here she was, being led out into the yard to be killed so that several thousand credulous dope-smokers could worship Haile Selassie and return to an Africa that did not want them.

The gun clicked behind her head. She was vaguely aware of a hen clucking softly behind her in the sideyard. *The Chicken of Death?* She thought. How amusing. Goodbye world, goodbye. So long sky, so long flowers, goodbye fr—....

"So where's Betty Sue?" asked Boss.

"She's back in Palmyra, of course."

"You're lying, I was just there."

"She was somewhere else, yes, but now school's started. How come such a sudden interest in your daughter after all these years?"

"Don't get smart with me. You know what'll happen if you start gettin' smart with me."

She said nothing. What was there to say?

"Let's go back to Texas. I heard about your boyfriend. He good as me?"

"I don't want to talk about it."

"Really? What happens when you have your bastard baby? You gonna take care of it, maybe? Huh?" Bill grabbed her upper arm and held it tight. Dauphine yanked it away violently.

"You don't touch me! I'm not married to you anymore." Bill looked surprised, then angry.

Dauphine hissed, "I don't want either of you! I don't need him and I don't want you! I'm leaving."

He tried to get on the bus with her, but Dauphine had the presence of mind to tell the driver that the man was bothering her. He glared at Candor when he tried to board the bus.

"Sorry, sir. You have to pay a fare." This provided a way out of the confrontation. But Candor pulled out his wallet and gave the driver $20.00. Candor got on the bus and sat as near as he could to his ex-wife, who had already made sure she was not sitting alone. For her efforts she had to listen to a talkative black nun from Benque Viejo, who wanted to know a lot about life in Texas. Dauphine's head swam with fear and anxiety over Candor's presence, but after an hour she got used to and even enjoyed telling things to the sprightly little nun with Coke-bottle lens glasses. Dauphine felt like a celebrity telling all the people on the bus about her life back in Texas. The little nun, Sister Angela, taught school at St. Catherine's Academy in Belize City. She had some old, old parents back in Benque Viejo who ran a small feed and seed store and a tiny little postage-stamp tavern adjoining it. During the trip back, a huge thunderstorm from the east forced the driver off the road. The sky grew darker, releasing ozone freshness to the jungle air. Most of the lightning was cloud-to-cloud, to everyone's relief. Candor made no attempt to speak to his wife, but she caught him looking at her somberly, sometimes grinning. He's a wolf, she thought. He wants to eat me alive.

Dauphine felt a hot tear course down her face. She was glad the tear was running on the side of her face next to the bus window. That way Sister Angela and William could not see her fear and anxiety. Dauphine blessed the storm for drawing attention away from her. The rain pounded the thin metal roof for thirty minutes, then the storm lifted. The day seemed much later than the three p.m. it really was. Ands the bus pulled into Belize City. The front of the terminal was lined with several cabs, one of whose driver's took Dauphine's bags with a scowl on his face. William saw her leave on the road through town toward Ladyville and the airport. Through Elena's generosity, all SAHSA, TACA, and Air Florida flights were instructed to board Crazy Caravan passengers for whatever destination they wished. Dauphine would catch the afternoon flight to Houston, then arrange a Greyhound bus trip back to Palmyra. It would take a long time and would be grueling to her, but there was no alternative. Her life had changed within the course of an afternoon. That morning she had been with Barry; now she was headed back, alone, to the U.S. She reflected bitterly on her situation. It seemed to her that not only could men not be trusted to stay; they also could not be trusted to stay away. She was saddled with the attentions of a man she now despised and feared, and she longed for Barry to defend and comfort her. But Barry was a thousand years ago from that very morning, when they had still been together. That was over now as well. The prospect of getting rid of Candor, especially if he chose to return to Palmyra, tired her. Doing without Barry and then having his baby anyway doubly exhausted her. She took a cab to Ladyville and went through customs. The friendly young customs official told her goodbye, and she waited in a tiny little sitting room with a T-shirt shack and souvenirs in it. A Mennonite lady and three black men sat talking about their children as Dauphine entered. From around the corner came Barry, holding a Coke bottle! Dauphine's eyes grew wide but she could not move toward him. Her ex-husband was also in the terminal. And the three of them would be together soon. Another unpleasant prospect.

LV At the Nursing Home

Pasha Tikhonov lay in bed facing the ceiling. There was no familiar radio here, there were no lawn ornaments, there was no wife looking for gypsies in the dark of night. How lovely and charming had been his wife's few faults! And how long must a man live before he finally knows that his wife is the only real gift God can give a man on this earth? He longed for even her nagging, her habit of overeating, her monumental and irrational fears. And the pleasures of her company he longed for, even more so. Aloneness was a terrible burden for a man who had not been alone for more than sixty years. Through the Great War, the Second War, the Bomb, the Cold War—he had lived through them all, laughing in his confident, hearty way. All problems he could solve. There were no real problems to him. But his wife Yelena's death was a problem he simply could not deal with. He shook his head all day; he hoped that he would turn around and see her coming in the screen doors complaining about the heat. But her death and this move had gotten to him. It really had gotten him. Something in his mind had cracked or split open, and whatever cerebral vial holds our desire to go on was shattered, allowing Pasha to prepare himself for death.

Every day he lit a holy candle and prayed to the icons of the Virgin and St. Methodius. The other people in the home were Russians like him. And their backgrounds were similar. But he did not care for their company even though he was extremely polite, remembering to pay call for call, loan for loan, favors for favor. But no one—not even the youngish Praskovia Petrovna, just in her sixties-- could bring him out of his shell. "What a shame," said the nurses. "He really does want to die." He scratched his nearly baldhead and flipped on the light. He had had two glasses of wine for dinner—far too much for him. They had helped to keep him awake. It was just as well, however; he needed to sign his will. Since Yelena was gone and he was not sure about any other relatives, he asked himself: "Who gave us the most pleasure and happiness while we were alive?" He stared at the ceiling again, then at the icon of St. Methodius. The next day he called a lawyer and constructed a revision of his will. The house, its contents, and approximately $2.9 million went to the nice man whose jukebox in his bar the old couple used to listen to on quiet evenings Pasha laughed. He found out the nice man's name was Mr. Fernandez, his investigator had told him. Ed was also getting ready to marry a woman named Brenda. That Pasha approved of also. The other half of his estate went to the Orthodox Church. As an afterthought he offered a Gypsy spokesman from New York $400,000 to the first ten gypsies who agreed to settle down in one place. He did this in memory of his wife. It was the least he could do for her after her death, and his. Which happened September 15, 1984. The next three days—the 16th, 17th, and 18th—dawned on a very shocked and surprised Ed Fernandez and his fiancée Brenda. They suddenly found themselves multimillionaires if they kept the Tropicala open. In the Harlingen office of the Tikhonovs' lawyer, Ed Fernandez found that his pullover was sticking to his back although he did not know whether the wetness was caused by nerves or the heat or both. When summoned to the reading of the will, Ed was almost afraid that there was some problem with it, that somehow he would be paying money for some kind of legal fee--that is the way it usually worked.

But when the will was read, all he could say was, "This must be some kind of a mistake. I don't know who those people are. ..Uh, were." After a few minutes of description, however, the lawyer finally made Ed recall a few instances of seeing the old couple briefly from the causeway or in town. Neither he nor anyone else in town had suspected that the eremitic Tikhonovs were, in effect, the richest people in town after Elena Muñoz.

After finally accepting the will's reality, Ed asked for a re-reading of any conditions on the document. Surely there must be some horribly debilitating or limiting codicils that would somehow take the money from him or limit his use of it severely.

"There is one condition," the lawyer said, pushing his glasses back up on his nose. Ed braced himself. The lawyer took a sip of water out of his coffee mug. "The will states that you cannot sell the Tropicala. You have to keep it in your or your family's possession for at least twenty more years. That's all."

Ed ran to a phone. Brenda would be at work.

Dauphine's wild hope was that the two men would not recognize each other, but that did not happen. Whether they recognized each other from their high school days or whether from mere animal rival senses, the two men faced each other down. Dauphine feared for both of them. She called a security guard from one of the airport's doorways. Her airplane was leaving. There was no time to breathe or think or do anything else. She could either get on the plane or forget both of them, or she could go with Barry, or she could go back to the U.S. with William. Three choices and no more. Until she created a fourth choice; she threw up and fainted. About an hour later she woke up the Maya Air Office where the owner had kindly given her a couch. Sister Angela and the two men were looking at her from overhead. She was ill, but she croaked a question.

"Would someone please take me to the Airport Motel? I have some thinking to do."

Sister Angela got permission to stay with Dauphine for a night. Then the following day Wanda came to the motel to stay with her. Dauphine talked and cried and agonized over her decision for two days. These days would determine the rest of her life, and she knew she would have to come to the right decision.

The next day passed with Dauphine's deep need for sleep not answered. She remembered vaguely saying goodbye to Sister Angela and hello to Wanda, who had a new tan. Dauphine was jealous and said so. Then she fell asleep for six more hours. When she finally woke on the morning of September 20, Wanda and Lanky and Petey were sitting at a corner table in a neighboring suite, playing Chinese checkers. Petey was laughing his gurgly laugh. Dauphine stumbled into the room. They looked up at her.

"I've made up my mind," she announced. Deep down inside, Wanda also knew that she would be making a decision soon too. Maybe it was all too soon.

Zillah and Otto got to talking about old times at Los Cocos but neither wanted to go back.

"It's this way," Zillah said, leaning her fold-up chair against the Winnebago and fanning herself with a rattan fan with a little Belizean cottage scene painted on it in egg tempera. "I can't go back home to that life 'cause it wouldn't no life. You can't either."

Otto sighed and agreed. He would not know what to do outside the service of Miss Muñoz and though he felt as loyal as ever, all the sudden changes and abrupt dislocations had disturbed his tranquility.

"I even miss der bird," he offered.

"Me too," said Zillah.

LVI Decision

To make matters short, Dauphine chose to stay with Barry. Barry begged her to come back to him, and that they would return to Palmyra if that were what Dauphine really wanted. Boss Candor was summoned to Dauphine's room. Lanky and Wanda were there with her just in case there was trouble. Candor took the news quietly, his eyes meditative, dark.

"I guess your choice is final?" he asked.

"Yes. There have been too many years apart. You never came to visit your own daughter, and I don't really know what you're up to now." Boss Candor fingered the sleeves of his red pullover knit shirt.

"I'm going to hurt you," he said quietly—almost as an afterthought—as he left. Wanda asked him what he could have meant.

"Oh, probably nothing," said Dauphine, but her eyes showed her fear.

"Oh my God," said Wanda. "What about Betty Sue?"

"He wouldn't, would he?"

"I don't know," said Wanda. "I wasn't ever married to him." Dauphine's spine shivered. She packed to go home on the next plane. Boss had left already, so Dauphine made a phone call to the States from the U.S. Embassy.

"Hi Mom! I'm so glad to hear your voice!" cried Betty Sue.

"Listen to me. Your father's coming to Palmyra. Don't get in the car with him! Don't even talk to him. Quick, put Marti's mother on the phone, I want to talk to her."

"But Mom, she—"

"DO IT!" shrieked Dauphine. Marti's mother promptly came on the line, and Dauphine explained the situation. Marti's mother felt sure that no one could enter her house uninvited, but she told Dauphine she would see to it that the sheriff would drive by every day, and she herself would take the girls to school every day. Dauphine said she would be home in a day and a half. When she hung up the phone she prayed that Boss Candor would return to whatever hole he came from.

Mary Ann woke up. That in itself seemed strange. So this was heaven! Only her head hurt where the young man had knocked her unconscious. At length it all came back to her. A radio was playing somewhere in her hazy half-conscious mind. She heard, of all things, the Sister Thompson Radio Revival Hour. The good Sister was now off the air but she had made tapes of some of her best shows, and they were being aired in Belize. Mary Ann's head throbbed. The feeling reminded her of the way her head felt after having been blasted in the ears chaperoning a school dance. She had gone home to her husband and lain on the couch. Back then he was still alive.

"Did you have a nice time?" he had asked casually.

"You're really cruel, you know that?" she had said. Her head felt like a pumpkin stuffed with excelsior for days after that. Now she was hot and sore and she wanted a bath. Looking up, she was the blue tint of the windshield. She was in the back seat of her car, and the key was in the ignition. The radio was her own car radio. She did not recognize the surrounding countryside, but at least she was alive. she switched off the radio and grabbed the sore spot at the back of her head, mouthing the word "Ooh!" noiselessly as she kneaded the bruise that lay under her hair. Suddenly aware that her captors might be nearby, she looked quickly around the car. No one was there. Apparently she was free to go. Before three hundred yards there was a sign that said:
BELIZE 15 KM

All the better for her. Corozal would have to be forgotten. Mary Ann had somehow escaped death. Maybe her philosophy about mankind was incorrect. She saw a torn envelope on the passenger seat beside her. Picking it up, she saw a scrawled message:

We're just looking for a sign from the sky.
We decided not to kill you for one reason only:
You were too vulnerable. Remember your promise.

There was no signature. What did it mean? Were they some kind of cult? Had some other unhappy people come to Belize before the Crazy Caravan? And what was her "promise"? That much was easy. She soon remembered she was not to tell what happened to her. She never did.

LVII Going Home and Kaan Ek

After saying goodbye to their friends and making a call on Sister Angela, Dauphine, and Barry boarded the TACA jet back to Houston. After an hour the plane landed back in the U.S. Dauphine rapped her fingers nervously on the chair's arm, almost as if she wanted to grasp it, throw herself out of the chair, and fly to Palmyra on her own wings. A black dread surrounded her, weighing her heart down and making rational thought impossible. She feared for her daughter's safety. Barry put his hand over hers, stilling the tattoo of her nervous fingers.

"What do you think he'll try to do to her?" Barry said, dredging up the unspeakable.

"He won't kill her; after all, she's his own daughter, but I don't know what he's capable of."

Dauphine told Barry about the happy years of their marriage then about William's growing brutality of spirit, his gradual refusal to support his wife and daughter. He seemed to enjoy the looks of fear and disappointment in his wife's eyes. When she had lost track of him, he had reverted to some kind of aging teen, a womanizer and a drunk completely out of control. Barry flinched to hear those words. After all, they had pretty much described him as he had been for most of his adult life. The same thought occurred to Dauphine but it was too late to change what she had said.

Near sunset, Janie and her archeological group scanned the hot green horizon of the Mexican jungle.

"It's got to be around here," she said. They were not too far from the Rio Grijalva, cutting its way through the mountains and forests quite certain of its destination.

"Maybe it's over this embankment," she pointed to her left. It rapidly dawned on her the embankment was the side of an ancient promenade of some kind. She crawled to the top of the hill. Gigantic stele and mounded temples looked benignly back at her. Janie Norworthy stood quietly with her mouth open. She also wet her pants. The large planet Venus stood over the plaza, shining like a silent jewel. The rest of the group clambered up the hill behind her. Janie later named the city Kaan Ek—Precious Star, after the planet Venus that appeared so beautiful in the night sky. The rest of the group, toasting one another with Dos Equis, agreed to the name. The excavations would begin the very next day. Janie had achieved her moment of triumph. Even though Susan Villas got the map for the expedition, it had been Janie Norworthy who pushed hardest to make the expedition a reality. Now she and Susan shared the moment of triumph, both reveling in the other's success as well.

They could forget about their job worries. Their careers would be made. As far as their eyes could see, there was no end to the ceremonial center. Ornate carved snakes writhed in the air at the temple crests. Janie would not sleep that night.

Chuck came upon Loren, who was sitting on the Foreshore point, looking across the bay towards Bird's Isle. The shadow of Bliss Lighthouse fell behind her.

"You're crying," Chuck said. Petey ran up behind him. He saw Loren crying and veered off towards Albert Street. He could not comprehend Loren's upset. He loved Belize City.

"I don't know why I'm acting like this, it's so stupid," she snuffled into her wrinkled blue Kleenex. "I'm just so homesick. I miss my friends. And school has started without me. Now I won't graduate from high school with Marti and Jeanine and Betty Sue."

Chuck tried to be supportive. He sat beside her and put his arm around her in an almost avuncular embrace.

"You know, I feel the same way. I want to go to school, too, and maybe we could go while we're here waiting for Elena to come back. Or maybe we could talk your parents into letting us go back. I could leave tomorrow, I suppose. Mom and Dad don't know I'm not in school, and I haven't told them about it. But I don't want to leave without you."

She still had her face covered with the Kleenex. Frigate birds hovered overhead. Gulls and pelicans fought for fish in the bay. Chuck put his face closer to hers and kissed her nose. She did not move.

"Maybe," he said, "we're not supposed to be going back."

"Don't say that!" shouted Loren. "You're mean to say something like that!"

"Maybe I'm not, though. Look at things the way they are, Loren. Maybe we'll go to school here, maybe we won't. But look at what Elena's trying to do here. You told me what you and your friends used to do, all that driving around and high school stuff. What if what Elena is doing is really important? What if we left and went home just when something really important is going to happen here?"

"I don't care about her stupid school, I don't care about her kooky visions! I just want to have a normal life like any other girl. And I want to be with you, too, but not here."

"If we go back, you and I will be split up. Remember that I don't live in Palmyra. I live in Houston."

"That's another reason I'm crying," she said. Two grackles battled in a yard not far away. Chuck and Loren stared out to sea, comforted by the other's touch. Petey was trying to steal mangoes off a tree in someone's yard.

Mary Ann decided to check into the hotel at the International Airport. It was time to go home, a little voice told her. She called her travel agent in Belize and cancelled all further plans. Yet she knew she would come back again, if only for a visit. All she could think about now was the comforts of her own den and bed. She even looked forward to going to her office. She strolled around the hotel and talked with some businessmen from Baton Rouge who were on vacation with their wives. It was nice to hear American accents again. Just as the band began to warm up, Mary Ann glanced at the lounge door where couples kept coming in. A man with graying hair walked through the door by himself. Mary Ann recognized him with a little cry: it was her lover from Coatzacoalcos. She rose and left her group without a word.

"Arturo," she said almost in a whisper.

He smiled, took off his sunglasses. Behind him in the parking lot she could see his little white Fiat.

Mary Ann's plans always had a way of changing.

LVIII Four Calls and More

"I'm not supposed to talk to you."

"Why not, honey? I'm your father."

"Mama told me not to talk to you."

"Can it be so bad if we talk over the phone?"

"I guess not. What do you want to talk about?"

"I don't know what Dauphine has told you, but I'm not a monster."

"She never said that."

"Why don't we get together and talk?"

"Uh-uh. No way."

CLICK.

An hour later.

"Hello?"

"Just checking, Betty Sue. It's me, Mama."

"Dad called."

"What did he want?"

"He wanted to talk to me."

"Did he say to meet him somewhere?"

"Yes, but I said no."

"Good. Don't leave Marti's house for any reason. We'll be in Palmyra in two and a half more hours."

CLICK.

"Are all the papers in order now?"

"Yes, Miss Muñoz. We need a little time to deal with the embassy here. They have the contacts to make everything a lot easier. You never know how deals are going to go in Guatemala."

"Okay, Mr. Arriaga, you can handle it, I'm sure. When do you think we'll be able to leave for Belize?"

"Two weeks tops. Probably a week and a half."

"You certainly have a grasp of American slang."

"I studied law at Loyola in New Orleans."

"I see. Call me when all the bureaucratic nonsense is over."

"Will do. See you later."

CLICK.

"I've been thinking about the future lately," said Ed Fernandez.

Silence.

"And what have you decided?"

"Well, we shouldn't be talking about it over the phone."

"Want me to meet you at the Tropicala tonight?"

"Yeah.... we meet there every night, don't we?" observed Ed, laughing.

"I guess we do....Do you love me?"

"I don't know. Who are you?"

"Silly bastard."

"Okay"

CLICK.

Even though Betty Sue was not supposed to leave the house, she figured there would be no harm in going to the pool in the backyard. Marti's mother had almost said no, but there was a clear view of the swimming pool from the drawing room table (where she liked to drink coffee and do the crossword puzzle from the Corpus Christi newspaper), so she said okay. Both girls were big and athletic. They could also scream like sirens. An abductor would have a hard time subduing them, let alone catching them. Marti's mother took a bite of toast. Certainly nothing could happen right there in full view of herself and her neighbors, who had also been alerted to the potential danger.

Marti got out of the bathroom first. She passed Betty Sue in the hall and said, "See you at the pool." Marti threw the towel over her shoulder and walked toward the sliding glass door. Her mother looked up from her paper as if to ask where Betty Sue was. The toilet seat coming down gave her her answer. Marti stepped out of the house into the searing Texas autumn heat. Summer sometimes never gives up here, she thought, feeling the blast of hot air and the odor of chlorine fumes.

When Betty Sue came out a few minutes later, Marti's mother noticed that her face was even brighter than usual. It must be because her mother's going to be here, she thought.

"I'd better go out and sit with you girls. You know your mother's going to be here in about an hour, and I don't want us to take any chances."

"Oh, that's all right. No one can bother us."

"Just the same, I want to--"

The middle-aged woman in the white caftan stood looking at the empty pool area. Marti's shoes were sitting skewed on the lawn next to the towel. A large black car roared down the road. Betty Sue screamed and grabbed the woman's arm.

"DAD'S GOT MARTI!! HE THINKS IT'S ME!!"

They ran into the house to call the police. Someone pounded on the front door. Marti's mother ran to her bedroom night table and got out her pistol.

"Who is it?" she said, her cheek to the wood of the door.

"It's Dauphine, Mary. Let us in."

The black car pulled into a dirty alley behind the Tetrapylon Video Game Parlor. There was a pickup truck rented from the Muñoz U-Haul on Highway 77 was loaded with what appeared to be a sheeted figure. The two dogs owned by the Tetrapylon's manager were barking their heads off.

A car screeched around the corner as the U-Haul pulled out into traffic, its driver confident that the girl could not be seen. Barry glanced at the truck briefly as he passed. He saw a misshapen lump in the rear of the pickup? Could it be . . . The . . .? Looking farther down the road, he saw no sign of traffic. The truck turned right at the next corner behind him. The lump in the rear tried to sit up.

Ed and Brenda Fernandez were driving home from Corpus Christi where they had been married at ten in the morning. A friend of Brenda's from high school was a witness, and so was the Justice of the Peace's wife. All the blood tests and other details had been worked out before. Ed Fernandez now found his life considerably altered. He was now the second richest person in Palmyra, and he would be the richest if the crazy Muñoz lady never came back. There had been plenty of gossip to that effect and his new wealth and its conferred status amused him.

However, he worried about Chuck for Edna's sake--her boy so far from home in a country she knew so little about. The kids, at least, were supposed to be returning soon. Brenda touched his shoulder lightly as he drove.

"What's wrong?" she asked gently. "You're not getting cold feet now, are you?"

"No, I'm worried about Edna. I'm sorry. It's just that her boy is stuck down in that place without any really stable adults to guide him. I guess I'd be worried too."

"Worry about it tomorrow," she said, whispering. "Save me your attention for tonight. I don't want you distracted. After all, it's my wedding day." Ed smirked and gave her a significant look.

Not too far from Cigüena Lagoon, Ed got out of his new Mercedes to check what he thought was a small air leak in his left front tire. The truth of the matter was that he was not used to the "flat" look of steel-belted radials and he assumed there were small leaks in every tire. Brenda laughed at him when he got out of the car, but she barely had time to chuckle once she heard Ed scream "Jesus!" and jump over the hood of the car. A U-Haul pickup truck came within inches of hitting the car and Ed himself.

"Goddammit!" said Brenda.

Soon a silver Mercedes and a rental car containing Barry, Betty Sue, and Dauphine were chasing the U-Haul over a series of back roads and ended up going south back into Palmyra. Marti finally untied herself and sat up in the bed of the pickup, screaming over the noise of the truck and the honking horns. She saw Ed's face contorted in anger. She saw his face change as he realized she was captive.

And Marti also felt horror when she saw an old bicycle and a mattress in the truck with her.

Her shriek carried all the way to the second car. She scrunched up into a ball in the far corner of the pickup.

William Candor did a stupid thing. He had been drinking to build up his courage, but it had impaired his judgment. He took the Highway 77-exit spur for Palmyra, essentially trapping himself in the town. Nearly a thousand late-season tourists screamed along Tooley Boulevard as the U-Haul ran red light after red light, cutting off the street crossing of kids in swimsuits or young women pushing strollers. The other two vehicles howled after them, closely followed by two Palmyra patrol cars.

Suddenly they were at the gates of Los Cocos and Candor slammed through the gate. They were at the Rise, and any position Candor took could be easily defended from the third-floor jalousie room. He also knew the house was empty now. But there was no time to react or think. Marti jumped out of the truck the moment Candor stopped. He chased her across the yard, tackled her, and hit her in the temple with the butt of his gun.

The other cars flew into the driveway as Candor pulled Marti's slumped and bloodied form to his chest. Her drooping face was aimed at his attackers.

Dauphine shouted his name.

"Bill! Bill! Listen to me! That's not Betty Sue! It's a friend of hers! Drop her, Bill! I'll do anything, but just drop her! DROP HER!"

The police pulled up behind them. Bill saw that Marti did not resemble either him or Dauphine, that she was not his daughter. He steeled himself. He would use this girl to get out, and he would kill her if he had to.

"SEND THE COPS OUT!" he screamed. "OR I'LL BLOW THIS BITCH'S BRAINS OUT, I MEAN IT! MOVE IT! "

The policemen moved back slowly, their momentum ruined. Bill backed up toward the thickly palmed yard. He dragged Marti by the armpits. Betty Sue jumped out of the car.

"Daddy!" she cried.

Candor turned his puzzled face toward her and stepped on something.

SQUEAK!

Startled, he shot wildly into the air and tripped over the source of the noise. The police and Barry and Ed were on him in seconds.

Who would have thought it? A policeman with a pot belly and apple cheeks picked the thing up and brought it to his partner. The ambulance that took Marti to Kenedy County General wee-oh'd off into the distance; the police car-taking Candor to jail left silently.

"A toy animal?" asked the sergeant.

"I guess so," said the other.

"Some crime fighter."

"Who? Me or the skunk?"

LIX Penúltimo

September eased into October; then six months, then a year went by. It began to rain in Belize during the nights, the soft patter tapping on tin roofs around Belize City. On No Name Cay, Elena sat up late nights trying to figure out how best to run her school. She now had a cup of black coffee and opened an old envelope postmarked from Coatzacoalcos. It was from Mary Ann, who everyone said had just disappeared.

"Dear Elena,

I'm sorry to go away without letting anyone know, but I ran into a man I met in Coatzacoalcos that night when so many disasters happened. I can't tell you all the things that have come my way. Arturo wants me to stay with him. He's fifty-five and slender. There's been no talk about marrying but he seems like the type--he has two sons from a youthful marriage. They all treat me like a queen. I know I'll never leave here, and I'm taking courses at the local autonomous university as soon as my grasp of Spanish is better. I seem to be learning faster than I ever thought I could.
I also wanted to ask if you could think of a possible buyer for my business in Palmyra. I need to sell it.

Be sure to tell me about your school and new life on No Name Cave.

Love,
Mary Ann Banks--hopefully soon--Quintano"

Elena folded the letter carefully. They had both been through so much during the caravan, she and Mary Ann, yet Elena felt she had never really taken the time to know Mary Ann better. But one day, maybe, the ex-realtor would come from Coatzacoalcos for a visit.

Out in the yard Elena heard the sound of José, the First Child, pulling on the padlocks on the front gate to see that they were secure. More and more material was arriving from the US, Japan, and Europe every day--telescopes, NASA publications, world literature books, art supplies, books on computers and camping and cooking: there seemed no end to stocking the two-story library which glistened with shiny black Polarized windows and a brilliant white stucco finish. Thinking about Mary Ann had led her to answer the letter right away:

"Dear Mary Ann,

I, too, don't know how to start this letter. I know that I won't bother you with too many details. It's enough to know that I got 100 orphans to feed, love, clothe, and educate. Some days I don't think I'll make it, but in my heart of hearts I know I am happy to be doing what I do. The days fly by so fast; I barely sit down for a breath before I realize it's time to get up again. As you know, I am preparing these children to be a vanguard to outer space. That is my duty to myself, the thing I wanted to find out by coming down here. And I have certainly found out what my duty is! It's strange that one part of my duty to myself in life is to do my duty to other people.

I miss Palmyra and Popol Vuh and horrible old Kuon. I miss the old life in general because it was so pleasant and, in its own way, carefree. But now, whether through design or just blind luck, I'm doing something else, wearing a new set of clothes and yet not trying to make myself a teacher mentality. I know I am to prepare the young generation to leave this world and move on to the next--and not because this world is so terribly polluted or in danger of war. Those are possible, certainly. It's just that there is only one more place that can give humankind a sense of wonder, and that's the rest of the Universe itself. Other than loving and caring for one another, that's the only thing that really matters--knowing what is truly out there and what its nature is.

All my life I have been unquiet. My soul has not been at ease. But now it is.

Philosophy has never been my department, so I leave the reasoning to you. I've had a revelation. I didn't think such things were possible anymore.

Otto and Zillah are still with me here, still working hard despite their (our?) ages. They will be retiring here with me as soon as I work out some kind of pension fund down here. Who knows? They may even live together to pool their income. Race doesn't mean much here. Otto and Zillah fight all the time, as you well know, but I think they'd be sad without each other.

Don't sell your business. Turn over the operation to Barry and Dauphine. You know they can handle it. Why don't you split the profits with them fifty-fifty? That way there will be an extra income for you and a job for Barry and Dauphine.

Chuck and Loren flew back to the States last week after helping me get everything started at No Name Caye. The children love them, and everybody went out to the launch to see them off to Belize City, which is about forty-seven miles from here. All the little ones cried and so did Chuck! Loren and he say they're coming back to work with me after a brief visit home to Chuck's parents who live in Houston. Lanky and Wanda are still here in Belize. Something is going on with L. and W. but I don't know what. They've been out here with Petey twice to visit Loren and Chuck, but I noted a certain tension between mother and father.

Please come see us and what we're doing here at No Name Caye. There's so much to tell you and not enough paper to write it all down. You know you're always welcome."

She signed the letter, read it over casually, then stuffed it in an envelope. She got out of her chair and went to the gigantic new porch with its white stucco sweep and cantilevered terracing down to the sea. The glittering night sky performed as if on a stage. All Elena ever had to do was to stare off into space and smell the sea air, and her mind would turn to sensations of immensity that the universe had to offer. The feeling was not religious at all; Elena did not believe in much that she could not see or feel. The universe was somehow even more mysterious to her when when emptied of its caretaker deity. In any case she was of two minds about the existence of God. Just like everybody else.

Leaning over the railing she saw to her left and right the transplanted coconut palms, their greenness turned gray in the somber moonlight. Shadow-fronds grew on white building everywhere. The wind ran in freshets between the stark-white buildings--the long low dormitories, the swimming pools, the still-unfinished observatory, the oddly terraced classroom buildings covered with plants, all windows facing the sea and the sky.

Room would be made for other students later; for now the orphans' education and care was her first concern. Many of them had had parasites and deficiency diseases. At first there had been a lot of nightmares and screams in the temporary tents that had been erected before the buildings could be completed.

Despite all her troubles, Elena was attracting the attention of NASA and of the Belize government. If there was any income to be derived from space, the government wanted to be in the deal from its inception. Elena liked that. She had government ministers and their families visiting at her new mansion/administration building, also called "Los Cocos" but looking (almost) entirely different. Elena insisted on jalousies. The wind was so strong and cool that it usually did away with the need for air conditioning, especially at night. And besides the buildings–four dormitories, recreation buildings, library, botanical complex, observatory, classroom buildings and mansion there was also a wharf and boat house, as well as a cleared space very similar to the kissing part of Sand Island, but just for being alone. If a space station were to be started, it would be on the mainland directly across from No Name Caye.

She now could hear José checking the emergency generator shed as the last part of his rounds. Most power came from windmills and abundant solar power, fresh water from huge rain cisterns. The initial investment for these independence-making machines had been high, but contributions had started coming in from people around the world, people who were starting to ask for sane policies for this world and a view to the future just as enlightened, humane, and foresighted.

Elena also decided that national governments are basically obsolete, and it is only the threat of nuclear war that maintains national borders and laws, which prohibit commerce and ideas from traveling between areas of the world. Elena also started exploring the worlds of physics and chemistry. She hired a professor to tutor her on subatomic physics. For the first time in her life Elena learned that common sense and cause-and-effect do not apply to the subatomic realm. That particular revelation upset her so much that she made a pitcher of margaritas and went out to her porch. She had promised herself that she would drink a great deal less than she had in her life before, but after reading *The Dancing Wu Li Masters*, she had a small relapse. Otto and Zillah often sat with her, and more often than not Elena got up to fill their glasses or snack plates. They usually chatted about less disturbing matters than quantum physics.

Zillah had taken to wearing red hibiscuses in her hair. They stood everywhere at attention in her graying hair. She also started wearing homemade muumuus around the house and in the garden instead of her dowdy old uniform. Elena had even heard her laugh once when Otto ran into the compound carrying a large conch and slipped on some wet grass. He was not hurt but his dignity had been ruffled. He grinned with embarrassment.

"You fell down," cackled Zillah.

"Ja," was what Otto said.

During the year the young Mennonite couple keeping Kuon let him go because he was sowing his wild oats all over town.

There were odd combinations of puppies, all half German shepherd, in the little Mennonite settlement not far from Altun Ha. His profligacy an embarrassment to all concerned, Kuon was released to the forest, where he fell into the hands of a detachment of the Belize Defense Force on maneuvers. One soldier who had worked at the customs office in Corozal recognized the dog from when Elena had first come into the country. The detachment borrowed a British launch and took Kuon to No Name Caye. Kuon was overjoyed to see Elena. He kept barking and running in circles. Elena immediately sent José to Belize City to order a whole box of rubber skunks. After all, as Dauphine had found, rubber skunks turned out to be pretty lucky. After José had left, Elena was sad that everything had been replaced or returned to her but Popol Vuh. Even Kuon that evening sensed sadness in his mistress, and he sat at her feet quietly. When José came in he had a rubber skunk already. By some miracle, one had been on the shelf of a Belize City supermarket next to some little plastic toys and novelties. José also carried something in his left hand. There was a sort of backdoor smirk on his face as Otto watched him hand the box to Elena, who looked at José questioningly and lifted the lid. Out flew a young but apparently lazy banana-beaked toucan. Now the house was truly a home again. There were no officials or guests that evening, so Elena played her new ondes martenot for Otto and Zillah and Kuon and the new bird. After a light snack of crackers and avocados, the discussion turned to the naming of the bird.

"Kaiser!" suggested Otto.

"Kaan Ek," said Elena, more suggesting than demanding, in honor of Janie's discovery.

"Amy," said Zillah, "--after my mother."

"But it is a male," said Otto.

"Amy," said Zillah, frowning.

The name was finally fixed as Amy. It was just as well, since the bird's aimless flying habits were like Popol Vuh's.

LX Ultimo

Chuck and Loren took Petey with them to Houston, and before their return to Belize they rode a bus to Palmyra.

"I'm sorry but neither of you can come with me," said Loren that evening in the motel. "I've got a date."

Chuck, the young newlywed, looked up with a combination of surprise, sorrow, and anger on his face. Loren laughed at him.

"Silly you. I'm going cruising with my old girlfriends." And she did exactly that. Marti and Betty Sue were going to a junior college in Brownsville. Jeanine was going to Austin to attend the University of Texas part time. She had gotten over her troubles and no longer blamed herself for Janie's desertion. She did not even see it as a desertion anymore; rather, she saw it as a change that had to happen. Her only regret was Janie's haste and cruel words.

Janie had returned briefly to pick up her personal possessions before moving to New Orleans to begin her appointment as an assistant professor of archeology. Jeanine left the Atwell house before Janie arrived so she would not have to look at her sister. Janie hoped that Jeanine would understand one day. Lenny was civil to Janie when he met with her by arrangement at the Red Arrow Cafe. The beach people were gone and there was a gray, early evening pallor over the world.

"I'm glad you didn't bring the children," said Janie. "I've made my choices and there's no going back now."

"You're right, Janie. I didn't want to upset them," said Lenny. Janie's discovery of Kaan Ek had been in papers all over the US and Central America, even in parts of Europe and Asia. Lenny knew what Janie had been doing, but Janie was curious about Lenny. "Have you found someone else, Lenny?" she said.

"Yes," was all that Lenny offered by way of an answer. The split was amicable, and Lenny agreed to send pictures of the children every year. When the children were old enough to understand why their mother left, it was decided, they could either choose to visit her or not as they pleased.

They kissed briefly at the door of the cafe as Janie's cab pulled up. She hugged Lenny one last time, feeling once more the familiar flanks of the man who had given her two children. She put her mouth to his ear and whispered, "I'm sorry." For Lenny, who was already late for work, that much of an apology was more than enough.

The four cruising teens hit Highway 77 with a burning mission to cause trouble. Once again in Marti's old car they passed Stanley Burgen and "Loretta the Hog" who were in a Volkswagen Beetle. They laughed and talked until they got to the stretch of road where they say Karen. They picked some wildflowers and placed them wordlessly on the spot. Nothing happened. Loren and Chuck and Petey flew back to Belize the next day. The four teens promised each other there would be adventurers in the future the way all young friends promise one another things before life takes them, darkens them, flings them over the face of the earth, and robs them of what few illusions they once had. But maybe, just maybe, Loren felt, they really would all be together again but for reasons they could not guess at now. Betty Sue promised to come for a summer vacation, and that was enough for Loren. Maybe Betty Sue would stay.... Loren would have to start hunting up some of the eligible young male teachers at Elena's school. There were about five possibilities. Loren prayed none of them would get tied down before Betty Sue's visit.

The Maddens and the Fernandezes became fast friends after the episode that became known as the Chase. After the birth of her son Barry Jr., Dauphine was often teary when she thought of Wanda, who ignored or did not receive letter after letter. Barry would occasionally get irked at Dauphine for getting wet-eyed when the subject of Wanda came up, but he never berated Dauphine. The Fernandezes themselves were not fools. They knew how beautiful friendship is and what it means to lose it. Brenda had started wearing slacks and swore like a fishwife again. Ed did not mind. They had a baby girl named Maria Ximena; and of course no one could have known it then, but Brenda was to have another daughter in two years, Remedias.

And now a last word about Lanky and Wanda: Lanky got a job as a driver on a cacao farm. He loved the work although it did not pay much. But he was satisfied to have Petey with him in his little house on the southern plains of Belize. Petey was one of the star pupils of his local one-room school. The other children wanted to touch his white skin a great deal at first, but they soon got used to him. Later, and at great sacrifice, his father sent him to St. John's College in Belmopan to finish his secondary schooling.

Wanda lived in an abandoned shack on St. George's Caye. She was a part time cook at a diver's lodge, and the rest of the time she painted seascapes, beautiful ones that became popular back home in some of the better galleries. She came to see Lanky and Petey once a month. They never came to see her, and that was the way she wanted it. Lanky, though angry at first, found Wanda more and more exciting every time he saw her. Without his opinions and notions and suggestions always chipping away at her, she was taking on a new, strong spirit. And she was just as lovingly maternal as ever. The separation had done both of them good.

Wanda would always say, if pressed, that she would live with Lanky again if she decided to and if it was all right with him.

"What would make you decide to do that?" Petey asked one day.

"Oh, I guess if a hurricane blew my house down I'd come back here."

"You really do love it out there, don't you, Mom?"

"Yes, I really do."

Even so, Petey had dreams. He dreamed about the man back in Tampico who had told him to be careful. He dreamed about Elena's space school (which he himself would one day direct after Elena Muñoz's death)--and he also dreamed of pleasant hurricanes that might one day goad his mother to rejoin his father.

The End